Readers love Anton Du Beke's sparkling fiction ...

'Beautifully written'

'What a triumph'

'A story full of true emotion, heart, poise and survival'

'I was enthralled from start to finish'

'Anton Du Beke has done it again'

'A truly fabulous read'

'The story of The Buckingham just gets better and better. Couldn't put it down'

ANTON DU BEKE

The BALLROOM BLITZ

ORION

An Orion Paperback
This edition published in Great Britain in 2023 by Orion Fiction
an imprint of The Orion Publishing Group Ltd
Carmelite House, 50 Victoria Embankment
London EC4Y 0DZ

An Hachette UK Company

3 5 7 9 10 8 6 4 2

A CIP catalogue record for this book is
available from the British Library.

ISBN (Mass Market Paperback) 978 1 3987 1009 2
ISBN (eBook) 978 1 3987 1010 8
ISBN (Audio) 978 1 3987 1011 5

Typeset at The Spartan Press Ltd,
Lymington, Hants

Printed and bound in Great Britain by Clays Ltd,
Elcograf S.p.A.

www.orionbooks.co.uk

To Hannah, George and Henrietta...
everything only works because of you!
Thank you.

List of Characters

Beyond the Buckingham:

Cathy Everly – ARP warden and member of the Women's Voluntary Service

Mortimer Bond – a captain of the ARP warden volunteer force

Vivienne Cohen née Edgerton – Raymond's sister-in-law

Stanley 'Stan' Cohen – infant son of Vivienne and Artie

Uncle Ken – Mary-Louise's uncle

Aunt Marge – Mary-Louise's aunt

Camille Bourchier – Mathilde's estranged mother

Mrs Law – Mathilde's elderly neighbour

Mr Cockfosters – entertainments director at the Imperial Hotel

Hubert Gove – director of the Imperial Hotel

Hélène Marchmont – former demonstration dancer at the Buckingham

Mrs Yorke – Cathy's landlady

Mary Burdett – matron of the Daughters of Salvation

Warren Peel – patron of the Daughters of Salvation

Malcolm Brody – an Australian airman and son of Emmeline Moffatt

Leah Elkamm – refugee child fostered by the Cohen family

Arthur 'Artie' Cohen – Raymond's younger brother, now sadly deceased

Alma Cohen – Raymond's mother

15th September 1940

Chapter One

Welcome to the Buckingham Hotel...

There were very few souls in London's high society who had not, at one time or another, entered the doors of the Buckingham Hotel's feted Grand Ballroom and stood in awe, taking in its ostentatious chandeliers, the elegant sweep of its glistening dance floor. There were even fewer souls who, on stepping into the arms of one of its troupe of illustrious dancers, had not felt their hearts take flight. This was the singular magic of the Grand Ballroom – and never was it more manifest than in those dark days of September 1940, when the good souls of London awoke each morning to find their city changed, when the only things in shorter supply than bacon and butter were wonder and joy.

But they didn't ration wonder, not at the Buckingham Hotel. You could not ration the human heart.

This afternoon, the ballroom was alive. On the dance floor, Mathilde Bourchier, the Buckingham's dark, elfin princess, sailed in the arms of Frank Nettleton – sometime hotel page, sometime ballroom dancer, sometime hero from the beaches of Dunkirk – while around her the ballroom filled with applause. Up on stage, the Archie Adams Orchestra were driving their latest number, 'Blue, Blue World', to its urgent climax – and Mathilde, who'd been lost in the song from the very beginning, was on the cusp of throwing herself upward in Frank's arms, to glide to the front of the dance floor and be presented to the assembled guests. The afternoon demonstration dances had been a fixture in the Buckingham Hotel since the ballroom opened its doors a decade ago, and for Mathilde – who had long been understudy to the troupe's principal dancer – they were her chance to show the guests what she was truly capable of, that she too could imbue a moment with magnificence, that there were stars in the ballroom beyond the troupe's leading players: the striking Karina Kainz, who'd fled from Vienna for a new home at the Buckingham Hotel; the imposing Marcus Arbuthnot, who'd once trained dancers for world championships and had returned to the dance floor to guide the troupe valiantly through these years of war. The demonstrations were Mathilde's chance to shine, perhaps even eclipse, the better-known dancers who dominated the Grand Ballroom, and they'd become so much more important in the months just passed – when an evening could be suddenly curtailed by the wail of an air raid siren, when a ball could be abruptly stopped and a shrill whistle blown, directing guests, cocktail waiters, ballroom dancers and musicians to the fortress of shelters beneath the hotel itself.

Joy.

Wonder.

Magic.

The world might have been on fire; the headlines might have preached about the calamity on the Continent and the madman whose eyes had turned, zealously, on Mathilde's little island nation; but Mathilde knew that, in the moment she completed her turn, arcing elegantly through the air above Frank's head, every soul in the Grand would be filled with the same rapture that buoyed her. Music was man's escape from the nightly horror of this thing they'd started calling 'Mr Hitler's Blitz'.

4

The ballroom was where people came to remember this feeling. The feeling that the world had once been filled with wonder and light – and that, one day, it would be again.

Not today, though – for, in the same moment that Mathilde swooped back to the ballroom's sprung dance floor, the same moment that the Archie Adams Orchestra brought their number to its end in a cavalcade of trumpets and piano, another music started playing outside the ballroom doors. It was the familiar music of the air raid sirens. The familiar *whomp* and *whirr*, spreading from police station to police station like the warning pyres of old being put to the torch.

Magic died in a moment.

Wonder, snuffed out like a guttering candle-flame.

Across the Grand Ballroom, dancers stepped out of hold; up on the stage, the white-whiskered gentleman Archie Adams – dedicated bandleader, with his ageless good looks and air of quiet calm – took leave of his grand piano and, with a single clap of the hands, marshalled his musicians.

'A daylight raid?' Mathilde whispered to Frank, stranded as they were in the heart of the dance floor. 'Frank, is it real?'

They'd come every night for the last week, pulverising the city from above while searchlights scythed through the black skies and the daring boys of the Royal Air Force took the battle to them. Since returning from Dunkirk, Frank, who spent three nights a week answering telephones for the Fire Service, had looked through the blackouts last night to see flames roiling somewhere beyond the palaces at Westminster, and willed the brave boys of the RAF on as their comet trails coloured the London skyline. Theirs was a battle like no other in history: a battle for supremacy in the skies.

'Of course it's real,' he said at last. After a mere moment's consternation, the ballroom had already sprung into action. 'Quickly, Mathilde. We've got a job to do.'

In the days when she'd been a fledgling dancer, mercilessly drilled to perfection by a mother who was indulging her own dream as much as her daughter's, Mathilde had never imagined it might one day involve being responsible for someone's life. But so it was. They'd been dancing to disaster all night long, and now the disaster had arrived. She turned on the spot and made haste to one of the guests standing by the dance floor balustrade, a young woman who served as attaché to one of the Norwegian King Haakon's ministers. Since the fall of Oslo, and the institution of that treacherous Quisling government, King Haakon and his family had taken up residence in Buckingham Palace, and so much of his government-in-exile now lived and operated out of the suites on the hotel's fifth storey. That was the Buckingham now: a world within a world, where dignitaries and ministers from fallen nations picked themselves up, put themselves back together, and got on with the business of resisting the Continent's new terror.

A terror which was, right now, raining from the London skies.

'Shall we?' she said, and gestured towards the ornate arched entrance of the Grand.

Mathilde took the attaché's arm and steered her away from the dance floor. Every other member of hotel staff – whether they were cocktail waiters, musicians, or just the audit manager who'd happened to look in on the ballroom when the demonstrations began – was helping to shepherd guests back through the archway from which they had, a mere half hour ago, emerged. A small band of others were taking advantage of the stage doors to hurry others on their way. There was once a time when no guest would have been permitted to see the dressing rooms and rehearsal studio behind the Grand, for fear that the ballroom's magic might suddenly have been dispelled, but things changed in a time of fire and devastation.

'I know the way, Miss,' the attaché said as Mathilde bustled her up the corridor, emerging into the hotel reception. Here, the black-and-white chequered expanse had been cleared of any obstruction, including the famous Art Deco obelisk which had stood here, an icon of the Buckingham Hotel, for a generation. No golden trolleys or potted ferns were permitted to pockmark the hall anymore, for fear of inhibiting the rush to the shelters.

'I'm sorry, ma'am,' said Mathilde, 'it's more than my job's worth to leave a guest alone. I'll see you to the stairs, then go back for others.'

The reception hall was a hubbub of activity. Staff who weren't escorting guests were generally instructed to remain at post until the last guest was secure and the rosters complete, but some were already streaming through to the Queen Mary restaurant, where the wine cellars had been converted into shelters for the staff. The guests were to be housed in the altogether more opulent surrounds of the old hotel laundries, converted this past year to a succession of suites almost worthy of the Buckingham's uppermost storeys. Walter Knave, the elderly Hotel Director – a shrunken, amphibious-looking man, in a suit that dwarfed him and spectacles that made preposterous protrusions of his eyes – watched from the check-in desks, wringing his mottled old hands together. Mathilde knew how he was feeling; the hammering in her heart seemed to keep time with the *whomp* of the sirens.

Marcus Arbuthnot, the Grand's regal leader, had a guest on each arm as he spun past Mathilde, heading for the passage-way that opened up behind the golden cage of the elevators. The way he looked now, a guest might have thought he had come to the Grand specifically for the purpose of shepherding guests to safety – but nothing could have been further from the truth. Marcus was a titan of the ballroom, a statesman of dance. Too old to join the steady roll of men being drawn into the war decimating the Continent, he had been hired a year ago to shepherd the Grand through what promised to be its most tumultuous years. A lifetime spent training young dancers, even shepherding them to glory on the world's stage, had, it seemed, given him an innate confidence in moments of terror such as this. Mathilde caught his eye across the spinning reception hall. 'One more time, my dear,' he mouthed to her; they were the words he used in the rehearsal studio behind the Grand, whenever he needed to urge the troupe through one more practise waltz, and they steadied her in the moment. She watched Marcus sallying on into the starrily lit passage that led to the shelters (praying that he was right, that this was but a rehearsal and not the last night of her life) and said, 'We're almost there, ma'am. Almost there.'

A figure, leaning into a walking cane meant for a much older man, emerged from the hall tucked behind the reception desks. The former concierge, Billy Brogan, more recently private in the British Expeditionary Force, had been one of the first into France in those early weeks of war. Now he stood, his body pitched at a slightly crooked angle (though significantly less crooked than when he'd first appeared on his return from France), his red hair growing back in tufts from its old military cut. Billy's body had been too broken to return to his division since Dunkirk – Mathilde had heard whispers that his mind was broken as well, for Billy had spent many long hours battling for life in the English Channel after the HMS *Othello* went down – but he'd been awarded a new role as head of the hotel post room. He emerged from there now, his face etched in deep, steadfast lines.

Mathilde hurried towards him. 'Billy, perhaps you can take the attaché to the shelters, while I help in the ballroom?'

'Can't, Miss Bourchier,' Billy announced, with a grim determination completely at odds with the happy-go-lucky boy the staff at the hotel used to know. 'It's my turn on the roster. John's out front, but I'm on the tradesman's entrance. Well, you can't abandon station. Look what happened at the Savoy.' The news had come yesterday: a group from the East End had marched brazenly through the Savoy to occupy its shelters in anticipation of the bombardment to come. Billy gave a wan, half-smile – and it seemed evident to Mathilde that he was trying his damnedest to summon up the fiery spirit of old. 'You get these guests safe, Miss Bourchier,' he grinned. Then he addressed the attaché directly. 'You'll be fine in the shelters, Miss. This hotel's got an iron skeleton. It's not going down.' A shudder ran through him. He'd thought that about the HMS *Othello* too – and then there he'd been, flailing in the water, clinging on to the wreckage, desperate for some passing fishing boat to sail by. 'Go on, Miss Bourchier. Quickly now. These Jerries won't hold fire for us.'

Mathilde looked back as she swept the attaché on. The reception hall was milling, as busy as any ballroom floor she had ever graced – only it was not joy in the air any longer. It was not wonder. It was panic, barely controlled. With the attaché on her arm, she slipped round the back of the golden elevators – and then she was gone.

Billy didn't wait to see her go. Angling through the bustle of other guests and staff, he limped along the Housekeeping hall, through the maze of other passageways, until he reached the hotel's side entrance. Here, past a room piled high with old boxes and crates waiting for pick-up, a broad doorway opened onto Michaelmas Mews, the narrow lane that ran around the periphery of the hotel and eventually opened up onto Berkeley

Square. The sun was shining along the mews; it seemed such an innocuous day for something so terrible.

Billy was standing there, listening to the whirr of the sirens, when the sound and fury of the first explosion reached his ears. He'd heard sounds like this too often, not only in this last week of constant bombardment, but all throughout his retreat from inland France. The German artillery had pounded the seaside town of Dunkirk; he still saw it, heard it, *felt* it in his dreams.

He shuddered.

He shook.

He felt the sea sucking him under, then spewing him out. He closed his eyes, but that only made the memory more vivid still.

He saw the sea on fire.

There was movement behind him. He turned, waving his cane as if to fend off some sudden assailant – but it was only Mrs Moffatt, the imposing Head of Housekeeping, tottering unsteadily forward beneath her tight curls of white hair.

'Billy,' she said, and took his hand, 'how close are they?'

Close enough, thought Billy. Not for the first time, he was thankful that all of his brothers and sisters – the Brogan brood, as so many called them – had been shipped out of the city with the evacuation last year. He squeezed Mrs Moffatt's hand, as if to give her strength. 'You ought to get to the staff shelter, Mrs Moffatt. Leave this to me.' Inwardly, he cursed. Billy Brogan would do whatever was asked of him – he'd done it in the British Expeditionary Force, and he'd do it for the Buckingham Hotel, which was where his heart truly lay – but there was something about standing sentry here that rankled. The enemies were in the skies above, not on the streets of London. Guarding the hotel against blackguards and thieves did not have the same ring of honesty and heroism that he'd felt doing his bit in France. Even that group who'd occupied the Savoy had a good point to make – in war-torn London, being rich was much safer than being poor. 'Mrs Moffatt, are you OK?'

He'd seen the way her face and neck had discoloured. The rush of blood to the head. Moments later, she was palming her way past him. She had to use the walls to steady herself. It seemed, to Billy, as if the earth was listing under her feet.

Then, she was out through the doors and into the sunlight that dappled Michaelmas Mews.

'Mrs Moffatt!' he cried out. 'Mrs Moffatt, what are you doing?'

Mrs Moffatt was not a small woman. Having long been in the depths of middle age, she had a doughy frame, ankles permanently swollen by too much work, and a waddling look to her when she walked that had, on occasion, put Billy in mind of a duck. That was why he was surprised by the sudden burst of energy with which she sprang past. That was why, when he staggered out into the Mews and watched her cantering for Berkeley Square, he could hardly believe his eyes.

'Mrs Moffatt! Mrs Moffatt!'

But his voice, if she cared to hear it at all, was lost in the thunder from above, as some defiant RAF boys banked over the rooftops in defence of the realm.

Billy heard some fresh hell being unleashed to the south – over the river, if he was any judge, and exactly where his mother and father would be hunkered down in the Anderson at the bottom of their yard.

He stood there a moment longer.

But that was as long as he could wait.

Whatever Mrs Moffatt was doing right now, she wasn't in her right mind. Nobody could be, to willingly rush into a storm like this.

Billy had never let one of his friends down before, so he

grasped his cane, grit his teeth against the old, nagging pain, and prepared to give chase.

By the time he reached her, she was standing in the middle of Berkeley Square, turning madly on the spot, her face upturned to take in the clear blue skies.

'Mrs Moffatt?' he called out, as he limped near. 'Mrs Moffatt, please?'

Berkeley Square was a riot of colour. Roses of iridescent hue stood alongside the irises and magnolia that bordered the green expanse where Mrs Moffatt stood. Billy felt a rush of summer scents as he picked his way to her, the beauty of his surrounds quite at odds with the palpitating fear in his heart.

The shrill scream of some falling incendiary sounded to the south. Billy cringed and looked upwards, just in time to see the shapes of three planes banking overhead. He knew, by instinct, that these were RAF boys. Mrs Moffatt seemed to know it too. She lifted her hand – and, just when Billy felt certain she was cheering, she clasped it to her mouth in horror.

'Mrs Moffatt,' he breathed, 'you've got to come inside.'

But she did not even look at him.

'Mrs Moffatt, it isn't safe out here.'

But she did not breathe a word.

'Mrs Moffatt?' Billy tried, and failed, one last time to get her attention. Only then, when her eyes remained fixed on the skies above, did he know it was futile. Mrs Moffatt couldn't stay out here, like some sacrifice to the vengeful gods above, and nor could he. He just couldn't do it alone.

The planes tumbling over Berkeley Square had already coursed across the rooftops of East London, but more roared in their wake. On the Whitechapel Road, where mothers swept children suddenly into their arms and made for the shelter of the old church halls, Lance Corporal Raymond de Guise looked to the skies and took his young companion Leah firmly by the hand.

Raymond de Guise, formerly the principal dancer at the Buckingham Hotel, had returned from his Salisbury barracks for five days' leave before his inevitable new posting – but he hadn't expected to be stepping directly into a theatre of war. Even so, a year in the armed forces had given him instincts enough to know he could cope with the sudden fluctuations of tension. That was life in the military: vast tracts of nothingness, punctuated by sudden flare-ups of drama, danger and death. As soon as the sirens had started to sound, he knew he had to act. Whether it was London or the Low Countries, being caught out in the open with the enemy incoming was no good thing.

At thirty-four years of age, Raymond de Guise stood more than six feet tall. His reflection, in the window of the florists where he and Leah had been browsing, showed a man with jet-black hair, cropped short to the scalp where it had once been a devilish, wild curl, a lean body and sun-burnished skin. He was wearing his standard issue uniform, graced now by his lance corporal stripes, as was required even when on home leave – but what use were a lance corporal's instincts when the terror came from above? He watched, in the reflection, as he crouched down to meet twelve-year-old Leah's face and said, 'Just stay with me, sweetheart. We'll get somewhere safe.'

No sooner had he said it than he heard the first planes screaming overhead. The sirens ordinarily pre-empted an attack long enough to reach shelter, but there was something about a daytime raid that discombobulated the system, throwing the engineers and signallers out of sync. Leah, who had been brought from her Polish home only months before the Nazis marched over the border, trembled and held Raymond tight. From one war-ravaged country, straight into the heart of another.

She'd been fostered by Raymond's mother Alma since her arrival at the Tilbury docks. Raymond didn't mean to let her perish here. There'd been too much perishing already.

'What about the flowers?' asked Leah, in her unformed English.

Raymond brushed back her hair, dark as his own, and looked into the chocolate buttons of her eyes. They'd been standing here, deliberating which flowers they ought to buy for Vivienne, Raymond's sister-in-law and the widowed wife of his brother Artie. Artie hadn't made it back from France; three months had passed, but the wound still felt raw. Too raw for flowers to pacify, thought Raymond, but flowers were all they had – and Leah had her heart set on the gesture.

'Here,' said Raymond. He picked up a bouquet of orange and lilac roses and quickly palmed coins into the hands of the florist, who dashed about bringing in her wares. 'Hold tight to them, Leah – and hold tight to me. We've got to move.'

Rags of people hurried down the Whitechapel Road. As Raymond started to run, steadying his pace so that Leah could keep up, he saw families vanish into side-streets, saw shop fronts go suddenly dark, heard shutters coming down and doors being slammed shut. At the Stepney Green Underground station, a huddle of panicked passers-by were piling down the stairs, only to be met by the crowd of travellers just disgorged by the railway below. 'It isn't far,' said Raymond. He knew these streets like the back of his hand; he'd take her through the back alleys if he had to. Though he'd spent the better part of his life waltzing his way through the ballrooms and palaces of Europe, winning prizes for his tango, his foxtrot, his elegant Viennese waltz, these rough-and-ready East End streets were where he and his late brother used to roam. He still remembered the switchbacks and shortcuts of his boyhood. He took to them now.

He had just hustled Leah off the Whitechapel Road when the first quake shook the London streets. Instinctively, Leah threw herself against the wall. By the time Raymond had whispered some calm into her ear, the second explosion was coming from the east. The Luftwaffe were trying to raze the dockland again. That was their principal aim, Raymond thought – cut the city off, blockade it from help, grind it into submission. 'Leah,' he whispered, 'Vivienne's waiting. They're safe at home, out back in the shelter. We could be too. We just have to get there.'

Leah picked herself up, tried to shake down her fear. It was only when Raymond gripped her by the shoulders and gazed into her eyes with his own rich, dark ones that his calmness washed over her. She nodded, nodded again, and clasped his hand. 'How far is it?'

'Mere moments, sweetheart,' he told her. Raymond had no daughter of his own, but in this moment she might have been his; his heart called out to hers. 'Vivienne's there, and Nancy's there, baby Stan and my mother too.' Just a Sunday afternoon, a chance for the disparate family to unite over tea and cakes and pretend, for a few hours, that the war was happening somewhere else. Nobody had expected the bombs to rain down in broad daylight. The night was when battle happened; when the sun shone down, it was meant to be calm. 'Just stay with me. Say no to the fear. I'm going to get you there.'

Raymond saw the effect of his words. The shimmer of tears retreated from her eyes; her jaw was fixed, the trembles gone. He drew back to his full height. 'Stand behind me,' he told her. He'd carry her if he had to; he'd carried his brother Artie in the end as well. 'Let's—'

But he never got the chance to finish that sentence, because before he took his next breath, the screaming of a falling bomb tore open the skies. Next second, the Whitechapel Road erupted in fire, smoke and devastation. A rampaging wall of dust and debris rushed outwards in an unstoppable wave. And all that Raymond could hear, through the ringing in his ears, was Leah's petrified scream as she buried her face in his breast, the once-perfect flowers soiled and sandwiched between them.

Mrs Moffatt was so absorbed by the smoke trails scarring the blue sky that she did not hear her name being called, nor the cantering of footsteps as two figures clamoured to reach her in the heart of Berkeley Square. The summer scents filled her lungs with every breath – but the only thing that filled her heart was terror.

Not terror for herself.

Terror for a loved one, in the heavens above . . .

'Mrs Moffatt?' a voice was calling. Billy's voice, she knew. He'd been here some moments before, but then – when she hadn't given in to his pleas and demands – he'd run away, left her there in the heart of Berkeley Square. Now he had returned, to find her sobbing and unmoved. 'Mrs Moffatt, I brought someone who might—'

Another RAF plane banked overhead, its guns ablaze as it stalked one of the Stukas over the skyline. To the other onlookers at the Buckingham Hotel, it must have been a thing of hope – to see the good old boys of the Royal Air Force rallying to repel the invaders – but, to Emmeline Moffatt, no sight could have incurred more terror. Her heart nearly stopped in her breast. She found that she could take no breath. Only when the planes had vanished, leaving their ghostly contrails behind, did she gasp for air. By then, the pressure was nearly too much. She staggered, uncertain of her own feet – and would have pitched forward into the grass on Berkeley Square, if hands hadn't reached out to catch her.

Not Billy's hands, she realised.

It was Archie Adams.

'Archie?'

'I went to fetch him, Mrs Moffatt. I didn't know what else I could do.'

'Emmeline,' came Archie's softly spoken voice. Only a voice like that, thought Mrs Moffatt, could unknot the fear that had been building in her breast. Only a man like Archie could remain so calm and in control, while war was being waged all around him. She supposed Billy had found him where he always went when the bombs rained down – with his Orchestra, in the shelters beneath the Queen Mary restaurant, his eyes closed as he listened to the gramophone gently playing; music, the only true escape from the terrors of this mortal world. The girls in Housekeeping said that Mrs Moffatt and Archie were more than friends, though of course nobody had ever seen them step out on an evening together. But Archie Adams was known to take tea in the Housekeeping Lounge after hours, and to have ordered a bright bouquet for Mrs Moffatt's birthday on Midsummer's Eve. The girls said they could always tell when Archie had paid Mrs Moffatt a visit, for she was less strict about punctuality at the morning breakfast, and paid less attention to the details as she inspected their work at the end of each shift. Those stories had evidently found their way to Billy as well. In any other circumstance, Mrs Moffatt might have been mortified – but here was Archie, quite possibly the only man who could set her back on her feet.

'Archie,' Mrs Moffatt whispered, 'he's up there, I know it. It's his turn, *his turn!*'

'Oh, Emmeline.'

'My boy,' Mrs Moffatt quaked. 'Fighting – fighting in the skies.'

How cruel, this feeling. How all-consuming, the fear that a love just found might so suddenly be dashed. Mrs Moffatt had only just rediscovered Malcolm, the son she'd been forced to give up for adoption when she herself was little more than a girl – and perhaps it was this that made the thought of losing him seem so acute. In her darkest moments, she felt as if she almost deserved it; why should somebody who'd never kissed a grazed knee, or brushed a boy's tangled hair, suddenly be gifted with the beauty of becoming a mother? At nights, she would lie awake, imagining the horror of his death: trapped in a burning cockpit, tumbling from the skies, nobody to hear his final words, no body to grieve over, just as – once upon a time – there'd been no baby to love. All of the knots inside her had become unbearable. She wanted to sail into the skies and sit beside him, to be his gunner, to mop his brow, to whisper in his ear that everything was going to be all right – that he was her brave boy, that she was proud of him, that she was sorry, sorry, sorry … but of course it was all so foolish. She was Emmeline Moffatt, housekeeper at a luxury hotel; the feeling of it was powerlessness, pure and simple.

She was glad to have Archie's arms around her.

Only Archie could lead her away from those darkest thoughts.

All of a sudden, she realised what she'd done, how irresponsible she'd been. It wasn't just she who was standing in the middle of Berkeley Square. Poor Billy Brogan was here as well – and that was because of her. She imagined how his leg, maimed somewhere in the English Channel, must have played hell with him as he lurched back along Michaelmas Mews, hurtling to fetch help. She could imagine how he'd marched through his pain, across the barren Queen Mary restaurant – where the tables would be laid out like epitaphs to abandoned afternoon teas – and down into the cellars. What courage it had taken for Billy to return. What courage for Archie Adams too. And it was she, Emmeline Moffatt, who'd put them in that peril – all because of that uncontrollable feeling in her heart, the feeling that to lose her son again would be the end of everything.

She clambered to hold on to Archie, who lifted her up and held her tight.

'Emmeline, dear?'

Mrs Moffatt trembled. 'They buried his best friend last week. Peter. He went down somewhere over Liverpool. There'll be boys being burned up tonight. They're saying none of them will last. It's suicide, Archie.'

'Now, Emmeline—'

He held her even more tightly now. For a fleeting moment, she felt like a cornered animal – but something in Archie's presence pacified her. Moments later, he turned her to face the hotel.

'There's nothing to say he'll be one of them, Emmeline. Nothing to say he won't be standing on solid ground by nightfall. Nothing to say that, when this is done, you won't be sitting in the pews at his wedding, or—'

Mrs Moffatt stiffened. 'Reading the rites at his funeral.'

'Emmeline!' Archie Adams raised his voice. 'Don't speak of it,' he told her, and braced her by the shoulders as some fresh hell was unleashed, somewhere in the north. 'It's but a moment in time. The foulest of moments, but a moment nonetheless. All things pass. But if you give in to those thoughts, they'll overcome you. So hold on to this instead: you and Malcolm, on a summer's day, your grandchildren around you. Life, Emmeline. Hold on to *life*.'

Mrs Moffatt whispered, 'I only just found him. I can't lose him again so soon.'

Archie had steered her away from the square's grassy expanse and was preparing to harry her back along Michaelmas Mews, when the doorman at the front of the hotel started halloing them urgently from the sweeping marble stairs.

'This way,' cried Billy. 'Quickly!'

Ordinarily, it was more than Billy's job was worth to be seen scrambling through the guest entrance. Ordinarily, were Mrs Moffatt and Archie Adams to be seen hurrying through the hotel's revolving brass doors, the displeasure of Mr Knave would have been severe. But today there was not a soul in sight as they passed beneath the hotel's grand white colonnade, past the empty taxicabs, up the marble stairs and into the reception hall.

Billy was the last to lope through. As he watched Mrs Moffatt and Archie head for the shelters, he winced at his aching leg, cricked his neck and took a long, laboured breath.

Another explosion sounded in the west; the scream of some incendiary returned the call from somewhere out east.

How long had it been now? It felt like hours, but surely mere minutes had passed.

In the skies, the battle went on.

Raymond de Guise clung on to Leah as the smoke and debris parted, revealing the ruin of the Whitechapel Road.

'It's OK,' Raymond said, his voice tinged with disbelief as he looked to the skies. 'Leah, we're OK.'

The tear-stained girl still had her arms flung around him. Bearing her aloft, he returned to the end of the side street, then cast his eyes at the devastation further along the road.

The incendiary had turned the Whitechapel Road into a crater. The road itself was impassable, a vast gaping wound, the shop fronts on either side obliterated beyond recognition. Tendrils of smoke were curling up from the centre of the crater. Ribbons of fire licked the place where the shop fronts used to be. Raymond saw curtains, miraculously undamaged in the blast, flickering in waves of wind and heat.

'Pssst!' came a voice. 'You two, get out of the road!'

With Leah still cradled in his arms, Raymond turned to see that one of the shops closest to him had opened its doors, and out stuck the face of an old haberdasher.

'In here!' the old man cried. 'I've a cellar.'

Raymond heard engines roaring. He looked down the barrel of the road, to see fire trucks approaching from beyond the impact site.

Then he saw a figure. A figure standing in the second storey of one of the obliterated shops, the bedroom in which she'd been cowering now opened to the world like a ravaged doll's house.

She looked so young, seventeen or eighteen years of age – though, through the dirt and the ash, Raymond couldn't be sure. What he could be sure about, however, was her panic. She was screaming, wild and untamed.

Raymond hurried to the haberdasher's door and, with some effort, detached Leah from his arms. Setting her down, he kissed her once on the brow. 'Stay here,' he told her. 'You'll be safe here.' The look in Leah's eyes told him she wasn't sure, so he dropped to his knees, embraced her again and whispered into her ear, 'Be brave for me. You've been so brave already. I'll be back in but a few moments.'

Leah snorted, trying hard to reabsorb all her tears. When she opened her mouth to speak, the words wouldn't come, so instead she embraced Raymond one last time, then retreated with the haberdasher into the sanctuary of the shop.

Raymond started to run. 'Hold on!' he cried out to the woman in the ruined building.

From the haberdasher's window, Leah watched him go. As the old shopkeeper urged her to follow him, down into his cellar,

Leah stood frozen in the glass. Raymond was but a stick figure now, dwindling in proportion as he approached the crater in the road. Smoke wreathed around him. He vanished and reappeared as he flailed his way through the shifting grey reef.

She'd always known Raymond de Guise was a hero. He'd defied death on the way back from Dunkirk. He'd led a rag of the last survivors across the Channel, even after the Continent was overrun, and been decorated for it since then – elevated from being a lowly private to a lance corporal, with the promise of more to come. The world had loved Raymond as a ballroom dancer; but the world *needed* him as a soldier. That, Leah supposed, was the difference.

She'd come a long way in her short life. It had been a year since she'd last heard from her parents, and all the whispers of what was happening in this thing they called the Third Reich only filled her with nightmares. But the people she'd found here in London had hearts big enough to fill that void. She hadn't voiced it until then, not even to herself, but she had started to love them. In a fractious world, constantly being torn asunder, love was the only thing there was.

And that was why, when Raymond de Guise reached the edge of the smoking crater and began to plot his way up the ruined building to where the girl was stranded, Leah's breast was filled with pride. That debonair Englishman was part of her family, for now and evermore.

She was still standing there, her heart filled with the emotion of it all, when the unexploded bomb in the crater ignited.

Raymond de Guise had not known there was a second bomb, sitting unstable on the Whitechapel Road. But he knew it now. It was the work of an instant for the flames to geyser up, like a volcano exploding; for the fractures in the road to spread out, rupturing yet more of the road's surface, its shock waves shattering the glass in the windows of shops further down the road.

Leah saw Raymond's dark figure tossed upwards like a rag doll, but she did not see him land – for, in the next moment, all she could see was the billowing smoke and dust, as the bright sunshine of a September afternoon was cast into deep, impenetrable shadow.

Chapter Two

'Wake up. Raymond, wake up—'

The ballroom was listing, like the deck of some ship in the heart of a storm. Every time he tried to take a step, Raymond de Guise lost his footing, half plunged to the freshly lacquered floor, then — at the very last moment — pulled himself up, rescued the waltz, and danced on. Around him, the balustrade tipped up, tipped down, then rose again. The great cavernous vault of the Grand was plastered in stars as vivid as those that speckled the night sky. The music came not from an orchestra but from the creaking of a ship's timbers, the metallic groan of iron struts shearing apart and scything against each other, deep in the belly of an obliterated hull. And in his arms hung not his darling wife Nancy, not his former partner, the celestial Hélène Marchmont — but his brother, bedraggled and drawn, pale of skin and even paler of heart.

Raymond took him into an even tighter hold. He could feel, now, how the dance floor was coming apart beneath him. Water was leaching up through cracks in the interlocking oak boards, sloshing over his dancing shoes with every step.

'Now, Ray,' Artie scoffed, 'you never held me like this before.'

Raymond danced on. If he was good enough, if he was fleet of foot and solid of mind, he could dodge the rising waters.

Dance would see him through whatever calamity was befalling the ballroom. But the moment he stopped dancing, he thought, the Grand Ballroom would fall. Plunge beneath the waves. Sink into the inky blackness, and take him with it...

'Watch out, Ray, the stage is sinking.' Artie gave his old, wolfish smile; God, how Raymond had missed it. 'You see, Ray, you've always been good with those feet. You always knew the right step. Always followed the music. But there's something else you got to do for me now. Listen to me, Ray, because these are the most important words I've ever said to you.'

Raymond didn't want him to stop talking. The sound of his brother's voice – he thought it had been lost forever. 'What words, Artie? What have you got to say?'

And Artie broke suddenly free of Raymond's hold, waltzed backwards across the listing dance floor, and called out, 'Wake up, Ray! You've got a job to do!'

Lance Corporal Raymond de Guise opened his eyes.

He could still hear the rush of the wind, still taste the salt of the sea, but the four walls that enclosed him were white and bland – and he knew, by the scent of carbolic and the clipboard at the edge of his bed, that he was lying in a hospital room, wearing a sweaty, white hospital gown.

A figure floated at the end of his bed. He had to focus on it to make sense of its edges. 'Nurse?' he ventured, and the voice he heard was hardly his own; his throat was dry and caked, and he was so parched he could hardly speak. 'Nurse?'

She came to him and tipped a glass of water to his lips. The taste of it was like nectar. She had to stop him from gulping back the lot, in case he was sick.

'Nancy,' he was saying, 'N–Nancy...' – and the nurse seemed

to understand, for moments later she hurried from the room, out into the corridor.

Where Nancy herself was waiting.

Nancy de Guise was feeling older than her twenty-eight years as she sat here, occasionally getting up to pace around the waiting area, then sitting down again, getting increasingly nauseous with every hour that passed. Nancy had always fancied herself a strong woman, but she did not feel it this morning. Every time she caught sight of herself in the window glass, she thought she was seeing somebody else: that was somebody else's wild brown hair, somebody else's glassy expression. The war aged a woman daily.

She'd been here since daybreak, the moment Leah turned up on the doorstep, an old haberdasher at her side. It had taken some time to learn which hospital Raymond had been taken to, even longer to learn that he'd been patched up and hadn't perished in the explosion on the Whitechapel Road. Six hours had passed since then, Nancy flitting in and out to brush the hair from Raymond's brow, to sit holding his hand and to whisper in his ear, and the sick feeling was still coursing through her. She just couldn't shake it. More than once, the nurses had brought her hot tea and toast, or offered to take her on a stroll to the hospital canteen – but the thought of eating just about anything turned her stomach this morning. Anxiety like this worked dark magic on the body. She supposed it was relief now, flooding through her. She just hadn't realised that relief could make her feel so unsettled.

'Mrs de Guise,' the nurse ventured, 'he's asking to see you.'

It was all she needed to hear. Moments later, she burst through the door – and there was Raymond, propped up on the end of the bed, the sheets sloughed off him as he searched through the pile of scorched, torn clothes on the bedside chair, looking for something to wear.

'Lance Corporal de Guise!' the nurse exclaimed. 'You're in no fit state – you mustn't get out of bed – you've taken a nasty tumble. The damage you'll do to that arm…'

Nancy had already noticed that it was in a sling. Another bandage was wrapped around his head, where ugly bruises coloured his brow.

'I need to get out of here,' Raymond began, his voice still hoarse. 'I can't lie around here all day, not when there's so much work to be done.'

'Don't put weight on that foot!' the nurse called out. But it was too late. Raymond had already placed his right foot on the ground and, the moment he leant into it, a terrible pain shot through him, causing him to crash back down to the bed. 'It's a terrible sprain,' the nurse went on. 'Lance Corporal, we're waiting for the surgeon. Doctor thinks you've been very lucky, but keep on like this and your luck's going to run out.'

Raymond breathed, 'Our luck's already run out, nurse. All we've got left is the fight.'

The nurse stiffened. She was about to issue some fresh order to Raymond – but then, realising that she had no business speaking to a lance corporal like this, she turned on her heel, declared, 'I'm fetching Doctor,' and vanished through the doors.

Nancy, who still felt queasy in the pit of her stomach, rushed to Raymond's side and helped ease him back to the bed. 'Raymond, please,' she beseeched him, 'just a little more time. You've been out cold for so long. Darling, I didn't know where you'd gone. I didn't know if you were living or dead.'

Raymond had a sudden vision of the ghostly, wraithlike Artie, waltzing in his arms.

'Where's Leah?' he asked, a rush of memories stealing upon

him. He fancied he could smell the smoke still. An image hit him: kissing Leah on the brow as he left her by the haberdasher's door.

'You've Leah to thank for it all,' Nancy explained. 'She saw it happen. Every last bit.' And she tried to tell him, then, how close he'd got to the bomb site, how the second explosion had tossed him up into the air, how Leah — ignoring the haberdasher's cries — tried to rush back out of the shop, and would have done exactly that if the doors hadn't already been bolted. 'She watched the ambulance men take you away. That was how she knew you were still living.'

'And she came to find you.'

'All on her own,' said Nancy, to whom the thing was both beautiful and cruel. 'Twelve years old, and she had to find her own way.'

Raymond crashed back into the pillow, fresh pain lacerating his body, and pictured her at the haberdasher's window as he turned to march into the ruin. 'I shouldn't have left her,' he whispered. Then he remembered the figure, stranded in the open face of the ruined building, and wondered: how do you know what the right thing is? Where does one responsibility end and the other begin? How does any man make the right decision in an age like this? What did it even mean to be a 'good man'?

'And Vivienne?' Raymond asked, suddenly. 'Did Vivienne make it through?'

Vivienne Cohen: she'd married Raymond's brother only a short year before, their wedding vows spoken on the very same day that Mr Chamberlain announced the country was at war. Raymond had known Vivienne the longer, but to him she had just been the spoilt rich girl with permanent rooms at the Buckingham Hotel, the step-daughter of the now-deposed head of the Hotel Board. It was Nancy who'd first seen the goodness in Vivienne; Nancy, long before Raymond, who'd seen the spark in her. They'd been friends ever since. It was Nancy, in a roundabout way, who'd introduced Vivienne to Raymond's brother. Strange, how the world turned. They'd been perfect opposites – Artie the East End scallywag, Vivienne the spoilt heiress – but, in finding each other, they'd found their better selves. Now all that was ruined, like the city in which they stood. But, of them all, perhaps only Vivienne truly understood the gaping loss Raymond felt in the absence of his brother.

He took Nancy's hand. 'Will you send word to my division? They're expecting me back.' He laughed, wryly. 'I don't suppose I'll make it, will I? Wherever the posting is.'

All the talk had been of North Africa, where the Italian armies – having freshly announced their allegiance with Nazi Germany – vastly outnumbered the British. Raymond hardly thought he'd be on the next transports now, not with his body in pieces, and his brain not far behind. North Africa seemed so very far away, when all he really wanted was to be back in the rolling, verdant pastures of France, his brother at his side, sending the enemy back where they belonged.

'I'll take care of it,' Nancy told him, putting her hands over his. 'Raymond, look at me.'

Raymond didn't want to, but something in Nancy's voice always compelled him to do as she asked. Raymond de Guise could live with a lot of things, but not disappointing Nancy.

She looked blurry and far away. He supposed that was the knock he'd taken to the head. He had to concentrate to bring her into focus.

'It's a good thing,' she told him. 'I know you don't want to hear it, but let me say it all the same. These injuries, they're a blessing in disguise. You need to be grounded, Raymond. You need a little time. If they sent you back into battle now, I know how it would go: you'd throw yourself, heart and soul, into the fight. You'd lose yourself in it. You'd take any silly risk that came your way, just to punch back at them. After what happened to Artie...' She wanted to say more. How he just hadn't been the same since Dunkirk. How he'd barely been able to take her in his arms. How he woke in the night, drifted downstairs to listen to his records – how the only respite he found was in music, not in Nancy herself. But, in the end, she didn't breathe a word. She told herself she *understood*, that it was all a necessary evil, the thing he had to go through to make sense of Artie's death – but the truth was that she didn't understand, because she couldn't. It wasn't Nancy who'd been there, stranded in the sinking vessel. It wasn't Nancy who'd been swept back onto the blasted beaches and held on to her brother as he died. She tried to think how she'd feel if it had been Frank, and perhaps that gave her an inkling of what this war could do to a soul – but the thought of it stirred such terrible emotion in her that she quickly cast the thought aside.

'Darling,' she ventured, 'I know how much you want to go.' She stroked his brow, her finger dancing around the place where the bandages were strapped. 'But look at you. Raymond, you're not the same. You're in a...' she floundered for the words, '...different kind of battle now. But here's the difference. *I'm* here, right here, in the trenches with you.' She was talking about whatever was happening in his mind, the black places his thoughts were leading him every night, the compulsion – which she was quite certain had come over him on the Whitechapel Road – to put himself in harm's way; but she might as well have been talking about the Blitz itself. Eight days without respite. The Germans were throwing everything they had at breaking London's spirit.

But London had a lot more to give.

So did Nancy de Guise.

'Raymond. Darling. I love you. If you love me too, do this for me – if not for yourself. *Recover*, Raymond. Recover, before you go back to the fight.'

There was movement at the door. Nancy looked up to find a middle-aged doctor in a long white coat standing in the frame, his face half hidden behind the steamed-up lenses of his spectacles.

'Listen to your wife, Lance Corporal,' the doctor intoned, his voice both gravelly and grave. 'You took a nasty bump there. The skull, I suggest, carries a couple of fractures, here and *here*. You're concussed, Lance Corporal. Add this to the ruin of that foot and the angle this arm was hanging off when the ambulance brought you in, and you can count yourself lucky it was just a beating you took. You might not have died yesterday afternoon, Lance Corporal, but you took a jolly good thrashing. Count your lucky stars Death had other souls to be collecting.'

Raymond had got used to gallows humour like that in his division. He looked from the doctor to his wife – and Nancy was buoyed up to see him incline his head in an almost imperceptible nod.

'Bed rest, Lance Corporal. I want the nurses here to keep a weather eye on you until we're sure this concussion's not going to turn more nasty than it ought. Then it's off home for you – and the care of your good lady wife.'

Nancy stood, as if to attention. 'You heard the man, Raymond. That sounded like an order to me.' She paused, as a sudden thought struck her. 'Can a doctor give orders to a lance corporal?'

In the door, the doctor had already turned round to leave his patient to his rest. 'This one can,' he grunted, with a wide grin. Then he was gone.

'You heard the man,' said Nancy, and settled down again by Raymond's side.

Raymond lay back on the bed, fixed his eyes on the ceiling tiles, and wondered how it had come to this.

That night, when the sirens came, he was lying there still.

It was three days later that a stumbling Lance Corporal de Guise accompanied his wife out through the hospital doors and to the taxicab idling by the kerb. In the East London air, the smell of the night before was strong. Smoke lounged like mist through the struts of warehouses razed in the bombardment. Construction workers filled the roads, ambulance wagons as common as taxicabs in the obliterated streets.

At first, the west seemed to fare better. By the time the taxi was taking them along High Holborn, the cityscape appeared less scathed. The damage along the eastern stretch of Oxford Street had come days ago, some semblance of order restored to the chaos – but the devastation at Oxford Circus was very real, very recent, and evident from miles away. Black columns of smoke still churned in the place where the great John Lewis & Partners store used to sit. As the taxicab drew near, Nancy averted her eyes – but Raymond could not tear himself away from the devastation. The smoke roiled. Flames still licked up the ruin that was left, even though a great horseshoe of firefighters remained on site, having battled back the blaze. The entirety of the store's West House was gone, the East eaten from the inside out. Raymond's fist instinctively tightened, causing Nancy – whose hand he'd been holding – to recoil.

It was only the sight of the Buckingham Hotel that brought Raymond back to his senses. That was exactly how Nancy had hoped it would be. The Buckingham stood, unblemished, at the head of Berkeley Square, its white façade made more brilliant still by the devastation they'd seen in the city beyond, the great copper crown sitting at the peak of its edifice as if reaching, defiantly, for the Messerschmitts which tumbled over it each night. Berkeley Square, where autumnal flowers were still in full colour and the grass a verdant green, seemed an oasis in the increasingly ruined city.

The taxicab drew up at the hotel's grand white colonnade, and before Nancy could guide Raymond out, the doorman had loped down the marble steps to open the door.

'Good Lord, it's Mr de Guise,' he began. 'Sir, it's been an age.'

The doorman was doing his best not to take in the injuries Raymond was wearing; the cane he was using to prop himself up as Nancy helped him out of the car, the way his arm was still strung up. Raymond was wearing his uniform, but his cap could not cover the dressing he still wore on the side of his head. The nurses had cropped his hair even closer to his scalp.

'Come on, Raymond,' said Nancy, as gently as if she was guiding an old man, 'we should take the tradesman's entrance.'

'Nonsense, ma'am!' the doorman replied. 'I'll not hear of it, and neither would Mr Knave. Mr de Guise isn't on the Housekeeping staff – with no offence meant, ma'am. He's not on the staff at all any longer – and, in my book, that makes him a guest.' The doorman stepped back, and beckoned them to follow him to the hotel's gleaming brass doors. 'In you go, Mr de Guise – and thank you, thank you from the bottom of our hearts.'

As Raymond followed Nancy through the revolving doors, he couldn't help think that, whatever the doorman was thanking him for, he hadn't done nearly enough to warrant it. All he'd truly done was survive – and even then not very successfully, for he hadn't brought his brother home, and too many others had perished on the way.

He tried hard to battle those thoughts away, and the music that was drifting up from the Grand Ballroom helped. From the

ANTON DU BEKE

middle of the black-and-white chequered reception hall, where
guests buzzed back and forth and porters, concierges and pages
busied themselves attending to their every need, he could hear
the Archie Adams Orchestra taking the ballroom through one
of their more energetic numbers.

There were still a few moments until his meeting with Mr
Knave. He took Nancy by the hand and drifted down the arched
hall towards the Grand Ballroom's doors. There, he slipped
through, and watched as the demonstration dances began.

Nancy's brother, Frank Nettleton, was leaner, more elegant
than Raymond remembered. He squeezed Nancy's fingers,
because she was feeling the pride of it too. The way he held
Mathilde Bourchier, their footwork speeding up as the foxtrot
took flight with the music, showed a young dancer coming into
the full command of his talent. A smile passed Raymond's lips,
and it lifted Nancy's heart to see it. He hadn't smiled nearly
enough in the summer that had just passed – but the ballroom,
as ever, was the opening to his heart.

'Marcus is a special dancer,' Raymond breathed, watching the
leader. There was happiness in it, but there was bittersweetness,
too – because this had once been *his* ballroom. Until war had
come and he'd taken the King's shilling, he himself had been the
King here. From the day the Grand first opened its doors, until
last autumn, this place had been his home. Now he was – what
had the doorman called him? – a *guest*.

'Come on, Nancy,' he said – and, catching Frank's eye as he
danced, inclined his head in pride, 'Mr Knave must be waiting
by now.'

He said his farewells to Nancy, who marched off to her duties
in the Housekeeping Lounge, and made his own way behind the
reception desks, and the hall where the Hotel Director's office
lay. He hadn't taken more than a stride when a middle-aged

reception clerk rushed up to him, declaring, 'I'm sorry, sir, but this area is reserved for staff. Perhaps I can help? Have you a query?' and tried to hustle him back to the black-and-white chequers. The clerk was new, of course. There was no reason why a middle-aged hotel attendant ought to have known the name Raymond de Guise, nor recognised him outside of the ballroom – but something in the idea still stung Raymond. It had been less than a year since he last danced in the ballroom. He'd stepped out in the Grand at Christmas, before shipping out for France. But so much had happened, it felt like a different world.

'I've an appointment to see Mr Knave.'

'Let me escort you there, sir.'

It was less than twenty yards to the end of the hall, and Raymond had walked it a hundred times before, but he acquiesced with good grace and allowed the check-in attendant to present him at Mr Knave's office door as if he was a royal attendant presenting some new visitor to court. Then the attendant scuttled away, and Raymond was alone with the Hotel Director.

The office had changed since he was last here. It was lighter, airier, in spite of the tape that criss-crossed the glass windows to guard against the reverberation of nearby bombs. Many of the old filing cabinets had been taken off for archiving somewhere else, and consequently Mr Knave had been able to introduce a snug little corner to the office, with two armchairs facing each other across a table of some Ottoman design – a gift, Raymond assumed, from one of the dignitaries now calling the Buckingham their home-in-exile. It was here that Raymond and Walter Knave settled.

Walter Knave was a tiny man, an imp in comparison to Raymond. His association with the Buckingham Hotel extended back generations, but his current tenure as director had lasted only a year. Upon his first arrival, pickled in liquor and very clearly a rushed appointment by the Hotel Board, few at the Buckingham had given Mr Knave any hope of carrying the hotel through wartime; but, looking at him now, Raymond saw a man much changed. The first thing he noticed was that there was not a drop of liquor in the office. No bottles of port, no magnum of Champagne, no crystal decanter filled with the finest whisky. Mr Knave was sober, and had been for months.

'Lance Corporal,' Walter began. 'I'm glad to see you well.'

Raymond had to smile at this, and Walter Knave smiled in return.

'*Well* is a subjective quality, Mr Knave. I've taken quite a bruising. In part, that's why I asked Nancy to arrange this meeting with you. You see, I'm told my division won't expect, nor *accept*, my return until the New Year. I'm stranded here in London, my body riddled with cracks and pains, until Christmas has come and gone. My part in this war isn't over, sir, but I've been put on hiatus. It's my *off-season*, if you like. And, sir, I'm looking for something to do.'

Walter Knave might have been an octogenarian, but he was no fool. There hadn't been a ballroom at the Buckingham the first time he was director here, but he'd quickly learnt of its importance to the institution. He'd had to learn all about music and dance; he'd been the one to hire Marcus Arbuthnot to replace Raymond at the head of the troupe, and in doing so he'd begun to understand the kinds of benefits the ballroom brought. It was because of the ballroom that the Buckingham had won so much of the new custom coming from the Continent's exiled dignitaries and governments. Without the ballroom, King Zog of Albania and his entourage wouldn't now be occupying suites on the second storey, nor hosting visitors in the Candlelight

Club most evenings – spending all of the gold, or so it was said, that they'd smuggled out through Greece. The ballroom was the beating heart of the Buckingham; it was through the ballroom that all the fresh riches of war were being poured. And Raymond de Guise had once been at the ballroom's heart.

'I should have thought,' croaked Walter Knave, 'that the thing you could do is *recover*, Lance Corporal.'

It was what Nancy had said. But what neither of them realised was that there was no recovery, no sitting around idly, twiddling his thumbs while London burned. 'I can't offer my services to the ballroom, Mr Knave – and, by the looks of it, my talents aren't needed there either. Marcus has the troupe drilled to perfection.'

'Well, he's trained dancers for world championships, as you know.'

'He's been to more finals than any other man I've known,' Raymond agreed. 'You made a very wise appointment. But, sir, I *know* the Grand Ballroom. I've lived it for nearly ten years. I've seen it through triumphs and disasters. I've helped countless young dancers reach the peak of their ability in the Grand. My hope is that, while my body knits itself back together, I might offer my services again – not as a dancer, but as a tutor. Somebody who might be on hand to help that young troupe, to give pointers and solve problems. Young Frank's footwork, for instance…'

Even as Raymond said it, he realised he was grappling at straws. Having seen Frank in the Grand just now, it was very clear that Marcus and Karina were doing an expert job at polishing young Frank up. If he wasn't quite at the peak of his prowess yet, surely it was only a matter of time.

In the end, though, what Raymond thought didn't matter – for Walter Knave had come to the same conclusion.

ANTON DU BEKE

'I'm afraid, Lance Corporal, that it's not a simple matter of
you waltzing your way back into the ballroom this autumn. The
Company has had to – how shall we say? – *reorganise* itself
in your absence. A certain balance has been achieved. A new
vision, under a new leader. If you sashayed back in there, it
might provoke a certain … uncertainty. Right now, they look
to Marcus to lead them; if you were there, the dancers might
become uncertain. Cracks might begin to appear. I cannot afford
those cracks.' Walter paused, for he had seen the displeasure
colouring Raymond's face. 'Mr de Guise, we're already being
challenged by the Savoy, the Ritz, the Imperial. They're coming
after our guests. It might not be war like you know it, but it's
war all the same. And it's the ballroom that keeps those guests
with us …'

'I could be an asset, Mr Knave. I've danced here for a decade.'

Walter was hesitant, but he shook his head all the same.
'Mightn't there be some other way to put yourself to good use?
Young Nettleton himself works three nights answering telephones for the Fire Service. We have ARP wardens and other
volunteers on our staff. Lord knows, London needs good men
on the ground. We can't leave it all to those up in the skies
above.'

Raymond ruminated on this for a time. The thought had, of
course, been in his mind already. He only feared his body was
not capable of the work that needed to be done. Yet perhaps
there was a way. There were old men and children among the
Air Raid Precautions department. An off-guard soldier with a
limp and a crack in his skull might just about do.

He was about to take his leave when Walter Knave added,
'There is *one* other thing, Raymond. I make no promises on
this, because of course you must see how your body fares as
we approach the winter months – but the Board met yesterday

evening and concocted a plan for this Christmas's festivities. Now, as you know, traditionally the Buckingham has held its balls on Midwinter's Eve. But Mr Hastings – and I should add that he has the full support of the rest of the Board in this – would like us to continue the good work we began last year.' Last Christmas, the ball had been dedicated to the influx of Polish refugees who'd found their way to Great Britain; in July, the Grand had celebrated the miracle of Dunkirk by hosting the Summer Ball in honour of its veterans and remembrance of its dead.

'What does he have planned?'

'Mr Hastings has had the Board sign off on an evening we're calling "ONE GRAND NIGHT". It won't be a ball this year, not in the strictest of senses. Our aim is to spend an evening auctioning the greatest dancers ever to have graced our ballroom to both our guests and prospective guests. It's hoped this might help us retain our most prized guests throughout the year, and draw new ones in for the years to come. Well, once they've seen the ballroom, why would they ever want to go anywhere else? How does the Imperial Ballroom compare to the Grand? We've already sent invitations to your old partner, Miss Marchmont, in the hope she might return – for one night only, you understand. Mr Hastings is writing to your old mentor, Georges de la Motte. We're quite certain that some sizeable sums will be paid for stars like these. And, of course, that isn't money we intend to keep as capital here at the hotel. It's to go to the war effort. To the relief of London's poor. We don't need the riches, Raymond – what we're after is the *reputation*.'

Inwardly, Raymond smiled. Walter Knave really was a consummate professional. Reputation was the life's blood of every luxury hotel.

'I'm quite sure, Lance Corporal, that your appearance in the

Grand for *one night only* wouldn't upset the delicate balance Marcus and Karina have instituted in the troupe. And I'm equally certain that, if you were fit enough to take part, there would be much merriment – and much wealth – generated by an auction for a night with the legendary Raymond de Guise.' He paused, because another idea had just struck him. 'And if you're not fit, Raymond – well, events like these do need compères. We're going to need an auctioneer. There are worse ways to contribute than this.'

The idea was circling in Raymond's mind as he left Walter Knave's office and returned, alone, to the edges of the Grand. By now, the demonstration dances were coming to an end. The guests in attendance were applauding the troupe as they disappeared through the dance floor doors, quickly followed by the stripped-down version of the orchestra whose music had filled the ballroom.

Yes, Raymond thought – and Nancy would have been proud to sense his heart lifting again as he drew in the smells of the ballroom – it would be good to dance here one more time, before he re-joined his division. It would be good to feel the sprung dance floor beneath his feet, and let the music fill him up. Good to take a guest in his arms, and know that he was bringing some magic to the world again.

But December still seemed a long time away. Who knew what might befall Great Britain by then? Would the battle in the skies be over? Would London have fallen, its fascists been freed, a new government sitting in Downing Street – just like the puppet governments now strutting around in Norway and France?

No, he thought, he couldn't wait until then. Three months was an ice age in this time of war. Between now and then, countries would fall, continents be overrun – and countless innocents, all with families and loved ones, would die.

So, yes, dance he would, if dance he could.

But first there had to be something else.

Something *more*.

Chapter Three

It felt churlish to complain about being weary, when not a soul in London slept the whole night through, but when Billy Brogan awoke early that morning – having spent half the night in the Anderson shelter out back, and the other half in fitful dreams of oceans on fire – he was exhausted beyond measure. Still, there was some comfort that came from sleeping in his old childhood bedroom – he'd had to give up his quarters at the Buckingham when he was shipped off to France – and breathing in the familiar scent of his family home.

If it wasn't for the clattering coming from downstairs, he might have slept all day.

The Brogan house always woke early in the mornings; Billy's father worked at Billingsgate fish market and, consequently, awoke long before dawn to cross the city in time for the deliveries – and his mother, used to looking after her gaggle of children, still kept to the same routines, even though the Brogan brood was now scattered across Suffolk. The problem was – Billy's father wasn't on shift this morning, and he was quite certain Frank Nettleton (who lodged here) wasn't due at the Buckingham until this afternoon. Besides, he could hear him snoring through the thin bedroom wall.

Billy picked himself out of bed, ignoring the protest of his leg, and used his cane to lever himself out of the bedroom and to the top of the stairs. The Brogan house, at No. 62 Albert Yard, Lambeth, was a higgledy-piggledy, creaking old property, its single staircase cutting back and forth so many times it was like forked lightning running through the building. Consequently, all that Billy could see from this high up was that there were lights on downstairs.

Lights and a lot of noise.

He came tentatively down one set of stairs, then tentatively down a second. His parents' door was still ajar – they left it ajar all night long, the act of a husband and wife with so many children they knew little fists would come knocking if they dared keep it closed – and, through the gap, he saw that they were sleeping. He couldn't begrudge them; they'd spent all night in the shelter too.

But if it wasn't Frank Nettleton, and it wasn't his mother and father, then who was it, clattering around the Brogan house at this ungodly hour?

Billy was suddenly very grateful that he was carrying his cane in his hands. Well, being disabled had to have some silver linings.

Downstairs, the Brogan house had only two rooms – the big living room, where the fireplace dominated the wall and his mother's table was used for breakfast, supper, and all sorts of odd jobs in-between; and the kitchen, with its larder off to one side. The stairs down which Billy was edging plunged into the narrowest of hallways, tucked behind the living room – but, from here, you could slip through a back door, into the larder, and therefore approach the living room from the kitchen door. This Billy did. It was only because of the clatter coming from the living room that the intruder didn't hear the clicking of his cane as he slipped through.

Through the larder, through the kitchen – and straight to the living-room doors. He stopped at the doorjamb, heart beating in panicked bursts, and gathered himself before he peered through.

A figure was at his mother's sideboard, flinging open drawers and ferreting through them, then smashing them closed angrily again. On the table, between his mother's sewing machine and his father's stack of newspapers – Mr Brogan was very diligent at keeping on top of the war news, and had been ever since Billy shipped out to France – was a china plate piled high with badly scrambled eggs, bacon and toast.

Billy's heart stuck in his throat. His father had read, and spoken at length, about how the privations of the war were driving people to theft. His own market, already devastated by the limits posed upon fishing too far from the coastlines, had been broken into on multiple occasions by profiteers seeking to make a quick return. But Billy had never imagined his own house might be the target of one of these thieves. It made his blood boil. The enemy was supposed to be on the Continent, not right here in his own front room.

He lifted his cane, grasping it like a weapon, and pitched suddenly into the room.

The figure was draped in a long, oversized brown coat – no doubt something else they'd stolen – with badly cropped red hair. Until Billy cried out, 'Put your hands where I can see them!', they'd been hunched over the sideboard, furiously attacking another drawer. Now, they turned round – revealing plump, heart-shaped lips, cheeks dusted in freckles, glittering green eyes... and a startled expression that perfectly matched Billy's own.

In fact, it might have been that Billy was looking into a mirror. 'Annie Brogan!' Billy cried out, in consternation.

'There's no knives and forks,' Annie railed. 'Billy, why's Ma moved the knives and forks?'

Billy didn't know whether to embrace her or start pummelling her around the head with a rolled-up newspaper – just like their father used to do, whenever they scrapped. Annie Brogan was the second eldest of Billy's siblings and, at fourteen years old, seven years younger than him. She looked a mess – with her oversized coat, badly cut hair, and general grubbiness, she had the air of a vagrant about her. The fact was, right now, she ought to have been in the Suffolk countryside where the Brogan children had been sent – to two neighbouring villages, with a house in each for half the Brogan brood; well, it had been so difficult to house all six of the evacuees together. It made him less mad to know that the food heaped up on the table was for Annie – but only *slightly* less, because she'd helped herself to eggs and bacon meant for three, and more toast than she could possibly eat. It was a good job Billy was used to lifting scraps from the hotel kitchens and room service trolleys – the Brogan family's ration-books couldn't have coped with a crime like Annie Brogan had just perpetrated.

'What's going on?' Billy stammered. 'Annie, what are you even doing here?'

'I'm having my breakfast,' Annie chirruped; then, with a frisson of darkness to her voice, '*if* I can find any knives and forks. What does Ma expect me to do? Trough it like a pig?'

Billy – who had seen Annie eating like a pig on more than one occasion – was still bewildered as he levered himself to the other side of the room, opened a cupboard, and brought out a knife and fork. Their mother had gone half-mad with rearranging the house after the evacuation; something to do with the empty nest feeling, Frank had said, and heart-breaking to see.

'Annie,' he said as he watched her start stuffing her face, 'you're going to have to explain. What happened? Why are you here?'

Annie looked up quizzically, face smeared in egg and bacon grease. 'To do my bit, of course.'

'Your ... bit?'

'Well, you've been under the weather, haven't you, Bill? All this unfortunateness with your leg. It hardly seemed fair that you were here, looking after Ma and Pa, when it's likely you're the one needing looking after. And what good am I in the country anyway? It was all right for a while. Gracie-May needed some ointment on her knee when she grazed it, and then there were bedtime stories to tell, and – Lord help me – bedwetting enough to drown in. But after a while all that stopped, and the rest were just getting on with it, happy as anything, and I thought – what's the point of *me*? All I'm doing is pottering around all day. Bit of schooling, bit of cooking, bit of cleaning. I reckoned I'd be better use doing that here, where it matters. So here I am.'

Billy whispered, 'Here you are,' in disbelief.

'I got the train yesterday afternoon. By the time I'd reached London, of course, those sirens started. So I've been in a shelter out east all night. It's a devil of a walk from there, Billy. I'm famished.'

'I can see,' said Billy. 'Your plate's nearly clean.'

'So, are you going to give me a hug?'

Billy was the eldest and, though he'd often adopted a benevolent uncle's role in his siblings' lives, he had never ignored a chance for some gentle teasing either. 'I'll wait until you've had a bath, thanks Annie. And maybe until you've borrowed some of Ma's lavender water as well.'

Billy fell into the chair opposite her. There was one piece of toast left and this he snatched before Annie could lay her grubby fingers on it. And it hit him then, how much he'd missed his brothers and sisters. That riot of voices, that squabbling mass, that noisy, adoring gaggle of them. He hadn't got to experience their absence when they first went away, for in the same moment he had been sent off to France – but in the last months, the silence in the house had been deafening.

He heard creaking on the floorboards upstairs. Somebody was awake – either his mother, his father, or Frank.

'Annie, they're going to be ...' Billy didn't know how their parents were going to react. Either elated or furious – both things were possible. 'You better have something to tell them. Something better than "I just jumped on a train." Make out like you have a plan. Something you're determined to do. They'll understand that, just like they did with me when I joined up with the Buckingham Hotel. Remember? Pa wanted me at Billingsgate, just like him – learn the ropes, work my way up, something steady and reliable, where a man could know his place. But I knew I could do better for us than that. I convinced 'em of it. You've just got to have the vision, Annie. If you don't, they're going to put you straight back on the train and—'

'I'm fourteen years old,' she declared, indignantly. 'They can't just put me back on a train. I'm a grown woman and I can—'

Grown woman, thought Billy. *Grown woman!* Not even Billy himself had been so sure of himself at the age of fourteen. Part of him wanted to rap his knuckles on Annie's head, just to knock some sense into her – and another part wanted to throw back his head and laugh. There was fire in the Brogan blood; it came from their Ma and Annie had it in bucket-loads.

'Annie?' came a voice from the bottom of the stairs.

And then, 'Annie, dear?' came a second, more incredulous voice.

Billy looked over his shoulder. There stood his father and, just a step behind, his mother as well. Both of them had faces etched in surprise. Both those faces transformed from bewilderment, to pleasure, to concern in a manner of moments. 'Annie Brogan,' their father began, 'what in the good Lord's name are you doing here?'

'Oh Annie, dear,' their mother cried out, 'Annie, what's happened?'

'Nothing's happened, Ma. I just thought...' Annie faltered. Billy flashed her a look and it was evident that the things he'd said had wormed their way into her brain. *Make out like you have a plan. You've just got to have the vision. If you don't, they're going to put you straight back on the train...*

'Ma,' Annie announced, overflowing with bravado, 'Pa. It just wasn't good enough, me sitting out there doing reading and arithmetic and collecting hens' eggs from the coop. Not when you three are here, labouring through these bombings and scrabbling to put dinner on the table. So I'm here to help out.' She forked another load of egg into her mouth – just, Billy was certain, so she'd have a little time to think. She'd have to do it fast, though – her plate was almost clean. 'It's high time I started helping this family properly,' she declared at last, 'and... and... Billy here's showing me exactly how I can do it. Aren't you, Bill?'

'Am I?' Billy whispered.

'Yes,' said Annie, with a hint of a glare in her eyes, *'just like you said.'* She popped the last corner of toast in her mouth and beamed. 'Billy here's promised he'll get me a job at the Buckingham Hotel. Then I'll be bringing another wage into this house, and we'll be living like kings. Isn't that right, Bill?'

Billy froze. It was the perfect trap, and Annie had sprung it flawlessly. He shuffled around in his seat, so that he saw both his mother and father full in the face. Before they rushed over to Annie to embrace her, they looked at him with expectation. He withered inside.

'Ma,' he said, 'Pa, get ready to be astounded. By the end of the week, there'll be two Brogans nattering with high society in the Buckingham Hotel.'

Billy had no idea how he was going to accomplish it. He'd thought of nothing else, all the way across London. There was a time when the long morning walk, over the river, up through Westminster and beyond, would have filled Billy's mind with ideas and schemes; now that he was forced to ride the buses to Berkeley Square each morning, his imagination seemed to be dulled. He was still none the wiser when he disembarked from the bus on Regent Street and loped the last stretch into Mayfair. Incredibly, last night's bombardment had not touched the opulent townhouses that surrounded the square. Not for the first time, Billy thought how London really was a city of two distinct halves – those who had money, and those who had none. Not even the Luftwaffe was the great leveller; somehow, even now, the poor souls of London seemed to suffer more.

All Billy could think, as he wended his way in through Michaelmas Mews, was that he might be able to pull a few favours in the Housekeeping Lounge. Nancy had always been a good friend, and now that she'd risen to a position of some authority – still, of course, under the aegis of the indomitable Mrs Moffatt – she might be able to bring some influence to bear. Billy and Raymond had got out of France together – or at least they'd tried to. Something in that bound the de Guise and Brogan families together; it just had to.

It was still early when he reached the Housekeeping Lounge, and the breakfast service – when Mrs Moffatt or Nancy gathered the girls and prescribed the day's duties to each – was almost coming to an end. As Billy limped his way along the hall, the door opened up, and out of it cantered Rosa Bright, Frank's sweetheart – who winked at him as she passed – and a group of the other girls, who all took lodgings in the hotel's rickety staff quarters, hidden in the attic space above the Continental and Grand Colonial suites. Among them, Mary-Louise slowed down. She had almost gone past when she stopped suddenly and took him by the shoulders. 'Billy, you look like you've seen a ghost.'

He hadn't often spoken to Mary-Louise. She'd joined the Buckingham when Billy was already bound for France, in that first flush of war when so many had suddenly changed their lives, left London or joined the war effort at home. Some of the chambermaids had gone off to the WVS, others to the Women's Land Army – and a rush of younger girls, like Mary-Louise, had taken their place. Only eighteen years old, Mary-Louise came from a sprawling South London family who were very glad she'd found some honest work at a time of such crisis. She stood Billy's full height, with strawberry-blonde hair pinned back in a bun (the same style that every chambermaid was compelled to wear) and eyes of the deepest chocolate brown. Frank and Rosa had said she could be spiky, but Billy himself had never seen this. He certainly didn't see it now; she was looking at him with an expression that spoke of softness, pride, and not a little gratitude.

'The other girls say it was you, Billy, who brought Mrs Moffatt back from Berkeley Square.' Billy wasn't sure of what she was speaking, until she added, 'The daylight raid. Rosa said Mrs Moffatt had wandered out, and you were the one who got her back to the shelters. And, well, I wanted to say *thank you*. The old bird hasn't been herself, not since the bombardment started. But to think that she just wandered out there, right into the eye of the storm...' Mary-Louise's voice had become full of emotion, and her rough South London twang became even more pronounced the more emotional she got. 'Well, Billy, that's all I wanted to say. Thank you.'

Billy knew how much Mrs Moffatt meant to the girls, though he hadn't, until this moment, known that they had started calling her 'the old bird'. To many of these girls she had become a second mother – or even a grandmother, since the gulf between Mary-Louise and Mrs Moffatt was so vast. Billy rather liked the way she was thanking him; it made him puff up his chest. For that reason, he decided he wouldn't tell her that it was really Archie Adams who'd done the talking and convinced Mrs Moffatt where she ought to be. Billy didn't have the right words, but everyone in the Buckingham knew the strength Mrs Moffatt took from Archie's friendship.

'Well,' Billy said at last, 'we've got to look after each other, haven't we?'

'Well, that's what I mean,' said Mary-Louise, and tried to hide the smile that had crept onto her features. 'You see, most Sundays I go up to my uncle's in Camden town. Uncle Ken normally puts on a bit of a spread – he always knows where to get the right stuff. I help with his boys and, well, it's just nice to be somewhere else, you know? Uncle Ken put me up once upon a time – my mother had thrown me out, you see ... but that's another story.' It sounded like a terrible story, but Mary-Louise was snorting with laughter. Not for the first time, Billy marvelled at how different families could be; his own, wild and unruly as it was, was just brimming with love. Not all families were the same. 'I don't know, Billy. I see you up and down these halls, and I'm not sure you really know what we all think of you – all you done in France, and now right here, under our noses. I know you got plenty of people looking out for you, but ...'

Billy blurted out, 'I'd love to.'

It was what Mary-Louise needed to hear. She'd started

blathering, just to fill the silence, and now she stopped. Her big, brown eyes were bright. She was still bracing Billy's shoulders, and now she tightened her hold. 'I'll send him a note. We can go up together, next time they're free. He'll want to know about France and Dunkirk and, why, everything you did. Aunt Marge makes the best Victoria sponge. Well, she's never short of eggs.'

Mary-Louise gave him a wink, then hurried up the House-keeping hall.

Billy stood there, discombobulated. He wasn't quite sure what to make of it – he certainly wasn't quite sure he wanted to talk about France and Dunkirk and all that had happened on those beaches – but a day out with Mary-Louise was surely going to be some sort of tonic. If only he could solve the puzzle of Annie's sudden return in the meantime...

Mrs Moffatt hadn't attended the breakfast service this morn-ing, but Nancy had remained in the Housekeeping Lounge, sorting through paperwork among the remnants of the morn-ing's breakfast. At least the staff of the Buckingham Hotel didn't go hungry. The boon of working here was that the hotel often fed its staff, which meant their ration-books could be put to good use filling their families' larders instead. The leftovers on the table in the lounge were worth a king's ransom. Billy wondered how many of London's poor were eating Continental croissants and greengage preserve. Black pudding was a delicacy in a butcher's shop window, but big chunks of it had been left uneaten on the chambermaids' plates.

'Billy?' Nancy ventured – and, rising from the table, put her arms around him. 'Are you well?'

Billy couldn't lie, not to Nancy, so instead he said, 'I've got a bit of a problem, Nance.'

Instinctively, Nancy kicked out a chair, drew the teapot over and poured Billy a steaming cup. Mrs Moffatt kept a drawer full of barley sugars which she liberally shared with her girls – it was almost a religious belief with Mrs Moffatt, that a barley sugar could cure all ills – and Nancy stepped into the office to gather a few. Billy had a sweet tooth; when she returned, he was stirring Royal Gardens honey into his tea.

'Is Raymond OK, Nance?'

Billy had thought Raymond dead once before; the thought that he had made it back from France, only to perish on a London street, was almost too cruel.

'He's going to be. But this problem of yours, Billy? Well, you're here for a reason?'

Billy laughed. 'I'd like to say it was just a social visit. Just old friends, sorting out the ills of the world over a good pot of tea and brown sugar.' He'd heaped brown sugar in, as well as the honey. 'But something's come up, Nancy – and I reckoned, if anyone could help, it would be you.'

Nancy had hardened. London was an ever-moving tidal wave of bad news this autumn; she braced herself for more. 'Billy, what is it? Is it your injury? Has something happened to you?'

'Oh no, Nance!' Billy exclaimed, surely with more bravado than he felt. 'I'm right as I've ever been. Leg's bothering me a bit, but you'd know all about that. It's nothing I can't soldier through. The hotel post room's light work – even enjoyable, now that sour old Mrs Farrier's upped and left. And, well, I reckon I got myself a nice day out on the horizon – I'm stepping out to Camden with Mary-Louise.'

Nancy's eyes brightened. Romance, she thought, for Billy Brogan? Well, the war had thrown up so many stranger things...

'Then what is it, Billy?'

Billy slurped at his tea, set down his cup and wiped his sleeve across his lips – the habit of the Billy Brogan of old, not the smart young soldier he'd become.

'It's my sister, Nance. Something's got to be done about my sister.'

Chapter Four

The music soared.

There wasn't a guest in the Grand Ballroom who didn't feel their hearts filled in moments like these. Now that the Buckingham truly was a home for so many – around the edges of the dance floor stood dignitaries from Oslo, the royalty of Albania, a Bordeaux baron and his lady wife – it felt as if the world itself was holding its breath, as Archie Adams tinkled the first ivory keys of his piano and the trumpets sounded their march. Queen Wilhelmina of Holland – who was visiting from Claridge's, and on whose residency the Buckingham Board had clearly established its sights – stood in a phalanx of black-clad ladies-in-waiting, while her son Prince Bernhard draped himself over the balustrade, awaiting the appearance of the famed beauties who danced on the ballroom floor. Karina Kainz, he'd been told, was a goddess worthy of antiquity.

Backstage, Marcus Arbuthnot – he of the russet gold hair, with eyes like a winter skyline – gathered the troupe. Marcus, who towered over the other dancers by half a foot, was in the early years of middle-age but still carried himself like a Herculean hero. When he opened his arms to the troupe, it felt like he was embracing every dancer at once. Frank Nettleton, who was diminutive in comparison, had often wondered if his own 'presence' could ever be as vast and impressive as Marcus's; probably 'presence' was something you were born with. Raymond used to say that a man could achieve greatness through dedication and hard work – but Frank very much doubted that Marcus's oozing confidence and style had been achieved through hard work.

'Dear friends,' he began, with that eloquent, theatrical air he had brought to the ballroom last year, 'one more time, for the Buckingham Hotel. One more time, for love and beauty. One more time, to show the world that good things survive. Through those doors, we will make miracles happen. Tonight, until the sirens compel us to the shelters – as surely they will – we shall take our guests into our arms and reveal to them the *reason*. The reason we must live. The reason that, in the darkest of times, we must not forget what it is to revel in the light…'

Alone among the dancers in the Buckingham troupe, only Mathilde Bourchier had not joined the circle. On the other side of the dressing rooms, she stood in front of one of the area's many ornate mirrors, turning herself this way and that as she tried to ascertain if the forest green silk gown she was wearing fitted her perfectly. Occasionally, her eyes drifted up and, in the mirror, she caught sight of Marcus pontificating – yes, *pontificating*, that was what it was – at the troupe, Karina Kainz standing at his shoulder like a Greek goddess, her thick blonde hair falling in curls. Getting herself ready for the night when all of this hubbub was going on was proving increasingly tricky. Mathilde wanted to centre herself. She wanted calm before the storm of the ballroom. Her old mentor Hélène Marchmont had been like that too – but the complexion of the ballroom had changed so dramatically since Mathilde first danced here, it was difficult to know where she belonged.

'You ready, Mathilde?'

Frank Nettleton had appeared in the mirror behind her. Marcus would tell her that she belonged in Frank's arms – the two young darlings of the Grand, rising together – but, in her heart, Mathilde wasn't so sure. There was nothing *wrong* with Frank Nettleton. If he sorted out that unruly hair, and did something about his poise during those difficult reverse turns, he'd be a thoroughly impressive young dancer. But Mathilde had been dancing since she could walk – her mother, who'd once haunted the ballroom circuit from Brighton to Blackpool, had seen to that. Frank had come to dancing so much later than Mathilde and, in her heart, she knew that it would always show. She liked him, but he wasn't the right partner for her.

Her eyes moved from Frank's face to Marcus, who was smoothing out the miniscule creases in Karina's gown. By God, he could be like a girl with her pony, the way he treated the dancers sometimes.

'Ready as I'll ever be,' Mathilde sighed, and turned round.

'Your heart isn't in it tonight. I can tell.'

Mathilde said, 'I'm a professional, Frank. If my heart isn't singing, I'll fake it.'

'But you heard what Mr Arbuthnot said. There are guests out there that Mr Knave's trying to woo to the suites. Steal some custom from Claridge's or the Savoy, turn the Buckingham into the centre of things…'

'Oh, Frank, you mustn't listen to all that.' Mathilde threaded her arm through his. 'Just dance, and ignore the rest. Just put on a show. When One Grand Night comes around, you'll want to be dancing with somebody special, won't you? It won't be the Buckingham troupe all in it together then – we'll be competing with each other for the best hand, the biggest prize. It will be you against Marcus, me against Karina…' At this, she allowed her eyes to drift over to Karina Kainz, who stood resplendent at the dance floor doors, awaiting the musical cue that would welcome them to the Grand.

Frank thought that Mathilde had, perhaps, missed the point of One Grand Night. It wasn't a gladiatorial contest, dancer against dancer; it was a show of unity, a way to bring some relief to Londoners who'd suffered so much – and if the hotel managed to impress enough to poach a few honoured guests from the Savoy and Claridge's, well, so much the better. He was about to explain as much when he saw the way Mathilde's eyes had lingered on Karina, and some other piece of the puzzle seemed to slot into place. 'Maybe you should talk to her more,' he ventured. 'I've been spending afternoons with her, when I can. She's helping me refine my oversway.'

Mathilda darted a waspish look at him out of the corner of his eye. 'I don't need refining, Frank. Not from her.'

After that, Frank tried to stay silent. Frank was proud, every evening, to be stepping out into the Grand. Even after a long summer of dancing, he still felt the magical rush every time the doors opened and he sallied out, to be swallowed up by the music. It was easier for Frank to revel in the beauty, because he'd never expected it in his life. As for Mathilde . . .

'I'm sorry, Frank,' she whispered. She'd relaxed at his side as they lined up to go through the doors. Frank detected a little shame – or perhaps embarrassment – in her tone. 'It's not your fault. It's not even *hers*.' Her eyes darted, again, at the elegance of Karina Kainz. 'I don't expect you to understand. But when I came to the Grand, the air was full of promises. Understudy to the great Hélène Marchmont! It felt like the world was at my fingertips. It felt like *I* could be a legend too. All those years of training, all those years of competitions and hardship and . . . and my *mother*.'

To Mathilde, it was almost a curse. But, whatever the story

was, Frank did not dare ask more. And he thought he understood, then, the way in which Mathilde was pinned: she'd been brought to the Grand to one day succeed Hélène Marchmont as the ballroom's queen. Then, when Hélène had been compelled to leave suddenly, the Board had not thought Mathilde quite ready for the post, and had opted, instead, for somebody with more reputation, more prowess, somebody who was more likely to win them the very best guests. Karina came with all of this pedigree and more. It left Mathilde waiting, and feeling further away from stardom than she'd ever been.

'You don't need to be the principal to be a great dancer, Mathilde,' said Frank. '*You're* great. You're already a-a-a legend.'

'Frank, you're stammering.'

He always did when he was nervous.

'What I'm trying to say is – we all *know* how good you are. The guests know it too. Just because it's Karina dancing with Marcus…'

Mathilde snorted, 'I'm not sure I'd want to dance with him anyway. All that syrupy nonsense, whispered in my ear. Who could stand for it?'

Frank thought that that 'syrupy nonsense' was actually inspiring. Marcus understood the emotions of the ballroom better than anyone; he was a very different kind of leader from Raymond, but nobody could doubt the amount of passion in the air when Marcus drew the troupe together.

Through the dance floor doors, the Archie Adams Orchestra reached a triumphant surge. 'That's our cue,' said Frank, and drew even closer to Mathilde. 'You'll be amazing,' he told her.

I know, thought Mathilde – and tried not to think about Karina Kainz as she and Frank cantered out through the opening doors.

The Grand Ballroom: the very heartland of dreams.

A myriad of lights shone down. Mathilde heard the wave of applause tumble over her. The pop of a Champagne cork as it arced across the room. Chandeliers flickered. Mirrors, high up in the curved vault of the walls, dazzled with lights like they were the heavens themselves.

Since the start of the Luftwaffe's campaign, the evening dances had begun earlier in the Grand, but the blackouts in the Berkeley Square windows made it seem as if it might be midnight already. Stepping into the Grand Ballroom could make you feel as if the rest of the world didn't exist. Here you danced, in a corner of the world carved out from all the rest, where all horror and darkness was banished and only music and light held sway.

Mathilde whirled in Frank's arms, gave herself to the music, let the Grand ballroom swirl around her in a riotous cavalcade of colour.

When the first number came to its end, the dancers of the Buckingham troupe left their partners and invited the guests onto the ballroom floor so that the true delights of the evening could begin. Every Buckingham dancer prided themselves on being able to make even the most inexperienced guest feel like royalty on the dance floor, but it seemed cheating, somehow, when Mathilde saw one of the minor Norwegian princes take Karina's hand and step into hold in the dance floor's heart. Prince Harald was far enough removed from the throne to never anticipate getting near it, but close enough that he had been awarded rooms at Bowdown House in Berkshire, to which most of the royals had absconded once the Luftwaffe's bombardment of London began. The young prince, however, was constantly tempted by the delights of the Buckingham and had returned to London to dance with Karina on more than one occasion.

Mathilde, meanwhile, found herself stepping into hold

with an altogether more unremarkable gentleman. Short and dumpy, with round spectacles on his even rounder face, he barely introduced himself as he took her arm. She supposed he was some member of the Norwegian ministry – the Buckingham was filled with them – and, if that was so, it rather explained his flat-footed, out-of-time dancing as Archie Adams struck up the next number. 'Dance With Me, Treasure' was supposed to be a quickstep – but, to Mathilde and her partner, it became an arduous trudge. Karina and her prince seemed to be dancing on air, soaring on the spirit of the music in the room; Mathilde was wading through treacle.

Consequently, she was grateful when, at the end of that number, her partner wrinkled his nose and said, 'Perhaps a little break – for a glass of Champagne?'

Sometimes the guests misunderstood the pact that was made on the ballroom floor – they took that spirit of togetherness, the air of romance, the thrill of the dance as something else, something *more*; it wasn't uncommon for a guest to become besotted with a particular dancer. But the way this man looked at her did not give Mathilde that kind of a chill. She supposed he was just looking for an excuse not to humiliate himself further on the dance floor – and so, to preserve his dignity (and because her place in the ballroom depended on her making the guests feel good about themselves), she followed him to a table by the balustrade, where a waiter bedecked in white with gold brocade almost immediately manifested with a magnum of Moët et Chandon.

'I'm sure you found me a boor on the dance floor, Miss Bourchier,' the guest said. His voice had a nasal quality, and he kept pinching the bridge of his nose, as if something was irritating him. 'I'm afraid I haven't spent as many evenings in the ballroom as you have. I look about me and I, er, see it for what it is – this beautiful *other* place, where different laws apply. A place of wonder and abandon. Just the sort of place one needs to retreat into this autumn. But I'm afraid I don't quite have the knack of it. I've got two left feet. Sometimes I struggle to walk in a straight line.' He punctuated his speech with a little snort of laughter, before clinking his Champagne flute against Mathilde's and toasting her good health. 'I suppose you're one of those who's been dancing since before they could walk, are you?'

'So my *mother* used to tell me,' said Mathilde – and there was the emphasis on 'mother' again, as if the word was riddled with spite. 'She was a darling of the ballrooms, you see. The great Camille Bourchier. She was out winning competitions while I was still in the crib – this was before my father left, you understand. They say she had the whole world at her feet.'

'What happened?'

Mathilde demurred, 'I'm sure you don't want to hear about my mother, Mr...?'

'Cockfosters,' the man replied.

Well, it certainly wasn't a Norwegian name. Now that she thought about it, there wasn't a hint of an accent in his voice either; the Norwegians she met all spoke the Queen's English as if it were there own, but you could often detect their ancestry in the way they stressed certain syllables, like music just a tiny bit off-key. For the first time, something bristled inside her. She looked over her shoulder. The ballroom was heaving tonight. There would be other guests to dance with, guests with whom she could truly show off what she was capable of. Let Karina Kainz get stuck with a tax inspector, she thought. *Give me a Crown Prince*.

'Your mother must be very proud of what you've achieved here, Miss Bourchier.'

'Oh, I dare say she is,' said Mathilde, draining her Champagne, 'but I haven't spoken to my mother in three years.'

'Oh,' Mr Cockfosters mouthed.

'There's no secret to it, sir. My mother took a tumble when I was small. After that, she could never compete. Dance, yes – but her idea of competing for the world championship was very much dashed. She was a tyrant after that, I'm afraid. One day I was merely her daughter; the next, I became her protégé. If she couldn't dance, well, *I* jolly well would – whether I wanted to or not.'

'And did you want to?'

Mathilde had given this question much thought over the years – she just hadn't expected to be speaking about it tonight, in the opulent environs of the Grand. She paused as Mr Cockfosters bowed to refill her Champagne flute. The fuzzy warmth of the first glass was already coursing through her body. Perhaps it was this that made her say, 'I always wanted to dance, that's true – but where my mother's ambition ends and my own takes over, I've never been sure. All I really know is that the ballroom's all I've ever known. I don't see my mother any more, Mr Cockfosters – well, once the devil's been sitting on your shoulder for too long, you start to want to shake him off. But I do believe that the yearning I have to be here comes from her. How much of it is nature? How much of it is the hectoring and bullying of my childhood? I suppose I'll never know. But my mother wanted to prove herself the best. I want that for myself as well.'

Mr Cockfosters made a steeple of his fingers and peered at her over the half-empty magnum. 'And *are* you, Miss Bourchier? Proving yourself the very best, here in the Grand?'

It seemed a question designed for this very evening. She looked, one more time, over her shoulder, down onto the dance floor where Karina Kainz was soaring on air, the prince's hand dancing on her waist. There was an angel, thought Mathilda. Every eye in the room seemed magnetically drawn her way.

The ferocity of the feeling inside her was almost too much to bear. This time, she took the Champagne bottle herself and refilled her glass, completely ignoring Mr Cockfosters as she did so.

Tall, blonde and beautiful – it was no wonder Karina had inherited the throne that once belonged to Hélène Marchmont. Mathilde, small, light and dark, could not compare.

Mr Cockfosters looked suddenly serious. 'I'm afraid I've rather unsettled you,' he said, and Mathilde detected a new frisson to his voice, a formality and confidence that had not been here before. 'I assure you it was not my intention – though the truth is, in a former role I interrogated the most Machiavellian men for the Metropolitan Police, and some of those old habits have not deserted me. Miss Bourchier, please don't think me a fraud – but our meeting tonight was no accident. My directors ordained it.' He reached into a pocket and handed Mathilde a little business card. It was a simple, stylised design in which the one word 'IMPERIAL' immediately stood out. 'I am the newly appointed entertainments director at the Imperial Hotel, Miss Bourchier. Now, you may find it odd that someone in my position can't perform a simple box-step without standing on his own feet, but do be assured that, what I lack in finesse, I more than make up for in business acumen. I came here tonight because your name has been whispered more than once in board meetings at the Imperial Hotel – and my directors would like to invite you to a meeting of minds in our ballroom next week.'

Mathilde didn't know whether it was the Champagne she'd drunk, but suddenly her body was lighting up with a new energy. The Grand whirled around her, a chaos of colours, with only Mr Cockfosters remaining in focus.

'A meeting?' she whispered, suddenly aware that this should be a secret. 'But what for?'

Mr Cockfosters pinched the bridge of his nose and smiled. 'Let me just say that the Imperial can see star potential, where the Buckingham sees only an understudy.' At this, he stood, smoothed down the creases of his dinner jacket, and stepped away from the table. 'Think about it, Miss Bourchier, and make contact with us if you can. There is more than one ballroom in London. And there is more than one way to capture your heart's desires.'

October 1940

Chapter Five

It had taken Raymond de Guise two weeks to bear any weight on his foot, and even now – as the early evening dark drew in, and Londoners from Berkeley Square to Brixton Hill hunkered down, anticipating the wail of the sirens and the aggressive reports of the ack-acks returning fire – he couldn't let go of his cane. He was standing in the hallway at No. 18 Blomfield Road, levering himself into his greatcoat – the second sleeve of which Nancy had kindly pinned back, to make accommodation for his arm – while Nancy waited somewhere behind. The terror of 'goodbye' was in the air. She'd said so little, but now he could feel the tension simmering – here, in their homely little hallway, where wedding portraits sat on a sideboard: Nancy and Raymond and, at their side, his best man Artie.

'How do I look?' Raymond said, trying to dispel the tension. There was a mirror hanging above the sideboard and, in its reflection, he saw himself, neither as a ballroom dancer nor a lance corporal, but as a veteran about to offer his support with the civic defence. At least his face had settled back into its old shape, his hair a shade thicker and darker, to hide the place where his scalp had been exposed. In the past two weeks the livid bruises he'd been sporting had faded away, and his foot – though still sore and prone to putting up a complaint – had started to heal. His arm was still weak, but it was not useless. It would take more than unexploded incendiaries to unman Raymond de Guise.

'I wish you wouldn't.'

Nancy's voice echoed along the hall. She was standing so close, almost near enough to touch – but when Raymond looked at her, somehow she seemed far away. She'd come off shift at the Buckingham just after midday and, ever since then, she'd clucked around the house uncertainly, as if she didn't know where she should stand, where she should sit. Now, though he'd suspected all along, Raymond knew why.

'Just give yourself a few more days. Another week. Raymond, you're not ready.'

Raymond said, 'The world isn't ready. None of us are ready. But I've got to, Nance. You see that, don't you? What use am I sitting around here? No ballroom, no regiment.' *No brother.* 'I can do this. They wouldn't have said yes if I couldn't. We've all got uses.'

'I didn't say you *couldn't.*' Nancy folded her arms across her breast. 'I asked whether you should. Not yet. It isn't time. How many times have I almost lost you in the last six months?' She stopped there. What she didn't say was: if you keep knocking on his door, Raymond, some day soon, Death's going to answer.

Raymond left his cane by the door and, only palming off the wall once, came down the hallway to kiss her tenderly on the cheek. 'I always come back, darling.'

Those words were so close to the words he'd said on his return from Dunkirk that something burst inside her. She put her arms around him and hung there for a time, until – when the moment had lingered too long – she drew away and watched him go.

After he was gone, Nancy busied herself in the kitchen. Then she marched around the house, fixing every blackout curtain in place, making certain that everywhere was locked tight. A stray window latch, of course, could not protect against a German bomb. A blackout curtain did not deter a Messerschmitt. But her insides were upended, she was unfathomably tired, and the thought of saying goodbye to Raymond every single night, not knowing if he was going to come back, was too much to bear.

She felt suddenly hot and dizzy. She'd hardly eaten today. That had to be it. Between that, the stresses of the Buckingham Hotel, and the thought of Raymond stepping out into the night before he was ready, she felt quite empty.

Tea and toast, Mrs Moffatt would have told her. Tea and toast could cure all the world's ills.

Well, it didn't feel that way tonight.

Raymond tried to ignore the pang he was feeling as he left No. 18 Blomfield Road and the taxicab took him to the north side of Hyde Park, where the great townhouses all hid behind their blackouts and the park's barrage balloons hung like great eclipses in the London sky. He wasn't blind to Nancy's feelings. There'd been moments – ordinarily in the dead of night, returning from the Anderson shelter at the bottom of their garden and unable to sleep – when he'd sat and listened to his records in the sitting room and knew, all of a sudden, that she was right. That, no matter what it did to his soul, he should stay there with her, and hold her tightly when the bombs came down, and drink up every moment they spent together until he was called back to his regiment and taken far away. But the nights were long with nothing to do. The fear took hold in the emptiness before the dawn. All he could see was Artie, fading from life. That was when he *knew* that, no matter what Nancy's misgivings were, he had to do this. If there was anything he could do to stop another family losing a loved one like Artie, he would give his heart and soul.

That was why he stood here now, outside a small black doorway on one of the green and pleasant boulevards north of Hyde Park, preparing to go in.

The door opened immediately as he knocked at it, and soon Raymond was waiting inside a spartan office – very evidently someone's sitting room, now put to a more civic use – where corkboards covered the walls, an Ordnance Survey map of London dominated the old hearth, and a dumpy old gentleman sat behind a desk, hammering away at a battered Olympia typewriter with half a chewed-up cigar dangling out of his lips.

The man barely looked up – so, for a time, Raymond was compelled to wait. Occasionally, he heard voices through the blackouts – people congregating on the boulevard, before hurrying on. Once, he opened his mouth to introduce himself – but the portly mole of a man behind the typewriter lifted a hand like a grandfather bidding his unruly grandchildren to silence, waited a second, and then returned to his feverish typing. Only several minutes later, when the man ripped the paper from the typewriter with gusto and added it to the pile teetering at his side, did he stand up, waddle round the table and, still chewing on his cigar, pump Raymond's good hand energetically.

'Lance Corporal de Guise, I presume?' he clucked, his baritone voice given a ghostly aspect by the cigar (and, quite probably, the thousands of others he'd smoked). 'Yes, you're on the list. I have to say, when they told me you'd taken a battering, I didn't expect you to be showing up with your arm still bound up and that cane you're propped up on. The doctors would make garters of my guts if they thought I was putting one of our finest in harm's way.'

Raymond wasn't sure about 'finest'. It seemed a lousy

expression for somebody who felt as if they hadn't quite done their duty – but here he was, all the same.

'The name's Mortimer Bond,' the dumpy fellow said. 'Former lance corporal myself, you know. Lance Corporal Bond, of days gone by. Plied my trade as an army medic after that – so I can tell you, now, that you shouldn't be standing here. But I'm going to let that pass – because I'll bet you'll only be standing on the doorstep at night's end if I dismiss you now, isn't that right?'

Raymond had been quite swept up in the little man's speech. Now he nodded, because nodding seemed the right thing to do.

'That's settled, then. Let's put you to some use. Even a three-legged donkey can pull a cart, isn't that so?'

'I'm not sure that particular picture image works, sir.'

Mortimer Bond took the cigar out of his mouth and ruminated, twirling it in his hands. 'I'm sure I've seen it, de Guise. On a farm, when I was a lad. Obstinate things, donkeys. They'll damn near look Death in the face, and all for the want of a carrot.'

Raymond tried to suppress a smile and was grateful when Mortimer Bond returned to his desk, studied the Ordnance Survey of London pinned above the hearth, selected one of the manifold red pins that dotted the cityscape and shifted it from one street to another. 'I've teams all over these quadrants. Wardens for reconnaissance and reporting. Rescue parties, when the worst comes to the worst. You'll have had gas training, of course, and no doubt that puts you in good stead. But what I'm really lacking tonight is—'

'I had it in mind that I could provide some use to the Fire Watchers Order, sir.'

The order had been announced in September, an auxiliary service to supplement the local brigades who ordinarily serviced London.

'Well, we'll be seeing about that,' Mortimer went on, 'but tonight I'm setting you on reconnaissance and patrol. It's fact finding, de Guise. Observation duties only. I don't want you scrabbling into any fallen buildings, not with a body as smashed up as yours. Look, I heard about what you did on the Whitechapel Road. As a matter of fact, I've the greatest respect for you lads who made it out of France in one piece. Hell of a thing, those beaches at Dunkirk. One for the generations. But, if you're anything like me as a younger man, you'll think it confers you some immunity against future disaster. I'm here to tell you it doesn't. We're a team here – a raggedy old team, old and young and *infirm*.' At this, his eyes glanced up and down Raymond. 'But we work as a team, because that's the way we'll get through it. I'm going to be handing you over to the custodianship of one of our other volunteers. They'll take you out onto Oxford Street, north side. Between there and the Euston Road, that's your beat for the evening, de Guise. Reconnaissance and reporting – am I understood?'

Raymond said, 'Yes, sir.'

'Good man. We'll see where this takes us after that – but, I must say, I'm damned pleased to have a decorated lance corporal on hand, even if it's just for a couple of months. That ought to inject some much needed rigour into operations around here. Oh, and, if you're hungry, the WVS has a canteen service running right in the middle of your quadrant. They'll over-sweeten your tea if they like the looks of you.' Mortimer Bond grinned. 'You're a handsome chap. I daresay you'll get a scone.'

His responsibilities to his new volunteer seemingly fulfilled, Mortimer Bond returned to his seat, used the dog-end of his first cigar to light up a second, and hurriedly fed another sheet of paper into his typewriter. The first puff of smoke was only just enveloping his head when there came the sound of the front door slipping open and footsteps approaching along the shadowed hall. Moments later, Mortimer Bond looked up, announced, 'This must be for you, de Guise,' and returned his features to the typewriter.

The door opened.

Standing in its frame, emerging from the blacked-out hall beyond, was a woman dressed in a grey lambswool coat. Raymond guessed her a little younger than Nancy. She stood as tall as Raymond's shoulder, with jet-black hair pinned back in a bun and her plump lips coloured with a deep crimson lipstick. Long and lithe – with something of an imperious air, in spite of her relative youth – she stepped into the office, gave Raymond a cursory look, and said, 'This our man, Mr Bond?'

Mortimer waved his hand airily, obviously too rapt in whatever he was typing to get back to his feet, or even glance up. 'Take him away, Cathy. The night hasn't yet started. Perhaps you'll have a chance to show him the ropes before ...' Mortimer brought his hands together, said 'BOOM!' with an amateur thespian's relish, and returned to his work.

'Follow me then, Lance Corporal. We've a bit of a march. Will you manage?'

'I'm sure I can make it to Oxford Circus, ma'am.'

The woman gave a spirited laugh, her teeth bright and white against the crimson lipstick. 'Then follow me,' she announced. 'The name's Everly, by the way, Cathy Everly. The patrol's down a man in my section – I'm afraid he kicked the bucket the night John Lewis went down – so we've been in sore need. I'll show you the ropes, if you can keep up.'

They'd already come down the shadowed hall together, and soon they were out in the bracing night air. Raymond, who felt he was falling a step behind for every three of hers, said, 'I'll keep up, ma'am. You won't have to worry about that.'

It was more difficult to do than it was to say. He followed Cathy along the edge of Hyde Park, passing through the Marble Arch and onto the western corner of Oxford Street – where the shops were all closed, and the last buses were grinding past as the blackout came into full force. There were still passers-by in the streets, and at Bond Street a group of young women were gathered at the door of a restaurant, hoping they might get in – but Raymond kept his mind focused on following Cathy Everly. She had a lordly air about her, as if she was used to people doing precisely as she requested; Raymond had seen this before, in the Buckingham Hotel, where the guests had rarely grown up without servants to do their every bidding. As for Cathy, she was brisk and to the point, and if ever Raymond was lagging too far behind, she made a point of telling him, 'We ought to be on site before the sirens. You'll want fortifying for the night ahead. It could be a long one.'

The 'site' in question was a vacant shop front off Great Portland Street, but before they got there, the vast ruin of the old John Lewis building reared up above them. What was left was cadaverous, the corpse of a building, its remaining walls and girders like the skeleton of the department store that used to be here. The site was cordoned off, and work teams had been industrious across the last days in clearing the rubble, then either bracing or bringing down the corners of the ruin that seemed most unstable. But it was difficult to believe that this was the place where, less than two years before, Raymond and Nancy had shopped together to set up their new home, the place to which all the various guests at their wedding had come to find gifts.

Cathy slowed as they passed the great ruin. She gazed up, the peaks of rubble as jagged as mountains against the stars. 'I was on duty when it happened. Not patrolling, not that night.

76

Well, there's still folks around here who think the Women's Voluntary Service ought to stay by the kettles, making the tea – or knitting cosies so the good, solid men of the ARP patrols don't get cold ears on a long night. I was at Control that night, answering the phones on Mr Bond's account, when the call came that we needed all hands. By the time I got here, the place was a furnace – and all those people trapped in the shelters underneath. You can scarcely believe they survived down there. It was an oil bomb. I've never seen such flames. But they got them all out. Too late to save the building, of course. The fire blew into the East House too, so there wasn't much left. But it's lives that matter, isn't it?'

'People can't be replaced,' whispered Raymond. He was still staring at what was left of John Lewis's western building. 'But there are many left to be saved,' he finally said, with more conviction. 'Where do we start?'

Cathy's eyes lingered on Raymond. She seemed to be considering every angle of him. Raymond had known that look before; his first captain had appraised him in quite the same way, back in basic training. Georges de la Motte, who had long ago taken Raymond under his wing in the world of the ballroom, had looked at him like this as well. 'Come with me, Raymond,' she said. 'There's something you should see.'

The East House of the John Lewis department store had not taken the incendiary's direct hit, and consequently much of it remained standing, a charred, smoke-blackened wreck. Workmen had sealed the ruins as best they could, and the store's workers had flocked here in the days after to warehouse what goods were left and secure the building, but Cathy knew the men standing night guard and, after a brief exchange, she was leading Raymond into the deathly husk. By torchlight, they moved through the smoky devastation, until soon Cathy was leading

Raymond up the surviving staircases, through the hollow halls, to emerge onto the building's roof. The smell of smoke was strongest up here. Ash had settled in banks against the building's uppermost walls.

'What is it?' Raymond asked.

'It's *everything*,' said Cathy. For the first time, she had a dreamy, faraway sound to her voice. 'You can see forever from here, Lance Corporal. You can see what's at stake. What's being lost, night after night. I'm sorry – perhaps this doesn't make sense to you, but ... I think it's good to remind oneself. And how better to remind oneself than to look at London like this, from on high?'

She led him along the building's rim. The blackout in central London was near perfect, but by the light of the moon Raymond could see the silhouettes of his city rolling in every direction. It was not so far, from here, to the palatial expanses of the Buckingham Hotel. *All of it at stake*, he thought – and knew, then, that, in spite of Nancy's fears, he was in the right place tonight.

There seemed something Cathy wanted to ask.

'You were on the Continent,' she finally ventured. 'Am I right?'

Raymond could hardly see her in the darkness. 'I was.'

The silence stretched out again, so much so that Raymond thought there was something Cathy wanted to say, some question she wanted to ask, some mystery begging to be revealed. In the end, though, she merely held herself and, with her quickly-becoming-familiar stiff upper lip, said, 'And you made it home.'

'There are thousands who didn't.'

Cathy fell back into silence. She was still silent, holding herself, when Raymond said, 'They say Dunkirk was a miracle, but it wasn't – it was hundreds of little miracles, all worked by human hands. There's no point any of us waiting for some divine intervention. We have to roll our sleeves up, do it ourselves. That's why I'm here. To make little miracles, every time that I can. To be one of the good men standing up for their city.'

'Good *women* too,' Cathy corrected him.

'Indeed,' said Raymond.

'The WVS do good work, supporting our boys. I was happy to be one of them at first. But there's only so much one can accomplish manning the canteens, or sitting by the phones. I don't care for baking and I'm a terrible knitter. When the chance came to join the fire-spotting, I seized it. Now I wouldn't have it any other way.'

'Forgive me, Miss Everly – but you don't have the feeling of a WVS girl about you.'

Raymond was thinking of the chambermaids who'd left the hotel to sign up, but Cathy interjected straight away, 'What *is* a WVS girl, Raymond? There's no barrier to entry, not in the voluntary service. There's plenty come from the gutter staffing the canteens, but there's plenty more, like me. Lowborn and high, they're all welcome in the WVS. I rather think it upends some notions that ought to have been upended some years ago. My father holds titles in Yorkshire. His family traces itself back to Cholmeley baronets. I could have gone back to his estate when the war came down. Instead, I chose *this*.' She opened her arms, as if to take in not only the entirety of London, but the vast open skies above. 'There's adventure in the family, Lance Corporal. My second cousin was one of those who went with Mr Shackleton to the ends of the Earth, then came back to fight in the last war. With a heritage like that, I could hardly opt out.' She paused. 'With a name like yours, you must have an interesting ancestry yourself. What is it you did, before the war, Raymond?'

Perhaps now was not the time to explain the true origin of

the name 'de Guise' – bestowed upon him by his old dancing mentor, as a way of sprucing him up for the Continental ballroom circuit – but Raymond could not help a breathy laugh when he said, 'Cathy, believe it or not, I was a ballroom dancer.'

Wryly, Cathy said, 'Well, I don't believe we've had one of those out on patrol. We'll be foxtrotting through the bombs, will we?'

Raymond's foot was putting up a particularly bitter complaint. He gripped the edge of the wall and said, 'I'm afraid I'm not much use in the ballroom this season. And besides, I'd rather be here, where it matters.'

'War truly is the great leveller,' Cathy answered, sagely. 'Here we stand, atop the ruins of London, the ballroom dancer and the aristocrat's wayward daughter, facing down the ...'

Cathy was looking up, taking in the stars, when suddenly she stopped talking. There was something wrong, she thought. Some different texture in the night.

Next second, the sirens started wailing.

She turned to Raymond. 'You get a sixth sense for it, when you're out in the night long enough. Here it comes, Raymond.' In the east, the ack-acks started returning fire, the silence of the night being torn apart yet again. 'How many nights is this? I count twenty-eight. They don't ever learn, do they?'

'Learn?'

'Yes,' said Cathy, and started picking a way back to the rooftop stairs, 'that this is *our* island and we're not to be trifled with.'

She was at the top of the stairs now, Raymond flailing behind her, his eyes on the sky.

'There's still time,' she told him. 'They've harried the east so much in the last few nights. We'll make it to station and see what's what. Go where we're needed.' She hesitated. Some ghostly feeling seemed to have stolen upon Raymond. He was staring up at the skies, searching for signs of the Luftwaffe scything across the stars. 'Raymond, let's move. Give me your hand.'

He shook off the feeling, uncertain why that cold, creeping dread had come upon him. Perhaps it was only that, this high up, he was so much closer to the destroyers. Shaking away even that thought, he loped to the top of the stairs. Beneath him, his foot screamed in protest; he pitched forward, steadied himself on Cathy's hand, and took a deep breath. 'My apologies,' he told her. 'Let's go.'

Cathy was still touching his hand. In the starlight, his wedding band dazzled. She stroked it with the tips of her long, graceful fingers. 'You're married?'

'Nearly two years, though I haven't been at her side for half of that. This war's upended us all.'

Cathy lingered on a thought, then withdrew her hand. 'Tonight's the last time you wear it out on patrol, Raymond. ARP aren't the only ones who go out under blackout. The city's full of good men putting up the good fight, but it's full of plunderers and profiteers as well. If anything happens to you out here, they'll have it off your finger without a second thought.' She ducked down through the door and back into the hollow, echoing shell of John Lewis. 'London by night isn't safe any more, Raymond – and we've got a job to do.'

Chapter Six

The truth was – though he'd never admit this to anyone, except perhaps Frank – it had taken Billy Brogan a little time to get used to life in the hotel post room. A little time, in fact, to get used to civilian life at all. Sometimes he thought he'd left it as one type of person, and returned to it another altogether.

He'd last worked in the post room the year before he was sent to France, but back then the office had been a dark corner of the hotel basements, where the domineering old Mrs Farrier had ruled the roost for longer than Billy had been alive. Since the construction of the hotel's guest shelters, however, the post room had been relocated to a disused store off the end of the Housekeeping hall. At least this place had windows – and at least without Mrs Farrier, Billy had been able to brighten the place up a bit. He even had a picture of his whole family, brothers and sisters included, propped up on the sorting desk. The portrait had been taken a couple of years ago, and in its centre Billy had his arm around Annie. She looked much younger here; it was funny how quickly they were growing up. That made him think of Patrick, Roisin and all the rest, and how long it had been since he'd seen them. Just another cost of this blasted war.

But for every damnation this war brought, thought Billy, it brought opportunity as well. It was Sunday morning, approaching noon, and the nervous flutter in his heart wasn't to do with last night's air raid at all.

He was due to meet Mary-Louise the moment she came off shift, so with the clock rapidly approaching midday he wended his way to the Housekeeping Lounge. The door was ajar so, with just a gentle knock, he limped on through – but the only person here was Nancy, who seemed increasingly flustered as she flitted around the room, setting it back in order for the girls' return. Billy wasn't sure, but he thought she looked a little peaky; her brow was shimmering, as if she'd been working flat out all morning, and her colour was pale.

'Nance, why don't you put your feet up, just for a second?'

Nancy barely stopped moving, even when Billy spoke. 'I can't, Bill. Far too much to do.' She took a breath. 'It's sweet of you to notice though, Billy. It's just these nights. I'm hardly sleeping. And Raymond out on these patrols when he surely isn't ready. Gosh, Billy, it was hard enough when you were all in France – but at least then I learned to push it out of my mind. At least then I didn't obsess over him dying every single night. Now, the world's just one long string of goodbyes. I feel pulverised.'

Billy limped over to the sideboard, where a kettle of hot water still stood on a tray. Moments later, he was presenting Nancy with a cup of tea and half an orange from the hotel kitchens. 'You don't see these out in the greengrocers, do you, Nance? Ever think it's funny, how they can get oranges through the blockade for the nobs, but not for the rest of us?' He faltered. 'Nancy, about Annie—'

'I've been giving it some thought.'

'I've never seen my Ma and Pa's house cleaner or brighter. Everywhere my Ma polishes, there's Annie to give it a second scrub.'

Nancy, who'd finally taken a seat, said, 'Mrs Moffatt's worried she's too young.'

'There's plenty of chambermaids started here just as young. She's fourteen. And, besides, she's a Brogan,' insisted Billy. The name didn't count for much, not in a place where kings and queens, dukes and duchesses, barons and earls regularly walked the halls – but it did stand for dedication and hard work. 'The Buckingham gave me a chance, Nance. I reckon it could do the same for Annie. She'd be good to you. She'd be loyal. She'd be—' *Out of the house*, Billy wanted to say, *and earning an honest living*.

But he never got the chance, because Nancy's face was breaking into a wan smile – and, as she said, 'I'm needling at Mrs Moffatt, Billy. It's her you'll need to convince, not me,' the door opened up and, among all the other girls streaming back in from their shifts, came Mary-Louise.

'Billy,' she said, ignoring the other girls who had started tittering. 'I'm not quite ready. You – you'll need to give me a few minutes. Can't go to afternoon tea in my work clothes, can I?'

When Billy said, 'I think you look fine, just the way you are', the tittering from the other girls rose in pitch. Nancy gave them an admonishing look, then turned to Billy. 'Mr Brogan, I expect the better thing is for you to wait for Mary-Louise somewhere less well populated. Perhaps out on Berkeley Square?'

Billy was flushing crimson red. He shuffled, awkwardly, back to the Housekeeping door. 'I'll see you soon, Mary-Louise,' he mumbled – and then he was gone.

Mary-Louise was wearing a simple floral day dress, but as she and Billy hurried for the Underground, even this made him feel severely under-dressed. Billy, who rarely wore anything other than his grey slacks and braces, allowed visions of Mary-Louise's family to tumble through his mind. He'd assumed they were good working sorts like the Brogans themselves – yet, as they came out of the Underground at Camden Town, then picked their way along the bustling high road to find the right house, he was gripped by the sudden fear that he was about to attend high tea with a family of upper-crust toffs.

'You'll love Uncle Ken,' Mary-Louise said as they followed one of the leafier avenues north, along the line of the winding canal. 'You remind me of him, you know. There's just something about the two of you. I can't quite put my finger on it.'

It certainly wasn't looks – because, when Mary-Louise led Billy to the door of one of the old terraces, Uncle Ken was revealed to be a rotund man of somewhat porcine appearance, with a balding crown and tufts of coarse yellow hair. Appearing on the doorstep, Ken gripped Billy firmly by the hand, declared, 'This is the lad then, is it?' and, with a twinkle in his eye, began to inspect Billy much as a farmer does a cow at market. 'Yes, girl, he looks dapper enough. And you've got some service behind you, have you, lad? Our Mary-Lou says they got you back from Dunkirk. That was a rotten affair, lad. A rotten affair.'

Billy stepped into the house. Somehow, it seemed so much more frightening stepping into this hall, where the wallpaper showed wildflowers and a shelf was lined with dainty porcelain pigs, than it had done taking up his first rifle in basic training, or marching through the fields of France, knowing that some Wehrmacht division was on his tail. The lump in his throat was a very real and present problem; he worried he'd even be able to speak.

The door closed behind him. Mary-Louise had been the last one through. She stood abreast of Billy in the hall and squeezed his hand. That gave him courage, at least. Mary-Louise had let her strawberry blonde hair down, and it bounced around her shoulders in full, dramatic curls. Unless Billy was very much mistaken, she was wearing perfume too.

'Come on, soldier,' laughed Ken, leading the parade down the hall and into the sitting room at its end. 'You can meet the family.'

The family comprised Thom and Jake, fourteen and twelve years old respectively. They were almost as eager to speak about Dunkirk as Billy was to avoid the subject altogether. 'What was it like on the beaches?' Thom asked, the moment Billy had been introduced. 'Were you awfully afraid?' Jake chipped in. Billy did his best to muddle through without either encouraging or refusing them, then followed Ken and Mary-Louise through to the kitchen where Ken's wife Marge was busy preparing tea.

Marge was the one related by blood to Mary-Louise, and Billy could clearly see the familial resemblance. Both had the same tall, slender frames; both the same strawberry blonde hair (although Marge's had grown paler with age, and thinner as well). But the real reflection was in their eyes, deep as the in-dulgent chocolate desserts served in the Queen Mary restaurant. Marge was just as familiar and friendly as Mary-Louise; dusting down her hands, she skipped across the room and planted kisses on Billy's cheeks. At this, he flushed crimson yet again.

'I hope you'll enjoy our little spread,' said Marge, dancing back to her work. 'We like to do what we can for our Mary-Louise. She's practically been a daughter to me and our Ken.'

Billy looked around the kitchen. The place wasn't large, but the doors opened onto an immaculately kept back garden, into which the afternoon sunshine was pouring down, and this gave it the appearance of somewhere much bigger. It struck Billy that, unlike many of the back yards he'd seen across London – cer-tainly his own at Albert Yard – Uncle Ken's hadn't been given over to a vegetable plot. Nor was there an Anderson shelter sitting here. Some of the summer flowers still clung on in the terracotta pots lined up against one fence, and a table had been optimistically laid on the small patch of lawn, ready for tea.

And what a tea it was.

Billy was uncertain if he'd seen anything quite as elaborate as this outside the confines of the Buckingham Hotel. Egg and cress sandwiches were piled in a miniature mountain. Chunks of sausage had been tossed with tomatoes in bowls. A plate held an improbable number of cold chicken legs, and an extra loaf of bread was cut up and slathered with butter so thick that it made Billy wonder if there was a war on at all. There was cream in a jug, a quiche brimming with bacon, and a wheel of cheese that wouldn't have seemed out of place on the Queen Mary's trolleys.

'Well, Billy,' Ken said, 'we didn't want to be miserly with one of our heroes. We're grateful for what you lads have been doing for us all.' He crossed himself, then looked at the skies as well. 'The least we can do is fatten you up for the fight, isn't that right? Well, come on! Let's get these plates filled, Marge. The lad looks like he could use some filling up. So could you, Mary-Lou.' He rolled his eyes jocularly and patted her on the belly. 'You're stick thin. They've got you working too hard down there.'

Billy was grateful for the food – not just because there was so much of it, but because it saved him from having to answer every question at length. As long as he kept chewing, he was able to slip around the questions about Dunkirk and about France, and what he might think happen next in the war. Sometimes, folks treated you as an expert, just because you'd been 'boots on the ground'. The only thing Billy felt like an expert in, this year, was sticking stamps on envelopes for guests at the Buckingham Hotel.

'Another chicken leg, Mr Brogan?'

Billy was about stuffed full, but the way Mary-Louise was

looking at him across the garden table – as if, every time he filled his plate and made a lovely comment to her Aunt Marge, it was just filling her heart – he nodded gratefully. Marge had made a collection of different relishes, and Billy chose one of tomatoes and mustard. He was spreading it liberally on the chicken leg when a thought occurred to him and he said, 'My sister's just come back in from the country. It's different out there, but there isn't fare like this. Annie said that wringing an extra chicken's neck could see a farmhand brought up on charges. I'm just ever so grateful you set all this aside for today. You didn't have to. We're not in want at the Buckingham…'

'I hear not,' said Uncle Ken. As if to stretch his legs, he got up and paraded around the edge of the garden; it seemed to Billy that, in truth, he was sneaking looks over his fences, to make sure he wasn't being overheard. 'All that business last year with that load of grubbers getting into that restaurant of yours. Well, you'll know more about it than me, but it seems there's some folks out there disgruntled about things. What is it they were chanting? We don't ration the rich, not in this country.'

Billy had been in France, so he'd only heard the story second-hand. Now Mary-Louise shook her head and said, 'They just stormed the place. You can scarcely believe it! The whole of the Hotel Board were taking luncheon, and then in they burst, with their placards and chanting and—'

'Boorish!' Aunt Marge exclaimed.

'Now, Marge,' interjected Ken, with a paternal air, 'things are a touch more complicated than that. Here, let me and Billy have a proper chat, man to man. I'm sure he's quite exhausted from all these questions.'

'Yes,' said Mary-Louise, with pride, 'let's leave the boys to business, shall we? Here, Aunt Marge, I'll help you clear up.'

Thom and Jake were more reluctant to help, but by the time

Marge had clipped them both around the ear they were clearing the table, ferrying everything back into the kitchen. Mary-Louise pointedly let her hand rest on Billy's shoulder as she passed. He was still thrilling from the touch of it – and wondering how on Earth a veteran soldier could tremble at the touch of a pretty woman, after all he'd seen and done – when he looked up and found himself alone with Uncle Ken.

'I'm glad it's just the two of us, Bill. I've been looking forward to meeting you. Mary-Louise has been chattering about you, off and on, all summer. As a matter of fact, it was me who suggested she get you up here. Well, it seemed like you were never going to do the necessary and ask her to step out yourself. Far too much of a gentleman, I gather – and, well, you've obviously had other things to contend with too.' Ken meant Billy's leg. Awkwardly, Billy shuffled it further under the table.

He thought he understood, now, why the rest of the family had left him alone. Mary-Louise's mother and father lived in South London, but evidently they hadn't been the closest of parents, and it was Ken and Marge to whom she looked for guidance. Billy had the distinct impression, as he sat here, that he was being *vetted*. It was nothing more than the concern of a father for his favourite daughter – or, in this case, a favourite uncle for his favourite niece – but Billy suddenly felt tense. He wanted to give a good representation of himself, but wondered if that was even possible with chicken in his teeth and tomato-and-mustard chutney smeared across his lips.

'I think very highly of Mary-Louise, sir,' he said. 'You don't have to have any doubts about me on that account.'

'I'm glad to hear it, boy.'

'I have to say, the truth is, I'm rather bewildered that she's sweet on me.'

Ken roared with laughter. 'A modest man, eh? That's what I

like to hear. Well, you've put on a good show, Billy Brogan. I trust you think we've put on a decent display too?'

There was something just a little *odd* about the phrasing of the question, some frisson that Billy couldn't quite identify. It felt odder still when Ken slunk into the kitchen and emerged from the larder with two bottled brown ales, pressing one of them into Billy's hands. Billy had only rarely drunk ales (though, at the Buckingham Hotel, he'd tasted the dregs of quite a few bottles of Veuve Clicquot), and found the taste of this particular brew rather dissatisfying – but, to keep face, he sipped at it slowly while he said, 'The best display, sir. You must have been planning this for some time. All of this, just for me and Mary-Louise.'

'Well, Billy,' said Ken, and lowered his voice a fraction as he shuffled his chair nearer, 'that's the perk of my trade, you see. I've been a wholesaler all my life. Selling goods into the groceries, right here in Camden town. The shopkeepers I work with are always very pleased with the work I do for them, the goods I put their way. They always save a little extra for Uncle Ken.' He paused. 'As a matter of fact, that's why I asked about your Buckingham and that to-do with the Queen Mary last year. Ration the rich!' he laughed. 'Well, it doesn't happen, does it? There's still fine dining in your restaurants, I shouldn't wonder. Fine dining – and lots of waste. I have to say, it rather shocks you to the soul – there's all those rich people, eating like there isn't a war on at all, and the rest of us just lining up in ration queues for a few cubes of butter. Well, that's England, am I right?'

Billy nodded, vaguely, but said very little. Then, sensing his discomfort, Ken changed tack. 'I know how it feels, son. Believe it or not, twenty years ago, I was right where you're standing. I got back from France myself. Saw my pals perish on the Somme. You come back home and everyone thinks there was heroism in it. And there was. Only, it's not the kind of heroism they're thinking of. It isn't derring-do and knights on white chargers. Most of the time, it's just putting one foot in front of the other. That's heroism, that's the thing that gets the job done – it's just that, if you weren't there, you don't know it. Well, *I* was there, Billy. *I* know what you're feeling right now.'

Billy was almost choked up when he said, 'I just want to do my bit.'

'There's more than one way to do that, son. Me, I'm too old to go off fighting again, but I do my bit here, wherever I can. Getting people fed, that's my business. All those old dears, standing in line all day for their milk and cheese. Well, I try and lend them a hand, try and do what I can. This rationing business – well, the Ministry of Food's doing what they think's right, but it's hardly fair, not when the rich don't get rationed.' Ken paused, because a thought seemed to have just occurred to him. 'Hey, Billy, there's waste up at that hotel, right?'

Billy nodded.

'Well, listen, if ever you feel like helping out, I reckon I could find some hungry families who'd lap up whatever those rich nobs have left behind. One man's leftovers is the difference between some poor old dear's life and death.'

Billy hesitated. He was no stranger, of course, to helping himself from the kitchen waste and the room service trolleys. The Brogan family had depended upon it, once upon a time.

'Sorry, Billy, I can see I've made you uncomfortable.' Ken stood, doffing Billy on the shoulder. 'I'm just looking for ways to do my bit, you see. And if it doesn't hurt anyone ... Well, have a think on it, if you would. I've people up here who'd be ever so grateful for a bit extra in their bellies at night. And this blockade – it's only going to get worse before it gets better. That's if it gets better at all.'

At that moment, Mary-Lou reappeared from the kitchen. She looked once at Billy, then at the skies up above. 'I hate this time of afternoon. You can feel it in the air. Evening coming. Darkness, somewhere out there, creeping towards us. Can't you just tell what it's going to be like?'

The sirens, thought Billy, anticipating the night to come.

'Winter's drawing in, my girl,' said Ken. He seemed to have quite forgotten the conversation he'd just been having with Billy. But then he said, 'Well, at least you've got full bellies to be going home with. There's countless out here who haven't.' And the wink he threw Billy at the end made him feel a kind of guilt he'd never felt before: like it was he, Billy Brogan, who was responsible for the ration books and empty plates around London; like he, Billy Brogan, was part of the problem, just because he was sworn to the Buckingham Hotel.

'Come on, Bill, let's get going. Otherwise we'll be camping in the Underground all night, and I just don't fancy it.'

There was still daylight enough to stroll in, and Billy wasn't certain he wanted to be back underground anyway – so, ignoring the complaint of his leg, they wended their way south, across the verdant pastures of Regent's Park. There were still signs of the devastation that had touched London Zoo, which had already been hit twice during the bombardments. 'Uncle Ken says they found a zebra, just cantering along Camden High Street. All the zookeepers had to come and hustle it back,' said Mary-Louise, with a snort of laughter. 'Well, you've got to see the bright side. A zebra, standing right outside the post office!'

Evening was too near, and in the middle of the park – when Billy stopped to rest his leg – a gust of wind, flecked with rain, whistled through. 'Mary-Louise,' he ventured, giving voice to the thought that had been niggling at him all along, 'your Uncle Ken's a good man, isn't he?'

'Oh, the very best,' said Mary-Louise. Her arm had already been threaded through his, but now she drew nearer. 'I can't tell you the things he's done for me across the years. Every row I ever had with my mother, every time my father threw me out and told me never to come back – there was Uncle Ken, ready to set me back on my feet. I owe him so much. There's plenty others who owe him as well, all over this part of town.'

'You see, he asked me to bring him bits from the Buckingham Hotel. Said he knows people in need, and maybe I could help.'

Mary-Louise hesitated before she shrugged and said, 'That's my Uncle Ken all over. Helping out however he can. He does shifts with ARP up here as well.' She paused. 'I suppose there *is* plenty at the hotel, Billy. Plenty that just rots or goes to waste. Ken just likes to do his bit. Lord knows, we all need some help these days. I know I do.'

'You, Mary-Louise?'

And, with a deep breath, she answered, 'I'm scared, Billy. That's all. The world used to make better sense. Now it's just uncertainty and fear, everywhere you go.' She stopped. 'Except right now, of course. I'm not scared now, Billy. Are you?'

Billy trembled. 'No,' he said.

But the fact was, he was more scared than ever. He was scared as Mary-Louise took both of his hands. He was scared as she closed the narrow gap between them and he felt the warmth of her body against his. He was even scared as she bent her neck to kiss him, full on the lips, and linger there – until, a full second more than was decent, she drew away.

'You *are* scared,' Mary-Louise chided him, with a grin.

'Well, maybe a little,' grinned Billy Brogan, in return.

When she kissed him again, though, he wasn't frightened at all. In fact, he felt light as the air.

Chapter Seven

The afternoon demonstration dances had come to an end only moments before, and Mathilde Bourchier was already backstage, wrenching herself out of the ivory gown she'd been wearing. It didn't suit her anyway; it had been made by the hotel seamstress for Karina Kainz, then cut short, tucked in and re-hemmed to fit Mathilde. It felt like wearing somebody else's skin.

'That was incredible, Mathilde,' said Frank Nettleton, who'd cantered from the dance floor behind her. 'Did you see M. Blanchet? And M. Moulin? They'll be bidding for your hand at One Grand Night, Mathilde, I'm sure of it.'

The two Frenchmen were infrequent visitors to the Grand Ballroom. They'd attended, with a coterie of their associates from the Free France forces, last Saturday night, when John Hastings of the Hotel Board and Walter Knave had hosted a grand dinner in their honour in the Queen Mary restaurant. Mathilde had to admit she had always been drawn to the glamour of Paris, and had hoped to one day dance there herself – but she wasn't certain that dancing with some stuffy government representative, who probably had two left feet, was recompense for missing out on the real beauty and magic of Paris after dark. She smiled at Frank and said, 'That's sweet.'

'And the other night, Mathilde, when President Benes was here—'

Mathilde stood, and shushed Frank with a finger to his lips. It was so difficult to get irritated by Frank – there was something in his puppyish enthusiasm, and his yearning for the dance floor, that brought out the light in everyone around him – but Mathilde couldn't summon the enthusiasm to join in today. It was true – as London filled up with the fleeing governments and outlawed dynasties of the Continent, more and more of these figures were being drawn to the Grand Ballroom's magical delights. Marcus talked about it as a moment in history they would never see again – when, one night, they might dance with a Scandinavian prince, and the next a minister appointed by the Belgian king – but Mathilde found it so difficult to get lost in the romance of it. One Grand Night was just that – *one* night. She deserved more than that. It had been promised to her.

But the way Frank looked at her with his soulful, puppy-like eyes, she couldn't deny him the joy of it. 'There'll be plenty of bids coming for you too, Frank. Who knows? It could be that you're dancing with a princess before Christmas comes.'

Frank's eyes opened wide. 'I'll be happy with anyone, Mathilde. I just want to be there.'

And that, thought Mathilde as she kissed him on the cheek and brushed past, was Frank Nettleton all over. As long as Frank could be on the dance floor, in the heart of the foxtrots, he'd be happy. Mathilde, meanwhile, wanted more.

She was almost at the dressing room doors when Frank called out, 'I was thinking we might practise. This afternoon. You never know who'll be in the ballroom tonight. Maybe, with a little more time to rehearse, we can capture someone's eye? Get some more interest firing for One Grand Night?'

Mathilde hated letting him down. Frank, she decided, was

one of the only good things left in the ballroom. But still she said, 'I'm sorry, Frank, I can't this afternoon,' and disappeared through the door.

The Imperial Hotel wasn't quite as grand as the Buckingham, but as Mathilde made haste along Knightsbridge, with the barrage balloons casting the streets below into deep shadow, she fancied that it wasn't so very far behind. Established a full decade before the Buckingham, the Imperial was almost seventy years old and sat like a miniature palace on the corner between Knightsbridge and Lowndes Square, where the gardens had been given over to allotment space at the behest of local residents. Four storeys tall made it several storeys smaller than the Buckingham, but what it lacked in style, it made up for in old world glamour. The old tsars and tsarinas of the Russias had called this their home away from home in its elder times, and in the last decade its Board had poured investment into the hotel, revolutionising its ballroom, building a second, anterior wing and securing its future as a rival to the Savoy, the new Dorchester, and the Buckingham itself.

Mathilde wasn't sure if she ought to be seen going in through the front doors, but ultimately decided that it didn't matter. In the opulent surrounds of the reception hall, where smells wafted in from the Continental Kitchen – the Imperial had become famous for its French cuisine – she asked one of the concierges to inform Mr Cockfosters that she had arrived, then sat back to take it all in. Porters buzzed back and forth. A great bronze cage opened up to disgorge guests from the elevators behind. The potted palms dotted around the reception hall made it seem as if the Imperial was a world apart from London – and indeed it was, for Mathilde could hear the busy chatter of half a dozen different languages as she waited for Mr Cockfosters to appear.

When he finally approached, throwing his pudgy arms open

wide from the opposite side of the reception hall, he was just as unremarkable as she remembered. Today, he had his shirtsleeves rolled up – like he was both a professional at this hotel, and a carpenter by trade – and his jowly cheeks flapped as he called out, 'Miss Bourchier, I'm delighted you could make it.'

Mathilde said, 'I wasn't sure that I would.' She thought of Frank Nettleton, his zest and passion, and how all he wanted to do was *be there*, in the Grand, while the chandeliers dazzled and the orchestra played. A little piece of her felt guilty for wanting more – for thinking that she was better than that. Life would have been simpler if she didn't have this yearning inside her, this desperation for *more* – not just to dance, but to be the very best, to call herself the ballroom's queen. But here she was and, now that she was here, it didn't unsettle her as she'd feared it might. 'But you did intrigue me, Mr Cockfosters. The idea that you'd seek me out. That's worth something to a girl.'

'Come with me, Miss Bourchier. There's somebody who's been eager to meet you himself.'

Mr Cockfosters led the way across the reception hall, and through a vaulted archway where two potted palms stood sentry, like the guardians of some exotic island. Here, at the end of a short hall, two great oak doors opened up, revealing the Imperial Ballroom.

Mathilde had danced here once before, but back then it had been nothing like this. In the intervening period, a new dance floor – as broad and gleaming as the Buckingham's – had been installed, and the small stage where Mathilde had seen the Tommy Dorsey Orchestra hold sway was now a grand, sweeping construction with room for a band almost twice as big. Up above, the chandeliers had been illuminated, spilling starlight across the boards. And there, in the middle of the dance floor, stood a lean old gentleman wearing a suit of midnight-blue gabardine, his face banked in finely sculpted white whiskers.

'Miss Bourchier,' the man intoned, with a voice that was at once booming and yet full of whispers. 'Charmed to meet you.'

They met each other at the edge of the dance floor, the smell of beeswax and wood varnish strong in the air. As Mathilde felt the gentleman's whiskers touch the back of her hand – he had bowed to plant a kiss there – Mr Cockfosters made a more formal introduction. 'Mathilde Bourchier, allow me to introduce Mr Hubert Gove – the Imperial Hotel's lauded director.'

'Thirty years in post, ma'am,' Mr Gove announced. 'I'm very pleased you agreed to meet with us here. But first, tell me, what do you make of our ballroom?'

Mathilde turned on the spot. It was always hard to judge the tenor of a ballroom when it was not bustling with dancers, musicians and guests, but right now she felt she could picture it as vividly as if an orchestra were playing and the dance floor filled with the great and the good. Something about the work they'd done to the place – the carvings in the pillars, the smooth finish to the balustrade, the long sweep of the cocktail bar – brought it so colourfully to mind. She breathed in and, when she breathed out, a ballroom full of dancers, caught in the storm of some wild foxtrot, seemed to manifest in the air around her.

'It's beautiful, sir,' said Mathilde – and meant it, with every beat of her heart.

'I'm glad you agree,' said Mr Gove. 'No expense has been spared, preparing the Imperial Ballroom for the battle to come.'

Battle? wondered Mathilde. Surely he didn't mean the battle taking place in the skies above London each night. The Imperial would have converted its cellars into shelters – though it was said that these grand old buildings were among the safest in London, their skeletons built (ironically enough) from strong

German steel – so he must have been speaking of some other conflagration. She decided to let the moment pass and, asking 'May I?', drifted onto the dance floor itself.

The feel of it beneath her feet was sublime. Dancing here would be like dancing across the clouds. She turned once, then again, stepping a little as if she was in some partner's hold. Oh yes, *now* she could imagine it, even more vividly than before.

'How do you like it, Mathilde?' asked Mr Cockfosters.

She noted that he was using her Christian name, for the first time.

'Oh,' she said, stopping her dance, 'I like it very much.'

'You might like it even more, if you were to dance on it each night,' said Mr Cockfosters.

Mathilde froze, then looked between them both. Yet, before she could pipe up, Mr Gove intervened. 'What do you know of the Imperial Hotel, Miss Bourchier?'

Mathilde said, 'The Buckingham. The Savoy. The Ritz and the Imperial. The only places a lord would stay in London town.'

'Indeed. The four homes-away-from-home for the great and the good in London town. Each with their unique properties to offer their guests. Each aspiring to be the biggest, the best, the most elegant and refined of London hotels. And now, each at war with the other.'

'War?' mouthed Mathilde. She'd heard businessmen speak like this before, but something in it seemed almost crude this year.

'The war for reputation,' Mr Gove explained. 'Let me take you back a little in time, Miss Bourchier. Think back a mere season. Most likely you already know that this hotel built quite a reputation on account of its Friday night cabarets. Our ballroom, we like to think, was already great – but our cabarets were what London spoke about.'

Mathilde had often heard of the Imperial cabarets. Colour

and light, music and dance – and the occasional carefully orchestrated scandal or two – had made sure they were often gossiped about in the London clubs. 'No more cabarets, Mr Gove?'

'Well, war touches everything, Miss Bourchier. It has changed the very complexion of London life.'

Mathilde said, 'And you don't just mean the bombs, of course?'

'You're a wise young woman, Miss Bourchier. The bombs may devastate us all – but they come and then they go. It's the bigger changes that affect a place like ours. Society itself is changing. You'll have seen this yourself, over at the Buckingham Hotel.'

Mathilde nodded. London, she thought, had become host to an even wider array of dignitaries than it had ever been. Families of great wealth and importance, kings and queens, presidents and their ministers – all had come to call London their home.

'But kings and queens, ladies and lords, do not stoop to cabarets, Mathilde – no matter how distinguished they might be. For people like these, only the very best will do. Elegance. Passion. *Refinement*.'

It was at this point that Mr Cockfosters intervened. 'So, you can see, a change of approach has been needed, here at the Imperial Hotel. Cabarets will not cut it. Our ballroom must become the draw of the town.'

'We must give them what they want the most,' Mr Gove went on, picking up the baton Mr Cockfosters had just handed over. 'Not just safety and security, but a taste of that old world, the memory of the indulgent lives they used to lead, the glamour, the beauty, the exquisiteness that they deserve. *That*, Miss Bourchier, is why we invited you here today.'

Mathilde took another perambulation around the dance floor. The feel of it beneath her soles was divine; not a penny had been pinched in their attempt to make it the equal of the Grand.

She turned on the spot, then opened her arms to face them. 'Gentlemen, I'm cautious to ask – but is it your intention that *I* should be a part of this?' She couldn't see why else they'd brought her here, not under such a cloak of subterfuge.

'Well, Miss Bourchier, there's a little bit more to our sugges-tion than that.' Mr Gove turned to Mr Cockfosters. 'Perhaps the time has come when we take Miss Bourchier into our confidence, Michael. And yet…' He put a musing finger to his lips. 'Perhaps I might first ask, Miss Bourchier, if you would promise to keep your meeting with us, and what we are about to describe to you, a secret? The world of the ballroom is, after all, so very small, and even a little whisper can become an unstoppable rumour. Might we have that guarantee?'

Mathilde believed she had nothing to lose. 'Be like Dad,' she said, parroting that summer's poster campaign, 'keep Mum.'

Mr Gove raised a smile, then demurred to Mr Cockfosters.

'We're late to this party, Miss Bourchier. There are no two ways about it. Everybody saw war coming, but we were, perhaps, too cautious in our attempts to profit from it.'

Profit from war. There was something ugly in that sentiment – but, the more she thought about it, the more she began to see it everywhere. That was what they were doing at the Buckingham too, and being lauded for it along the way. Why should the Imperial be any different?

'I suppose we believed in the might of the British Expeditionary Force too much,' said Mr Cockfosters, 'but, whatever the reasons, hotels like the Buckingham have got a head start on us in capturing the more lucrative guests who have flocked into London.'

'We are late to the gold rush, Miss Bourchier.'

Mr Cockfosters smiled, with a gentle incline of the head; he couldn't have put it better himself. 'The Imperial doesn't need to simply win new custom, Miss Bourchier; it must unseat guests from places they have become comfortable, places which they have started to call home, and bring them to our own halls. To put it plainly – it isn't enough that the Imperial shines; the shine of our competitors must be irredeemably tarnished. We must prise our custom from the grasp of our competitors.'

Mathilde thought she understood. She whispered, 'From the Buckingham Hotel…'

It was at this point that Mr Gove laid a hand on her shoulder.

'Indeed, Miss Bourchier. We are, of course, incredibly sad that it has come to this.'

Mathilde didn't know if it was sadness that was coursing through her, but the sense of an opportunity hoving into view was certainly invigorating. She looked, again, around the ballroom. Yes, she could quite imagine dancing here. Surely that was what she was here for? Surely that was what they meant?

'But the Buckingham is shining,' she said. 'Even without Raymond de Guise, the Grand is *alive*.'

'And that,' Mr Cockfosters declared, 'has been our problem. How to tempt guests away from the finest establishment in town?'

'Unless, of course, it wasn't the finest anymore?' Mathilde ventured, trying to sense where this conversation was going.

'Our sentiments exactly,' Mr Gove intervened. 'For some time now, Miss Bourchier, we have been awaiting something that could undermine the calm and constancy of the Buckingham ballroom. Something that might devalue it in the eyes of the guests…'

'And we believe we have found it.'

Mathilde felt, suddenly, as if she was in some trap – as if she hadn't been invited here as potential principal dancer, but so that some dreadful surprise could be sprung on her.

Mr Gove saw the look of panic that flitted across her face and said, 'Marcus Arbuthnot.'

Those two words filled the entirety of the Imperial ballroom.

'Marcus?' ventured Mathilde. 'But what of him?'

'A gentleman,' Mr Gove began. 'A celebrant. A champion. A star.'

'And, very possibly, the weakness in the Grand's armour.'

'Once upon a time, we thought that, if there was a sordid little secret that could blow apart the sanctity of the Grand, it would be found in Karina Kainz. All that Austrian glamour – perhaps it was hiding a connection to something altogether more lurid. But, alas, it was not to be. Miss Kainz, as you know, was interned last year and put in front of a very strict tribunal. They found no reason to suspect her of any misdeed.'

Mr Gove paused, allowing Mr Cockfosters to pick up the telling. These two could form a vaudeville act, thought Mathilde. It was like they were speaking with one voice.

'But Marcus?' Mathilde marvelled. 'The weakness in the Grand's armour? I'm not sure I really understand.' He'd been kindness personified, since he joined the Company last year. You could wryly smile, sometimes, at his theatrical flourishes – but you couldn't deny his generosity, his encouragement, the sense of camaraderie he'd brought. 'Sirs, Marcus is the absolute *darling* of the dancing world. He's been a champion. A tutor. Mr Cockfosters, Mr Gove, he's a *gentleman* ...'

'But we believe he is not without his secrets.'

'Indeed,' Cockfosters went on, 'a little rudimentary research reveals that, in 1931, Marcus trained a young partnership, Victor Grace and Meghan Barr, to glory at the Exhibition Paris. According to all of the literature – and you can read it for yourself in *Dancing Times* – it ought to have been the beginning of a glorious romp around the Continent. Meghan and Victor should have won that year's World Ballroom Dance Championship. But they did not.'

'And why not?' picked up Mr Gove. 'Well, it seems that Marcus abandoned them. Indeed, it seems that Marcus abandoned dance altogether. Nothing more was seen of him in the ballroom until he reappeared, quite suddenly, in 1933, picking up where he left off with new dancers to tutor and instruct. Of course, we all know the rest – how he took his partnership to glory in Bad Nauheim in 1936, how the world was once more filled with rapture for his talents. But of the years 1931 to 1933, there is not a whisper. Marcus Arbuthnot, it seems, simply vanished from the face of the Earth.'

'The question,' Mr Cockfosters went on, 'is *why*.'

'Well,' Mathilde stuttered, 'it could be almost any reason.'

'It has to be something of real severity. Marcus was at the peak of his profession. Then he simply vanished.'

'We believe,' Mr Cockfosters said, 'that Arbuthnot's history holds a secret, one he has worked feverishly to protect. A secret problematic enough to force him to flee from the ballroom world for two whole years. A problem perhaps *sordid* enough that, were it to be revealed, might ruin him. And everything around him.'

At last, Mathilde began to see. She really was in the middle of a web, the heart of a trap – only it wasn't a trap designed to ensnare her; she was being invited to ensnare another.

'Let me see if I have you right, sirs. You wish to put a bomb in the heart of the Grand Ballroom. You wish to sully its reputation – perhaps even do away with one of its stars – and, in the aftermath, poach the Buckingham's guests to your own hotel.'

Mr Cockfosters face flushed red. At least he had the decency to be embarrassed; Mr Gove simply looked imperious, and intoned the words, 'Business is warfare, Miss Bourchier. And all is fair in war.'

Mathilde wasn't sure if this was true. It wasn't fair when the sirens went off each night. It wasn't fair, when you saw the ruined homes and shops. The ruined lives.

But in the *ballroom*? Well, perhaps that was different. People did not die from dance. You didn't waltz away to meet your maker.

'We're offering you the world, Miss Bourchier. You are the talent of your generation. The Imperial Ballroom could be yours. All we would ask is that you help us in this endeavour. You're close to Marcus Arbuthnot. You've won his trust. Draw from him the truth that kept him from the ballroom for those two missing years of his life. Reveal that truth to us. Allow us to use it to unlock all the riches of the Buckingham Hotel.' Mr Gove hesitated before he went on, for at first he could not tell what Mathilde was thinking. Then he saw the way her eyes had opened fractionally wider, and the dazzle of the chandeliers' light in her irises. That, he decided, was the twinkle of somebody grasping the full potential of the opportunity in front of them; the dazzle of somebody seizing the day. 'Then come and dance with us, Miss Bourchier – and see out this war in elegance and beauty, right here in a ballroom that you may call your own.'

Chapter Eight

'Now listen to me,' whispered Billy Brogan, halfway along the Housekeeping hall and struggling to keep his sister from bolting ahead. 'You're bright and you're bold, but that isn't enough, not in a place like this. You've got to be...'

'*Refined!*' Annie scoffed, barely able to control her laughter. '*Upper crust!*' And she started strutting along the hall in one of the worst impersonations of an aristocratic lady Billy had ever seen. She threw back her head so hard it was pointing at the ceiling, and her walk was so prim she looked as if she had a broom handle stuck up her skirts. 'Calm down, Bill. I know what I'm doing. I'm not completely useless, you know. What's a chambermaid do, anyway? Change some bedsheets? Plump some pillows? You think I haven't been doing that since I was a nipper? You think I wasn't doing it every morning, out in Suffolk?' Annie stopped her strut and turned to see Billy standing in the middle of the hall, a despairing look on his face. 'Bill!' she roared. 'It's like you're *embarrassed* by me or something! I come from the exact same spot as you, Billy. Ma and Pa taught me just the same. I can do this standing on my head.'

Annie was striding purposefully along the Housekeeping hall – *Good Lord*, thought Billy, it was like she'd been working here for years already! – and Billy's leg screamed at him as he tried to keep up. Eventually, biting back the pain, he was able to plant himself between her and the door of the Housekeeping Lounge. 'You're *just* like me, and when I first came here, I didn't know a thing. *Yes*, it's changing beds. *Yes,* it's tidying up. *Yes*, you can do the job in your sleep – but, Annie, the job isn't the job. That's what you don't understand.'

'The job isn't the job?' Annie's face creased up. 'Billy, I reckon you took a proper bash to your head. Or is that just the way the rich speak? *The job isn't the job!*' She snorted with laughter again. 'Billy, what are you so worried about?'

Billy braced her by the shoulders and was about to explain when, all of a sudden, the door to the Housekeeping Lounge opened and a succession of chambermaids began to spill out. It was almost lunchtime, and Mrs Moffatt stood on the threshold, counting the girls as they hurried past. In the hubbub, Billy caught Mary-Louise's eyes. They flashed at him so warmly that he was almost too distracted as he said, 'Now, listen to me, Annie – and just, for once, accept what I'm saying as gospel. No questions. You're not in Lambeth Yard any more. What matters here isn't how well you fold a sheet, or how diligently you polish the armoire – though that's important too. What *really* matters is the way you comport yourself. You've got to be discreet. You've got to be *invisible*. The guests don't want to imagine you're a real person, with a life of her own – they just want to imagine their rooms get cleaned by magic.'

'Magic?' Annie spluttered.

None of it seemed to make any sense. Billy could hardly blame her; there'd been a time when he was constantly caught out by the strange rituals and traditions of the upper crust as well.

'Just show them you can keep quiet,' said Billy, who was pretty certain this was an impossibility. 'Show them that you can keep a secret. Imagine you've seen something in a guest's room – show them you wouldn't be chattering about it to all and sundry. Show them you've got some common sense.'

'Common sense?' grinned Annie. 'That's why they've kept you around so long, is it?'

Annie had a devilish twinkle in her eye as she brushed off Billy's hands, turned on her heel and, looking up at Mrs Moffatt's matronly face, gave a dainty curtsey and extended her hand. 'Annie Brogan,' she declared, 'at your service!'

Billy's heart sunk. It was just the most preposterous beginning.

'Mrs Moffatt,' he ventured, 'I think I should say—'

But Mrs Moffatt had already held up her hand. 'Thank you, Billy. We'll take good care of her from here.'

And Annie skipped after her, blowing Billy one last kiss over her shoulder as she went.

Billy hung his head in the hallway. The way he was feeling right now, there wasn't a shadow of a doubt about it – he'd be taking Annie home at the end of his shift, and telling their Ma and Pa she was going to have to find some other way to make a steady wage.

He was still standing there, felling pretty hopeless, when he felt movement behind him – and, turning round, discovered that Mary-Louise had been waiting there all along.

'You all right, Bill?'

'It's Annie,' said Billy. 'I reckon she's about to show us Brogans up.'

Mary-Louise grinned. 'I'll bet she does better than that. My money says I'll be showing her the ropes before October's out.'

'Here's hoping,' said Billy, glumly. 'Hey, listen – I've been thinking, about your Uncle Ken, and…' Billy was carrying a satchel and, when he opened it up, it was to reveal a half-stick of butter wrapped in paper, another paper bundle filled with rashers of bacon, and a cloth bag of apples. A pocket was stuffed with sugar cubes too. 'Well, he put on such a good spread for us, didn't he? He didn't have to. I was up thinking about it and, well, I reckon I kind of owed him a favour in return. Do you think it's enough?'

Mary-Louise leant in to kiss Billy on the cheek. 'More than enough. I reckon there'll be some old dears round his way very grateful for this, when he shows them. I'll take it to him, shall I?'

Billy nodded, and hoisted the satchel off his shoulder. 'Just cram it in your quarters, until shift's over. I might be able to scrounge up a bit more, between now and then.'

'He'd love to see you again, you know.' Mary-Louise paused. 'So would I.'

'Well,' Billy said, and found himself shuffling from foot to foot with nerves, 'that's the other thing. See, there's a matinee on, *The Great Dictator*. Charlie Chaplin, you know. Well, I thought it might be a nice afternoon if we were to—'

Mary-Louise's chocolatey eyes opened wide. 'Billy, you don't even need to ask.'

As Billy watched her hurry off, bound for the guest rooms on the second storey, his heart was suddenly so full that he quite forgot what was happening, right now, behind the doors of the Housekeeping Lounge. It was just as well – there was nothing he could do for Annie now. Billy had been like her, once upon a time – young and headstrong, and quite oblivious to the kinds of rules you had to live by in a place like the Buckingham Hotel.

He only hoped she could learn faster than he had.

Annie Brogan took her seat in the Housekeeping Office, tucked behind the Housekeeping Lounge, and was delighted to see that a plate full of shortbread biscuits and barley sugars had been provided. Nowhere that served this amount of sweet treats could be as formidable as her big brother Billy had been insisting. Quite clearly, he'd just been trying to frighten her. She took a piece of shortbread and tucked straight in.

Mrs Moffatt was fixing a pot of tea, humming to herself as she did so, so it was Nancy de Guise who first settled with Annie – and promptly found herself showered with shortbread crumbs, spraying from Annie's lips. 'You do get the fine stuff here, don't you, Nance?' Annie scoffed, choosing another piece. 'It's not like this in Lambeth Yard, I'll swear on that.'

Nancy flicked a crumb out of her eye. The truth was, delectable as the hotel shortbread was – the Queen Mary had one of the finest pastry chefs in the world – the thought of all that sweet, buttery goodness seemed rather revolting to her this morning. She could hardly comprehend why, because she was so used to indulging in a little shortbread with Mrs Moffatt while they worked through the rotas after the end of each day's shift. Perhaps it was just that she could see the insides of Annie's mouth as she chomped away.

'Annie,' Nancy ventured, not unkindly, 'I think it's wisest if you call me Mrs de Guise while you're here. Do you understand? I know Billy's a close friend, but while we're at work, we must observe the formalities.' Nancy glanced over her shoulder, to see Mrs Moffatt waddling back into the room. 'Mrs Moffatt, this is Annie Brogan.'

'*Miss* Annie Brogan,' said Annie, clearly delighted with herself for having observed these 'formalities'. 'How do you do, I'm charmed.'

Nancy furrowed her eyes. Annie was evidently trying very hard indeed, but her intonation was so off-key it was almost as if English wasn't her first language.

'Now, Miss Brogan, take your seat,' Mrs Moffatt began, 'and let's go through some of the particulars. That's the particulars of this job, and the particulars of your own talents. Then we can see what kind of match we've got on our—'

Mrs Moffatt was just settling into the third armchair, when the telephone sitting on her desk started trilling. Annie, recoiling at the surprise sound, seemed to have a bright idea – and was herself reaching for the receiver, when Mrs Moffatt brushed her hand out of the way and took it herself.

'I'm attentive and work under my own steam,' Annie explained to Nancy. 'I use my noggin,' and she tapped her head, 'to get the job done.'

As Mrs Moffatt's voice buzzed in the background, Nancy ventured, 'Has... er... has our Billy been rehearsing for the interview with you?'

'Oh, I wouldn't hear of it,' said Annie, incredulous. 'He's been telling me about *knowing my place* and being *invisible* – but I said to him, look Billy, I can do almost anything those other chambermaids can do, and in half the time. I can change beds and polish taps, and fold towels like the best of them. I know I can, because I've been doing it for all my brothers and sisters, all of my life. Just because it's a lord and a lady doesn't change a thing. We all sleep the same way. We all sit on the pot.'

Nancy felt quite queasy. Annie, she decided, was certainly a Brogan – it was just that, after so many years of working at the Buckingham, Billy had learned to temper his more vocal excesses. Annie was a girl with eagerness and spirit, but she lacked almost any sense of the occasion. Polishing her up for the Buckingham Hotel would be an even greater endeavour than polishing Frank up for the ballroom.

Before Nancy could continue, Mrs Moffatt put the telephone receiver back on its stand and looked at them both with an ashen face. 'Mrs de Guise, you'll have to continue with our Miss Brogan alone,' she said. She was already gathering her coat from the hook by the door. 'Put the girl through her paces, Nancy. If she's a shadow of her brother, she deserves a chance. I'll be back by late afternoon.'

With that, Mrs Moffatt was up and out of the door.

Nancy, feeling fresh dizziness – really, *what* was this that kept sweeping over her? – hurried after Mrs Moffatt, out of the office and across the Housekeeping Lounge. 'Emmeline,' she called, keeping her voice low so that Annie (who was very definitely eavesdropping) might not hear. 'Has something happened?'

'Yes,' said Mrs Moffatt. 'No,' she continued, in something of a fluster. 'It's Malcolm, Nancy. He's on leave. Two days on the ground. He's left the airfield. In fact, he's in London right now.'

'That was him on the telephone?'

Mrs Moffatt could hardly get both arms into her coat sleeves, so Nancy set about helping. 'You get calls like that – you think that's it. He's gone down, somewhere over the Channel, or in some farmer's field, and ... Sorry, Nancy. My heart's racing – and all he's done is invited me for luncheon.' Triumphantly, she fed her arm through her sleeve and started buttoning her coat. 'Lunch, with my son. Doesn't it sound ridiculous? Doesn't it sound just ... beautiful?'

Nancy touched her on the arm. 'It does, Emmeline. Even more beautiful than that.'

'And you can deal with our young Miss Brogan?'

Nancy glanced back at Annie, who was eagerly pushing more shortbread into her mouth. 'Oh yes, Emmeline. I'm certain I can deal with her.'

'Then thank you, Nancy. Thank you again.'

After Mrs Moffatt had gone, Nancy took a deep breath and returned to the office. Inside, Annie – sensing her interview was about to recommence – was feverishly trying to swallow the mouthful of shortbread she'd just optimistically crammed in. In the end, she reached for Mrs Moffatt's mug of tea and hurriedly slurped it back as Nancy approached.

In the doorway, Nancy stalled. Here was that dizzy feeling again. She propped herself against the doorjamb, closing her eyes as she let it pass.

When she opened them again, Annie Brogan was peering at her owlishly.

'Are you all right, Nan ... Mrs de Guise?'

Nancy nodded, but the fact was her heart was fluttering. She tottered across the room, and dropped into the armchair, where within moments Annie was serving her a hot cup of tea from the pot, with three brown sugar lumps dropped straight in.

'Drink that up,' she said. 'It'll see you right.' She paused, concern furrowing her face. 'What is it, Mrs de Guise?'

'Oh, Annie,' Nancy returned, 'I'm just run off my feet. Up all night worrying, then hurrying around these halls all day. I haven't been eating properly, that's all. I can scarcely keep anything down.'

'Aye,' said Annie, piling some barley sugars on Nancy's saucer, 'exhaustion'll do that to you. But you know what else will?'

Nancy looked at her, through the steam of her tea.

'I reckon you ought to be seeing a doctor, Mrs de Guise. I've seen this plenty of times. My Ma got like it with every last one – and there's enough of us Brogans that I got used to the signs. Feeling tired, feeling funny, dizzy spells – and not wanting a chunk of this shortbread, when it's probably the finest shortbread I've tasted in my whole life? That's not right. Not right at all! So I'd lay bets on it, Mrs de Guise. You're pregnant.'

Nancy's eyes widened. She'd imagined this interview might go any number of ways, but not quite like this. 'Annie?' she said, in shock, dismay, and disbelief.

Annie crashed back down in her seat. The shortbread was all

gone from the plate now, so she started scraping up the crumbs. 'So what are you thinking, Mrs de Guise?' she beamed. 'Have I got this job, or not?'

The Balderton Grill sat on a bustling corner hidden behind Bond Street, only a short stroll from the Buckingham Hotel. By the time Mrs Moffatt arrived, she was completely out of breath – which was faintly ridiculous, because, having taken the table Malcolm had booked, she had to wait half an hour for the big, blond airman to arrive. The frantic rush had half been in her head, and half in her heart.

As she waited, she got to fretting about the way that she looked. The invitation had come so suddenly that she was still in her work clothes, with only a forest green cardigan thrown over the top to disguise the fact that she'd come directly from the Housekeeping Lounge. In the back of a silver spoon, she fixed her hair; then, when it refused to stop being unruly, she fixed it again. Of course, even this was preposterous – she was not a young woman, invited to take dinner with the potential love of her life; she was a middle-aged (some might say *old*) mother, about to have lamb chops with her son.

When he arrived, she almost jumped out of her chair. She was still shaking when the waiter came and rearranged it behind her. By the time that had happened, Malcolm too was sitting down. He stood at least a foot taller than Mrs Moffatt, with sandy hair and eyes that were the perfect mirror of her own. She'd last seen him at the start of summer, when all the talk was of the fall of France and the fisherman's fleet which had gone out to relieve the soldiers at Dunkirk. Malcolm was an airman with the Royal Australian Air Force, part of the six squadrons dispatched to Britain when war was first declared. Accordingly, he'd flown reconnaissance and resistance missions over the Channel, as that valiant fleet of fishermen brought the BEF back from Dunkirk. Mrs Moffatt's heart had almost burst with the fear of it then; this autumn, it felt ready to burst every night.

The first thing she did was take his hand. 'Why didn't you tell me you were coming? I'd have ... baked a cake.' Well, *that* sounded useless. 'I'd have put on a nicer dress, and that's just to start. I could have got you rooms at the Buckingham Hotel.'

'I barely know where I'm at hour to hour, Emmeline,' Malcolm said, in his rich West Australian brogue. Malcolm, adopted by a Suffolk couple soon after he was born, had been taken to the country outside Perth when he was barely old enough to speak. There he'd grown up, running wild across the family's new farm, often dreaming of the England he'd left behind. 'Sometimes, all you'll get is an hour's call and it's off to the skies.' Malcolm faltered, not knowing if he should give voice to the words that now came to his lips. 'It's getting bad, Emmeline. Nobody wants to say it, but we can all feel it. Two of us went down this week. That's two boys from back home who'll never drink a beer in a Fremantle pub again. My pal Seamus got winged. He brought his bird back home safely, but it puts the scares on you. Ma, they're *strong*. And they're relentless.'

The waiter had brought menus. Mrs Moffatt waited until he had passed on before she said, '*You're* strong. *You're* relentless too.'

'That we are,' said Malcolm, 'but for how long?' He shook himself, then started scouring the menu. 'I'm famished, are you? I reckon I could eat a whole lamb, let alone just its chops.'

'They not feeding you up there, Malcolm?'

Malcolm grinned. His smile – that came from Mrs Moffatt as well. These were the little things that brought her joy; his voice, his eyes, the way his cheeks dimpled, ever so slightly, when he smiled. She hadn't been able to do much for the boy, not when the Sisters at St Maud's were so eager to lift him out of her arms and send her on her sinful way, but it felt special to know he'd inherited these parts from her.

'Oh, they feed me well enough. They have a whole WVS division waiting on us. Actually, Emmeline, that's part of what I wanted to tell you today. That's part of why I've come into town.' His smile was growing even broader, but then the waiter reappeared – and whatever this secret was had to wait while they made their order. Everything was off-ration here, as it was in most of London's restaurants, but much of the menu had also been redacted, like one of those horrible letters soldiers sent home from the front. As luck would have it, there were lamb chops enough that Mrs Moffatt and Malcolm could take one each – and this on top of healthy helpings of potatoes, parsnips and gravy. The gooseberry tart looked like it might be perfect for dessert.

Then, when the ordering was done, Malcolm blithely announced, 'Emmeline, I'm getting married.'

Mrs Moffatt near choked. She reached, again, for his hand.

'Her name's Sarah. She's one of the WVS girls out at the airbase. Stuck on canteen duties, but she's in and out of the planes as well – has her heart set on being a mechanic, would you believe?'

'You never said anything. I didn't know you had a sweetheart, Malcolm!'

She was almost giddy with joy for the younger man. At thirty-five years old, Malcolm had 'bachelor adventurer' written all over him; the thought of him finding love in such dark times was a tonic for the soul.

'I didn't,' he explained, 'not until a few short months ago. After Dunkirk. But then there was Sarah, and … well, you've been in love, Emmeline. You know how that feels.'

It could feel like you'd come home, or it could feel reckless and wild; Mrs Moffatt had known both those kinds of love. She'd fallen hard for Malcolm's father, only to end up abandoned and with a child inside her; falling for her husband Jack, who'd perished the last time war came around, had been a slower, steadier affair – but no less deep and meaningful for that.

'Tell me about her,' she said.

For this, Malcolm didn't really have the words. 'Prim and proper, I suppose you'd say.' It was strange to see her son blushing; he looked almost cherubic when his cheeks flushed red, in spite of his size. 'She's good for me, Emmeline. She's helping me keep my head, when I'm up there.' He looked up at the restaurant's ceiling, but really he meant the vast open battlefield of the skies. 'She's got me thinking about what comes after – what life could be like. And ... I want you to meet her.'

Mrs Moffatt's heart felt full up. She was breathless, trying to get out the words, when the waiter reappeared to serve lunch. The lamb chops, such as they were, were tiny – but she would have happily slurped up nothing more than bread and gravy right now, for her mind was on something else.

'I know it's fast, but the world's changing so quickly – I want to marry her, in case—'

'Don't say it,' said Mrs Moffatt, and clutched his hand.

'I have to,' said Malcolm. 'They're saying half of us might not come out of the fight. It'll be worth it, to bloody Mr Hitler's nose and show him this island's not for taking – but who knows who'll come through and who won't? You throw yourself at them, night after night. It's like rolling the dice, every time I fly. And I want to marry her now, in case I never can. I want you to meet her, Emmeline. I want to have that moment in my life, whether I live on – or whether I burn up in the sky.'

The brutality of those words had shocked Mrs Moffatt, but once their fire had burned away, she saw it for what it really was:

just one man's frank, honest assessment of what was happening in his life.

'We *are* going to come through it, aren't we, Malcolm?'

Malcolm could not hide behind a mask, not now, not sitting in front of the mother he'd spent his life dreaming of finding. 'It's on a knife's edge, Emmeline. But we'll resist them to the last.'

The chasm inside her opened. 'We sit in the shelters, night after night, then come up to the ruins – to see what's happened to London. All those people suffering, it can't be for nothing – can it?'

Malcolm had no answer. Instead, he took a deep breath and declared, 'I want you to leave London.'

Silence separated them, deep and vast. Silence, and the steam curling up from the gravy boat the waiter waltzed through and set down between them.

'What?' Mrs Moffatt whispered.

For the first time, Malcolm seemed flustered. In silence, they poked at their plates – but it seemed, all of a sudden, that neither of them had much appetite. The only reason Mrs Moffatt started eating at all was the guilt of it – here she was, with a plate of beautiful food in front of her, while the ration queues stretched on outside every grocery store in London.

'I want you to go to the country,' Malcolm finally ventured. 'Now, Emmeline, I know I've got no right to say it. I know we aren't mother and son, not in the usual way. But I spent my life wondering about you, and I've spent the last two years getting to know you – and, well, you *are* my mother. My English mother. And I don't want you here, not where you have to look this *thing* in the eye every night. If the RAF fails, if London falls...'
He swallowed his mouthful awkwardly; even to speak of it felt something akin to treachery – because of course he should have

been unwavering in his belief that the RAF would be victorious, the enemy routed, the Kingdom restored to safety. 'If all of that happens,' he said, his voice low so that the neighbouring tables did not hear and think him a coward, 'then the Nazis are coming. I've already lost one mother in this lifetime. I don't want to lose another, not when you've only just come back into my life.' He took a deep breath. 'So I want you to go.'

Mrs Moffatt contemplated it, her face almost without expression. Then she said, 'I can't, Malcolm. I've got duties here. Things that matter. My girls. My hotel. My friends there, they're all I've ever had in this life. How could I just...' Her words petered out – because Malcom mattered too, didn't he? He was her flesh, her blood, her whole heart. And here he was, begging her to survive.

'Your friends would understand, Emmeline. Your girls would get by.'

Mrs Moffatt trembled, 'We're meant to be in this together. All of my memories are in that hotel. My closest companions in life. Archie's there, Malcolm.'

Malcolm fixed her with a questioning look. Archie Adams. He'd been there, the first time Malcolm met Mrs Moffatt; he'd chaperoned her, all the way out to the airbase where Malcolm was stationed. He'd been there ever since as well – at dinners they'd shared, and once for a walk in the park.

'You'd stay here, in a city of ruins, for Mr Adams?' whispered Malcolm, uncertain if he had it right.

'He has his Orchestra,' she explained, though something told Malcolm there was more to the feeling than this, 'and I have my girls. That's how it's always been.'

Malcolm set down his knife and fork. 'You and Mr Adams, it's more than friendship?'

Mrs Moffatt's hands were shaking, so Malcolm took hold of them.

'Emmeline?'

'I don't know,' she finally said – and, when she tried to draw her hands away, Malcolm held on, as if for dear life, as if he wouldn't let her slip through his fingers, nor hide from the truth. 'I've never been lucky in love, Malcolm. First your father, and then my Jack... but with Archie it's easy. It's dinner and pots of tea, and sometimes an afternoon matinee. It's been like that for a little time now. Why change things? He's dear to me, that's all.'

'He's more than dear, Emmeline. I saw it from the start. I can see it right now.' He paused. 'If you're willing to stay in London, and all for his sake, then it has to be more than companionship. It's love. It's the same thing that's put my feet on the ground this autumn. It's the same thing I'm fighting for, every time I take flight. So why not tell him? If you're really willing to risk everything, isn't it time?'

Mrs Moffatt whispered, 'Why risk the heartache again? I'm older than you are, Malcolm. You don't know how that feels. Everything's fine now. Everything works. Why take that chance?'

And Malcolm, who stroked the back of her hands gently, said, 'Because we're standing on the edge, Emmeline – we're on the cliff's edge, and who knows what comes after? It's something Sarah said to me. It's the reason I knew we had to be married. One night, we were out walking out beyond the airbase, and she told me that we're all going to die – every last one of us. It could be tonight, she said, or it could be tomorrow, or it could be many happy years from now. But there's no denying the fact – death's coming for us all. But if we get to love in the meantime, well, maybe it's worth it. Maybe it's worth all the heartache and pitfalls of life, if we get to say that we loved someone and that they loved us too.' He took a deep breath.

'So if you're really telling me you want to stay in London, to sit out the bombs every night, to risk it all – then it had better be because love is calling on you too, Mother. It had better be because you've seized that chance.'

It was the first time he'd called her 'mother' like that, but Mrs Moffatt didn't get the chance to bask in the beauty of it, because now a hundred other thoughts were tumbling through her head. Love and death – and, in the middle of it all, Archie Adams, sitting behind his ivory white grand piano, gazing at her across the Grand.

The gooseberry tart was here. For a few minutes, that would be distraction enough.

After that, she thought, the world would have to change.

Chapter Nine

The cars had careered into each other an hour after the blackout began. In the darkness where Regent Street and Great Portland Street met, one wreck sat stranded in the intersection, while three wardens from the ARP patrol crouched at the other, nervously trying to keep the concussed driver awake. The black Austin had been caught between the oncoming car and a lamp post; its bonnet was crumpled, its front doors bent beyond opening. It wasn't the first this evening, and no doubt it wouldn't be the last.

Up above, the sirens were in full song. The sky was open and clear, a full moon illuminating such great swathes of London that the Luftwaffe had seized their opportunity for an all-out assault. In the east, searchlights criss-crossed the skies above the docks. The steady report of the ack-ack fire made an unholy chorus with the sirens.

Twenty yards along Oxford Street, Raymond de Guise stood on the corner, waiting for the ambulance service to arrive. He'd been standing here too long already, and there was still no sign of its approach. Nervously, he looked to the skies. It was going to be a devastating night, there was no doubt about that. The beautiful, crystal-clear nights always were. 'An Englishman prays for rain,' Mortimer Bond was often heard to say, for the cover of clouds was the best deterrent against the Luftwaffe's advance.

Back along the road, voices swirled – 'We need to get him out of there, Sam; that's a steady stream of blood he's losing' – but most were drowned out by the explosions rending the night apart somewhere in the east. He tried not to let his mind dwell on his family, his mother and Leah, and especially his sister-in-law Vivienne, alone in her shelter with his nephew Stan. A great part of Raymond de Guise thought he ought to have been with her, that it was what his brother would have wanted; another part knew he ought to be with Nancy, holding her tight. And yet, what better way was there to honour his brother's passing than to be standing here, where he was most use? With that thought in mind, he flexed the muscles in his leg, lifting his foot off the ground. The sprain had healed, but whatever bruising it had left behind was lingering. Most mornings, when he returned to Nancy – often just as she was stirring to head for the breakfast service at the Buckingham Hotel – it had started swelling again, and he'd have to sleep with it propped up on pillows just to be fit for the following night.

There came the sound of another explosion. That wasn't in the east this time; Raymond felt as if he could almost feel the shock wave rolling over him, just like the crashing waves of the English Channel some months before

'That's closer,' came a voice behind him.

He turned. Cathy Everly, and a group of the other WVS from the canteen behind John Lewis, had rushed down to the site of the collision to provide support. Raymond smiled at the sight of her. In the weeks since she'd introduced him to the ARP patrols, he'd crossed her path several times – even patrolled with her twice. She was, he was quickly learning, one of Mortimer Bond's most dedicated troops; Bond, though not directly in control of the activities of the WVS, had seemingly co-opted Cathy as one of his own. 'She's good on the ground,' he'd said one night. 'Dedicated to the last. You won't find many officers with as much street knowledge as Miss Everly. She could take you from bombsite to bombsite, hardly even opening her eyes.'

The WVS had brought blankets; two of them were tending to the survivor from the first car, while others waited with the driver from the more crumpled vehicle, trying to make him as comfortable as they could before the ambulance arrived. Cathy seemed to have detached herself from the latter group and picked her way to find Raymond at the intersection.

'How are you bearing up?' she asked him, the words distant against the thunder of the night.

'I haven't fallen over yet, Cathy,' Raymond shuddered. He saw that her eyes were suddenly directed over his shoulder and, turning, saw another silhouetted car appear along Oxford Street. This time, instead of slowing down to help, the car saw the wardens attending the collision, turned around in the road, and vanished along one of the northern thoroughfares.

Cathy shook her head ruefully. 'They've been circling all night. Watch out for them, Raymond.'

He gave her a pointed look, inviting more explanation.

'We saw them outside one of the boarded-up shop fronts just beyond the WVS station. As soon as the blackout comes down, out they all come – it's like rats, when the ratcatcher's away. Like foxes on my father's estate, after the hunt has moved on. The blackout draws them in. Looters, Raymond. When they come to write the history of this winter, they'll rhapsodise the everyday goodness of Londoners – but let's not forget that not all of us were in it for the common good.'

Cathy's last words were rendered mute, when a vast quake shook the city somewhere in the north. At the site of the wreck, every man stopped what they were doing and looked to the north.

So did Raymond. The rose glow of fire was suddenly apparent over the rooftops of Fitzrovia, the night sky turned to churning golds and red.

'That was near,' he whispered.

Inside the wreck of the Austin, the driver had started crying out. Whether it was pain or panic, Raymond could not tell – and nor did he wait to find out.

'With me, Lance Corporal!' one of the other ARP wardens was shouting, gesticulating along the barren road. Then he turned to hurry across Oxford Street, heading into the north's maelstrom of fiery light. 'All hands!'

It had been several days since Raymond last used his cane, but he soon wished he'd brought it tonight. The other ARP wardens were surging into the northern streets, but as soon as he took off after them he started floundering. Spikes of fresh pain ricocheted through his foot whenever he landed badly.

The ARP warden who'd clamoured for him looked back, saw Raymond staggering and cried out, 'Stay with the casualties, de Guise!'

'You said *all hands*,' Raymond protested, and took off again.

He didn't get far. The other wardens were already leagues ahead, but his ankle turned painfully underneath him – and it was only Cathy's sudden appearance beneath his shoulder that stopped him falling.

'I don't need propping up,' he grinned at her.

'Call it a three-legged race,' she replied, with a flash of her iridescent smile. 'You must have had those in your schooldays.'

'I prefer to imagine us waltzing,' he said; after all, she'd practically taken him in hold. 'Or – make it a quickstep. That's looking serious.'

By his intonation, Raymond seemed to want to take off after the wardens streaming north. It was Cathy who held him back.

'You received an order, Lance Corporal. I'm sure you followed your every order in France. Well, the same goes here. We're with the casualty. I'm sure you wouldn't want a record for insubordination following you back to your division?'

At first, Raymond wasn't certain whether she was teasing him or being deadly serious; the regal look in her eyes might have been interpreted either way. All he truly knew was that the thought of staying here attending to a casualty did not sit comfortably in his heart. For all the invaluable work the WVS was doing, his place was certainly somewhere other than this.

He was about to tell Cathy as much when the cry went up, a bell started ringing, and he and Cathy turned to see the ambulance's approach.

In moments, two young men were leaping off and hurrying towards the site of the collision. Behind them came two more veteran fire officers, carrying the bolt cutters and various other tools that had been radioed for some minutes ago. Raymond hurried after them, with Cathy holding him upright as he came.

For a moment, as the ambulance men and fire officers did their job, all that Raymond could do was stare, incredulous, at this shopping promenade where, a few short weeks ago, young lovers had congregated, wives had gone shopping, city clerks and railway workers had stopped for lunch. This, thought Raymond, was London. It wasn't Occupied France. It wasn't Dunkirk, where he and his brother had waited on the beaches, listening to the scream of incendiaries in the town, watching the planes dogfight above. London: a place of war. The thought was almost too difficult to imagine. It kept slipping away, whenever he pinned it in place.

At last, the fire officers completed their job, extracting the man from the crumpled Austin. Soon the ambulance crew were checking the man's injuries, wrapping him in blankets – and then, once they were certain they might move him without causing further injury, ferrying him gently to their waiting wagon. 'Are you sure you don't need to go with them?' Cathy asked, still holding on to Raymond's arm.

This time, he was quite certain she was teasing. 'I've wasted enough nights in hospital.' He looked to the north, where the orange glow of fires was spreading over the rooftops in precisely the same direction the other ARP wardens had taken flight. 'We could still be some use – but I may need your help to get there, Miss Everly.'

'We might be some use here too, Raymond. Look…'

The ambulance had wheeled away, taking its injured with it, and in its wake, the WVS girls were ready to flock back to their station. No doubt, just as Raymond had said, there would be survivors from whatever inferno was raging in Fitzrovia to the north; the girls would need to make sure there were enough supplies on hand to deal with a sudden influx. But it wasn't them to whom Cathy was pointing. She took Raymond by the arm, angled him round, and directed his gaze to one of the lesser roads heading north. There, the same vehicle they'd seen circling the crash site some time before had pulled into the darkness underneath one of the shop fronts. Raymond could only make it out by the man's cigarillo flare, but the driver and a companion had climbed out of the car and now loitered around its bonnet. *Watching.*

'I'll tell him to put it out,' said Raymond, 'that ought to put the frighteners up them – that they know we've got their number.'

He was about to march in their direction, ignoring for a moment the pain in his foot, when Cathy strained on his arm. 'You mustn't.'

'What?'

'What's the use in shooing them away, like a stray cat? You understand what they're out here to do, don't you, Raymond? It's men like that who crawled through John Lewis after it was hit – taking everything they could find of any value from the shelves. If it isn't the cash box, they'll go after the fine china. I've seen looters in and out of a corner shop down by Piccadilly – bags full of corned beef, bags of potatoes. Almost anything has a value. Look, off they go ...'

While Cathy had been talking, the first man had snuffed out the light of his smoke. Now just a pair of indistinct shadows, they scurried up the road and out of sight.

'Come on, Raymond. It wouldn't do to catch them for something as tiny as a cigarillo light. Better to wait and *watch* – and then, the moment they're in somebody else's shop, filling their suitcases, we'll have them. Two more off the streets.' She stopped, uncertain if it was a look of disappointment on Raymond's face. 'I know you'd rather be with the wardens, Raymond, but this is—'

'It's not that at all,' said Raymond, whose look had not been disappointment but anger. 'There's men losing their lives to win this war, and others turning a profit from it.' He took a stride forward. 'Come on, Cathy – I might need you to lift me if I stumble, but I'll be beside you, every step of the way.'

The men had left their car in the shadows between two shop fronts, so evidently they didn't mean to go far. It was a dark green Ford, with license plates to indicate it was scarcely two years old, and this made Raymond even more furious still; whoever these men were, they were clearly not impoverished. They might not have been driving a Rolls Royce to the scene of their crime, but Raymond knew countless families who had never owned a car, let alone one as well-kept and polished as this. Part of him thought they ought to wait here, laying in an ambush for their return – but Cathy quickly disabused him of the notion. 'Catch them red-handed,' she said. 'Fingers in the pot. That's the way to do it. A statement from a loyal lance corporal – and one from a valued member of the Women's Voluntary Service,' she added with some modicum of pride, 'and they can rot in a prison cell like they should be doing. Let them enjoy their rations in *there*.'

It wasn't immediately evident where the men might have gone. This part of London abounded with small shops ripe for pillaging, but in the immediate vicinity none of them seemed to have been damaged. For the moment, all that Raymond and Cathy could do was walk a quiet circuit, listening out for the sound of breaking glass, the tell-tale whisper of pillagers at work. Not an easy task, set against the riotous music of the night. Sometimes, shadows darted in the place between shop fronts. Sometimes, London rats emerged from their hidings and (because even rats were terrorised from above) took flight for safer corners – but, for a time, Raymond and Cathy saw no other soul.

'You learned to keep your head, when you were in France,' Raymond said, as he and Cathy returned to the pillagers' car and began another circuit, to explore some further streets. 'Even at Dunkirk, it wasn't like this.' He looked up; the sky was clear above the narrow street they wandered, but then the conical glare of searchlights burst over the rooftops, like a volcano erupting. 'In France, when they came for you, it was brutal, nasty, short. Here, it doesn't end. And it's not infantry and gunners suffering it, not soldiers at all. It's grocers and haberdashers. It's city clerks and railwaymen.'

It was the mention of Dunkirk that had made that glassy look come over Cathy's eyes, Raymond was sure of it. He remembered standing with her in the ruins of the John Lewis East House and it being just the same. Dunkirk was the horror that dogged Raymond's every footstep. To almost everyone he met, it was the triumph, the happy ending, the hope that inspired them. But not so to Cathy Everly. The mention of the word seemed to rip her from the current moment and plant her there, on the same beaches where he'd been, with his brother Artie and young Billy Brogan at his side.

'You know,' said Cathy, 'you still haven't told me the story – of how you got back…'

They hurried along the next shop fronts, twisting round a corner where an old public house sat, the corners of its blackouts revealing that some drinkers were still gathered within. Raymond could not begrudge them it – a pint of ale, a drop of brandy, could work wonders for the soul on a night like this.

'That's a long story,' Raymond panted.

'I should like to hear it,' Cathy went on, reaching, at last, the final corner, round which the waves of heat rampaged. 'What you all went through out there. What it took to get you all home…'

Home. He sensed something more meaningful in the word, but did not stop to ask, for he was suddenly quite certain he had seen figures darting across the road some distance ahead – and, gritting his teeth through the pain in his foot, he picked up the pace.

'There,' said Cathy when, at last, they reached a crossroads. The corner was dominated by the frontage of a broad post office, flanked by shops of various design: a cobbler's, a tailor's, a bookseller going by the name 'Geraint & Jones'. It was beyond those shop fronts that the ruin began. Raymond wasn't sure what the shops had once been, whether it was one or a collection that had been razed together – but he was quite certain this wasn't a recent devastation, for no fires licked the walls, no smoke curled from the detritus. Indeed, the shattered windows had been boarded up. So too had the door – only, now, it stood ajar, allowing glimpses of the darkness within. The board which had been nailed across the front was propped against the wall – as if the enterprising hands which had levered it free might soon decide to hammer it back into place – and, from within, came the sound of footsteps.

'It might just be rats,' said Raymond, looking sidelong at Cathy.

'It's not rats,' she said.

They skirted the shadows on the edge of the road until, at last, they reached the open doorway. Then, into the ruins they slipped. If there had been any doubt that they were alone in the building, it quickly vanished; it wasn't just footsteps they could hear within, but the sound of wrenches and hammers, as if there were joiners at work. 'They've been here before,' whispered Cathy. 'This has been planned. There's nothing here to steal – nothing except the shop fixtures. That's what they've come for now. Timber and metal brackets, the brass of the cash register – there's value in all of it.'

It had taken some time to get used to the new darkness inside the building, but now Raymond saw what Cathy meant: the downstairs of the shop had already been stripped clean, perhaps some nights before; the men were at work somewhere above, unscrewing shelving from the walls, ripping out electric cabling and tightening it into rolls.

'They're not just opportunists, then. It's not just stupidity – it's malice, organised malice...' It would have been easier to forgive some passer-by reaching into a ruptured shop front to help himself from the shelves than it was men who'd come here for the express purposing of picking the corpse of the building clean. This was organised labour; pointed, planned, deliberate. Not for the first time, Raymond thought of his brother Artie's sacrifice at Dunkirk. Artie was no angel – he'd done his fair share of skulduggery, even served his own stretch in Pentonville as penance for it – but he'd still stood up and done the right thing. It broiled in him as they picked their way through the ruin and came to the bottom of a set of stairs.

'What was it like?' she asked, breathlessly, as they took the first step.

'What do you mean?'

'Dunkirk. Trapped on the beaches, with nowhere to go. The fear of it, I mean. The Wehrmacht advancing from behind. You were *stranded*…'

Dunkirk again, thought Raymond. Something in her desperately needed to know. 'When we reached the beaches,' he explained, 'command was already loading the destroyers. But it was only the sick and wounded. They had Red Cross on the ships. That was the plan – get those that needed it most off first. And who can argue with that? Except time was ticking. Ticking, ticking, ticking. Counting down the hours of our lives.'

The noise of the sirens made it difficult to hear.

'We were fortunate – or, at least, we thought we were. We were onto some of the first fishing boats that made it across, then ferried onto the HMS *Othello*. I thought we were free. But then…'

Raymond stalled; he was certain he could hear a tiny voice beyond the door. Or was it just the wardens, shouting from the street outside? It was so difficult to tell.

'Then what?'

'The *Othello* went down,' he told her. 'You'll have read about it. Even then, I was lucky. My brother and I were thrown up, back on the beaches. But…' He stopped. Together they had reached the top of the stairs. There was more devastation here, and it occurred to Raymond for the first time that it was the rear of the premises that had been hit in the bombardment. One of the hallways here was nought but a landslide – but, in the other direction, where the living quarters above the shop used to be, a door stood ajar. From inside spilled the pale light of a lantern.

Raymond was stealing towards it when Cathy whispered, 'Your brother died on the beaches, didn't he?'

He lifted his finger to encourage her back into silence.

'But Raymond, what – what happened?'

Raymond was certain the hammering of tools beyond the doors had come to a sudden cessation. He held himself still, gripping Cathy's arm to demand the same – but, at that precise moment, some reverberation rolled across the London skyline and, once it had passed, the drumming of tools returned. Raymond inched closer to the door, careful not to show his face to the lantern light. When he looked back, he could see Cathy staring at him with a strange intensity. It took him some time to understand she was still expecting an answer to his question.

'He was injured when the *Othello* went down,' he whispered. 'Alive when we washed back up on the beaches, but he never stood a chance. I stayed with him until the end.'

He'd done more than that. He'd buried Artie, in a lonely field, with his own two hands. One day, he meant to go back and retrieve his brother; one day, when the war was done. But how many people made promises like that to themselves? He found himself running his hand along Cathy's arm, for her face was etched in such sadness, and he supposed it could only be for him. 'It's been a hard time, hasn't it?'

She nodded as she clamoured, 'But *you* got back. You were stranded in France. Weeks, with the coast overrun. And you still made it back – didn't you, Raymond?'

'I'm here,' he said, with a simplicity that belied all the peril and drama of the last six months – and, in return, Cathy whispered, 'Then others might be out there, mightn't they? British soldiers, who got left behind? They might be living still. Just stranded, without a soul to help them home…'

The door flew open.

Raymond and Cathy had been too lost in their whispered conversation to realise the hammering had stopped again; too rapt in this memory of Artie Cohen and his bitter end in France to realise the lantern light, too, had shifted. Now, caught off-guard in that quiet moment, the door swung back, connecting directly with Cathy's face. Cathy flew backwards, staggering into Raymond as she fell – and out of the doorway two men, considerably older than Raymond, scrambled, wrenches in hands, a box of tools swinging at their side. 'Out of my way!' one of them snarled as he reeled along the hallway, back towards the top of the stairs. 'Out of my way, you bastards! Can't a man get a minute's peace in this sodding city?'

Raymond had dropped instantly to his knee, to reach for Cathy and make sure she was all right – but now he looked over his shoulder at the fleeing men. 'Stop!' he thundered. 'Stop right there!'

'Bloody pigs,' one of the men seethed as they reached the top of the stairs.

'Let's seal it up, Terry, lock 'em inside, see how they like that!'

Raymond looked down. Cathy had been grasping his hand, her eyes screwed up against the shock of the fall, but as he watched she visibly relaxed, her eyes widening to take him in. 'After them, Raymond. After them, my—'

He had started hoisting her back to her feet, but evidently her ankle, too, had turned over in the tumble – and now she crashed back to the floor, wincing in pain. Besides, it was already too late; Raymond could hear the retreat of the men's voices as, breaking back through the shop front, they took off up the road. At least they hadn't stopped to hammer the boards back in place, he thought. No, they were too cowardly to try something like that.

'A decent pair of wardens we make,' said Raymond grimly as, finally, he was able to help her back to her feet. 'How much does it hurt?'

'I'm still standing,' she laughed. 'Look, they left their lantern light.'

'A warden's first priority,' said Raymond, 'to protect the black-out. Onward!'

Raymond and Cathy had to prop each other up as they hobbled into the room where the looters had been working. They hadn't got away with much, it seemed; the shelves they'd removed from the walls were still piled up, ready to be ferried away, and a steel strongbox – perhaps the shop's safe – had been levered out of a hole in the cracked wall. 'By God,' said Raymond, 'they'll take anything.'

'The city's at war,' said Cathy, 'but it doesn't have to be at war with itself. It makes one sick – after everything you did at Dunkirk. You and your brother and ...' Here she faltered, before suddenly saying, 'And all the fishermen, sallying out to bring you back, while others just want to grow fat and rich on the misery of it.'

As Cathy had spoken, Raymond had knelt down to take the paraffin lantern from the spot where it had been left. His fingers were dancing about its burning rim, searching for the valve he could turn to kill its light, when Cathy's hand darted down and took his. At first, he was uncertain why. Then he realised something had dazzled her eye in the lamplight. She lifted his ring finger now, and the wedding band that still glimmered around it.

'I told you, that first night, that you oughtn't to wear it. Not out here, not on patrol. Look around you,' she said, sadly, 'they'll take anything they can find. That door might have flown back, knocked you out flat. They'd have had it off your finger in a second. And all those memories bound up in it, all that love and joy – it would all be *gone*.' She let his hand fall and, reaching under the folds of her overcoat, she pulled out a simple silver chain – on whose end dangled a silver ring. 'If you must carry it with you, keep it out of sight.'

Raymond studied her closely. 'Cathy, are you married too?'

She shook her head. 'It was my grandmother's. She made a gift of it when she passed, in case my day ever came.' The lantern light died. On the shop floor, there was blackness, rich and heady with the scent of paraffin oil. 'Well, we've seen the worst of this city tonight. How about we go back out there and see its best? Every warden, every WVS girl, every good, decent Londoner, standing up for what's right? There's plenty of them. I think I should like to be among them right now.'

Both Raymond and Cathy were limping as they reached the top of the stairs; both limping as, having replaced the boards against the ruin's door, they picked their way back along the road. The dark green Ford was gone from the place it had been parked. No doubt they would try again another night. 'But that's all we can do,' said Cathy, 'one night at a time, doing our best, trying always to do what's right.'

'To put one foot in front of another,' said Raymond.

They both smiled. 'Quite literally, tonight,' said Cathy.

The night was yet young; together, each one propped up on the other one's shoulder, they strode out to meet it.

Chapter Ten

This time, there was hardly a flutter of nerves in Billy's belly as he walked with Mary-Louise up the Camden Road and through the red brick terraces to her uncle's house. Part of that, he supposed, was because Mary-Louise's hand was in his, and the feeling of this was certainly formidable. But the other part, perhaps the greater part, was what he was carrying, wrapped in wax paper, in the satchel over his shoulder.

Uncle Ken shook him eagerly by the hand the moment he stepped through the door. It was only the second time that Billy had crossed this threshold, but something in the atmosphere made it seem like he'd been here every Sunday since he was a boy – as if, perhaps, he'd grown up here, bobbing in and out of Mary-Louise's house, clambering over the garden fence for picnics on a Saturday or Sunday dinner. Aunt Marge covered him in kisses, and Thom and Jake stood in line, ready to shake his hand. This was more than an honour welcome for a return-ing soldier, thought Billy – who, though he flushed red with embarrassment, had to admit that he rather liked the feeling of being held in such high esteem; this was like the return of a prodigal son. Probably they were going over the top to make him feel part of the family – but this Billy liked too; it meant Mary-Louise had been speaking of him, since the last time he came ... and that could only mean that she held him in the highest affection as well.

Of course, he already knew *that*. She'd whispered it into his ear as they curled up, together, in the chambermaids' quarters last night.

On the kitchen table, Uncle Ken opened the wax paper packages Billy had brought and rubbed his hands together in admiration.

'That's a nice piece of venison. Shot on some lord's estate, I should think, for those nobs at the Buckingham Hotel.' He flashed Billy a smile. 'A pair of partridges. Oranges. Figs.' There was more. Billy had brought two pounds of sugar lumps, and a cloth bag of candied lemon slices. 'These are delicacies, Billy.' He held up a candied lemon as if it was a treasure found in some old pharaoh's tomb. 'Oh yes, you won't imagine what these old dears have been doing without. A man cannot live by bread alone.'

'And there's precious little of that to go round,' chipped in Marge, who was busying herself brewing a pot of tea.

'I'm just glad I can help, sir,' said Billy.

There hadn't been deceit in it, not really. This was the fourth time Billy had set aside a few bits and pieces for Uncle Ken, and the truth was it was no different to Billy siphoning off a few scones, here and there, for his own brood back in Lambeth Yard. He'd been doing that since he was Annie's age, just starting out as a hotel page – the leftovers on the room service trolleys had just been too tempting, and when Billy found out they were bound for the rubbish bins, well, it had almost seemed a moral obligation to put them to better use. Now, looking at the venison that Marge had put on the chopping block while the tea stewed, and the bag of figs – which had been deemed just a little too soft for the refined palettes of the Queen Mary restaurant – he wondered why he had any twinge of guilt at all.

It was only when the tea was served – and Mary-Louise was happily slathering a scone (from the Buckingham Hotel) with gooseberry jam (home-made) – that things began to feel strange.

'Look, Billy,' said Ken, 'I can't have you bringing this stuff to us for nothing at all.'

'What do you mean, sir?'

'Come on, Bill, you're a clever lad. It just doesn't sit right with me – no matter what feelings you have for our Mary-Lou – that you should be providing for us. I'm still the man of this house, aren't I?' Ken was wearing a grin altogether too big for his face. While Marge and Mary-Louise flitted around the edges of the kitchen, he heaved himself up, left Billy at the kitchen table, and tramped out to the cupboard under the stairs. After some moments ferreting around inside, he returned with an old tobacco tin. Inside it was a tightly bound roll of pound notes. 'Here, Billy, I'm not too short at the moment. Work's been kind to me, and our Marge has been taking in washing as well. Let me give you a couple of bob – just our way of saying thanks for all you've been doing.'

Billy was so perplexed that, at first, he didn't put up a protest when Ken pressed two pound notes into his hands. The sum was so big that he was certain there'd been some mistake, but Ken was already lumbering back to the cupboard with his tin, so it was easy for him to ignore it when Billy called out, 'Ken, I can't take this – I haven't done anything, it's only a few bits, it's not mine to sell and …'

The reason Billy tapered off, though, was not Ken at all; it was because Mary-Louise, appearing at his shoulder with the freshly slathered scone, bent down and whispered in his ear, 'It's just Uncle Ken. He likes to be straight with people. It's his pride, Billy. Let him have his pride.'

This, at least, Billy understood. The scone was a nice distraction as well. He'd just bitten into it, feeling the tart gooseberries explode around his lips, when Ken returned to the room, still talking as if he'd never stopped. '...because that's the thing nobody talks about, isn't it? That's the thing we're not allowed to say. All these rules and regulations, all this telling people what they can buy and what they can't, it's ruining lives. Can't anyone see that? Since when did the King of England get to tell the good working families of this country what they can and can't have for supper?'

Ken dropped down into his seat, realised the scones had arrived, and started tucking in. Here was somebody, thought Billy, who hadn't let the rules and regulations interrupt his meals one jot.

'An Englishman's got a right to his freedoms,' Ken orated, 'but we've got a Prime Minister telling us to give those freedoms back. Well, I don't think that's in an Englishman's spirit, do you, Billy? We're descended from lion-hearts.'

'Billy's *Irish*, Uncle Ken,' Mary-Louise interjected. 'I told you...'

Ken looked momentarily startled. Laughing, he reached across the table and doffed Billy around the shoulder. 'Well, the Irish wouldn't stand for this either! It's freedoms the Irish want – isn't that so? And here we all are, just rolling over and handing back every right we have. We're a scared species, Billy, don't make any mistake about that. There's kids going hungry out there because of it. Old dears, who've suffered enough in this life, who can't even have a proper dinner on account of this lot. And that's why I say it, Billy – *thank you*. This lot you've brought, it's going to make some sorry souls very happy. And that's on account of *you*, son. You can be very proud.'

'I'm sure Billy's got a lot to be proud of, Ken,' said Marge – who had now packaged off the butchered venison, then divided the figs into smaller cloth bags. 'He's a bloody hero, and no mistake.'

'Well, a hero's still allowed a day off here and there. Here, Bill, take a look at this.' Apparently, the tobacco tin wasn't the only thing Ken had produced from the cupboard under the stairs. Now he opened his hand and out fanned six paper tickets for a place called the River Brent Racing Stadium. The ticket was a simple design: today's date, a list of times, and a small silhouette of a greyhound in the corner. Ken's signature had been scrawled on each.

'My treat, Billy,' Ken beamed. 'Well, if you're going to be part of the family,' and he flashed a look at Mary-Louise, 'it's only fair we introduce you to our traditions. What do you say?'

'Hendon's got a fine tradition for the greyhounds,' Ken said as, a cramped car ride later, he marched the family into the shadow of the stadium on the Hendon high road. 'It's up here they first did the mechanicals – that's the dogs chasing a contraption, not a real live hare. That's before my time, of course – but the way my grandpa talked of it, those were the glory days. His old man used to catch hares for the races – and a good few for the pot as well.' He winked at Billy, though Billy – walking hand in hand with Mary-Louise – was not entirely sure why. 'Well, here we are. Isn't she a beauty?'

The River Brent Racing Stadium was only five years old, and sat overlooking the scrubby parklands that stretched north of Hendon, and the new road constructions – abandoned with the declaration of war – beyond. From outside, it wasn't so very glorious – but, as soon as they'd stepped through the turnstiles and Billy got to appreciate the scale of the grounds from within, he understood why Ken had been rhapsodising so effusively. In the heart of the grounds was the long oval track around which the greyhounds would chase a mechanical hare; but around *that* were a bustle of stalls and shops, bookmakers clamouring for bets to be placed while also hawking hot teas, teacakes and – in one corner – hot griddled sausage.

'There's some of these tracks had to close,' said Ken, as he led the family through the growing throng, 'but that only makes them more special, don't it? It's all these restrictions, you see. The government's called up all those boys, but most of them are sitting in billets, waiting to be deployed – when they could all be back at their jobs, keeping everything ticking over. Well, at least *our* place is thriving, isn't it, Marge?'

'*Your* place, Ken?' asked Billy.

'Now, I don't *own* it, Bill. But it *feels* like mine, you know? I come here enough. All my old pals like a good bet on the dogs.'

Ken had already seen some of those old pals – and, with his wife and children in tow, he marched off through the amass-ing crowd to join them at the railing. Halfway there, he had a sudden thought, ducked back over to Billy and pressed another pound note into his hand. 'Have a throw on me, Bill. I'll have that back if your number comes in, of course ...'

Then he was off again, straight into the heart of a group of men who tossed their caps in the air in some exuberant greeting.

'Your uncle's a popular man,' Billy said, as he and Mary-Louise gravitated towards one of the stalls. With hot teas in hand, they returned to the terrace. Down on the tracks, some of the handlers were leading a succession of greyhounds into their stalls. An engineer in a flat cap and tweeds was fiddling with the metallic rail along which the mechanical hare would soon course.

'This is his world,' Mary-Louise said. There were seats at the track-side, and Mary-Louise guided him there, before the horde descended. 'He's been coming since he was a lad. Used to bring me too, every time I came to stay. I think that's why he suggested it today. It's like a tradition – or a … baptism. For you, Billy.'

Billy snorted. 'I've already been baptised. My Ma and Pa wouldn't have had it any other way.' But he knew what Mary-Louise meant: she meant to the family; as if, after today, Billy would be one of them at last. 'You think I should put some money down, then?'

Mary-Louise thought it would be an affront to Ken not to – so, before the first race began, they got hold of one of the race cards, pretended that either of them could make sense of the odds in the gazette at the bookmaker's stand, and chose three hounds. Mary-Louise, who seemed to have some rudimentary knowledge of form, chose 'Irish Rambler' – but Billy suspected it was more because of the name than it was any particulars belonging to the dog. After that, she started calling Billy her 'very own Irish Rambler', and this pleased him no end – not the rambling part, nor even the Irish, but the idea that he belonged to her, that he was her 'very own'. Billy chose his own bets purely on the basis of their names: 'Archduke Revelry' sounded like just the sort of drunken shenanigans he'd seen happening among the toffs at the Buckingham Hotel, while 'Runaway Girl' put him suddenly in mind of his sister Annie.

'Do you think she'll get on?' Billy asked, as they returned to their seats, betting slips in hand. 'She's there today. Nancy promised her a trial – just to see if she can cut the mustard. But I know my sister. She's got an attitude about her. It's like she knows best, wherever she is. By the end of the day, she'll be giving the girls lectures on how to polish a brass bedstead, how to get the shine onto a silver spoon…'

Mary-Louise laughed. 'That sounds like somebody else I know.'

It took Billy a second to understand that Mary-Louise meant him.

'I wasn't there, when you started out at the Buckingham, Bill. But from everything I've heard, it sounds like you were quite the little lord, strutting up and down, busying yourself, getting in everybody's business.' She gave a sly grin. 'Under everybody's feet...' She prodded him in the ribs, just to make sure he knew she was joking. Then she said, 'I reckon, as long as she works hard, your Annie'll be fine. She just needs to get on with the girls. And she's a likeable girl, isn't she?'

Billy wondered if she was. She'd been plaguing Billy all of his life. But wasn't that the job of a little sister? He smiled and, in the corner of his eye, saw movement on the race track. 'Here we go, Mary-Lou. Keep your eyes peeled. If your Irish Rambler or my Runaway Girl strike lucky, we might have to go dancing tonight.' He slapped his leg. 'Well, I'm sure I could hobble around the dance floor a bit, with you hanging beautiful off my arm.'

Ken and the family had evidently decided to leave Billy and Mary-Louise to have some quiet time together, but as soon as the race started, Billy could hear Ken's voice soaring above the cheers of the crowd. 'Go on! Go on, son!' Ken was hollering. And Billy knew, straight away, that whatever bets Ken had placed had been on other dogs: Archduke Revelry and Runaway Girl seemed so disinterested in the mechanical hare that they lolloped along at the back of the pack, while some more sprightly hounds coursed at the front.

'We've still got a chance, Billy!' Mary-Louise thrilled. Irish Rambler was out in front, drawing snout-to-snout with a tan hound that, by the racing card, Billy knew as 'Victorian Darling'. 'Look at him go, Billy. He's nearly there! He's going to do it!' Mary-Louise was on her feet, hoisting Billy up too. 'Go, Irish

Rambler!' she cried out. 'He's at the finish, Bill! He's going to …'
The thrill in her voice had reached such a pitch that Billy was
borne up by it; what a thing it was, to see Mary-Louise as
unbridled and excited as this. She wasn't like this, sweeping the
corners of some minister's bedroom at the Buckingham Hotel.

But then the thrill died. 'Oh, *Billy!*' she exclaimed – and,
next second, she tore their betting slips clean in two. 'Victorian
Darling took it. Billy, that was *so* close.' She slumped back down.
'Reckon you might still want to take me dancing, Bill?'

Billy was about to tell her that he'd go dancing with her any
night, when through the crowd of jubilant and despairing spec-
tators, Ken emerged. His own face was radiating with victory.
'Victorian Darling's done it again. I tell you, Mary-Lou, I'm
going to buy a share in that dog.' Ken slumped down. 'How'd
you fare, Billy?'

Billy shrugged. Then, with a cheery shake of the head, he said,
'I don't think I believe in beginner's luck, sir.'

'Well, listen, Billy, I've been talking to some of the old
crowd …' he nodded over his shoulder, where a group of men
the same age as Ken were gathered at the railing, eagerly waiting
for the hare to be re-set and the next dogs led into the traps,
'… and they reckon things are getting even more stretched. They
all got friends and families trying to stretch things out. My old
pal Earl over there, his ma lost her ration book and has been
scrounging ever since. Do you know how long it's taking her to
get that book replaced? Well, I'll tell you, Billy – a woman can
starve in half the time.' Ken's fists were bunched. Then, when
he opened them, he started kneading at his legs, as if trying to
contain his fury. 'Blast it, Billy, people are dying out here. They
give us shelters to protect us from the bombs – but what do they
give us to protect us from *them* and their stupid rules?'

Billy said, 'But what about the blockade. And the U-boats. And…'

Ken shook his head. 'Come on, Billy, you know better than that.'

And he really did. Because there was food aplenty in the Buckingham Hotel, wasn't there? The Queen Mary didn't ration the lords and ladies who dined there every lunchtime. In the Candlelight Club, you could still get cocktails and canapes. An exiled king didn't have to stand in line to get his sausages. All he had to do was pick up his bedside telephone and put a message through to the hotel kitchens, where the larders remained perennially full.

'It's not their fault. Poor buggers,' Ken cursed. 'And here I am, stuffing myself with an extra scone for elevenses like I'm the King of England. I've got to do more for them, Billy.' He sat up straighter, as if an idea was only just occurring to him. Meanwhile, on Billy's other side, Mary-Louise stiffened, her fingers tightening where they were entwined with Billy's own. 'Listen, Billy, what's the hope you can lay your hands on a few bits more for me? A regular kind of thing? What do you think?'

'Regular?' Billy wondered.

'I could make it worth your while, Billy, if that's what you mean.'

It wasn't what Billy had meant at all. He'd faltered only because it seemed so *formal*, somehow. Lifting a few bits here and there – well, that was just grazing; that hardly mattered, not when it was only going to go to waste. It was the thought of *regularity* that gave him a shudder. It was the thought of taking payment for what was just a good deed.

'I just don't know how much waste there is at the hotel, sir,' he prevaricated.

'More than these poor sods have got,' grumbled Ken. Then

something occurred to him. 'More than's on the shelves at Cochran & Sons, one of my stores down on the high road. Jump up, Billy, son. I'll *show* you.'

The crowd was still cheering for the next race when Billy and Mary-Louise followed Ken back across the stadium, out through the turnstiles and up the high road to his waiting motorcar. This time, without Marge and the boys, Billy sat up front, while Mary-Louise luxuriated in the empty seats behind.

'You see, this city we live in, there are two sides to it. There's those that are rich and those that aren't. But when you live in one half, it's easy to imagine the other just doesn't exist. If you're bedding down for the night in Buckingham Palace, you don't think about those poor sods sleeping rough on the Common. When you're in your boarding house in Whitechapel, you don't think about those who are dining on caviar and rare steak in the Savoy. All you know's your own. It's safer that way. Because the fact is, if those that have nothing realised how easy the other lot have got it, there'd be an uprising.' They'd come to a crossroads – and, while the engine idled, Ken looked sidelong at Billy. 'It's a wonder this country didn't see revolution, when you scratch beneath the surface. But I'm not talking about civil war, son. I'm talking about an old couple who've given their all for this country, and all they've got for dinner each night is a heel of bread. Not even any butter, because by the time they get through the ration queues, it's all gone.'

A little further on, Ken turned his motorcar into a side street, where the houses were crouched under an increasingly sullen autumn sky. Here, he stopped. Then, taking a wax paper parcel – one of the pieces of venison – out of a bag in the boot of the car, along with a string bag of oranges, figs and sugar lumps, he hurried to one of the doors, rapped his knuckles on the wood, and waited.

In the car, Billy fidgeted uneasily. Mary-Louise could sense the tremors moving through the seat; she leant forward, put a hand on his shoulder. 'What is it, Billy?'

Billy wasn't sure. He knew what he was being asked to do, and somehow it was more than just intercepting the hotel waste and putting it to better use. But he also knew it was *right*. All those rich folk in the Buckingham Hotel, they had enough. It was only by the grace of God that his own family weren't on the breadline; all it would take was a direct hit on Billingsgate, and suddenly his father would be out of work. What then for the Brogan family? What, then, for his mother and father, for Annie and Billy himself?

'I've been lucky, haven't I?' he whispered.

'Is that what it is? Is that what's bothering you?'

He felt his insides churn. 'It's true, isn't it? All my life, I've been in and out of the Buckingham. They've never been in want, so neither have I. And then ...' He looked through the window. The house door had opened up, and Ken was chatting with a hunched man on the step. Billy's eyes misted over as Ken presented him with the package; moments later, the man had gripped Ken by the shoulder and was nodding his head fiercely, trying not to let his emotions spill out. The two men held that pose for the longest time; then they joined hands. Billy heard Ken saying, 'I'll be back soon, Reg' before he turned and loped back towards the car.

'That's Reg,' Ken said, sliding back into the seat. 'Lives there with his wife, and her parents. His old man's in the back room too. Hasn't worked since the last war, on account of his lungs. Well, it ruined so many of us back then. You see, Billy, when Reg came to me, that whole house – all five of the poor blighters – were living on a couple of eggs, a few rashers, some porridge oats and whatever apples they could scrounge up. It isn't just rationing they've got to get their heads around, you see. It's supply and demand, Bill. Old lads like them, they can't stand in queues all day – and, if they do, it's only to find out the shelves are near empty by the time they get through the door. That lot at Westminster will tell you rationing helps. They'll say that's what it's designed for. But I'm here to tell you there's too many falling through the cracks. The system's broke. It's down to men like me to patch it up.'

Billy was silent. His belly felt full – *too full* – and the sensation was bothering him. It felt like sin.

'Look,' Ken went on, 'I know what it's like to be hungry. I sat in those trenches in Flanders, surrounded by all my pals, and all we had to eat was what the mess could scrounge up. I knew lads who ate rats, Bill. I know what it's like to be poor too – because I came home from those same trenches where I'd turned skinny as a rake, and I didn't have two pennies to rub together. This rationing they've started, it's the thin end of things. It isn't going away. Once they start taking away your liberties, they've no need to give them back. That's just a lesson from history, Bill. And we're living that same lesson today.' He paused. 'And then I think of places like the Buckingham Hotel…'

'There's plenty left on the room service trolleys, Uncle Ken,' Mary-Louise chipped in. Her hand was still balanced, delicately, on Billy's shoulder. 'The chambermaids always rustle stuff up to the kitchenette. I'll bet I can get you bits too.'

'That's a good girl,' said Uncle Ken, and gave her such a fatherly smile that it stilled Billy's heart. 'But it must be a damn sight easier for you, Billy – sitting in the hotel post room, as you are. Head of it, so they say. Nobody breathing down your neck all day, like poor Mary-Louise here. Free reign of the hotel. It must be easy enough to package some bits up and send them on their way, straight out of the post room door.' He paused one final time. 'Look, Billy, it's up to you, son. I'm a good man, and I'm not going to ask you to do anything that doesn't feel right.'

Billy exhaled. Those were the words he had desperately needed to hear. 'I know you're a good man, Ken. I'm a good man too. It's just that—'

'But I reckon, in your heart, you're like me,' Ken went on, as if he hadn't heard Billy's interjection at all. 'We fought for our country, didn't we, Bill? We shed blood. We lost friends.' Billy's mind tumbled back to those beaches, and the last time he'd seen Private Artie Cohen, disappearing into the water as the HMS *Othello* sank. 'When you've been through something like that, you end up wanting to do good deeds wherever you can. Now, me, I'm too old to fight Nazis – but I'll never be too old to stick up for those who need it, those who're struggling to get by, day to day. I reckon those toffs at the Buckingham Hotel could get a little less fat, perhaps – indulge themselves a little bit less – and not even know it. It wouldn't be much – but these people, *my people*, need butter and bacon to put with their bread.'

There was silence in the car.

The silence lingered.

Then, when the silence had gone on too long – and Billy Brogan seemed a hundred miles away from that little Camden back-street – Ken said, 'Here, you think on it, son. I'll take you back there, shall I? Back to the *Buckingham Hotel*.' And he said the two words with such unutterable emphasis that it was almost like a curse.

The darkness was coming when, at last, they reached Berkeley Square. The sirens sounded for the first time as Ken's car followed the square around, grinding to a halt in front of the hotel's fabulous white colonnade. There, Billy poured out his thanks – and, taking Mary-Louise by the hand, ventured into the shadows of Michaelmas Mews.

Inside, the hotel was buzzing with activity. Guests and staff were flocking to the shelters, as the music in the Grand died away and the diners flocked out of the Queen Mary. Billy supposed that he and Mary-Louise ought to head to the shelters too, but instead they stood at the bottom of the service stairs, watching as the hotel emptied around them. Then, at last, they were alone – with only the footsteps of the doorman and other guards echoing from the vacant reception hall.

Into the silence, Mary-Louise whispered, 'You do it for your family, Billy. Maybe it's OK to do it for other people too?'

And that was the thing, thought Billy. Why should *he* be any different? He didn't even have wealth to protect him from life's harsh edges, like all the guests here did. He was one of them – one of the people Uncle Ken looked after. Wasn't it a betrayal of his own kind, if he didn't lend a hand?

A thought had been niggling at him as Uncle Ken drove, in silence, back across the Euston Road. 'Did you know what he was going to ask me, Mary-Lou?'

Mary-Louise's eyes widened in surprise. 'Not at all, Billy. Never. I – I don't think Uncle Ken even knew. It's just his fury. It's just the way his heart works. He can't see folks in need without needing to do something about it.' Mary-Louise paused. Then, with a deep sigh of affection, she said, 'I like you, Billy. I'll like you whatever you decide to do.' She touched him on the chest. 'I know you've got a good heart in here, Billy Brogan. Whatever you do, I know it will be the right thing – not just for them, but for you as well.'

The hotel was so eerily silent now. Billy ruminated on what she had said for some moments. Then he said, 'I suppose we should be going to the shelters.'

He took her by the hand, as if to guide her that way – but Mary-Louise's feet were fixed firmly to the ground, and it seemed she didn't mean to leave. 'If the shelters are filling up, Billy, that means the kitchenette's empty. That means nobody might see if, well, we took a walk upstairs. To my room.'

Billy had been introduced to some outlandish ideas today, but none seemed more outlandish than this.

Mary-Louise's room . . .

It thawed the ice that seemed to have taken him in its grip. It warmed him from within. It turned his furrowed expression to a smile as he took her by the hand. 'I think I should like that,' he whispered – though there was no need to whisper, for he and Mary-Louise were the only ones around.

'I think we both will,' said Mary-Louise.

Then, up the empty hotel stairs, they started to climb.

Chapter Eleven

At nearly sixty years old, Doctor Evelyn Moore – distinguished, grey, and with a deep, gravelly voice that instilled confidence in every soul it touched – had been serving the residents of the Buckingham Hotel for twenty years, ever since he returned from the field hospitals in Flanders and sought out a life in which his days wouldn't be spent attending catastrophic surgeries, or stitching up traumatised soldiers just to send them back into battle. In that time, he had attended the bedsides of ministers and lords, prescribed ointments and medications to dignitaries from home and abroad – and even, on one memorable occasion, had the solemn duty of certifying the death of a notable Hollywood starlet. The one thing he had never been called to do, however, was to attend to a floor mistress from the Housekeeping department at her private address, having first been sworn to keeping it a secret from the Board who employed them both.

Now, with the late October night throwing its cloak across London – and the anticipation of air raid sirens already heavy in the air – he stepped out of the bedroom at No. 18 Blomfield Road and, striding into the bathroom to wash his hands, waited for Nancy de Guise to emerge behind him. This she did, some moments later, and with great decorum headed downstairs to the sitting room.

There, while she awaited Doctor Moore, Nancy made sure the corners of the blackout blinds were in place, then busied herself with the pot of tea she had made earlier. She'd been working hard to keep her heartbeat in check, calming herself by simply going through the mental checklist of all she had to do to support Mrs Moffatt at the Buckingham this week – but somewhere along the way all those thoughts fragmented and drifted away. This, she supposed, was the biggest moment of her life. She didn't know whether she was in freefall, or being borne up high.

Fortunate, then, that she heard Doctor Moore's footsteps on the stairs, and turned to see him appear at the sitting room doors.

'Tea,' he prescribed, 'and don't scrimp on the sugar.'

This, Nancy could do – but her hand was certainly trembling as she passed Doctor Moore the cup and saucer.

'By everything you've told me,' Doctor Moore pronounced, as they settled down, 'I should think you've another seven months to prepare yourself for this. Mrs de Guise, your reaction is quite ordinary, I can assure you. It's only in romance stories that these things are met with unadulterated, rapturous delight. The real world allows for more nuances and contradictions than the pages of *Woman's Own.*'

The tea was helping. Tea always did. That was something Nancy had acquired from Mrs Moffatt. She only wished she had Mrs Moffatt here now, to dispense barley sugars at will. Nancy was eight years old the last time she'd had a mother; perhaps it was that hole in her that made her cry out for Mrs Moffatt now.

'You must think me a bad mother already. Doctor Moore, it's not that I'm not excited. I am. It's that—'

'You weren't expecting this, were you, Mrs de Guise?'

She steeled herself. 'Raymond and I started talking about it the moment he got back from Dunkirk. I don't know – now that I think about it, it seems the very worst moment to dream about bringing a child into the world. But the idea of it, the promise and the hope – I think that's what called out to me. That's what was making me start to … hunger for it. Yes, hunger. That's the word.'

Doctor Moore said, 'You're approaching thirty, Mrs de Guise. The human body is a thing of wonder. It knows what it wants.'

'I just didn't think it would happen so soon.'

How to say this to a man, even if he was a close friend and trusted doctor? How to say it, even to herself?

'Doctor Moore, Raymond hasn't been himself, not since Dunkirk. Not since his brother perished out there.' She stood and gravitated to the blackout blinds, gazing at them as if she could see through them, to the waiting city beyond. 'He's been here, of course – but he hasn't been here. Do you understand what I mean?'

Doctor Moore said, 'I've seen many soldiers like it, Nancy. Grief can take hold of a soul. But your husband is young. He's strong. He just needs time.'

Nancy nodded. How many people had told her the same thing? Even Mrs Moffatt had put an arm around her, in the safety of the Housekeeping Lounge, and lovingly whispered the same words. The problem was, all they saw was the Raymond de Guise who went out every night, defying the storm from above, defying the protests of his own body, to do his bit for London; they didn't see the man who came home and simply sat there, listening to his music; the man who slept fitfully, when he slept at all, calling out Artie's name in the dark; the man who had gone weeks at a time without touching his wife.

They saw a hero, but Nancy saw a damaged soul.

That was why she hadn't thought it would happen – not so

quickly, not so soon. That was why the principal feeling flooding through her wasn't elation or wonder. That was why all those other fears that would soon begin niggling at her – what might happen to her job, what might become of her when Raymond went back to his division – were being kept at bay. She was in shock. She wanted to reach out for Raymond, to share it with him, to luxuriate together in the fact that there would soon be a person in the world who was comprised of them both – would it be Nancy's head and Raymond's heart? Raymond's passion and Nancy's dogged determination? – but she couldn't begin to imagine how she might tell him, nor how he might react. A few short months ago, it would have been jubilation. But who knew how a man might feel, while he was still locked in the prison of his grief?

'I don't think it's good for him, Doctor, to be out there every night, to be putting himself in harm's way. He says he's doing it for his country. I think he's doing it for his brother. Because he's here and Artie isn't.'

Doctor Moore considered it carefully, then set down his tea and said, 'Perhaps it's your child who could anchor him again. He's lost one loved one – but to gain another? One love is seldom a replacement for the last, but we all have voids that we must fill.' Until now, he'd been speaking with tenderness; now there came a new severity to his tone. 'You must think of yourself as well, Nancy. It's you who'll nourish your child. It's your body that must bear this. Don't forget that.'

Nancy thought she knew what he was saying, but what Doctor Moore didn't understand was that she and Raymond were as one. When he danced on air, Nancy danced on air. When he struggled through the days, so did she. That was just the way it was. The way it had been since the beginning. That was just love.

And yet ... once upon a time, she'd have told him about her

pregnancy in a heartbeat. She would have told him already, the moment young Annie Brogan planted the seed of the idea in her head.

Now she wasn't so sure.

The sirens started sounding soon after Doctor Moore took his leave. For a time, Nancy prowled the empty house, one hand cupped around her midriff – though, of course, no real change had happened in her yet – and imagining how it might be: she and Raymond, the man that she loved, and the son or daughter gambolling between them. The image was fleeting, but when she could hold it in mind, it was an image so perfect that it filled her heart, dispelling all of the other fears baying at her.

She should tell him.

She needed to tell him.

It was just that . . . she'd feel better, somehow, if she could tell somebody else first, somebody who wasn't Doctor Moore. Her first thought went to Mrs Moffatt. Every woman and girl who'd ever been a chambermaid at the Buckingham Hotel would have thought the same; she was mother to them all, solver of problems, the calmest of heads in the middle of life's infinity of crises. And yet – a child would change things irrevocably; a child might take her away from the Buckingham Hotel; it might give rise to conversations she wasn't yet ready to have. How many girls had left Housekeeping since the declaration of war, and even through that uncertain summer before? Too many to mention, thought Nancy. The Housekeeping staff looked so different to how it had done, four years before, when she herself had come down from Lancashire to take up her post.

But if not Mrs Moffatt – who else?

Seconds later, Nancy was stepping into her lambswool coat and, opening the front door, resolutely ignoring the siren's song. Was venturing out like this foolhardy? Was it more foolhardy still, considering the life she was carrying inside her? The battle seemed distant tonight, though she was not sure how much of this was just her own wishful thinking. She ought to have been in the Anderson shelter, her own body the shelter around her unborn child.

But there was somebody else. Somebody who would know exactly what she was feeling. Somebody who'd walked this road before, and was out there now, walking it alone.

Vivienne would understand. She only hoped she could pick her way there, through the blasted night.

'They're flying out west,' said Cathy Everly. 'We might get lucky tonight.'

Raymond heard her voice before he saw her. On the north side of the John Lewis ruins, an assortment of volunteers from the WVS were gathering in anticipation of the night to come. The rest centre was not overflowing yet, but the night was still young. One of the volunteers had spent the day feverishly cooking casseroles in her own kitchen, and the mobile canteen was laden down with them – more than enough for the wardens on patrol and those routed out of their homes. In her hands, Cathy had two steaming cups, and she pressed the second into his hands. 'It's cocoa, Raymond. I trust you like chocolate.'

Raymond took the mug. 'Whatever's warm on a night like tonight.'

He could feel the breath of winter in the air. It had come so quickly, and there was something unnerving about it: a winter at war. One year ago, he'd barely begun his basic training. Now, the war was here, on the streets where he lived.

'I think the rest centre can spare me tonight,' said Cathy. 'Shall we?'

Shall we. The echo of those same words, spoken on the

ballroom floor, sounded through Raymond. It almost felt as if he should offer her his arm. 'Let's,' he said. 'Mortimer's got me south of here tonight. My old heartlands. Come on, Cathy, I'll take you on a tour around Mayfair.'

In truth, he was glad of the distraction. It seemed, tonight, as if he'd left home under a cloud: Nancy, not long returned from the Buckingham, with her classic Lancashire hotpot bubbling in the stove, had wanted to talk. He could sense it – unspoken words could be like flies, buzzing around your head – but he had no stomach for it, not tonight. She'd want him to stay home, to sit in the shelter with her, to burrow himself away while the rest of the city burned. This was an idea he could not embrace.

By the time they crossed Oxford Street and into the richer townhouses beyond, searchlights were criss-crossing the eastern skies. 'They think they've got us surrounded,' said Cathy, as they followed one of the Regent Street arcades. 'How many nights is it now?'

'They took a day off at the start of the month. Put their feet up for an evening.'

That still made it more than forty nights of bombardment since this thing started. Cathy said, 'Poor dears, they needed their beauty sleep. It's hard work being routed every damn night.' She paused. 'Listen, Raymond – about the other night . . .'

'Yes?'

She had something she wanted to say, but it would have to wait – because, before she breathed a reply, they had emerged onto the open expanse of Berkeley Square.

There stood the Buckingham Hotel. It did not look nearly as grand as it used to, not with the blackouts in place, the whole edifice sealed up like a mausoleum – but there was no denying its grandeur. Its spectacular white façade still stood out against the blackness of the night. Its great copper crown still reflected the light of the moon hanging up above the rooftops. Perhaps he ought to report that, as a diligent warden of the ARP, but tonight it was enough to stand here and take it all in.

'What are you thinking about, Raymond?' Cathy asked.

'Home,' he whispered.

'What do you mean?'

'Do you ever think about *home*, Cathy? What it truly means?'

Suddenly and unusually stiffly, she said, 'It's where I hang my hat.'

Raymond gave her a pointed look.

Cathy just sighed. 'I suppose, if you were to ask me, I'd talk about my father's estate. But I haven't set foot there in a year. I have digs over in Holland Park. It isn't much. I have the attic chambers. But it feels like mine...'

'This place felt like mine, once.'

Up above, some Heinkel or Messerschmitt arced across the sky, vanishing into the west. Instinctively, Raymond and Cathy pirouetted, to watch it go. Then their eyes returned to the face of the Buckingham Hotel.

'The windows on the left-hand side of the colonnade – they're draped in black now, so you might think it's a store room from the outside, but that's the Grand Ballroom. I danced there for almost ten years of my life. I know every square inch of that dance floor. I danced with queens.' He stopped, for an image of Marcus Arbuthnot and Karina Kainz, of Mathilde Bourchier and Frank Nettleton, had entered his mind. 'It was *mine*,' he said, wistfully. 'But then I took the King's shilling. I was the lord of the ballroom; then I was a private, with a rifle and a pack, marching through France. That's why I said it, Cathy. *Home.* This was my home. The Buckingham Hotel. Now I'm somebody else. Now I—'

'Don't have a home?' ventured Cathy.

And Raymond thought of where Nancy would be, right now – in the Anderson shelter at the bottom of their garden, alone perhaps, or with their neighbours beside her. It was like a knife had pierced him in the side; that was where he ought to be. *That* was supposed to be home now. And yet… the thought of those four walls, closed around him like the hold of the HMS *Othello*; the idea of sitting there, helpless, with nothing to do but console each other that everything would be OK; the thought that he was leaving other people to burn, while he hid. No, he could never do that.

'Home's just different now.' *Home is Nancy*. He gave a wan smile, guiding Cathy's gaze back to the Buckingham. 'I might dance there yet. The management are organising an event, an auction to raise funds for the families being bombed out. One Grand Night…' And he began to tell Cathy all about it, and how – even if he wasn't fit to dance there – it would be Raymond de Guise hosting the evening: an enchanted night, to take with him wherever he next went. 'I should like to take to the dance floor one more time, before I ship back out. If my body holds up, that's what I'll do.

'I used to dance,' said Cathy.

'You did?'

'My father practically demanded it. Elocution, the ballroom, etiquette. We were drilled in it from the time we were babes in arms. I can dance a fine quickstep,' she gave a smile, 'but I'd hazard you wouldn't keep up.' Then she paused. 'In all serious-ness, Raymond, my father was adamant we learn these things. It made us marriageable, you see. Heaven forfend a woman should want to do something more than marry! All he knows, right now, is that I'm in London on charitable business. He thinks I'm weaving baskets for the poor like some Victorian.'

Explosions obliterated the silence in the west.

'It seems an honourable thing to do for a place like this,' said Cathy, 'to raise money for the poor.'

'The Buckingham has a fine Board. But don't forget that a little reputation goes a long way in Society. The Buckingham's reaping the rewards of its generosity, even now. This summer, they held a ball in honour of the Dunkirk veterans. One Grand Night is the next step. The Buckingham, home to runaway governments and kings – but it hasn't forgotten the rest of us...'

Not like it's forgotten me, Raymond thought, then chastised himself for being foolish. It was good that life in the ballroom went on without him. The ballroom had to thrive.

'Raymond,' Cathy ventured, 'if you wanted – that is to say, if you felt like you needed to put a little practise in before One Grand Night – there's still dancing in London. They're dancing right now, in the Midnight Rooms. They're dancing through the sirens at the Starlight Lounge and the Ambergris. I can't claim to be as elegant as those you'll have courted in there,' she tipped her head at the Buckingham, 'but I'd be a proficient partner. Proficient enough to get you back in the ballroom, I'm sure.'

Raymond watched the skies. For a time, there were only stars to be seen. 'There's a thought going round in my head, Cathy. It's hard to even spit it out.' But he tried, nevertheless. 'I'm not even sure I *could* dance any more. I want to – but it's as if the only reason I want to is so that I can pretend it's yesteryear again. If I'm dancing, there isn't a war. If I'm dancing, everything's full of promise and potential. If I'm dancing, Artie isn't...'

Cathy snagged him by the hand. 'I know what that feels like,' she said.

Raymond detected some change about her. She was trembling. Her bewitching green eyes were flaring open. There was something fierce, manic even, in her look.

'Dunkirk,' she whispered, 'I had a friend who didn't come

back too. It's like – like there's suddenly a window in your heart. Everyone can see in. The gale's roaring through. But you, Raymond – you're like me. The window's shattered, but you've rolled down the blackout blinds. You've shuttered it up.' She stopped. 'You should dance, Raymond. I think it's all right to pretend it's yesteryear, just for a song. It feels good to pretend.'

Those last five words were loaded with some meaning Raymond could not decipher. But there was no doubting the look in Cathy's eyes. It was the look of some deep and lasting realisation; the look a man in a desert might give, when stumbling upon an oasis. *It feels good to pretend.*

She was still grasping his hand. 'So what do you think, Raymond? Should we dance?'

At that moment, the shriek of some falling incendiary obliterated all other noise. A fraction of a second later, the sound of some titanic eruption came from the west.

'That was closer,' said Raymond, taking his hand from hers. 'Come on, Cathy. Dancing might have to wait. There's no pretending about what's happening tonight.'

Nancy heard it too. Rising from the Underground at Whitechapel Station, she stepped out onto the deserted thoroughfare and, turning her face to the sky, saw the lurid orange glow in both the east and the west. It was indiscriminate tonight. Some nights, you felt as if the bombers up there knew precisely what their prize was: it was the palace, or it was the docks. But some nights, you felt as if they would drop their bombs on anything lying below. To them, shopkeepers and factories, motorways and royal parks – all were as good as the other. On nights like this, the best thing you could do was run and hide.

So she started running.

It was silly how much Doctor Moore's news had already

changed the way she thought. She wondered if she should run quite so fiercely along the Whitechapel Road, for fear of bouncing her baby. She wondered how the nightly terror might, in some way, infiltrate the budding mind and heart she was growing. She wondered – and tried not to wonder – what the world might look like when she met her child for the first time.

At least, by running, she was running away from those fears. She was still blotting them out when she reached the terrace door and hammered on the wood, trying to make herself heard above the sounds of the bombardment. Vivienne, she supposed, was hunkering down with Stan in the Anderson shelter out back – and, if that was so, there was no chance she'd ever be heard. All she could do was keep trying.

She was fortunate, then, that, moments later, the door opened a crack – and Vivienne's frightened face appeared in the shadows beyond. There was a moment of hesitation, the after-effect of sheer disbelief, before the door drew back. 'Nancy, what on Earth—'

'I've been foolish,' Nancy said, the tremor in her voice a mirror to the quaking city, 'but I had to come. Vivienne, please.'

The door was open in an instant, Vivienne reaching out with the hand that wasn't holding Stan to pull her through. Then, just as quickly, the door was slammed shut again, the latch fastened, and Nancy was being harried down the hall, into the cubbyhole beneath the stairs.

'Stan just cries in the shelter,' Vivienne said, her own voice heavy with exhaustion. 'It's the way it echoes in there. Or it's me – he can feel the tension in me. But he doesn't sob underneath here. He'll just sleep. Won't you, darling?'

Vivienne was right; Stan, the small miracle, at eighteen months old, had his head lolling on her shoulder, sleeping through the storm.

Vivienne Cohen looked older every time Nancy saw her, but that was just the effect of this last year of war, the death of her husband mere months after they were married, and the long nights caught between bombardment from above and the squalling of Stan from below. Vivienne was still scarcely twenty-three years old, but the lifetimes she'd lived were told in the rigid mask of her face. The auburn hair which she'd once kept short – in defiance of the step-father who'd manipulated and controlled every aspect of her life – now hung in thick curls around her shoulders, but the ostentatious gowns and jewellery she'd once worn were all, now, accoutrements of the past. The only thing that brought Vivienne's former life to mind was the perfume she wore – there were still a few drops left in the old Chanel bottle she owned. Even her accent, heavy with the sounds of her native New York, had faded this last year. Nancy had sometimes wondered if it was one of the manifold ways her heart was contriving to keep Artie alive; sometimes, she spoke with his exact inflection.

The cubbyhole beneath the stairs was scarcely big enough for two. With Stan sandwiched between them, beginning to look like a facsimile of his father – his hair coming in thick now, his eyes as dark as Artie's had been, with the same wolfish expressions even as he slept – there was no room to move. But at least, under here, the war seemed far away; the devastation was dull, muffled, unreal.

'You shouldn't be here, Nancy. What on earth were you thinking?'

Now that the adrenaline of her flight was wearing off, Nancy knew Vivienne was right. 'I couldn't be alone, Vivienne. Not tonight.'

'And what if I hadn't been here?' Vivienne seemed on the edge of fury; it was only her weariness that stopped it from being real.

'I *should* be at the Daughters of Salvation. That's where I was supposed to be tonight. It's only by chance that I'm not.'

The Daughters of Salvation: the charitable organisation that Nancy had helped Vivienne found, back when Vivienne was a virtual prisoner at the Buckingham Hotel and looking for a way to exploit her step-father and the allowance he gave her each month. In the years between then and now, the Daughters had grown from its home in a disused chapel hall to occupying the sprawling HJ Packer building, once a chocolate factory, on the edge of the Limehouse basin. There they provided shelter, sustenance – and, wherever it was needed, nurses to help people who, like Vivienne had once been, were in thrall to opiates, alcohol and worse. Since Artie's death, Vivienne had been at the Daughters less often than she had once been – but it was still the anchor in her life, still a monument. Warren Peel – once an addict, now a benefactor – and the rest would be there tonight, in the shelters underneath the complex; they said it was one of the safest corners in East London, but nobody could bely the fact that the HJ Packer building sat in the centre of one of London's worst hit districts.

'Well, you're here,' said Nancy, wrapping her arms around herself defensively. 'Maybe we don't have to fight about this.'

Vivienne's eyes darted around as she tried to make sense of Nancy's words. 'Nance, I'm not fighting with you. As a matter of fact, I'm happy you're here. You've no idea what it's like to sit these things out alone, night after night after—'

The words had been on Nancy's lips for some time; she'd thought to hold them in a little longer, waiting for the moment to be right, but out they came: 'I'm pregnant.'

Now there was silence, but for the muffled echo of the bombs.

Nancy was holding herself. 'I've been feeling it for weeks. Dizzy and worn out, and just not myself. I thought it was because of Raymond. He's out every night, Vivienne. He'll barely accept a night off. So when you say I've no idea what it's like, to sit these things out on my own – well, I do, Vivienne. I do.' She steadied herself, while somewhere another incendiary landed, tearing someone else's life apart. 'I should be euphoric. I should be dancing on air. But instead I'm…'

'Crossing the city, during an air raid, just to have somebody to talk to.'

There was a momentary silence. Then, when it had lasted too long, both Nancy and Vivienne started laughing. It was laughter tinged with madness, laughter tinged with disbelief – but at least it was laughter.

'I thought you'd be the one to understand,' Nancy shrugged. And, in reply, Vivienne rocked Stan in her arms.

'You can't keep news like this secret, Nance, not forever.'

Nancy said, 'Well, *that* much I did know,' and made a mime of her swelling belly.

'When I found out I was expecting,' said Vivienne, 'I went to Mrs Moffatt. I remember thinking how she'd helped so many girls across the years – and maybe she could help me too. Why don't you go to her?'

'I couldn't – not now, not with things the way they are at the Buckingham. She's relying on me, Viv. What if I go in there and tell her I'm pregnant, and everything has to change? What if there's no job for me at the end of this? It's strange enough to have me in that role as a married woman – but as a mother as well?' Now her thoughts were hurtling into exactly that area from which she'd tried to keep them: alone, at home with a child, Raymond gone back to his division – years away from home, if he ever returned. 'I don't know why the fear's got hold of me like this. I half-raised Frank, didn't I? Our mother died, and he needed me – so there I was. But… a child, in wartime, with no work and no father?' She realised, now, exactly why she had come to Vivienne. Because Vivienne was a vision of some possible future: widowed at a tender age, huddled up with her baby while the bombs rained down.

Vivienne had realised it too. With great tenderness – the same kind of tenderness that in her, darker, more unruly days, Nancy had shown her – she said, 'Sometimes, I wake in the night – when I've slept at all – and feel as if he's still lying there beside me. I still don't sleep on his side of the bed. It's like I can feel his warmth there, when I'm on the edge of sleep. At first, it unnerved me. Now, I think, it's starting to give me strength. Like he's still here with me, geeing me on, telling me I can do it.' Vivienne paused, because what she had to say next was the most important of all. 'And I *can* do it, Nancy. So could you, if it came to it. But it hasn't happened to you – not yet. You're lost in thoughts of what might come to pass. But there are hundreds of possibilities, hundreds of chances for it not to happen.'

As the words washed over Nancy, she could feel their effect. She'd been falling, falling into dark thoughts, but Vivienne was helping her take flight.

'But all of those possibilities, Nancy, start with the same thing.'

Nancy knew what it was. 'I have to tell Raymond.'

'I remember telling Artie. Unmarried, practically penniless – I thought we'd be judged from all corners. And perhaps we were. But the way he looked at me when I told him – well, nothing else mattered. I could see the love.' She paused. 'It's Raymond, Nancy. He loves you. He's lost right now, perhaps he can't see more than a few feet in front of him – but it's still love. This could be the thing that brings him back to himself.'

The bombardment lasted for a long time after that. One hour turned into the next, while the sirens wailed on and, here and there, reverberations shook the London night. By the time the all-clear came, Nancy had caught a few short snatches of sleep, her head resting against the bare brick of the wall, and Stan – having slept through the worst of the night against Vivienne's shoulder – was desperate for the chance to scrabble around the sitting room, among the old portraits of his father.

It was not yet dawn when Nancy returned to the Whitechapel Road. Not yet light when the first Underground train started grinding its way back west, with Nancy aboard its empty carriage, whispering quiet apologies for the desperate night she'd just put her baby through. As soon as she got home, she'd start thinking about the shelter at the bottom of their garden. She'd find old blankets to go with the mattress she and Raymond had carried inside. Perhaps she'd decorate it, fill it with more magazines and books – cut flowers, if she could rescue some from the tables at the Buckingham Hotel. Those were the sorts of things that could make a night more bearable. If she was well, then her baby would be well; that seemed self-evident to Nancy.

The sun was rising on another shell-shocked day as Nancy scurried back through the streets of Maida Vale. Who'd be a mother in a time of war?

The moment she stepped through the door, she knew Raymond was back. This, at least, stilled some of the mounting dread she'd been feeling as she walked up the road. There were his boots, still covered in the dust of his night's travails, and there was his overcoat – and, by these things, she knew he was alive.

He was in the sitting room, where she had known he would be. Fast asleep in his chair, he almost looked content. The gramophone had been left playing, its needle now turning empty circles in the air, so she quietly stole past him, slipped the record back into its sleeve, and the needle back into its clasp.

It was as she was fussing with the record that Raymond opened his eyes.

'Oh, Nancy,' he said – and she could hear some note of desperation in his voice as well, 'Nancy, you're back…'

She crouched at his side and took his hands.

'I didn't know where you were.'

She could hear how much he himself had been fretting at her absence, and it clawed at her; she spent her nights in fear for him, he spent his in fear for her – none of it seemed fair or right. The only answer was to spend them together, each and every last one. He'd do it, she knew, if she told him about the baby. He'd see the risks he was taking, the peril he threw himself into, and understand: there's more than one world that matters; there's *our* world too, Raymond, there's *our* child.

'Raymond, listen,' she said, and stroked the hair – which had grown back so unevenly since that terrible September afternoon – from his brow. 'I was with Vivienne. I got caught out when the sirens came. But it was good to see her, Raymond. She opens my eyes. This last month, it's been hard, hasn't it? Harder than any I've known. But we're still here, we're still strong and alive – and, Raymond, there's something I've—'

There came the creak of a floorboard.

Movement on the stairs.

Nancy let go of Raymond's hand, rising back to her feet. Another floorboard creaked; then the sounds of footsteps, tolling down the staircase. She was about to ask Raymond who it was when a figure appeared in the sitting-room door. She was tall, as tall as Raymond's shoulder, and her jet-black hair fell in waves around her shoulders. Startling green eyes were set in her heart-shaped face, discoloured by a graze along her left cheek.

'Nancy,' Raymond began, still rubbing the sleep from his eyes, 'this is Miss Everly. Cathy Everly. It's been the strangest night.

We were out on patrol when the bombs started falling. Some time after midnight, we got the news – Cathy's lodgings were bombed out. Three houses, just gone. Well, I couldn't leave her to the rest centre, Nancy – it wouldn't have been right.'

Nancy wasn't sure why she was suddenly feeling so guarded. Perhaps it was just the words that had been on her tongue, the life-changing news she'd been about to tell him. Or perhaps, she thought – as she marched across the room to take Cathy's hand, to plant a sisterly kiss on her cheek, to tell her that 'our house is yours, for as long as you need it' – it was something else, something altogether more unknowable, something she couldn't quite put her finger on.

'I'll make the tea,' said Nancy, 'and there's crumpets in the kitchen. Miss Everly, we'll set you back on your feet – you can count on it. But tea first – then we can worry about the rest.'

As she bustled down the hallway, into the kitchen, she felt almost like Mrs Moffatt: anything, even life's worst calamities, could be set straight, if you started with a nice cup of tea.

She looked back. 'There's greengage preserve...'

Cathy was still standing in the sitting room doorway, and now she turned Nancy's way.

'Anything you have, I'd be most grateful.'

And it was then that Nancy knew why this scene looked so off-kilter. It was then that Nancy knew why something here didn't seem right. She shook it off at once, because of course there was a perfectly reasonable explanation for it.

But Cathy was standing there in Nancy's own nightdress, with Nancy's own bed-socks, and Nancy's own pin in her hair.

'I'll just fix the tea,' said Nancy, and retreated into the kitchen with a gnawing feeling in the bottom of her gut.

November 1940

Chapter Twelve

'One more time!' Marcus Arbuthnot announced, and started energetically box-stepping with himself in the middle of the dance floor.

The dance troupe at the Buckingham Hotel had been rehearsing ferociously every afternoon for a month, taking advantage of those few precious hours between the end of the afternoon demonstrations and the start of the evening's dancing. 'One Grand Night is but six weeks away,' Marcus announced as he moved, with some imaginary partner in hold, across the dance floor, finishing with a theatrical flourish by the orchestra's stage. 'Let's make it the night of our lives.'

At the balustrade, Mathilde Bourchier watched with a mounting sense of unease. Two weeks had passed since her meeting at the Imperial Hotel, but scarcely an hour had flickered by without her harking back to their words, and that insidious meaning. It would have been easier, she supposed, if she had some reason to hate Marcus – but it wasn't even as if it was Marcus who had usurped her rightful place at the head of the troupe. That honour had gone to Karina Kainz – who was laughing gaily with Frank Nettleton among the huddle of other dancers, every one of them thrilling with the promise of what One Grand Night might deliver. Even *that* hadn't been Karina's fault. Decisions had been taken at Board level. To them, Mathilde had been an irrelevance.

Well, she wouldn't be irrelevant soon.

'To the dance floor!' Marcus announced. 'The ballroom remains closed this evening, so today is ours.' He strode to the stage, where a gramophone player sat on a small walnut table beside Archie Adams' grand piano. 'Ladies and gentlemen, the tango, if you please ...'

He was about to drop the needle into the groove when the sound of a silver spoon ringing on a Champagne flute announced Walter Knave's sudden presence in the ballroom. Mr Knave, elderly and diminutive, had never had the sort of booming general's voice that could command silence in a place as vast as the Grand, but the ringing of the Champagne glass brought everyone to attention. Marcus himself sashayed off the dance floor, to stand at the head of his troupe. Here, he gave an ostentatious bow to Mr Knave as he tottered forward. Mathilde was not sure, but she was certain Frank was stifling a snigger; they loved Marcus in the ballroom, but nobody here had ever quite got used to his extravagant, courtly ways.

'Mr Knave, to what do we owe the pleasure?'

'Gentlemen, ladies,' Walter began, 'it's been a little while since I checked in on proceedings in the Grand. But the Board gathers tonight, and the clock is ticking: only six weeks separate us from One Grand Night. How are we faring?'

Marcus swept around. The dance troupe at the Buckingham Hotel was twelve strong, but only six of those were permanent dancers on staff. He flitted between them – 'Frank has perfected his poise in his Viennese waltz, Karina has been soaring on air' – and landed, last of all, at Mathilde's side. When he put his arm around her, she felt both proud and shameful; sometimes, Marcus seemed to hold her in the highest esteem, but other times he hardly seemed to notice she was there. It was the most vexing combination. 'Mathilde, here, will be like starlight on the evening, Mr Knave. The way she's gliding through her promenades. It would take a well-seasoned dancer to know *why*, but there won't be a soul in the Grand Ballroom who doesn't judge it beautiful beyond compare.'

Mathilde felt that gut stab of shame again. It was what Marcus did: used his eloquent language and wild imagery to make his troupe feel like they were the very best on Earth. But it didn't work on Mathilde, not any more – not when it was Karina dancing with Marcus at the head of the troupe, and Mathilde permitted only to perform in their wake.

'I came to tell you that we are already inundated with interest for the evening,' Walter explained. 'The notices we commissioned have been seen, we're told, by many tens of thousands of potential patrons – and the letters of note we've received are evidence of that fact. Our very own Mr Brogan is inundated with them coming into the hotel post room. We've expressions of interest in you, Marcus, of course – and early bids already placed for the return of Hélène Marchmont. We haven't yet permitted an early bid on a dance with Raymond de Guise – though, according to Mrs de Guise, it seems he might yet be strong enough to take to the dance floor. But it's you, Karina, where the real attention lies ...'

Karina Kainz said, 'Truly, sir?'

Walter Knave inclined his head in acknowledgement, even as Mathilde looked the other way.

'I rather thought that an English rose might be the star of One Grand Night. I feared to waltz with me might be seen as a waltz with the enemy.'

'Nonsense, my dear!' Marcus interjected, throwing his arms open wide. 'Are we so uncivilised, now, that we don't see goodness and beauty, wherever it is? Next thing they tell us, we'll be outlawing the Viennese waltz itself. No, my dear – why should we be surprised? You are, after all, our *star*.'

In that very instant, what shame Mathilde had been feeling at what she'd been asked to do melted away. Karina, their *star*. She'd heard it so many times, and always in Marcus's syrupy, showman's voice. She decided, then and there, that her course was set.

The feeling only hardened in her as Mr Knave left and the rehearsal continued. Every time Marcus took Karina into hold, to demonstrate some nuance of a pivot in reverse, or the delicate balance that a hesitation brought to a dance, she felt it more keenly. Frank, in whose arms she performed an unbridled tango, noticed it too. 'You feel so rigid today,' he told her, with a tremor in his voice that told her he was nervous of saying it. 'Your head's not in the room. Are you well, Mathilde?'

'Very well, Frankie,' she said, forcing herself to be as sweet as she could.

'Then what is it?'

She stepped out of hold. 'It just isn't my day.'

As evening approached, and the dancers departed the ballroom – for rest, recuperation, or yet more work – Mathilde remained behind. One after another, all the other dancers disappeared through the backstage doors – Frank Nettleton was off to work a shift answering telephones for the fire service – until, finally, only Marcus and Karina remained on the dance floor. By the looks of them, they were embroiled in some private heart-to-heart; theirs was the dance that would open One Grand Night, theirs the moment that would set the tone for the entire event. Mathilde didn't begrudge them their eagerness to get it right – she'd been in enough ballrooms to know that a moment like that could transform a guest's appreciation of the next few hours, or else undermine it completely – but the way they conversed, then took each other in hold, turned about the empty dance floor, and conversed again, made her feel practically invisible. She wasn't sure why she was surprised; she'd been feeling that way since the very beginning.

The moment Karina departed, Mathilde wended her way to the edge of the balustrade. Marcus, as was his wont at the end of every session, had taken up a notebook and pencil and begun to inscribe notes in his flowery, cursive script. Those letters had just as many grandiose flourishes as Marcus himself. Mathilde had often wondered what notes Marcus compiled on her own dancing.

He was deliberating some finer point, repeatedly closing his eyes to picture the dance, then tightening them as he imagined it happening in some other way, when he saw Mathilde.

'Like an angel,' he declared, 'about to descend to the dance floor. Mathilde, my dear, is there something you wanted to ask?'

It was now or not at all. She'd been agonising over the question for weeks. In dance, though, you so rarely made a conscious decision; you simply let yourself be carried where the music took you, where the melody and motion combined. It would have to be that way now. *Stay in the moment*, she told herself. *Just see it through*.

She reached the parting in the balustrade, then dropped down the steps to the ballroom floor.

'I'm not good enough,' she started.

This was a declaration worthy of setting the notebook down for. Marcus placed it on the edge of the orchestra's stage and rolled over to her, his sky-blue eyes furrowed in curiosity beneath his perfectly coiffured russet-gold hair. 'Mathilde,' he said, with a patricianly air. 'My Mathilde, what's wrong?'

'I'm not feeling it properly, Marcus. It's been the same thing for weeks. I can't hold the dances in my head.' She gave a deliberate pause, just as she'd planned. 'I'm letting Frank down.'

'My dear.' Marcus folded her slender hand beneath his Herculean own. 'I've heard countless young dancers say the same thing. There isn't a champion I've trained who hasn't, at some point or another in their lives, felt precisely the way you're feeling now. And I'll say to you, now, what I said to Marianna Brown, and Emily Woods, Pauline Dew and Geoff Neville – you don't hold a dance in your head, Mathilde. You hold it in your heart.'

He was right, of course; dance was not a riddle to be unpicked and solved – it was an instinct to be followed. But instead Mathilde said, 'I feel like I need you, Marcus.'

He did not reply, merely inclining his head so that she would fill in the silence.

'I've had some incredible tutors in my time. It started with my mother, of course. Camille Bourchier.'

'Of course!' said Marcus. 'She and I crossed paths, all those years ago. I always thought she'd return to the ballroom, one day. Alas, it never came to pass.'

'She sent me instead,' Mathilde smiled, wanly. 'She taught me everything. And then there was Bernard Potts – and, of course, Hélène Marchmont, when I first came here. The truth is, Marcus, I didn't think I needed a tutor any more. I thought I could just follow the music, wherever it went. But I've been falling apart. I should appreciate it if you didn't tell the rest of the troupe, but I wondered if you might do me the honour of some...'

It seemed that Mathilde's instincts were correct; flattery truly was the way into Marcus Arbuthnot's heart. He arched one knowing eyebrow and said, 'Private tuition, Mathilde?'

Mathilde smiled, as if embarrassed. 'I don't want to blame

Frank for anything. He's such a talented dancer, and with hardly any formal instruction. He's a *natural*. But I should like to feel the dance, as it were, from your own arms. I thought that, if you felt the way I moved, you might steer me a little better.'

'You've a keen dancing mind,' said Marcus. 'I heartily approve. But one moment, Mathilde – a change of shoes is required.'

Evidently his brogues had been causing him some discomfort, for Marcus sashayed off the ballroom floor, into the dressing room, and was gone for some moments.

While he was gone, Mathilde dared to chance a look at the notebook he'd left open by the grand piano. In Marcus's inimitable script, each dancer had been afforded half a page of notes. Frank Nettleton's poise was 'exceptional, a delicate sergeant-at-arms in command of his every move', but Marcus had noted that perhaps he needed to 'refine the expression; the eyes are but windows to the soul, and Mr Nettleton's soul remains puppyish and given to delight'; Karina's notes were all to do with how she passed the weight from foot to foot in the moment after one of their dance's hesitations. Other dancers had lines devoted to the intimacy of their holds, or the speed of their changes; Marcus had noted that one remained 'half fallen angel, and half clockwork doll' and the word FEELING was underlined in pencil so fiercely that it had scored the page.

Alongside her own name, however, there was only empty space. She was still struggling to imagine what that meant – had he found her dancing perfect today, or did he simply not care? – when Marcus returned, wearing his second pair of dancing shoes, and evidently much happier for the change.

'Shall we?' he asked.

Mathilde smiled graciously and stepped into his arms.

There was no doubt it was different from dancing with Frank. Frank, filled with vigour and a young dancer's bravado, had settled into himself of late – but there was still an air of the unexpected, a frisson of uncertainty when he took her into hold. Frank had first fallen in love with dancing in the clubs, where he'd embraced the wild, exuberant jitterbugs and jives which were, by increments, making their way over from the United States – but Marcus had been reared on the classics, and in his comportment and poise it showed. Every step he took was in honour of the greats who had gone before him – those pioneers of ballroom dance who had first described its steps; even the stately, regal expression on his face had been rehearsed in its every detail.

There was always a new feeling with a new partner. Different bodies slotted together in different ways; each had to compromise to accommodate the other. That was something her mother had once taught her: no dancer can be perfect, not without the perfect partner. Marcus was taller and broader than Frank, but that wasn't the only thing that changed the sensation. As he danced, he *knew* that he owned the ballroom, and that every eye was on him. That was the difference. That was the mark of a veteran of the dance floor.

The song they'd been dancing to came to its close and, as Marcus went to adjust the gramophone player, Mathilde ventured, 'I'm grateful you have the time for me. I know how many other dancers you've tutored.' She stopped, because Marcus was now circling her, lifting her arms and arranging them at each joint, then inspecting her poise. 'Marcus, do you ever get *tired* of it?'

His face was a horrified mask. 'The man who gets tired of the ballroom is tired of life.' He went to slip the needle back onto the gramophone record, then gracefully positioned himself in Mathilde's arms. 'Watch me for the hesitations. Let me show you a little something you might take back to dear Frank.' Then, as the first measure of music began and they leaned in to the dance, he furrowed his eyes and asked, 'Is that the problem, my dear? Do you think you're *tired* of it?'

'Oh no!' Mathilde's voice flurried up – and, for the first time, she wasn't being fake. 'I'll never be tired of it, Marcus.' *Never*, she thought. 'But you've come so far, trained so many dancers – you've seen the whole world...'

'Aha,' said Marcus, as he turned her on the dance floor, 'but there is always a new adventure. The Grand came calling at the right time in my life. To everything there is a season. Here, I can dance again – without having to turn my back on that which has defined my ballroom life...'

'Training young dancers,' said Mathilde.

'The cream rises to the top of the milk!'

With this elliptical saying, Marcus spun Mathilde so that she felt almost giddy.

'I have been awarded prizes for my quicksteps, my dear, but the greatest joys in my dancing life have come from seeing those under my instruction shine. As you will do, Mathilde, on One Grand Night. Imagine the feeling you'll have – to be here, on this dance floor, your talent the prize awarded to some lord for the evening. A foxtrot with Mathilde Bourchier – worth its weight in gold!'

He was filling her with such rhapsodies that it felt wrong to continue deceiving him – and yet then he said, 'One day, Mathilde, you'll dance with the stars, I promise,' and suddenly her conscience scuttled back to the dark corner into which she'd previously cast it. *I don't want to dance with the stars,* she told herself. *I want to <u>be</u> the star.*

'Mathilde,' Marcus said, breaking out of hold, 'you're every bit as talented as the dancers I took to the World Championship in 1936. Every bit as talented as those I've seen set sail for the stars at Brighton and Blackpool, at Milan and Vienna. But there's something holding you back. I can feel it in your body. I remember, long ago – in fact, it was the first time I encountered our own Archie Adams. 1929, perhaps. Archie's Orchestra were rising stars in their firmament, about to secure the residency right here in the Grand when it opened. I was tutoring the stars of the day. Yes, there was a dancer much like you, back then. She was trapped in her own head. Archie and I took to her one side one night, thinking we might lead her through some dance and music together, away from the prying eyes of the competitions. But it wasn't a dance problem she truly had. It was an affair of the heart, one that was stopping her from giving her all to the moment – one that was trapping her in devilish thought.' He whirled away, to silence the music at the gramophone. 'Speak to me, girl.'

Marcus's words were so similar to Frank's observations, earlier that day. The truth was, the thing holding her back was the only thing she couldn't speak to him about; the thing she had to do, if she was ever to claim her heart's desire. She supposed he could feel the conflict in her body, as they danced; had he access to her head and heart, he would have seen the battle being waged inside her right now.

But he'd given her an opportunity, and she didn't mean to waste it.

'It's not that I'm tired, Marcus. It's more … sometimes to love something, maybe you have to remember that other things exist. You can't eat caviar every day and still taste the sumptuousness of it. There was a time, perhaps four years ago now, when I decided I didn't want to dance. My mother, she'd been pushing me so hard – and I took off and, for six months, I didn't step into a ballroom or even a dance hall. Then something just changed and it called me back. But … didn't you leave the ballroom, for a time? I'm sure somebody told me that once? That you took yourself off and just didn't dance for – what was it, a year? Two?'

Right there and then, she saw the almost imperceptible flickering of his eyes; the way his cheeks burned a different hue, just for a second, before he recovered full control of his senses.

'Well, Mathilde, my history is long and storied. It bores me, so often is it told. To dance at our best, we mustn't look back, nor even forward – we simply have to exist, right here, in the moment we're given.'

He wanted to go on, but Mathilde intervened, 'But you must have had a reason, Marcus, for just taking off like that? You were on top of the world! The dancers you were instructing just before you took off, didn't they win the Exhibition Paris? And then that was it – you were gone!' She could see how it was troubling him – Marcus's face, ordinarily sparkling with theatrical delight, had almost no expression at all. Perhaps it was best, now, to bring it back to the state of her own mind. 'So you must know how it feels. You were on top of the world – but you still needed a break.'

'Is that what you're trying to tell me, Mathilde, my dear? That you don't want to dance for the Grand?'

'No!' she exclaimed, seeing for the first time the dead alley into which she seemed to have stumbled. 'No, it's not that. It's just – I think I've been missing something. I'm beaten up by it. Maybe it's just the war. I thought you might know how it feels.'

'The truth is, Mathilde, that I didn't plan to step aside in 1931. Meghan and Victor were glorious at the Exhibition Paris. They should have gone on to the World Championships themselves. I still believe it was within their grasp. But human beings are notoriously fickle creatures. It was Victor himself who asked me to set them free of my instruction. And so I did.'

Mathilde's heart sank, in unison with his. Was that it? Was

that the entire story? But why, then, the two years in the wilderness? Marcus Arbuthnot lived for the ballroom. He had been at its giddiest heights. In 1931, there would have been no end of young dancers desperate for his tutelage.

'What did you do all that time, Marcus?'

'I nursed my heart,' he said. 'Mathilde, if you want to step away, you must tell me now. One Grand Night is but six weeks away. The ballroom would reel without you. Mr Knave is already accepting bids for your hand. We'll let people down if we step aside now – if that's how it must be, then let us do it soon, so that the damage is but small.'

'I'm sorry, Marcus,' she said, 'I've upset you. I thought we might be … kindred spirits, somehow. I don't want to leave the Grand, Marcus. I just thought you might understand the feeling of it.' By the way his face softened, she knew that he had accepted it as an apology. Perhaps, now, if she pressed her advantage just one more time, he might yield. 'Two years away though, Marcus – did the love of the ballroom stay with you? Didn't you have to find it again?'

Marcus had been about to take her in hold again, but now he stepped back. 'I've told you, my dear. Dancing is not about the past, nor the future, but the beauty of *now*. It has never served me, in my life, to ruminate on what used to be. But let me simply say this: sometimes, we all need to step away.'

He was stepping away, right now. She could see it, plain as day.

'Sleep, Mathilde. We all need sleep. It's the curse of these days, with the bombs raining down. It's no wonder cracks begin to show. Cracks in our dreams. Cracks in our talents.' He strode across the dance floor, up through the balustrade, and hovered among the tables arrayed around the Champagne bar. 'Rest your body and your mind, Mathilde – for we dance tomorrow. The ballroom needs you at your very best.'

Then he was gone.

Mathilde slumped against the balustrade, caring not at all for her posture or poise. Well, there was nobody here to see.

Then she looked around, surveying the beauty of the Grand. It was, she knew, the very best ballroom in London. Neither the Imperial nor the Savoy could compare to the great arches of its vaulted ceiling; the way the dance floor kissed the feet as they skipped upon it; the pure, crystalline magic of those dangling chandeliers. And it hit her, then, that *this* was the place she wanted to call home. This was the place where dreams came to life.

Perhaps it was how spurned princesses felt in days of yore – sold off, by marriage, to some faraway kingdom where they could call themselves queen, without ever feeling it in their hearts. She wanted to be queen *here* – but it was the Imperial that had opened its arms to her, and so it seemed that it was the Imperial where her future lay.

She just had to destroy all this first. To bring down its beauty. To carve apart One Grand Night and the Buckingham's reputation with it.

How heavy could a heart feel?

She had, at least, learned one thing of use this afternoon. Marcus Arbuthnot hadn't left the world of the ballroom by choice; if what he said was true, then it didn't take much imagination to know that he'd been pushed out – pushed out, somehow, by the man he'd tutored to victory at the Exhibition Paris.

But if that was so, it was a secret he'd been keeping for almost a decade. A secret that, even now, he was guarded enough not to let slip. And a secret that she could no longer probe him about – for she'd pushed him too far and, in doing so, she feared, already revealed a sliver of her purpose.

There had to be somebody else who knew. Men can keep secrets, she thought, but not when other people were involved in them. Secrets like that always leaked out. Light always got in, through the tiniest of cracks. And whatever this story was, it didn't belong to Marcus alone – now she knew it belonged to Victor Grace and Meghan Barr as well.

There had to be others. Dancers who'd been at the same Exhibition, or just dancers who'd been at the heart of the ball-room scene in 1931.

It was then that she remembered what Marcus had said, that there was at least one other person in this hotel who'd known him back in those earlier, formative times. She turned to the stage – empty now, of course, but for the grand white piano which sat there, regally awaiting the night's performance and the appearance of the one man who could turn its eighty-eight keys into a joyous, jubilant cascade.

Archie Adams.

Chapter Thirteen

'There you go, Mrs de Guise – job done at half the price, fit for any king to lay his head!'

Nancy had known she was taking a risk when, in concert with Mrs Moffatt, they invited Annie Brogan to work some shifts in the Housekeeping department. The girl had come across as brassy and bold as the other Brogan they knew – but they were so fond of Billy, and knew him to be such a hard worker, that taking the chance on Annie seemed sensible enough. It was only now – five shifts later, each one of them when one of the other chambermaids had been taken sick, or else asked to be excused for some personal reason – that Nancy was truly giving in to the doubts she had. Until now, she'd been telling herself to go easy on the girl – and constantly reminding herself that she, Nancy, was depleted, exhausted, her own mind hardly on the job after everything Raymond was going through – but it was going to be difficult to go easy on her today. They stood in the Trafalgar Suite on the hotel's third storey, the curtains drawn back to reveal the splendour of Berkeley Square – where the russet gold leaves had finally shed, and winter was revealing itself bit by bit – and the gothic spires of the Church of the Immaculate Conception. But there was no denying the disorderly mess the suite had been left in. Ordinarily, it wouldn't have been a problem to enter a suite where the bed was badly made, the windowpane stained, and a smear of dried dirt from a guest's shoe marked the pristine sheepskin rug – but Annie Brogan was declaring that she had *already* done her work, and to Nancy this was most confounding. She didn't dare let her eyes drift down to the ornate French dresser, because she was quite certain no attempt had been made to clean the wine stain from its surface. No, she thought, this just wouldn't do.

'Annie, let's have a talk.'

'Anything you like, Mrs de Guise,' Annie declared – and threw herself onto the end of the badly made bed, further disrupting the bedcovers.

'Annie,' Nancy ventured, sitting softly beside her, 'a few questions, my dear. I don't see a laundry bag in this suite. Did you change these bedsheets?'

'Not today, ma'am. They've barely been slept in, so I straightened them out and did a proper tuck-in round the corners.'

Nancy cringed. 'And this earth trampled into the sheepskin…'

Annie held her hands up. 'Not me, Mrs de Guise. It must have been the fella that sleeps here.'

There were other questions Nancy had meant to ask. She could see that an effort had been made to polish the brass fittings – she could smell it, too, because the delicious scent of vinegar was strong in the air – and that the windows had been cleaned (the smears on the glass were testament to that), so there was no doubt that Annie was trying. It was just that 'trying' wasn't good enough in the Buckingham Hotel. Nancy herself had had to attend every room at the end of each of Annie's shifts, trying to kindly show her the way things had to be done. There'd been improvements along the way, but not quickly or fully enough that she could keep it up much longer.

So she decided to give it one last go.

'Annie, the guests who stay at the Buckingham Hotel require a certain level of elegance and polish. Do you understand what I'm saying?'

Annie shook her head with the air of a sage elder lamenting the idiosyncrasies and indulgences of today's youth. 'These lords and ladies, Mrs de Guise, they all go to the toilet like the rest of us.'

Nancy summoned up the last of her patience and said, 'They do, Annie, but what they expect from us is a certain level of service that is, perhaps, above and beyond how you and I might do things in our own homes.'

'I been tucking the beds in on *both* sides, Mrs de Guise.' Annie was almost rolling her eyes at the very notion. 'I don't know how they can even get into a bed like that. They'll have to untuck it first – so it's all a waste of time. The things we have to do for your "betters", Nancy!'

Nancy said, 'It's Mrs de Guise, Annie.'

Annie gave a mock startled expression.

Nancy could have screamed, but the girl was so proud of her accomplishments that she could hardly bring herself to say a cross word. The only thing for it was yet more patience. The problem was, given how tired she was, she wasn't certain how much she could magic up.

She got to her feet, clapped her hands, and declared, 'Annie, you and me, we're going to make this room fit for a—'

Then she felt the churning.

Moments later, Nancy herself was bent over the ornate French dresser, spilling the contents of this morning's breakfast over the sparkling mahogany. It had come over her suddenly, this time – and she'd thought, across the last few days, that these sensations were passing. Knotted with worry about Raymond as she'd been, she'd hardly given herself a second thought, even tricked herself, at moments, into believing she wasn't really pregnant at all. But here was the evidence, in all its lurid glory.

Annie was standing at her shoulder, with an expression of wide-eyed wonder.

'Annie,' she spluttered, 'I think, perhaps, the cloth, if you please.'

So much for showing the girl how to make up a lord's bedchamber.

'You been to the doctor yet, Nance?'

'It's Mrs de Guise,' she corrected, gratefully taking the cloth Annie had offered. 'And it's nothing to worry about. It's the stress of the bombing, and staying up all night worrying about my husband. Not a word of this to anyone, Annie.'

'Oh no, Nan – Mrs de Guise,' Annie declared, seemingly filled with pride at having become Nancy's unwitting confidante. 'I wouldn't dream of it!' She was looking down at the mess on the dresser when a puzzled look came over her face. 'Look!' she said, and pointed with a flourish at the surface, 'I didn't get that wine stain out after all!'

'Well,' said Annie ruefully as she strutted into the hotel post room, chomping on a glistening red apple from one of the room service trolleys, 'Nancy's pregnant.'

Billy, who had only just returned to the post room himself, set down the two cloth bags he was carrying, gave Annie a startled look, then ducked urgently behind her to close the post room door. 'Annie! What are you talking about?'

'I told her she was, and now she is. So that's what's happening. Of course, she says it's just *worry*, but our ma's worried almost every day and night, and I've only ever seen her be sick like that when she's cooking up another Brogan. So there you have it. Mrs de Guise is going to be a mother. And a fine mother she'll make too,' Annie gave a sly look, '*if* she can stop harping on about tucking in both sides of the bed.'

Billy opened the door again, made sure nobody was loitering outside, and limped to his desk – where he promptly began hiding the two cloth bags.

'Annie Brogan, what are you talking about?'

'It's just like I said, Bill.' She paraded into the room, one curious eye on the bags Billy had just hustled away, and added, 'I just seen her making a mess of a lovely old dresser – just like Ma when our Gracie-May was on the way.'

Exasperated, Billy said, 'You want to be careful with information like that. You let something like that slip and it can ruin a whole load of lives – and that includes yours, Annie. Nobody likes a secret-spreader. Trust me about that – I should know.' Billy didn't like to dwell on his own earlier years in the Buckingham Hotel – when, as a page, he'd been privy to just about every secret from the most elegant suite to the back of the hotel kitchens – because he hadn't always been discreet with the whispers and rumours he'd picked up along the way. But that only made him more determined to make Annie see. 'It's Nancy's business, Annie. We don't have a right to be chin-wagging it all over the hotel.' He stalled. 'But that's big news, Annie. Mrs de Guise and Raymond and – Annie, *what* are you doing now?'

The news of Nancy's pregnancy seemed to have sustained Annie's interest only until the end of her apple, whose core she delicately popped in her mouth. Still crunching it, she sidled around Billy and started worrying at the bags under his desk with her foot. Now that she was here, she could see a small packing crate too – one of those that usually turned up at the hotel kitchens, overflowing with fresh fruits and vegetables. Inside it were wax paper packages, half pound bags of sugar, jars of preserves, and paper bags whose surfaces had turned transparent with grease.

'What's all this, Bill?'

'Never you mind,' Billy said, and shooed her away.

But the look on Annie's face was of a young woman who would not be deterred. 'What are you doing, opening a grocer's?'

It wasn't like Billy Brogan to get filled with ire, but if it wasn't for his limp he might have carted Annie directly out of the room. Instead he said, 'It's hotel business, and mind your own! This is a post room, Annie. I've got things to package up.'

'Yes,' said Annie, her face a picture of innocence, 'but I thought it was all letters for lovelorn ladies, or terribly important notes for them ministers upstairs. Jars of orange marmalade and lemon curd! Billy, you want to be sending a jar or two home, that's what you ought to be doing.'

With evident irritation, Billy reached under his desk, produced a jar of Royal Green's Lemon Curd, and pressed this into Annie's hands. 'Here, tell Ma you just found it lying around. And get out of here, won't you? Some of us are highly valued members of staff at the Buckingham Hotel, don't you know? Some of us have got work to be getting on with.'

It was the first thing Billy had said that brought a look of dismay to Annie's face. 'Do you think they'll keep me, Billy?'

'You keep that mouth of yours shut about Nancy and they just might,' he said. Then, sensing he'd pushed her too far, he limped across the room and put an arm around her. 'You're a Brogan, so if they don't like you, they'll have me to answer to. Just do your best. Keep listening to what they tell you. They'll see what you're worth soon enough. Just look at Nancy herself – you don't reckon she stepped into the Buckingham a floor mistress, do you? No, Annie, Nance wasn't too different from you. Maybe a couple of shades smarter. Maybe her head was screwed on just a little tighter than yours. Maybe—'

'OK, Billy!'

'Nancy didn't get where she is today just by marrying Mr de Guise. She had grit. Determination. She worked hard, she got their respect. Annie, I know how it looks – it's like, in the Buckingham, there's only one thing that counts: class. But I promise you, you don't have to be a toff to find a place here. What really matters, whether you're upstairs or down, is *reputation*. Work on your reputation, Annie, and the Buckingham's yours for the—' Billy was cut off at that moment, because the telephone of the post master's desk had started trilling. 'I got to get that, Annie. There'll be a telegram got to go out. Look, I'll find you in the kitchenette at the end of the day. You go on up there and make nice with Rosa and the rest of the girls. You'll want them to like you too.'

Annie was only just out of the door when Billy took up the receiver. 'Buckingham Post,' he declared, in his best impersonation of some lord's stately squire. 'William Brogan speaking.'

'Bill!' came a familiar voice.

Billy's eyes darted instantly to the post room door. 'One moment,' he said, then forced himself across the room, where he checked Annie was still disappearing down the hall, then turned the key in the lock.

Back at the telephone, he said, 'Ken?'

'That's right, boy. I thought I'd get on the telephone after all. Took me a bit of a time to get the check-in desk to put me through to you – they're busybodies up there aren't they, son? Always trying to get their noses in another man's business?'

Billy's heart was pounding. 'Ken, you shouldn't call here. I don't want anyone asking after you. You understand, don't you? This is my work. I don't take personal calls.' He stopped, shaking his head fiercely to try and shake out the bad feeling. 'I haven't forgotten, Ken. I'll be there at six, just like always.'

The boxes and bags Annie had so keenly spied constituted the seventh – or was it the eighth? – collection Billy had made in Ken's honour. He called them 'collections' because, in Billy's mind, this made it permissible – collections, after all, were for charity. That didn't stop him feeling the frisson of fear every night when he filled his bag and walked, brazenly, out of the tradesman's exit, up Michaelmas Mews and away. There were more 'leftovers' from the Buckingham Hotel – he called them 'leftovers', even though most of this was simply lifted from the shelves in the larders – stored beneath his bed back at Lambeth Yard. Tonight, he'd round it all up and wait on the corner for Ken to drive through. He had to do it when his father was out on ARP duties, and his mother in the shelter out back; the elder Brogans wouldn't have stood for it, even though Billy had been helping them out with bits from the hotel for years. But it was difficult for them to know the true scale of things at the Buckingham, not without having seen it with their own eyes: only Billy knew how much the guests at the Buckingham gorged themselves each night, while on streets not so very far away, people starved.

'I know you haven't forgotten, Bill, but I had to get on to you. There's something you might be able to help me with.'

Billy, who was under the impression he'd been helping Ken out enough already, said, 'If I take much more, Ken, I'm bound to get noticed.'

'Oh, Bill! Bill, you've got me wrong. You've been doing us proud. I've a stack of letters here from some grateful old boys, and all directed to you. Not by name, of course – they knows not to get you in trouble. But everyone's saying how handsomely you've done them. There's food on plates tonight that wouldn't have been there without you. And, you see, that's what I'm call-ing about.'

Billy rather liked the idea of some old dears sitting around for a dinner of sausages and mashed potatoes, when previously it might only have been the mash, and thinking about it settled his stomach somehow. What he'd learnt was: the world wasn't the same, from high and from low. What was charity to those old dears with their empty kitchen cupboards was heinous theft to those in power at the Buckingham Hotel. It was just what those protestors had meant last year, when they marched into the Queen Mary with their placards: the rich didn't get rationed, not when they went for dinner every night at places like the Queen Mary restaurant. The rules the government had made to be fair to everybody *always* hit the neediest worst. What Billy was doing just redressed a little of the balance.

'Look, Bill, all these bits you're getting for our old dears, well, it's really got me thinking. The Buckingham Hotel's got to have other goods in it, doesn't it? You're sitting on a vein of gold you've hardly started mining. And I was chatting to some of my shopkeeps last night, and they said – well, Ken, if he can get us some other bits, I'm sure we can shift that. People are in want of butter and bacon, that's for sure, but why should it be that only the nobs get to have a little tipple of Champagne after blackout? Why should it be that you have to sit in some expensive restaurant to have a nice slab of pâté? They're up there, dancing in their silks and lace – well, can you get a roll of silk or any decent lace in a draper's?' Ken paused, and the telephone static crackled. 'What do you think, Bill? Can you help me out?'

Billy paused too. The tinny buzz from the telephone receiver was like a fly trapped in the confines of his mind.

'Bill, are you still there?'

Champagne, thought Billy. Silks. Pâté and lace. The niggling sensation, which he'd been stamping out ever since he first dropped a piece of venison and string bag of figs onto Ken's kitchen table, came back to him now: people didn't *need* Champagne to get by, did they? Perhaps they envied others a big slab of pâté, but they didn't *need* it. And silks and lace – what use were they?

And why was he now so silent? Why couldn't he just say what was in his mind?

Billy took a deep breath and said, 'I'm not sure, Ken. Champagne? Silks? It's not exactly bacon and butter. I thought we were helping folks out.'

'It's just levelling the scales, Bill. It's about being fair. Now, I know you're loyal to that hotel, and that's down to you and your good character. But have they been good to you, Bill? Them, who every night drink Champagne worth more than you get paid in a month? Them, who dance around that ballroom of theirs in gowns worth more than every piece of clothing you've ever worn, put together? Billy, you're a clever lad. You know what I'm saying.'

'I can't just take ball gowns, Ken. Bacon and figs, blackberry preserve – at least that feeds folks...'

'Now, Billy,' said Ken, and for the first time Billy could detect some sort of sternness in his voice, 'I never took you for a fool, son. I wouldn't have our Mary-Lou stepping out with some fool. I took you for a loyal soldier, who knew what was what. It's called the *economy*, Billy.'

Billy's knuckles were whitening around the telephone receiver, he was clinging on so hard.

'You know you're not the only one helping my shopkeepers out, don't you Bill? There's a whole load of us, all ready and willing to lend a hand to those that need it. I've got a couple of farmers a short ride north from here, some lads in the warehouse

– some more at the markets. Even one or two out-of-bounds types going off into the woods for a few off-ration hunks of meat. And, you see, some of those lads, well, they might like a nice bottle of something on a night. Some of their missuses might fancy a nice gown. So instead of going to them with a roll of pound notes, a man like me might need to go to them and say – help me out with a few strings of sausages, and I'll stand you this fancy bottle of wine, courtesy of Mr William Brogan of the Buckingham Hotel. You see, Bill? You've got to keep things running smoothly. If you don't, those lads clam up or get scared, or else they go off and start supplying somebody else – somebody who *does* treat them right, with some nice smelling salts fit for a king. It's like in times gone by, you see – nowadays, the good old British pound isn't the currency they're after. We're back to bartering for what we can get.'

'But Ken…'

'Listen, Billy, if I don't get the bits I need to grease this particular engine, it's going to clam up. It's going to stop working. And if it stops working, well, who is it that suffers? It isn't me. It isn't you. It's not those lads who've turned away from me, and all because I couldn't help them out with the truffles and chocolates they wanted. No, it's them further down the ladder – it's them old dears who just want a little extra on their plates at the end of the day; them old boys, who've done their bit for their country, only to end up starved at home.' Ken paused. 'I thought you wanted to be part of the solution to all this, Billy. Or did I have you wrong?'

'No, no,' said Billy, cupping his hand around the receiver as if, even now, he might be being eavesdropped upon. 'I want to help. I've got the bits here waiting. It's just… ball gowns, Ken. Wine and Champagne. It doesn't feel the same. It's *not* the same.'

'Now, Billy,' snapped Ken, 'you've hardly been listening. You get these bits for me, and the good you're doing, it all trickles down. Some supplier of mine gets a nice bottle of Moët. So he cuts me a deal on the stuff he's got out back, the stuff he's holding on to. Then I can get that onto the plates of those that need it.'

Billy wanted to say: *and what's in it for you, Ken?* Because he knew, all of a sudden, that this couldn't all be about charity. That nice house Ken lived in, and that nice spread he'd put on for Billy and Mary-Louise – that crisp pound note he'd given Billy, to have a flutter on the greyhounds – it had to come from somewhere.

'I've never minded buttering someone's bread, Ken. You know that. But ball gowns and Champagne? This is my livelihood…'

For a pregnant moment, there was silence on the line. Billy had never known that silence could be so deafening.

'Livelihood, Bill,' Ken finally spat, his voice ripe with disappointment. 'Here I am talking about people's *lives*, and there's you fretting over *livelihood*. Well, how about this, Bill, old friend – your livelihood's up in smoke anyway, if anyone rumbles what you've been doing for me. Think on that a moment, son. You wouldn't like it if a little message were to land on the desk of your Mr Knave – or, say, the head of the Hotel Board? What's his name – John Hastings?'

Billy's blood ran cold, because Ken seemed to know everything there was to know about the Buckingham Hotel. And he realised, in that moment, that he'd known from the very beginning; he'd known what Billy was, and what he was worth, the moment he stepped through that front door in Camden. All of the days out, the money, the friendliness – it had all been leading him to this moment. Billy wasn't Ken's friend; he'd been like a lamb, being led into the slaughterhouse.

He took a breath.

He was a soldier, wasn't he? He wasn't somebody to be pushed around. He'd survived France. He'd come back from Dunkirk. He'd fought for his country then, and there wasn't a chance he wasn't going to do the right thing now.

Billy Brogan had never been a fighting man. Neither a uniform nor a bayonet had changed that. But, where his blood had once run cold, now it burned. He'd be a fighting man today.

'Now you listen here, Ken,' he snapped. 'You can't bully me. I'm not for bullying – do you hear? There'll be no Champagne from me. There'll be no silk and lace. Who do you think you're speaking to? I'm a Buckingham man, through and through. I'm a – I'm a Brogan, and Brogans do right!'

Perhaps the silence meant that Ken was taken aback. Billy was just about feeling proud of himself when a crackling voice said, 'Yes, a *Brogan*. That's right – that's what you are. But, of course, there's more than one Brogan at that hotel, isn't there?'

Billy's eyes flashed to the door through which Annie had disappeared. His heart, racing a new wild rhythm, jumped in his breast. 'What?' he whispered.

All of his newfound fire had vanished.

'Look, Bill, we've got a good thing going on here. If you want to end it, then end it. But I reckon there's another Brogan at the Buckingham Hotel who might be a good fit for what I need. In and out of the bedchambers, isn't she? A nice, sweet girl like that – she could go anywhere she wants. Well, that's what these chambermaids are taught, isn't it? How to be *invisible*.' He paused, and Billy felt certain it was deliberate – like an actor, letting the thought sink in. 'Annie, isn't it?' he said, with a cheeriness laced in menace. 'Yes, what if I got on to Annie instead? I'm sure my Mary-Louise could introduce us. Sit her down, tell her what big brother Billy's been up to – and how, if she doesn't keep it up, poor Bill will wind up in trouble with management. What do you think?'

Lamb to the slaughter, thought Billy.

He closed his eyes, and all he could see was that lamb, trotting happily into a trap.

'Well, Bill?' asked Ken. 'Have we got an agreement?'

The telephone receiver was trembling in Billy's hand. 'I can't get anything by tonight, Ken. It's too soon. I need to work this out.'

'See that you do,' said Ken.

Then the line went dead.

Two sets of emotions did battle through Billy: shame, at what he'd walked into; and anger, at how he'd been trapped. In the end, it was his anger that won out. Billy limped across the room, walking cane in hand, slammed the post room door shut behind him, and started to march.

His anger wasn't dimmed by the time he reached the service elevator. It was hardly dimmed as the floors ground by and the doors opened again, revealing the dark interior of the hotel's hidden seventh storey, the warren of staff quarters in the attics that nestled above the ceilings of its most extravagant suites.

The light at the end of the hallway was the chambermaids' kitchenette. Billy heaved himself through. In a big horseshoe of old armchairs, all arranged around a table where a pot of tea and crumpet crusts sat beside a backgammon board and a pile of weekly magazines, the chambermaids were gathered. Frank Nettleton was sitting with his sweetheart Rosa, both of them cramped into the same armchair, and they leapt up at Billy's appearance. So did Mary-Louise, who'd been sitting in the window seat with one of the others, unwinding from the morning shift.

'Billy!' Rosa exclaimed, grabbing him by the arm and trying

to hustle him to the backgammon board. 'You're just in time – Frank's about to get himself trounced. Maybe you can help him out.'

Billy shook off her arm. 'Sorry, Rosa, maybe another time.' He looked up, his eyes fixed on Mary-Louise. 'I need to talk to you.'

Some of the girls started giggling, as if anticipating some grand romantic gesture ('It would be just like Billy Brogan to propose!' sniggered somebody), but Mary-Louise could tell that Billy was serious. 'Is everything all right, Billy?'

He shook his head. 'I need to speak to you now.'

Mary-Louise said, 'Go on, Bill.'

'*Alone.*'

Mary-Louise crossed the kitchenette, looped her arm through Billy's, and together they went back to the hallway. Pointedly – and to another chorus of titters – Billy closed the kitchenette door.

He fixed Mary-Louise with a look. Those chocolate brown eyes of hers – now that he was here, it was easy to get lost in them, but they held unfathomable secrets.

'I just talked to your uncle.'

Mary-Louise looked at him, dumbly.

'I'm going to ask you this one more time, Mary-Louise. Please don't lie to me.' *If you lie,* thought Billy, *I'll believe you, and then where will I be?* 'Did you know, Mary-Louise? Did you know what your uncle wants from me?'

'Billy, we talked about this. I didn't know a thing. It's just my Uncle Ken. He's only trying to do a bit of good where he can.'

Billy blurted out, 'He wants me to steal Champagne.'

'What?' Mary whispered, inching closer to Billy.

'He wants me to take ball gowns and wine.' He stopped. 'You *did* know, didn't you? That's why you took me out to Camden the first time, isn't it? That's why we went to the dogs. He wanted somebody stealing from the Buckingham for him – not just odds and ends, not just waste and leftovers. Champagne. Ball gowns!' Billy was almost shouting, but remembered, at the very last moment, to lower his voice – because surely they were listening, from the chambermaids' kitchenette. With this in mind, he whisked Mary-Lou further along the hallway. 'He set me up so that I can't stop, so that I have to do what he told me. Did you help him, Mary-Louise? Is all this a lie?'

Mary-Louise brought her hand back, as if she might slap Billy – but Billy was too quick; he grabbed her by the wrist.

'Your precious Uncle Ken told me that, if I didn't do what he wants, he'll get you to introduce him to Annie – and make her do it instead.'

'But I wouldn't, Billy!' Mary-Louise protested. 'That's not the kind of girl I am!'

Dispirited, disgusted, Billy dropped her wrist. 'Then how, Mary-Louise, did he know about Annie?'

Billy stepped back from her. Only half a yard separated them, but it might as well have been the ocean. 'Billy, believe me – there's been some mistake. I didn't know a thing. I'll – I'll talk to him. I'll make him see he's not making sense. He's a good man, Billy. I know he is.'

Billy was done. He pushed past her, levering himself by his cane back towards the service elevator.

'Billy!'

Mary-Louise's cry had prompted somebody to open the kitchenette door. In its portal stood Frank and Rosa. They looked about ready to cheer, quite certain that Billy Brogan had just got down on one knee.

Mary-Louise caught Billy just as he was stepping into the service elevator. She was about to step through when she saw the look on Billy's face and said, 'Billy, you have to believe me. I didn't know.'

'Your uncle's a profiteer, plain and simple,' he sighed. 'And now I'm at his mercy.'

'Billy, what will you do?'

He wanted to believe her. He wanted it more than anything else in the world. He could feel his mind contorting itself to have faith in what she said – but something hardened in his gut, some little voice whispered in his ear that the risk was too great.

'I'm going to find my way out,' he breathed.

Then he reached out to pull the bronze gate across the elevator doors, pressed the button for the ground storey and dropped out of sight.

The last thing he heard, from above, were the voices of Frank and Rosa as they rushed towards Mary-Louise, full of joy and expectation.

But there was no joy in Billy Brogan's heart, and there wouldn't be again – not until he picked his way out of this most devilish of traps.

Chapter Fourteen

Dancing Times, April 1930. Yes, this was the one.

She'd tracked down a bundle of the old magazines from a stationers on the Charing Cross Road. She'd watched the bombs fall like meteors across the river last night, and in the morning the stationer was standing in front of his shop, between the ruins on either side. 'I didn't think I'd have a customer today,' he'd said, 'not least for this kind of thing. What's your interest?'

'I'm looking for something,' she'd said, 'and, besides, it's nice to get lost in a dream, isn't it?'

Slightly mysterious, the shopkeeper thought, but a sale was a sale. He'd take whatever he could in times like these. It was only by God's grace that he had any magazines to sell at all.

Now, she sat on her bedstead, sorting through the box she'd brought home. It was a small room, with a bed and a fireplace and a writing desk tucked into the shuttered window. And here it was, the thing she was looking for:

RAYMOND DE GUISE, KING OF THE BALLROOM

He looked so young and carefree in the photograph, a matinee idol in evening wear and sculpted black hair. *Dancing Times* had first been published in 1894, a magazine devoted to the

Cavendish Rooms on Cavendish Square, but since then it had grown to chronicle all the highs and lows of the worldwide ballroom scene. 'Raymond de Guise,' read the copy, 'returns from his Continental tour, in the company of his friend and mentor Georges de la Motte. Mr de Guise, twice crowned champion in Brighton, had his most recent success at the Hotel Acacias...'

His face peppered these pages. She lingered over each photograph, tracing them until she found the one she admired the most. September 1930: 'Raymond de Guise is reported to have been appointed principal dancer at the newly inaugurated Grand Ballroom at the Buckingham Hotel. As the Buckingham Hotel follows the Savoy in embracing ballroom culture, the Buckingham Board has high hopes for its new star...'

Her slender fingers traced around Raymond's image. Moments later, those same slender fingers were gently – perhaps, one might say, even lovingly – tearing the page from the magazine and folding around the edges until only the portrait of Raymond remained.

On the mantelpiece, above the hearth, an empty picture frame was waiting – empty, that is, except for the frayed edge of the photograph that had once been there, a photograph that was now curling into nothingness in the fire which flickered in the grate below.

She was humming to herself, the tune of some Cab Calloway classic, as she crossed the room and slipped the image of Raymond into the frame.

It was only as she stepped back to admire it from the middle of the room that her eyes caught sight of the photograph wilting in the fire. She could still see the image, as the flames lapped at its every side. There the figure was, standing in his own infantry uniform, with his own matinee idol good looks and his own proudly sculpted black hair.

But then he was gone, turned black by the fire – and, on the mantelpiece, it was Raymond, *her* Raymond, who remained.

Raymond was sleeping as Nancy left. Last night the bombardment hadn't been as fierce as in days past, and that had meant Raymond returning three hours before dawn. She'd been awake, of course. It was the morning sickness moving through her – nobody ever told a woman that, to an unborn child, there was no such thing as 'morning' or 'night'; it could strike you at any time. Tonight was different from nights past; tonight, he'd stolen into bed alongside her, and there he fitfully lay as she arose, tried to settle herself with tea and toast, then departed their home into the paling light.

She arrived at the Buckingham before the girls appeared for breakfast in the Housekeeping Lounge. Mrs Moffatt, of course, had been here before dawn – but, as Nancy entered, it was not to find the lounge already prepared for the chambermaids to descend. The teapot was warm and a plate of shortcake biscuits had been laid out (then half-eaten – there was nothing Mrs Moffatt adored more for breakfast than shortcake), but apart from this the lounge looked precisely as it had done the night before.

Nancy looked at the grandfather clock propped in the corner. In an age before Nancy came to the Buckingham, it had taken pride of place in the Benefactors Study, where the Hotel Board gathered for their monthly meetings, but since it had fallen into disrepair it counted the seconds between chambermaids' shifts. They would all, Nancy noted, be here in a few minutes time.

Mrs Moffatt sat at the head of the breakfast table, nervously chewing the end of a pencil, a leaf of paper in front of her and a good number of others screwed up at her feet. So consumed was she that she didn't, at first, look up as Nancy approached.

'Emmeline?'

Her name startled her out of whatever missive she was slaving over. As if jolted from a dream, she flurried up out of her chair – quite a sight, Nancy thought, for somebody of Mrs Moffatt's doughy size and shape – and started collecting up all of the half-finished letters.

'Nancy, dear, you took me quite by surprise.'

'The girls will be here soon,' Nancy said. 'Maybe we should…'

She'd meant to launch straight into the day, to blot out everything else and get on with the task at hand – the task of making sure the engine of the Buckingham Hotel ran smoothly for another day – but, all at once, those ideas abandoned her. In the vacuum they left behind, Nancy felt stranded – stranded and alone.

She wasn't making a sound, but her eyes were filling with tears. She could no longer see Mrs Moffatt, but Mrs Moffatt could see her.

'Nancy, dear, what is it?'

'I'm pregnant.'

There it was: another blurted-out confession. How silly was she? It was as if she couldn't approach the subject slowly and methodically, with careful reason and thought. That was how Nancy liked to think she'd lived her life: ambitious and adventurous, but always with her feet on the ground, always with a good deal of thinking before she'd taken each step. Everything planned. It felt as if the only way to speak about it was to throw yourself completely off the cliff-edge, and hope, just *hope*, that somebody else would catch you.

'Nancy, come through,' Mrs Moffatt said. She'd forgotten whatever frenzy she herself had been in and, leaving the balls of paper and half-finished letter behind, took Nancy through to the office, where they sat in the same armchairs in which Mrs Moffatt had comforted dozens of other girls – and at least one, Vivienne, who was in exactly the same condition as Nancy herself. 'Have you known long, dear?'

'A little time,' Nancy said. It was good to hear the splosh of tea in a cup that somebody else had poured for her. She realised, now, that it had been an aeon since anyone had done anything for her – even Raymond, whose energies were devoted to his nights on patrol. A simple cup of tea could be a gift greater than any other. 'Oh, Emmeline, I'm being a fool. I don't know why it's touching me like this. I ought to be thrilled. I am! What's not to be thrilled about? A married woman, expecting her first baby. So why do I feel so ... confused?'

'A baby will shake you to your core, Nancy. That's just the way it is – as natural as the air.' Mrs Moffatt had taken her by the hand, but this only brought more emotion to Nancy; this was a motherly touch – the sort she would soon be giving – but to feel it herself was such a beautiful thing. 'Nancy, you're scared. Why are you scared?'

Nancy held herself rigidly. She didn't *want* to be scared. It was so unlike her to feel fear or trepidation. Ordinarily, she was the one who rushed headlong into the things that she wanted. The one who made things happen. Being afraid was like standing on unfamiliar ground.

'What does Raymond think?'

Nancy shook her head, ruefully. 'I haven't told him, not yet.'

Mrs Moffatt almost recoiled – not simply at the notion, but at the strangeness that underpinned it. Nancy and Raymond were knotted together; what one knew, the other knew. They'd been oceans apart in their relationship and marriage, but they'd still been bound, one to the other. 'What's happened, Nancy? What are you keeping from me?'

So she told her everything, everything she'd told Vivienne and more: how she was quite certain it wouldn't happen so quickly, not with the way Raymond had been; how he was distant from her, even when they were in the same room; how he'd nearly perished and perished again, forcing himself out on patrol each night. And then – because it was Mrs Moffatt, and Mrs Moffatt could hear anything without blanching, she whispered, 'I don't want to be like Vivienne, Emmeline. Alone with my baby, hiding under the stairs, waiting for the bombs to come down. By Christmas, Raymond will be back with his unit. Chances are, he'll be in North Africa when our baby is born. There's every chance he won't come home – just like Artie.' She stopped. 'How can I be alone, Emmeline? I couldn't work. No husband, a child that depends on me ...'

'Now, listen here,' said Mrs Moffatt, and gripped her more firmly by the hand. 'A working mother's not unheard of. There are widows out there, too many to mention. Poor girls whose husbands have run off and left them to fend for themselves.' Mrs Moffatt's mind whirled back in time – to when that had been her, unwed and with child, the Sisters taking her baby away, not to be seen for more than thirty long years. 'There are ways. There have to be. The world is changing. War changes everything. But listen to me, Nancy – you're not there yet. Raymond's brother gave his life to defend this country – but it doesn't mean Raymond's going to do the same. That's the picture you've got to hold in your head.' She paused. 'You have to tell him, Nancy. You know that, in your heart, don't you?'

'I've tried to. But he's so swept up in his patrols. It's taking every piece of him. I got back, one morning, determined I'd tell him – but he'd brought someone home from his patrol that night. She'd been bombed out, needed a place to stay.' Nancy thought, again, of Cathy Everly standing there in her nightdress, Nancy's old pin in her hair. That had been the pin Nancy wore on her wedding day; the one her mother wore, when she married Nancy's father. 'Every time I want to tell him, something gets in the way.'

'It's your head,' said Mrs Moffatt. 'That's what's in the way, Nancy. Your thoughts and fears – they're clogging you up, like hairs in a drain.'

Nancy smiled for the first time that morning. Hairs in a drain: only a woman who'd spent her life scrubbing out the bathtubs of the feted and wealthy could come up with an image like this.

There were footsteps in the lounge, the doors opening as the first chambermaids began to arrive for the breakfast meeting. Mrs Moffatt's eyes turned wide with realisation – and, announcing, 'We're running late, girls, you'll have to muck in!', she bustled out of the office, across the lounge, and started gathering up the papers she'd left behind. She was happily tossing them all into the office bin when Nancy, who had rushed out to join the girls laying the table, saw one ball of paper still lying on the floor. While Rosa and the rest flurried around her, she whisked it up and took it back to the office.

She was about to drop it in the bin when she saw the words, 'Dear Mr Adams,' scribbled out at the top of the page, 'Dearest Archie' written in their place.

The Housekeeping Lounge was now a hubbub of activity, as the girls crashed about, laying the table, sorting out the toast racks, pouring out jugs of milk and cream. But Nancy, sensing something else in the air, pushed the office door half-closed and said, 'Emmeline?'

Mrs Moffatt saw what was in Nancy's hands. Quickly, she snatched it away and buried it in the bin. 'Oh, dear, it's nothing

– just me being an old fool. Well, I've hardly been sleeping either, Nancy. The difference is – I'm not growing a child…'

Guilt was coursing through Nancy: she'd walked into the Housekeeping Lounge this morning and opened her heart, and in doing so she'd made Mrs Moffatt snuff something else out, something she'd been doing for herself. 'Emmeline, I had no idea you were in the middle of something personal. I thought – rotas, or staffing, or advertisements. And here I am, leaning on you again!' To Nancy, it always felt better when there was somebody else she could help; at least, now, she felt galvanised; at least, now, there might be straightforward answers. 'Emmeline, what's happened?'

'Oh, it's nothing, Nancy, nothing you need to waste a second thinking about.'

Nancy made certain the door was closed, with nobody listening from the other side, and turned on her heel. 'You've spent all morning listening to me, Emmeline. Let me listen to you for once.'

Mrs Moffatt sank into one of the armchairs. After a second, Nancy sank into the one beside her. The temptation to take her hand, just as Mrs Moffatt had taken hers, was strong. She resisted it for only a moment.

'It's Archie,' Nancy ventured. 'Something's happened with Archie.'

That might have been the only combination of words that could make Mrs Moffatt smile. A wearied smile it might have been, but at least it was a smile. 'Oh, Nancy, that's exactly what *hasn't* happened.'

'What do you mean?'

'Nothing, Nancy. Nothing's happened with Archie – and that's… that's what I was writing to him about. I can't seem to find the words, every time he comes here for a cup of tea. I've hovered around the backstage doors, down at the Grand, but I've never found the courage to go in.' She shook her head, wearily. 'But it seems like I can't find the words to write to him either. I've been trying for weeks.'

Nancy knew, of course. She knew the warmth between them, the friendly looks, the way Mrs Moffatt had come to rely on his regular stop-ins to the Housekeeping Office as something by which to measure her day. But Mrs Moffatt's affection for Archie Adams had never been spoken about like this, not in terms as clear as day. It had always hung in the air, a topic of chaste gossip for the chambermaids – and yet, here it was, bringing tears – of frustration? – to Mrs Moffatt's eyes.

'Do you love him, Emmeline?'

Mrs Moffatt rolled her eyes. 'I'm nearly sixty years old.'

Nancy said, 'And?'

'And I ought to know better!'

Yes, thought Nancy, it really was frustration – frustration with herself. 'What's age to do with this?' she said – and, yes, it truly was better to think about somebody else and their heartaches; she'd been spending too much time thinking about her own conflict, her child, Raymond, catastrophising about the future. This, at least, was something to get lost in – something she could try and fix. 'Emmeline, every day you sit in here with one of the girls and their problems. You pour them tea and give them barley sugars and you help them see things straight. Well, let me do the same for you.'

There'd already been tea, but Nancy marched to Mrs Moffatt's desk drawer, produced a handful of barley sugars, and started unwrapping the wax papers. 'You want to tell him how you feel. You want things to change between you.'

'It's Malcolm who got my mind whirling. He's in love, Nancy. A WVS girl, from out on the airbase. I haven't met her yet, but he's found somebody, somebody he wants to spend the rest of his days with. Isn't that the most wonderful thing?' She trembled as she popped a barley sugar into her mouth. 'So, you see, it's him who got me thinking about it. He's up in those skies, night after night – and every time he gets into that cockpit, he doesn't know if he's coming back safely to the airbase, or if he's plunging out of the sky.' Her voice had become shrill; she took a breath to steady herself. 'He said he's just going to seize it, live his life according to his heart, for as long as he's got. Could be fifty years. Or maybe he'll die tonight—'

'Emmeline,' Nancy said, 'he won't die tonight' – and, as she said the words, she heard the hypocrisy in them. She heard the lie. Raymond left every evening, and the same fear infected her; how much worse would it be, to know he was soaring above the rooftops, dogfighting the enemy?

'So I got thinking,' Mrs Moffatt went on, 'and I worked it out, just the same as I'd work out a rota or the best route through the hotel. How many weeks do you think we each have on God's green Earth, Nancy?'

'I'm not sure I understand…'

'If we're lucky enough to live to eighty years of age, we scarcely have four thousand Sundays. Four thousand Saturday nights. And I've already pottered through three thousand of them. That's one thousand Sunday mornings left, if God gives me the time. Twenty summers. Twenty more times I'll watch the leaves turning russet and red out on Berkeley Square. Twenty more times I'll hoist the Norwegian Fir Tree in the reception hall for Christmas.'

Nancy couldn't help but smile; she truly believed, with every fibre of her being, that Mrs Moffatt would be running the Housekeeping department until the day she passed on, soundly in her sleep.

'The first part of my life was rather full, Nancy. I had Malcolm at such a young age. Lost him too. I was married to my Jack, and the Great War took that life away from me. But what have I done since then? I've ... worked. And I've pottered.'

'You've helped hundreds of girls find their way in the world.'

Mrs Moffatt nodded fiercely – because, of course, this was the achievement which had given so much worth to her life.

'I know, I know ... but what have I done for *me*?'

Mrs Moffatt had barely been able to utter the words. It seemed such a sacrilege, to be thinking of herself.

'It hasn't been the same at the hotel, not since Maynard Charles left.' Maynard Charles, the old Hotel Director, had counted Mrs Moffatt among his closest friends; she'd practically been a sister to him. 'But Archie and I ... I want more, Nancy. This war just makes it feel like life's speeding up. Like the hours are ticking down. Not just for Malcolm and everyone else at his airbase. Not just if you're in a Spitfire, hurtling through the sky every night. For the rest of us too. For *me*.'

'Then you have to tell him.'

The irony was lost on neither of them – both with secrets they knew they could not keep from the men that they loved, both stuck in traps their own minds had concocted.

At last, Mrs Moffatt said, 'Do you know, I used to think that men and women could be friends. Just close friends, caring and loving – and without a hint of romance. But I see it for what it is now: it was just me and my fears, pushing it away, denying my own heart – and all because I couldn't bear the thought of being hurt. I truly thought it was better to live without love than take the risk. But Archie's never been just my friend. I understand that now.' She stopped; some misty look had come over Nancy, a look Mrs Moffatt didn't quite understand. 'What do you think, Nancy? Is it possible he thinks we're just friends too? Can a man and a woman ever really be friends?'

Nancy was still lost in her reverie. Something Mrs Moffatt had said had cast her back in time – and now she was standing in her kitchen door, looking down the hall at Cathy Everly, jet-black hair bouncing around the collar of Nancy's nightdress, her mother's pin sparkling in her hair.

'I think you just *know* when it's more than friendship,' she said, feeling her way with the worry forming in her own mind. 'It's in the air when it's love, isn't it? It feels … different, somehow.' She paused. Yes, she thought, you'd just *feel* it, when something had changed. 'Emmeline, if it's love, *real* love, he'll be feeling it too. There's every chance Archie has dozens of these letters, screwed up and shredded, as well. But it takes one of you to break the silence. Will you do it, Emmeline? Will it be you?'

Mrs Moffatt sucked on her barley sugar. 'I will,' she said, with a sudden flourish of certainty.

'I don't think love's something we do,' said Nancy, 'I think it's something that happens to us. It comes from above. When it touches two people, that's when lives get changed – that's when worlds get built …'

The landlady was knocking at the door, but in the apartment, the music was playing. It was one of his favourite records – he'd played it for her that time he invited her, with hardly any prompting at all, back to his house – so now it was one of her favourite records as well. Cab Calloway. He was an American musician, and this number – 'Hep Hep, the Jumping Jive' – one of his most triumphant recordings. In what little space there was, she danced around the room, her eyes on the framed picture on the mantel.

It was only when the landlady's knocking became too insistent that she went to the door.

The landlady, a beady-eyed shrew of a woman, prodded a finger in her breast and said, 'The sun's hardly come up. I can't be having music this loud when I'm digesting my eggs. How many times have I told you about my constitution?'

'Oh, Mrs Yorke,' she said, Cab Calloway still filling the air around her, 'we all have to live.'

'Live? *Live?* Turn it down this moment, or I'll have my son show you the door.'

She jived back across the room, to lift the needle from the gramophone.

'Mrs Yorke, can't you see? I've been out all night, out in the storm – but I'm alive and I'm happy and …'

'You've lost your marbles.'

'Oh no,' she smiled. 'It isn't that, Mrs Yorke. It's because – well, we're in love.'

And she stepped back from the hearth, like a stage magician revealing his act. There, on the mantel, lit up by the flickering flames from below, was the picture of Raymond de Guise: black hair, broad shoulders, debonair in his evening wear.

'Oh, Mrs Yorke,' she said, with a peculiar smile, 'it's a mad, mad world.'

Chapter Fifteen

It was difficult to imagine a life without music.

The demonstration dances were done, the dancers dispersed, the musicians already on their way out of the Buckingham. Some of them had taken other jobs since war was declared; the Orchestra was made up, now, of veteran players, old enough to have avoided the call-up to war – but not so old they couldn't lend a hand in the Civic Defence, manning telephones, walking patrols, or protecting the blackout, the barracks, the barrage balloons. But Archie Adams remained true to his piano alone. In the rehearsal studio behind the Grand, he sat at the keys and allowed his fingers to roll up the octaves. Something spirited, he decided; something that sounded like a coming storm – only, not the storms that ravaged London each night, but a storm of colour and wild abandon. That would be the thing to set his heart free. He'd felt it in a cage these last weeks. He needed to unlock the door.

And yet, when his fingers reached for a chord, they found only a minor key – and all of a sudden, his mind was reaching out into the infinite possibilities of his Orchestra, constructing a melancholy riot of trumpets and trombone, percussion and soaring, mournful sax.

Archie opened his palms and let them sprawl, discordant,

across the piano. No, he thought, a minor key wouldn't do for today. He didn't want the music to follow *him*; he wanted to be the one following the music, to ride it up from this knotted feeling that had been dominating him so much and into a sky filled with colour and light.

Why, then, was the only thing that came out of his fingers so sombre? It had been all right during the demonstrations; then, at least, he'd had his Orchestra with him – to steer the ship in the right direction, to correct the strange courses of his heart. Here, alone, he seemed to be losing touch with the music he wanted to create. It was like reaching for an apple on a high branch, being able to touch it with your fingers but not quite grasp it. If he was to compose a song now, he would have to call it the 'Maudlin Waltz'.

He was about to hang his head – but, of course, that wouldn't do. Archie Adams was not the kind of man to hang his head. Some bandleaders were given to overwrought fits of emotion – they said it was what made their music so memorable – but Archie was known for his statesmanlike calm; it was only in his music and performance that he ever let his emotion pour out. And, at the end of the day, wasn't that what music was for? As a way of channelling the wild, unbridled passions that could define a man? Why did he have any need to let his feelings out any other way?

Only when the music died...

Archie flurried up from his piano stool. No, he thought, there *was* another way to unknot whatever it was solidifying in his breast. A cup of tea, some barley sugars, a piece of shortbread – and a long, meandering chat about the day-to-day nothings of life. That was as good as any music to make you step out of the world for half an hour; to forget the coming of night, and all the ruin it might bring.

He had gone three strides across the rehearsal floor before another sinking feeling hit him. By God, he was behaving like a child – and he, an esteemed gentleman of fifty-three years of age. A man ought to have left wild somersaulting feelings like this behind long ago. And *of course* a visit to the Housekeeping Lounge for tea with Mrs Moffatt wasn't going to cure this feeling keeping him and the music apart.

How could it?

He turned back. The ebony and ivory keys of his piano seemed, suddenly, to be grinning at him with a mouth full of cankers and rot. That was such an absurd image that he almost laughed out loud. The piano was his friend. His lifelong companion. By God, he'd even found a way to play during his stay at a field hospital near Arras, back during the Great War. They'd sent him to a local farmhouse during his recovery, to free up a bed for the next poor soul being ferried back from the Front, and there he'd tickled the keys of an ancient upright owned by the grandfather of the farm. Music had been a restorative back then, just the thing to take him out of the hell that was Flanders. 'And you'll do the same now, old friend. No minor chords. None of that flat, melancholy nonsense. Something bombastic. Something,' he declared, for an idea had hit him out of the blue, 'that we'll play at One Grand Night. The Archie Adams' Orchestra's next greatest hit.' He spun round as he skipped back to the piano stool, reaching out as if he might pluck a title for this new composition out of the air. 'I have it! *This Grand Life!*'

A little cough, somewhere behind him, plucked him out of this reverie. Archie Adams turned round, and discovered that – at some point – he had stopped being the only one in the rehearsal studio.

Mathilde Bourchier had stepped through the doors, and there she stood, quietly studying him, as if she had something to say.

Archie had never quite *understood* Mathilde. She'd come to the ballroom two years before, when Hélène Marchmont and Raymond de Guise were still in their pomp, and at first she'd seemed quiet, studious, hanging off every word Hélène used to say. In the last year, however, he thought he'd detected some sort of tension in her. Hardly surprising, when the newspapers narrated the fall of Europe and, every night, the war was being fought above the rooftops where you slept. Mathilde had always seemed made for the ballroom, but in the last few months, she seemed somehow like a piano key that could no longer be finely tuned. When it was played as part of a bombastic sequence of chords, it sounded good enough; but when the refrain was more delicate and each note stood out, there was no mistaking that it wasn't quite *right*.

She wasn't quite right as she stood there now. Archie could feel it.

Over the years, he'd had to talk to various musicians who felt the same. Music and dance were two arts inseparably intertwined. There'd been a saxophonist, Louis Kildare, who played with the Orchestra for years – gone, now, of course, like so many other young men to the war – and, one summer, he'd lost his grasp on the music he loved so much. There'd been a trumpeter, once, whose passion for the instrument died on the day he lost his dear father. Music and the soul, they grew out of each other – and Archie knew it was the same for dance.

'Mathilde, dear, I didn't hear you come in.'

'I'm sorry, Mr Adams. The truth is, I didn't actually know anyone was here. I couldn't hear you playing.'

Archie wondered just how long he'd been in his own world, trying to spirit up a tune.

'Did you want to dance?' Archie asked. 'Is that it?'

Mathilde shrugged her shoulders. 'Oh, Mr Adams, I've hardly

ever wanted to dance these last few days. I don't know what it is. It's something inside me, something I can't put my finger on.' She wandered a little further into the room. Archie couldn't help but wonder if some of this despondency was Mathilde's natural dramatic flair, for she certainly seemed to be putting on an act. Or perhaps this was the act she'd been performing all these days *slipping*? Perhaps the mask of outward calm and joie-de-vivre she'd been wearing for so long had grown threadbare, revealing the unsettledness within? Archie knew how that could feel, now more than ever. 'I suppose I *could* dance a little. Would you play?'

The idea appealed to Archie immediately. He'd been sitting here, hovering between his 'Maudlin Waltz' and the idea of 'This Grand Life!' and getting nowhere. But if his focus was on Mathilde, if he was sitting at his piano in aid of somebody else, perhaps that was the distraction he needed.

He settled back on the piano stool, then started up with a simple waltz, accenting the first beat of the bar, rolling his fingers up and down the keys.

Behind him, Mathilde started to step forward, then to the side, then back again, arms outstretched as if in the arms of some imaginary dancer. For the first time that day, Archie smiled. Yes, at least his fingers worked when he was playing for somebody else. Emmeline Moffatt would know this feeling – that feeling of being ready, willing and able to do anything for somebody else, but never quite finding the courage to do it for oneself.

No, he thought, *don't dream of Emmeline, not now…*

Mathilde looked courtly, dancing with her ghost. Archie could only imagine who she was picturing in her arms, for she was surely holding somebody in her imagination. Marcus Arbuthnot, no doubt. All the young dancers wanted to step out with the King of the Grand. Archie had often felt sad for Mathilde, that she'd never had the chance to dance with Raymond after

Hélène's departure from the Grand. That was what she had been being schooled for; that had been the path lain out. And yet, if there was anything to learn from the last twelve months, it was that the course of human history does not submit easily to rigid design. History, he decided, was very much like music, in that respect. Sometimes, it simply took flight.

His fingers leapt and darted, driving the waltz to some new urgency.

And inside he felt the sweetest release.

Here came the music now...

Mathilde felt the waltz move into another gear, and allowed her feet to carry her onward. Archie probably thought she was dreamily imagining dancing with Marcus Arbuthnot – or even swooning over the idea that she might get to dance with Raymond de Guise on One Grand Night – but nothing could have been further from the truth. The thing that dominated her thoughts was not a man at all: it was the question of how devious a dancer she could truly become.

She'd come into the studio, fully aware that Mr Adams was here – for she'd watched him wend his way in after the demonstrations, and had been lingering outside ever since, trying to find the courage to follow. Ever since that meeting with Marcus in the Grand, when she'd tried to lever open the secret of those missing years, the shame of what she'd been trying to do had niggled at her. This came as no great surprise, for Mathilde had never been tasked with something quite as poisonous as this – but she would have been lying, too, if she hadn't admitted that she felt some frisson of intrigue. The riddle of Marcus Arbuthnot had been preying on her day and night, tantalising enough even without the prize she'd been promised.

And now ... *Archie Adams.*

It would not be like deceiving him. Not really. Mathilde had never had anything but the highest regard for Mr Adams – and, even now, as he geed her on from the piano, his gentle words of encouragement half-drowned by the elegant music he was concocting, she felt nothing but warmth. She didn't think he'd find anything untoward in the questions she wanted to ask. To Mr Adams, it would just be reminiscing about times past. If he happened to let slip some information that might lead her one step closer to the truth – well, that simply couldn't be helped.

'Mr Adams,' she said, and promptly stopped her waltzing.

At the piano, Archie's fingers came to a halt. He looked round. 'Is it helping, Mathilde? To free up the heart a little? To free up the soul?'

Here was her moment.

Pointedly, Mathilde shrugged.

'Tell me, Mathilde – what's the song you're singing, in *there?*' Archie had turned round on his piano stool, to indicate her heart. 'It's what I tell my musicians. When they're just not right, when they're out of sync, when things just aren't *feeling* good … what's the song they're singing? You see – and call me a sentimental old fool if you like, Mathilde, because that's what I am – but I believe we're singing to ourselves all of our lives. Somewhere inside us, it's buzzing away, that song. Sometimes it's in a minor key …' His fingers fell to the keyboard, to run along an A minor scale. 'Or sometimes it's bright and major.' And now came G major 13. 'Bach called it the happiest chord, but sometimes I prefer a …' And his hands bounced out a simple turnaround in C. 'My point is, if we listen to ourselves closely enough, we can *choose* which song we sing. Or, in your case, my dear, the steps we dance.'

Mathilde wasn't sure why, but she had the distinct feeling that this heartening lecture was not meant entirely for her – as if Archie was talking his way out of some knotted feeling of his own. Regardless, she pressed on: 'Mr Arbuthnot says that lots of dancers start feeling this way. He said there was a time when you and he worked together and one of his dancers felt the same. 1929, he said, just before the Buckingham opened the Grand...'

Archie thought for but a moment; then his whiskers parted, to reveal a sentimental smile. 'It was the first time I met Mr Arbuthnot. My Orchestra were touring. Two weeks in a ballroom in Brighton, as I recall, for the competitions down there. It's strange, is it not, how small the worlds of ballroom and dance truly are.'

'Marcus said it wasn't a dance problem she had. That it was an affair of the heart.'

Archie froze. 'Well, I'm sure I didn't pry into the young lady's private affairs. My talents have always been with the piano. I'm afraid affairs of the heart are quite uncommon for me, and...'

He had started blathering; Mathilde was almost certain she could see him flushing red – cool, statesmanlike Archie Adams, hot around the collar. He didn't look quite as pink even in the middle of his Orchestra's most frenetic numbers.

Mathilde said, 'It isn't an affair of the heart, not for me.'

'I'm afraid I...'

Mathilde could have kicked herself; this conversation had somehow got tangled. It wasn't heading where she had meant it to go at all – and, not for the first time, Mathilde wondered if she was quite as devious as this scheme demanded. Then she looked at Archie again. She'd stumbled on some unseen emotion, she was certain – as if the song Archie Adams was singing to himself was itself off-key – and perhaps she would have gently asked him about it, seeking to help the man who gave so much of his heart to others, if only the more pressing matter of Marcus's disgrace hadn't been at hand. 'Mr Arbuthnot had his own time away from dance, didn't he?'

Archie said, 'I believe he left the ballroom, once upon a time – but he's here now, that's the important thing. That's just the thing this hotel needs, a man of his calibre. Mathilde, if you're fearing for the ballroom, know that we're all nervous too. But what else is there to do, but dance on? Mr Arbuthnot isn't going anywhere. The Grand will continue to thrive. You have a place here too. We'll get through this together.'

This wasn't quite where Mathilde had envisaged the conversation going either, but somehow it seemed right. 'But if Mr Arbuthnot's heart can give up on dancing – even if just for a couple of years? If someone that successful can turn away from the ballroom, what does that say about the rest of us?'

'I'm sure Marcus had his reasons.'

Mathilde seized her moment, striding forward to close the gap between herself and Archie. 'Do you know what they were? I mean, if you met Mr Arbuthnot just before he left … you and he were friends?'

'For a time.'

'And was he very different back then?'

Archie screwed his eyes at Mathilde, as if trying to understand why she needed to know.

'I just need to know I'm not *finished*,' Mathilde said.

The shame hit her when Archie stood, left his piano stool – and came to stand before her, one hand clasping her shoulder like a father. She knew he would not fold his arms around her, for Archie Adams was far too gentlemanly for that – but something in the gesture made her think of the father she'd never truly had. And no sooner had she thought of that, then the guilt at the deception she was perpetrating bit even harder. Indeed, so strong was the shame that she might have turned tail and fled, forgotten about the enterprise altogether, if only Archie hadn't suddenly said, 'I have some photographs of that old time, if you'd like to see? Something to restore the faith? Mathilde, we all have ups and downs in our careers. Ups and downs in our lives too, of course. The question is whether we rise to them, or whether we get washed away. Come with me, let me show you how two old hands did it.'

She didn't have to follow him far. Mr Adams kept a small property off Lincoln's Inn fields, but everybody knew that his true home was here at the hotel – and it was here that he kept his most treasured possessions. In the dressing room, at the bottom of his cupboard – beneath sheaves of music, and the boxes where he kept his old compositions – was another box, a tea chest meant for travellers. It was this that he drew out for Mathilde to see.

'My first bow tie,' he said, withdrawing a jet-black ribbon and holding it to his collar. Archie had worn bow ties ever since his earliest days as an entertainer; to see him without one would have been like seeing a man stripped naked. 'A card from my first bandleader.' It was a simple postcard, and on it a simple message of pride and good luck – but evidently it meant the world to Archie. 'And here, my photograph album.'

It was well-thumbed, which meant that Archie – who, everybody knew, was given to sentimentality, for what good musician is not? – had often dipped into these memories, but the particular photograph album he drew out, with its burgundy cover and gold lettering, had gathered some dust across the years. Perhaps Archie had not thumbed through this particular item in some time.

'Here we are,' he said, revealing pages of black-and-white images. Most of these pictures seemed to have been taken in a ballroom with vaulted arches – smaller than the Grand, not quite as polished or ostentatious, but with its own venerable charm. 'The Brighton Ballroom,' Archie began, wistfully, '1929. I'd been leading my Orchestra for four years by then. Marcus, of course, had been tutoring much longer. There he is, right there. Do you recognise us, Mathilde?'

They'd changed in the decade since, but not beyond recognition. And the thing that struck Mathilde, as she gazed at these photographs, was that they had got to live their lives in exactly the way they wanted; they had thrown themselves into their hearts' desires, indulged the passions of their youths – and, in that way, directed the courses of their own lives. For a time, she was lost in the photographs, thinking of how magical that was – for how many of us truly get to spend our lives pursuing the thing that makes us happiest? – but, some time later, still gazing at pictures of Archie and Marcus in that different, bygone time, she started to think how *unfair* it was that everybody else had to watch from the side-lines, that good, perfectly talented people got shuffled to one side so that a paltry few could shine.

She was so lost in this thought that she didn't notice, until Archie was trying to take the album back, that there was another figure lurking in the background of one particular photograph. There she was, brooding over the charmed life of Marcus Arbuthnot – a man, it seemed, who'd never known failure, a man who never knew what it felt like to be second best – and giving in to that feeling of injustice and *spite* (yes, she could acknowledge it was spite), when she saw another face peering at her from the corner.

'Oh,' said Mathilde. 'Oh.'

'Mathilde?' ventured Archie.

'Oh, it's nothing,' Mathilde began – but, of course, it changed everything. Because that face staring back at her, that face captured in the corner of the frame, was one she hadn't looked upon in four long years, but one which still seemed to dog her every step. And if she'd been there, back then – in the same ballrooms, around the same competitions – then that meant she might know something about Marcus Arbuthnot that Archie did not.

Mathilde didn't like the road these thoughts were leading her down, but there was no refuting the logic of the idea. Because this person was exactly the type to have revelled in the gossip and the whispers, exactly the type who would have delighted in every little rumour, who would have taken pleasure in the disappearance or demise of one of her old competitors in the ballroom scene.

'Mathilde,' Archie ventured, 'you look like you've seen a ghost.'

'Not quite,' said Mathilde.

The sick feeling was already rising in her gorge, because she knew, suddenly, what she was going to have to do.

She was going to have to pay this woman a visit.

Her mother.

After all these years, she was going to have to speak with her mother, Camille.

After she was gone, Archie tidied his things away and returned to his baby grand practise piano. This time, when he spread his fingers across the keys, the music came more easily. Perhaps it was only that he'd stepped away for a time, or that he'd listened to Mathilde spilling her woes. Or perhaps – just perhaps – it was that advice he'd given her. It was advice his first bandleader had given him, many long years ago. 'We each have our own songs, Archie,' he'd said. Alexander Elliot had known more than a little about how to manage an orchestra; he'd known more than a little about how to manage a heart as well. 'We're singing them all our lives. Sometimes, we just need to listen. And, well, if the song's getting too gloomy, if it's getting too slow or bogged-down or repetitive – well, *we're* the musicians; *we* get to decide where the song will go. Sometimes, you don't want to listen to a funeral hymn. Sometimes you want some joy. So make the song joyful. Reach for the music. You know how to do it with an orchestra, Archie, but that's the easy part. The harder part is doing it with a life.'

It sounded so simple. Change a life in the same way you changed a song. He let the piano show him how, starting with something sombre and reflective, then rolling up into 'He's Got Swing'. Then he smiled.

Could it be that easy in life?

Could you really just change your own song?

Or was that a young man's game?

All at once, he decided he would try. He picked himself up, marched across the studio and out, across the black-and-white chequers of the reception hall, through the winding hallways of Housekeeping – until, at last, he had reached the door of the Housekeeping Lounge itself.

He was about to knock when something shifted inside him. The song, he told himself – it was all off-key, all out of time.

Just like his heart.

How could a musician's heart be keeping such syncopated time?

It was Archie's good fortune that nobody came to the Housekeeping door. If it had drawn back and Emmeline Moffatt had been standing there, there was every chance the song in his heart would just stop – and all that would remain was the unending silence of a ruined friendship, a ruined life. No, it was much better that his feet were taking flight; much better that his song was carrying him back to that space behind the Grand Ballroom and the piano that was waiting.

By the time he sat down again, the rhythm of his heart had

steadied. By God, he'd been a fool. He'd forgotten it all, forgotten the simple, singular truth that all the best improvising musicians knew: that a song was a kind of controlled chaos, that when a song started soaring it was unstoppable; that, once you'd played those first few bars and thrown yourself into the music, there was no knowing where it might go.

Archie mopped his brow and straightened his bow tie.

Just like life, he thought, ruefully, and started to play.

Chapter Sixteen

The thought had come to him in the creeping November dark, that, the longer he left it, the more difficult it was going to be. It was just the same as speaking to Mary-Louise: the longer the silence went on between them, the more difficult it was to even think about looking her in the eye again. That was why Billy Brogan knew: with every delivery he made to Ken, the more perilous the trap in which he was pinned. This afternoon, for the third time, he'd made up a package – this time containing six bottles of fine white wine, a Parisian vintage from 1928, three wheels of Blackjack's Fine Lancashire Cheddar, and a French chicken liver pâté – that left the hotel post room by the delivery doors. As far as the ledger books at the Buckingham Hotel showed, it would be nothing more notable or mysterious than a member of the Norwegian ministry delivering a parcel to a Cotswolds country estate; only Billy Brogan would ever know where that package was truly delivered.

But it could not go on.

He'd spent long nights wracking his brain for some way out of his predicament. In his lowest moment, playing backgammon with Frank across his parents' dining table while Annie fluttered back and forth, pontificating about the proper way to address a duchess at the Buckingham Hotel, he'd thought about marching (as if he could even march!) up to Camden and confronting Ken. He was a soldier, damn it. He'd fought in France. He hadn't come home to get ensnared in some filthy profiteer's little swindle. He hadn't come home to line the pockets of some racketeer while good men perished in the service of their country. Artie Cohen – now there had been a good man. Artie had done his share of criminal things. He'd even served a stretch in Pentonville – all for robbing some railway sleepers, or breaking into a rich man's townhouse. Billy couldn't remember which because it hardly mattered: Artie had made his mistakes, served his time, then lifted his head proudly and gone on to greater things. The very greatest, as far as Billy was concerned. And here was he, Billy Brogan, suddenly the servant to some lousy spiv.

He wished Artie was here now. Artie would have known what to say to a man like Ken. Artie would have followed Billy north to Camden, then given him a piece of his mind. Well, Artie had been like that. He had the charm, but he had the wolf in him as well. He had the devil.

And it was in thinking about Artie Cohen that Billy had realised there was one other person he could turn to for help. One other person who'd been there with him, on the beaches at Dunkirk, then returned to a changing world.

That was why he was levering himself along Blomfield Road in Maida Vale, searching out for the gate that read 'No. 18'. That was why he was rehearsing the words, 'Raymond, I need your help.'

He hadn't got there before the sirens started to sound.

Inside the warm, cosy confines of No 18. Blomfield Road, Nancy was summoning what reserves of strength she had left, after a long day working the suites at the Buckingham – a day that felt even longer now that she had to shadow Annie Brogan's every move – and making Raymond a light supper of potted ham and boiled eggs. The smell of the eggs as they boiled was enough to turn Nancy's stomach; sensations like this had been getting more and more persistent in the past few days. This morning, she'd looked at herself in the bedroom mirror, and fancied she could see the first signs of her body changing shape, a slight swelling in her belly. That was why she knew she couldn't wait a moment longer.

Raymond had slept the morning away – but, when she returned from the Buckingham, she'd found him proudly polishing his boots by the back door. Every brass button on his overcoat was shined to perfection. Now, ready and dressed for his night on the streets, he was sitting at the dining table, diligently reading that morning's edition of *The Times*. Much of the talk, of course, was of the ruin being made of London – and of the assault on Coventry which had near razed it to the ground some nights ago. But there was always other news: the British fleet victorious against the Italians in the Mediterranean, Malta besieged and under consistent attack. Raymond's own division had set sail for North Africa, where the attritional battle went on.

Nancy put their plates down and settled opposite him. The thought of eating was nauseating, but she knew she had to do it; now that she was eating for two, it was more important than ever.

'Nancy, sweetheart, thank you,' Raymond said, earnestly, and began to eat.

She liked seeing him like this. It was one of the few moments since his return from France when she truly felt as if she was looking after him. He'd devoured half of his plate before Nancy had touched hers. She quietly moved one of her eggs onto his plate, and he looked quizzical as he cracked its shell.

'You've got that look again, Nancy,' he said, with a smile. Then he reached across the table and took her hand. She could see, once again, that he wasn't wearing his wedding band; it was on the bedside table in the room directly above. 'It's just another night, the same as all the rest. I'll do what I have to do, and I'll be back before dawn.'

Nancy's face had blanched. She wondered why she couldn't just blurt it out, the same as she'd done to Vivienne and Mrs Moffatt. The reason had always seemed slippery – it evaded her every time she tried to pin it down – but at last, across the dining table, it resolved itself: she could count on Mrs Moffatt and Vivienne to say and do the very right things – but, somewhere along the way, she'd lost that faith in Raymond.

Her fingers were curling, turning her hands into fists. This feeling – she hated it with a passion every bit as fierce as she hated the German bombers soaring above. A year ago, perhaps even six short months, she wouldn't have felt like this. It was this war, and what it had already done to Raymond – what it was doing to both of them, right now.

Well, she ought to be stronger than any war. She ought to have faith in the love that they shared. *For better and worse, in good times and bad*. Love was supposed to shine through.

And it occurred to Nancy, then, watching Raymond scrape out the last white of his egg, that perhaps she herself was doing him a disservice. Raymond had never let her down in the past. He'd stood tall and proudly beside her. Perhaps it was Nancy who was the problem – denying him the chance to be the good man she knew him to be, keeping this knowledge from him, the knowledge that would light up his world …

'Raymond, there's something I have to tell you.'

'I know you're afraid. I know it's hard, being alone in the raids. That's why I was thinking – what if Vivienne was to live here, Nancy? Vivienne and Stan, out here with you. Then nobody has to be alone while I'm on patrol.' He paused, and though Nancy tried to start speaking again, she was a fraction of a second too slow before he went on, 'I think it's what Artie would have wanted. The four of us, keeping each other close until all this is over.'

Here was her chance. 'Raymond, it wouldn't just be the four of us.'

He was nonplussed. 'What do you mean?'

'It's five, Raymond.' And, pushing her chair back from the table, she cupped a hand around the belly that was starting to swell. 'I'm going to have a baby.'

There was silence in the room, broken only by the clinking of knife and fork as Raymond set down his cutlery. The next instant, he was on his feet, rushing round the table, and dropping to his knees at her side. Grappling for her hand, and stroking the hair away from her eyes with his other hand, he said, with a breathy whisper, 'How sure are you?'

'I'm sure, Raymond. I've seen Doctor Moore – two times now. There isn't any doubt. You're going to be a father. I'll be a mother, not long after Easter comes.' She clasped his hand and brought it to her belly. 'Raymond, I'm scared.'

'Scared?' He reeled back, with eyes full of amazement. 'Oh Nancy, why would you be afraid?'

She couldn't voice it, not like she wanted to. How could you tell a man: I'm scared you'll die, like so many others are dying, and leave me alone?

'It's just such an uncertain world,' she said – and the relief at his reaction was bringing tears to her eyes. That look of wonder on Raymond's face – it was like he'd been marching through some blasted wasteland, and suddenly come across a garden in full colour. 'To bring a child into all this, when we don't know if there'll be an England. When we don't know what London will look like by Christmas, let alone by the spring when he's born.'

Raymond braced her by the shoulders. 'A spring child,' he declared, 'to renew our hope and faith in everything that's splendid and good. Nancy, why didn't you tell me?'

There was concern in his voice, but it could not keep the smile from his face. God, but it felt good to see Raymond smile. She allowed her head to fall on his shoulder. 'You've been so distant. So consumed. I wasn't sure if you'd...'

She could not say the rest, but she did not need to, because suddenly Raymond said, 'There'll be a world, Nancy. London isn't going to fall – not if I can help it. There are tens of thousands who think the same. If we lose the battle in the skies and they launch an invasion – well, it's like Mr Churchill said, we'll fight them on the beaches, and in the streets – in the ballrooms and the back yards. We'll have a world, you and I – and our child.'

She'd thought Raymond's determination to join the Civil Defence unwise – but hearing him speak like this restored that piece of her that knew it was worthwhile. 'If it's a girl, I was thinking about Eva, after my mother. If it's a boy...'

'Arthur,' Raymond said.

'After your brother,' Nancy replied.

The beauty of it took Raymond in its hold. He reared up, lifting Nancy in his arms and, ignoring the niggling pains that still existed in the aftermath of September's injuries, he whirled her around the room. There, flying around the home they'd made together, Nancy wondered why she'd ever been afraid. Of *course* Raymond would rise out of his despair; of *course* he would come home at the end of every patrol; of *course* he would return, as soon as the war was over, and fashion this life with her, the life that they had promised.

In the world beyond No. 18 Blomfield Road, the sirens started wailing.

Raymond set Nancy down. With haunted eyes, they looked at the blackouts. The sirens were so familiar, but they still brought death and destruction every night. He squeezed her by the hand. 'To the shelter,' he said.

She was straining on his hand, as if to lead him that way, when she noticed Raymond's boots were fixed to the ground.

'Raymond, aren't you coming?'

Raymond was saved from answering because, in that same moment, there came a rapid, insistent knocking at the door. Nancy felt his fingers detaching from hers; then he marched into the hallway, snuffing the lantern light on the way, and tentatively pulled back the door.

Cringing from the sirens above, there stood Billy Brogan. 'Billy?'

Billy gave a salute – and immediately Raymond reached out and brushed it away. Billy had served for longer in France than either Raymond or Artie; as one of the territorials signed up at the start of that last blessed summer of peace, he'd been among the first sent into France. Raymond might now be a lance corporal, but there was no way he was going to think of Billy as a subordinate.

'Mr de Guise, I'm sorry, I know this isn't a good time.' Together, their eyes turned to the starry vaults above. 'I had to see you. I need your help.'

'Help, Billy?'

That voice belonged to Nancy, standing in the hallway at Raymond's rear. Billy craned round Raymond to see her there. Perhaps he was just imagining it, but there was such a strange expression on her face that he couldn't quite work out if he'd walked in on Raymond and Nancy having some heated argument, or perhaps a tender heart-to-heart.

'I'm sorry, Mrs de Guise. I've picked a rotten moment. Maybe I should—'

'Nonsense, Billy!' cried Nancy, sensing he was about to depart. Then she hustled up the hallway, past Raymond and took Billy by the arm. 'Raymond and I were just about to head out to the shelter out back. Whatever it is that's troubling you, we can talk about it there.'

Billy was uncertain what the new tension was in the hallway. Nancy strained on his arm, but Raymond was unmoving. Then he took a step past Billy, moving towards the doorway. 'Nancy,' he said, 'I've *got* to go.'

Billy, still oblivious to what conversations had gone on before he rapped at the door, watched Nancy's face blanche. 'Raymond, please – not tonight. Not after everything we just said.' *Not*, she thought, *after everything I've just felt.* 'It isn't right. They'll fend for themselves tonight. It's just one night.'

Raymond's face had hardened. 'Nobody fends for themselves, Nancy, not in war. We fend for each other. Isn't that right, Bill?'

Billy opened his mouth, but only silence came out. Perhaps that was for the best; whatever was going on here was too far from his understanding.

Raymond strode back down the hall, bent down and kissed Nancy on the cheek. This time, there was no mistaking how brittle she seemed as he kissed her. She'd already released Billy's arm, and now she wrapped her own arms around her breast, as if building a barrier to keep Raymond away. Pointedly, she did not kiss him back.

'I made you a promise, Nancy. I'll be back by morning.'

'Just go,' she said and – keeping something else within – hurried along the hallway and into the backyard at the other end.

Billy was left in shell-shocked silence. 'I'm sorry, Mr de Guise. I didn't mean to ...'

Raymond was staring after Nancy, as if in a trance. Then, with a flourish, he seemed to come to some decision. He seized Billy by the arm and together they slipped out into the night. 'You're welcome to go to my shelter, Billy, but ...'

'I need to talk to you, Mr de Guise. I just need to.'

There was fervour in his tone, a different kind of urgency to any Raymond had encountered in France. 'Then march with me, soldier. Tell me everything.'

Though the sirens sounded, Raymond and Billy did not yet hear the sounds of devastation as they picked their way south, through the wide boulevards of Maida Vale, over the railways at Paddington, and into the grand environs north of Hyde Park. There was silence enough, between the sirens, for Billy to tell him all.

And what a sordid story it was. It was only now, giving voice to it in the company of a man he respected as much as any other, that Billy saw what a fool he'd been. 'I thought it was kindness at first,' he tried to explain. 'Kindness from Ken to me – and, well, kindness from me to him as well. Just a helping hand, just a little gesture to say thank you. And for Mary-Louise as well ...'

Raymond, who listened to the full story with compassion, said, 'Do you think she knew all along, Billy?'

It was the question to which he had no answer. 'I want to trust her. I really do.' *I want to believe that what she seems to feel for me is real.* 'But it isn't my concern, not now, not after what Ken said about Annie. Because that's how he's got me trapped. Champagne and silk. Ball gowns and lace. It was never about bacon and butter, not for Ken. He talks about it like it's charity, as if every bad thing he does has a good end to it. But he's feathering his own nest too, Mr de Guise. I know he is. And now, if I don't keep feathering it with him…' He faltered. 'Annie's my sister. I can't have her drawn into it. I should have been cleverer. I should have seen where this was going…'

They were almost at the wardens' office, where Mortimer Bond was waiting. Up above Hyde Park, the barrage balloons loomed, blotting out both the stars and the lights of aircraft aflame.

They stopped on the corner outside the office, where Raymond clasped Billy's shoulder and told him, 'Your heart has been in the right place, Billy – hold on to that.' *You've been a fool, but a good-natured fool – and when was it ever different, with Billy Brogan?* 'Have you thought about the police?'

Billy wrung his hands. 'I can't, Raymond. It would be the end of me.'

Raymond understood this. 'It wouldn't make a difference that you have a good heart, not to the law.' They wouldn't make allowances, not even for his service record: a crime against the system was deemed a crime against every good common Londoner. 'Rationing's there to spread out the suffering,' Raymond ventured. 'But there are men like Ken the whole world over – they find the chinks in the systems, exploit it to their own advantage. I've seen them right here, on the streets of London. Men going into the bombed-out buildings and taking every scrap they can find. You won't believe this, Billy, but I even saw it all over the dancing world. A favour to a judge, a nice bottle of Champagne, a secret withheld. Well,' he heaved a great sigh, 'there's more than one way to win a competition.' He stopped. 'Billy, hold tight. Do what you must – for now. But listen to me: don't take a penny from him in return. If he tries to pay you, don't take it. It will rile him – it always riles men like Ken when you won't let them keep you in their back pocket – but it's critical. When you start taking money from him, you're a profiteer as well. Better to be bullied and enslaved than to be a profiteer...'

'Yes,' said Billy, finding some strength in what Raymond had said, 'yes, Mr de Guise.'

'There's only one way out of this for you, Billy.'

Explosions sounded, somewhere out east. Raymond and Billy looked that way, searching for the sudden columns of smoke above the East End of London, the rose-gold glow of the fires.

'What way, Mr de Guise?'

Raymond had to raise his voice, for suddenly engines were gunning – and from the door of Mortimer Bond's office a stream of wardens erupted and started racing for the trucks that lined the road.

'It isn't just you who has to get out of this, Billy.' Raymond clasped his shoulder again, and looked into his eyes – hoping that, together, they might summon up some of that steadfast, stoic determination they'd somehow found on the beaches at Dunkirk. 'One way or another, Ken's enterprise has to be put to an end.'

Chapter Seventeen

Raymond was still watching Billy as he limped away into the night – the walk from Maida Vale had exhausted the boy; Raymond could see it with every step that he took – when a cry came from the office door. 'Lance Corporal!' There, in the shadowed doorway, stood Mortimer Bond himself, short and dumpy and recognisable by the cigarillo flare between his lips. As Raymond watched, he cupped a hand around it, shielding its light from above.

'Reporting for service, sir!'

Raymond's mind was a whirl as he followed Mortimer Bond into the office. 'They're hitting the docklands with everything they have,' Mortimer was saying, while his telephone trilled and footsteps pounded the building's halls. 'We've calls for back-up flowing through. I'm sending you out east tonight, Lance Corporal. It's where you're needed...' Mortimer Bond's attention was suddenly piqued by footsteps outside the door. Moments later, another ARP warden appeared, dressed in his steel helmet and serge blue overcoat. 'Humphrey – just the man. Lance Corporal de Guise needs a ride to the ops station out east. Room for one more?'

The new warden nodded. 'We're sitting in each other's laps already. One more won't hurt.'

'Then hop to it, lads. It's getting dicey out there.' They were at the door when Mortimer Bond called after them, 'Hang it, I'm coming on this one too. There's nothing this old body can't do that your young ones can.' Then, together, they hustled out of the office.

Raymond had been aboard a good number of transport wagons in France, but none of them quite like this. These were just delivery trucks, postal vans and Morris commercial transports, requisitioned or donated to the cause. All along the road, the vans were loading up with ARP wardens like Raymond, and WVS volunteers from the station on the edge of the park. Engines burst into life and disappeared into the blackness beneath the barrage balloons.

Raymond was clambering up into the van's dark interior, to find a perch among a dozen other ragged souls, when a voice cried out for him further down the row. He whipped his head round. The sharp cones of the searchlights were lighting up the sky above Hyde Park now.

And there was Cathy, hurrying with a crew of WVS girls into another of the waiting vans.

'I thought I'd better join this one, Lance Corporal,' she said. 'I wouldn't want you taking another tumble without me being there to pick you up. One good turn deserves another, after all.'

Raymond looked above – whether to God, or the brave RAF lads scrambling into battle, he did not know. 'Here's hoping luck's with us tonight, Cathy.'

'Oh,' she said, before she disappeared into the wagon, 'you don't need luck, Raymond. You've got me. Stay safe! I'll see you out east.'

Then she was gone, and so was Raymond, into the cramped interior. Soon, the black vistas of Hyde Park were rushing past. Soon, the boarded shop fronts of Oxford Street and the roped-off ruin of John Lewis. In the back of the truck, pressed against each other, the wardens exchanged wearied and stoical glances.

They'd seen this before, thought Raymond, night after night after blasted night.

But something was different in him now. His mind wheeled back. How long had it been since he was crouched at Nancy's side, the marvel of their unborn child sandwiched between them? Less than two hours, he guessed. And here he was, coursing to the epicentre of another disaster, steeling himself for the devastation and danger he'd find at the other end.

For perhaps the first time tonight, he heard her words: 'Raymond, please,' she'd said. 'Not tonight. Not after everything we said.'

It had taken two hours for those words to penetrate him. Two hours for him to see past the course of action he'd been set on and understand that, with the news that he was to become a father, the world had unutterably, irrevocably changed. He shook his head fiercely, as if trying to banish some loose thought. He'd heard Nancy saying those words, but he hadn't listened – not truly, not when it mattered, not when she needed him most of all. And now he was here, in a van hurtling towards disaster, while she was there – alone in the Anderson shelter, alone except for their child growing inside her.

Raymond started shaking.

'Lance Corporal' the warden named Humphrey began. 'Are you well?'

The words lifted Raymond from the crevasse inside him. He couldn't put this right now, not in this exact moment. He was needed here – the other men *needed* him here – and here he was. *Put one foot in front of the other*, he told himself – just the same as he told himself when something wrong-footed him on the dance floor, and he needed to rescue the waltz. *One foot here, and the next foot there. Focus on what's in front of you. It's all you can do.*

The way across London was longer than it ought to be, for more than once the convoy had to fan out in a multitude of diversions, to avoid newly destroyed roads. Consequently, it was almost an hour later when the back of the postal van opened, and Lance Corporal Raymond de Guise stepped out into a landscape of fire and blackened brick.

The other transports were coursing past, following the Whitechapel Road. Raymond turned on the spot, a perfect dancer's pivot. He knew these streets well. They were the streets where he'd been raised, the streets where he and Artie had once roamed. Now that he saw them through the reefs of black smoke, pitted with cauldrons of fire, he felt untethered, ungrounded – unable, somehow, to tell left from right.

He was going to be a father, he told himself.

Nancy was going to have his child.

And here he was, listening to Mortimer Bond begin to bark orders as the other wardens tumbled off the transports and fanned out across the road.

Fire trucks had appeared, vanishing into the smoke up ahead. The wardens already on the ground were organising the new arrivals into bands, then setting out in a compass of different directions, bound for different pockets of the inferno. Raymond was still marvelling at the destruction when, out of the miasma, he heard Mortimer Bond calling his name, 'De Guise is one of our stalwarts – a lance corporal waiting to join his division.' Behind Mortimer, two of the wardens who had already been on the Whitechapel Road appeared out of the dust. 'Round them up, Raymond, every one you can. There's a situation further south.'

'It's the old HJ Packer building,' the warden behind Mortimer explained. 'The damn place caved in, but the bomb hasn't gone off, not yet. We've people trapped inside.'

Though none of them saw it, Raymond's face paled. The HJ Packer building – he'd been there before; in fact, he'd spent his last Christmas Day there on the old factory floor, helping the charity who occupied the property feed the queues that lined up outside. The Daughters of Salvation – his sister-in-law Vivienne's enterprise. The same charitable institution which had brought Vivienne and Artie together. That had given purpose to Artie's life.

'Lance Corporal!' Mortimer Bond boomed. 'Can you hear me?'

Raymond came out of his reverie, lifting his hand in a half-salute. 'Yes, sir!'

'Then follow after! There isn't a second to lose.'

Two dozen ARP wardens took flight, weaving south past houses carved open, roads turned to rubble, around craters where gas and waterworks had been exposed and other Civic Defence volunteers were rushing to prevent further damage being done. It was only as they reached the wooded fringe of Stepney Green itself that Raymond felt he could see beyond the choking dust. Here on the green – where portions of land had been turned to allotments, and the cane wigwams that had been ripe with summer's bounty looked like the totems of a forsaken world – the air was clear.

Across the allotments they came, through the second fringe of trees, and back to the streets. There was less devastation here and, for a time, Raymond was able to believe it was all a mirage. When he looked up, however, the sky above the rooftops was orange. Flames licked the sky. 'It's the docklands,' said Mortimer Bond – who, out of puff, had stopped to count the wardens as they rushed past. 'They haven't been hit like it since September. Come on, de Guise, we've work to do!'

Raymond hustled him along, down one street and up the next – until, down the long, straight barrel of the White Horse Road, they saw the silhouette of what had once been the HJ Packer Building, a crumpled monument of iron girders and fallen masonry ringed in the fires of the docklands beyond.

Raymond had barely fallen into its shadow when another portion of the exterior wall peeled back, devastating the neighbouring building. Wardens and WVS scattered as brick and mortar came down like hail.

'How many have we got inside?' Mortimer Bond puffed, catching up with one of the wardens already on site, Raymond marching in his wake.

'It's hard to know, sir. There's a lady over there says she's part of the team that runs the place. She was one of the first out. According to her, they've been taking in waifs and strays since summer – they turned the basements into shelters for the homeless.'

Raymond turned on the spot. In the glowering dark he could make out a plump woman with wild white hair sitting on the open back of a delivery wagon, a mug of something hot in her hands. Raymond hardly knew the woman, but she'd been there on the day of his brother's wedding. He wracked his memories for her name, and finally it popped into his thoughts: Mary Burdett. It had been Mary who ran the Daughters of Salvation before Vivienne discovered it – Mary who was the stalwart at Vivienne's side as it grew from humble beginnings into the empire it was today.

'Sir,' Raymond declared, 'I'll be right back.'

The WVS had been on site since moments after the first wardens arrived. Raymond bounded over to where they were giving sustenance to the survivors and called out, 'Mrs Burdett?' At the last minute he realised that the WVS girl tending to her was none other than Cathy. Somehow, the van driving the back-up volunteers out east had beaten them to the site. Cathy gave him a meaningful look and squeezed his hand, even as Raymond knelt at Mary's side.

'Mr – Mr Cohen?' Mary stammered, and it was then that Raymond knew she'd been concussed, or else was shell-shocked by the blast; Raymond might have shared a dark, brooding look with his brother, but he hadn't used the name 'Cohen' in half a lifetime. 'Is it you?'

He took off his ARP helmet, revealing himself in full.

'It's Raymond,' he said. 'I'm Vivienne's brother-in-law. Artie was my brother.'

Mary Burdett came to some sudden realisation, and grasped him by the hand. 'Oh, Mr de Guise. It's gone – all gone!'

The hue and cry of wardens in action was filling the road. Raymond looked around.

'They're sending everyone back,' Cathy intervened, over Raymond's shoulder. 'In case it blows.'

'Mary,' Raymond pressed on, the smell of the Bovril she was drinking filling the air between them, 'I need you to remember – how many are in the Daughters tonight?'

Mary shook her head. 'Too many,' she whispered. 'Too many to count. Sixty-eight heads, if I'm right – and then Warren and the girls. The staff, you understand. They were all in the shelters. Only a few of us were above, battening down. We just didn't expect it, Mr de Guise. We didn't expect it to come so soon.'

Raymond reared up. 'Take care of her, Cathy. Get her back from here.' The ambulances had already arrived. Three of them formed a small ring at the end of the road, anticipating the casualties to come.

'What are you going to do?' gasped Cathy, her voice suspended somewhere between fear and indignation.

'I know this place,' said Raymond – and, though a flash of Nancy with her hand cupped around her belly came into his mind, so too did an image of all those trapped souls, sealed underground, waiting for somebody to find them. 'I know where those shelters are. I have to help.'

The doors of the HJ Packer building had been lost in the blast, but at a gaping maw in the southern wall, Mortimer Bond was deep in conversation with another warden. The gap was just about wide enough for two men to stand abreast. Beyond it, the darkness swirled with dust. As he approached, a warden appeared, soot-stained and choking, a limp body in his arms. Raymond knew this face too. As a second warden rushed to help ferry the fallen man away from the ruin, Raymond remembered his name: Warren Peel. He'd been one of the derelicts Vivienne had first been intent on helping, the wayward son of the financier whose later investment had allowed the Daughters to flourish. He'd saved himself from the gutter, risen with the Daughters to do some good in this world – but neither riches, nor honour, were shields against the Luftwaffe's might. He watched as the wardens carried Warren on.

'Sir,' Raymond said, reaching the gap in the brickwork, 'I know this property. I can help.'

'You're better out here, de Guise,' said Bond, chewing his whiskers in place of his cigars. 'Marshal the men – the road needs clearing, and fast, if we're to get the survivors away before this thing blows.'

'Respectfully, sir, there won't *be* any survivors if we aren't quick about this. I can be quick, sir. I can find my way.'

'It's a wreck in there,' the other warden ruefully said, 'my men are in and out, but the back wall's down. It's a mausoleum.'

Raymond drew a breath, filled his breast, and said, 'Let me *try*, sir. What are we here for, if not to try?'

Mortimer Bond and the other warden shared a long, doubtful look. 'The man's got a point,' Bond eventually said. Then he wheeled round. 'Torches!' he exclaimed. 'Get this man a torch!' A small electric light found its way into Raymond's hands. 'No heroics in there, Lance Corporal. If men are dying tonight, don't let it be you.' He whistled, summoning three other wardens, who quickly reached the maw. 'Listen up, you chaps – Lance Corporal de Guise here has knowledge of this property. Stay with him, each man in sight of the other.'

Raymond was the first through the gap in the masonry. Inside, the air was heavy with coarse, dry dust. It took mere seconds for it to coat his lips, his tongue, the insides of his cheeks. Soon, it was riming his eyelashes like hoarfrost – and, the more he rubbed it away, the more he scoured it into his skin.

His torchlight picked out the mountain of fallen brick that used to be the Daughters of Salvation's western wing. The old factory floor's inner partitions were gone. In places, the beds which had, earlier this very evening, housed recovering addicts, or derelicts from the streets, were either crowned in rubble or completely subsumed. Raymond's torch arced across them, and he saw that half the office where Nancy used to come and help Vivienne with the ledgers had been crushed by a falling girder. 'They found the young man in there,' one of the wardens beside him said. 'He hadn't gone to the shelters – he'd stayed with his books.'

It was work that had killed Warren Peel, then. Raymond's heart felt heavy and hot – but at least, now that he was standing near the old office partition, he could imagine the factory floor as it used to be. When Vivienne had first acquired this property, it had been standing empty since the chocolatiers who owned it left London behind. The floor where chocolates had once been mixed, then wrapped and packed, had been an open, rubbly mess, with a flight of rickety stairs leading to offices on a gallery above. All that had changed in the months that followed. Partitions had been raised, to build dormitories and small chambers where the sick and the needy could come. The old kitchens had been refitted and broadened, built big enough for Mary Burdett and her team of young volunteers to chop vegetables, peel potatoes, and make the nourishing soups with which they fed not just the local vagabonds, but every needy soul who came to the doors. And the basements, once full of the clutter of a factory too small for its purpose, had been diligently converted into shelters fit to withstand the fiercest blow.

He closed his eyes, ignoring the grit, and tried to picture it how it had been. Then, opening them to the gloom again, he swung his torch beam around, illuminating a landslide of crushed partitions, ruptured floorboards and brick. Beyond that, he was certain, a staircase led down.

'Where did the bomb land?' he asked.

The wardens swung their own torches around, the light dancing over the mountain of rubble and twisted girder where the west wing had once been.

Raymond exhaled, long and low. 'Well,' he said, darkly, 'at least we're not going to be disturbing it. Come on, boys. Let's dig for their lives.'

'Dig for victory,' snorted one of the others.

Raymond only hoped it was victory they would find at the bottom of that staircase – victory, and not sixty more souls lost to this night of blood and fire.

*

There were survivors in the buildings that bordered the Daughters of Salvation. As the ARP wardens led them out through the ruins, Cathy and her fellow volunteers swept them up, throwing shawls and blankets around their shoulders, then hurried them along the White Horse Road. Some hundred yards away, a cordon had been established. Here sat the mobile WVS canteen.

With her arm around Mary Burdett's shoulder, Cathy hurried down the road, the scream of some Stuka arcing overhead. Every time a reverberation moved through the city, Mary's body seemed to go limp; her tremendous weight fell across Cathy's shoulder, and she had to stand there, frozen in the road, until the terror had passed. 'Quick sharp, Mrs Burdett,' Cathy said, the warmth in her voice giving way to an urgent impatience. 'The sooner we get to the station, the safer you'll be.'

It seemed to take an age to reach the cordon. Mary, who'd already been checked over by one of the ambulance attendants, gravitated towards the mobile canteen – where, soon, she was being revived with another hot Bovril and an oatcake sticky with honey.

'Stay here, Mrs Burdett. You'll be safe with the girls.'

Cathy had turned on her heel, preparing to pass back through the cordon and reapproach the Daughters of Salvation, when one of the other WVS volunteers, a middle-aged lady with the demeanour of a battle-hardened headmistress, said, 'Miss Everly, stay with her, please. The old girl needs a shoulder.'

Cathy's glittering green eyes flitted between Mary Burdett and the ravaged silhouette of the Daughters. 'Mrs Pritchard—'

'There's nothing you can do down there, Miss Everly. You have your job – now hop to it.'

Cathy returned to Mary Burdett's side, touching her shoulder consolingly. Her heart and mind, however, remained fixed on what had become of the old HJ Packer building. 'The shelters,' Cathy ventured, 'will they survive?'

'Those shelters are built to last,' Mary said, nodding fiercely, as if it was important not just to convince Cathy, but to convince herself. 'Everything was reinforced, the moment we knew war was coming. Mr Cohen saw to it himself. Rounded up some of the old lags he used to run around with, gave them some honest work. There wasn't a shoddy thing about it. It was pristine.'

Cathy whispered, 'So they might be alive ...'

'Every last one of them, every last one, except poor Warren. I told that boy he was to follow the rest, get down that staircase – but he wouldn't listen. He just wanted to keep at his work. But what's the point in saving a soul, if we throw ourselves away, Miss? What's the point of that, I ask you?' She stopped. 'Have you ever lost someone you love?'

And Cathy said, with a wistfulness that bordered on reverie, 'I have, Mrs Burdett.'

'Then you'll know how it feels. I've seen too many poor sods slip out of this world. I didn't want to see it of Warren. We helped him, once. He came back from the dead, I tell you – only to perish here, tonight! It doesn't make sense. Just doesn't make sense ...'

Something Mary had said ripped through Cathy. *He came back from the dead – only to perish here, tonight!* And, all of a sudden, she was picturing a dark-haired hero on the beaches at Dunkirk, a last desperate attempt to make it home to those that he loved ...

She wheeled round. Raymond was in the HJ Packer building now, the unexploded bomb somewhere underneath him, breathing in the dust of the dead. 'Mary, I'm sorry, I've got to go.'

This time, she was halfway along the road when she heard the screaming from behind. She turned back. A new face had appeared at the WVS station: a small woman, with rich auburn hair. The woman had thrown her arms around Mary – but now, despite the protestations of the volunteers manning the mobile canteen, she was on her feet again, her legs pumping wildly as she rampaged along the road towards the devastated building.

'Cathy!' came the thunderous voice of Mrs Pritchard. 'Stop her!'

Cathy acted on instinct, reaching out and catching the woman's sleeve as she flew past. The two of them wheeled around each other, like dancers in the middle of the street.

'It's *my* building!' the woman exclaimed, in a strange accent redolent of a brash New Yorker Cathy used to know. 'Let go of me this instant! I'm the director of that establishment!'

Cathy released her hold on the other woman's arm. 'I can't let you go in,' she gasped.

'You can,' the woman declared, 'and you will. You've no right to manhandle me. I came as soon as I heard.'

'Madam, there's an unexploded bomb.'

'Then all the more reason to get those poor souls out of there.'

Cathy looked over the American woman's shoulder. Faces were still watching from the mobile canteen, but yet more survivors from the neighbouring wreckage were streaming out now, and the volunteers at the station were rushing to their aid. And it occurred to Cathy, then, that if she truly wanted to get close to the building, if she *really* intended to be there the moment he came out, if she was going to be any use if the brave fool needed her again, then there was no better way than acting as escort to the charity's proprietress.

Mrs Pritchard's voice still boomed along the road – but, emboldened, Cathy turned a deaf ear to it. 'Come with me, madam,' she said, 'but stay sharp. They've got a team in there – they might disturb the bomb at any moment…'

*

The other wardens had ferried shovels and barrows across the ravaged factory floor. Now Raymond, his hands in leather gloves, set about heaving the first sections of rubble aside.

Four of them worked together: two at the cliff-face of shattered timbers and brick, two racing with the barrows to deposit their loads against an exterior wall. Raymond's left arm, so much weaker than the right, jarred as he lifted one of the partition boards from the heap, but by gritting his teeth he soldiered through the pain.

There was a long way to go.

After some time – he had no way of knowing how long, for time seemed meaningless in this dark vault – the wardens he was working with switched round. Two staggered off into the cleaner night air, lungs filled with dust; two more arrived to take their place, joining Raymond in his labour. And still Raymond pushed on, levering boulder after boulder aside, straining on a mangled bedframe, side-stepping a pillar as, freed from the rubble buttressing it, it crashed to earth like a falling tree.

'Lance Corporal, you should take a rest,' came a voice – but Raymond did not reply. He was here now. Committed to the dance.

It was then that he heard the cries from below.

Raymond froze, a length of wooden partition in his arms. He cocked his head, listened again. 'Help!' a voice was calling – and then, underpinning it, there came a rhythmic clanging, as if a man was hammering at a metal pipe. 'Help!' the ghostly voice echoed. 'Is anyone out there!?'

Raymond redoubled his efforts. It seemed that he was not the only one who heard the voice, for soon the wardens manning the wheelbarrows had abandoned their posts as well, rushing to his side to carve a trail through the last walls of rubble.

And at last, there it was: the staircase leading down to the shelters, itself filled like a basin with timbers and shattered brick.

One of the girts that had been holding up the factory roof had bent when the building collapsed, forming a crude archway over the stairs and holding the men back as they fought into the stairwell itself. One at a time, they contorted themselves under the girt, passing back the bricks and chunks of debris blocking the path ahead. Raymond, labouring under an armful of roof slates, reared up choking from the stairwell, accepted a cup of water passed to him by one of the other men and, half drinking it and half using it to swill the grit from his mouth, returned to his work.

'Help!' came the voices from below.

'We're here,' said Raymond, while into his head flashed an image of Nancy, afraid and alone in the Anderson shelter at home. 'We're coming!'

He shifted a smashed tabletop aside – and there, at the bottom of the stairs, he saw the basement door.

Bricks had been piled against it. He heaved and kicked and scrabbled them aside. Then he was straining on the handle. It stuttered back an inch, then two – then finally a whole foot, revealing the clamouring faces behind. Raymond reached out his hand and drew the first man, a vagabond in only his shirtsleeves, through.

'How many are you?'

'All of us,' came a girl's voice, and one of Mary Burdett's young volunteers stepped into the ailing lantern light of the stairway. 'We're all alive!'

It was then that a strange, acrid smell touched Raymond's nostrils. He thought, at first, that it was just the smoke of fires beyond the Daughters of Salvation, wafting through the ruin on a rising wind. But there was another scent here, different to the one he'd been imbibing all night.

A moment of horror later, with the survivors battling up from the stricken shelter below, he realised what it was.

'Quickly!' he thundered. 'Gas!'

Up above, the wardens grabbed hold of the first survivors as they streamed through the ragged gash in the wall.

The charity's director was locked in conversation with Mortimer Bond, the ARP officer still remonstrating with her to get out of the way while the wardens did their jobs, when the first survivors started appearing. Tearing herself away from the barracking Bond, she started counting heads, acknowledging both volunteers and residents by name as the WVS volunteers rushed the first survivors up the street. Motorcars were already on standby to take them further afield. Hot drinks and honey biscuits were being doled out at the mobile canteen.

It was then that the horrifying cry rippled up the line, bursting out into the night.

'Gas!'

Cathy Everly froze. That one word, the word every warden feared, was enough to silence the crowd. Even the charity's director – brash enough to have brushed off Mortimer Bond and start taking charge of the evacuation herself – was suddenly still.

Cathy drew in a breath. She couldn't scent the gas herself, not yet. Perhaps that meant there was time before something terrible happened.

'Up!' Mortimer Bond was crying. 'Up, up, up!' He caught sight of Cathy, standing dumbfounded in the dark. 'Are you counting heads, Miss Everly? How many have we got?'

'That's twenty out so far, sir.'

'The old bird said there were sixty-eight, and that's the thin end of it. There might be more.'

Cathy strode forward. 'Sir, I want to go and help.'

More survivors tumbled past them, old men draped on shoulders, two of the charity's volunteers labouring for breath.

'Absolutely not, Miss Everly. We have this under control.'

Suddenly, she said, 'Raymond's in there.'

Mortimer Bond's eyes bugged out. 'And we couldn't ask for anyone finer to marshal this lot. The man's got drive. He's got fire. He's got the luck of a favourite son. That's our lance corporal. He's got God's good grace.'

'God's good grace won't save him,' she snapped, suddenly furious beyond measure. *I will.*

Mortimer Bond could turn from a benevolent grandfather to an outraged sergeant major in an instant. 'Step aside, Miss Everly – leave the men to this. I believe you're needed at the end of the road.'

Chastened, she turned on her heel. The White Horse Road was flooded with survivors now. Wardens, caked in grime, were being attended to by other WVS girls, even as those who'd escaped the shelter were being ferried away. She should have gone to join them. That was her duty. That was her role. And yet...

Raymond.

'No, sir,' she declared, turning again to the place where Mortimer Bond was standing. By now, he was on his radio, demanding an engineer. 'I won't leave him. Not again. Not like I left him on those beaches. He needs—'

'Beaches?' mouthed Mortimer Bond. 'Miss Everly, I believe the gas might have touched you. You're speaking in riddles.' He let his radio fall at his side and looked her square in the eye. 'I'm ordering you to step back – to step back and settle your mind.

You have a job to do. People are depending on you. I suggest you take up your post and…'

The rush of heat.

The violent blossoming of colour.

The sound of an explosion like the very air being wrenched out of the world.

Over Mortimer Bond's shoulder, Cathy saw the portal through which the survivors were emerging turn, suddenly, to a violent fandango of oranges, reds and white. A geyser of flame lanced upwards, through the devastated roof of the building. Every crack and window was suddenly illuminated in red.

The survivor coming out of the doorway found himself cast suddenly forward on an invisible tide, while flames turned the inside of the Daughters of Salvation into a tornado.

'Run!' screamed Mortimer Bond. 'Fall back!'

It was what the wardens were already doing.

But Cathy Everly had other ideas.

Raymond heard the explosion. From the door of the shelter, where he was helping the vagrants up the stairs, he looked up. At the top of the stairs, he could see the hurricane of fire engulfing the factory floor.

One of the other wardens was at his side. 'Was it the bomb?' he gasped.

'No,' said Raymond, and prayed the bomb wasn't just behind, 'the gas.'

He cast his eyes around the shelter. More than thirty had already gone up the stairs, but the two basement rooms were still crowded with survivors. His heart beat in syncopated rhythm. Then the dancer in him took over.

Dancing in the Grand meant keeping your head. Dancing in the world's most garlanded ballrooms meant holding your nerve. Talent was part of it, natural timing and skill – but so was thinking on your feet, recovering when you were wrong-footed, finding some other way to make the dance sublime. Once upon a time, that had been Raymond's job – to take some guest in hold and, no matter what the vagaries of their talent, to make them feel like they were the Queen of the Ballroom. Too often that meant carrying a dance when things went wrong. He'd never not succeeded yet. He'd been through triumphs and disasters. There was always a way. *Always*.

'Round them up,' said Raymond, with a division leader's authority, and hurtled back to the rubble-strewn stairwell.

Halfway up, he could feel the rush of heat. He had to bend low against the waves of it to crawl under the girt and reach the top of the stairs. There, he saw the western half of the old factory floor consumed in fire. The walls themselves were turned to curtains of flame. They raged and danced.

Smaller fires had taken hold wherever the piles of rubble remained – but at least there was a zigzagging path, cleared by the wardens as they blazed a way through the wreckage earlier in the night. The fires had nothing to take hold of here. With a little luck, perhaps Raymond could run to the exit and out into the night. He gazed around. Yes, he thought, they could dodge the fire.

It was the smoke that would kill them.

It was already billowing up. Great plumes were being dragged out through the fallen roof, but the air around him was already oily and black. Even as he watched, it started to solidify. He blinked and, suddenly, had only a vague idea where he was. The exit from the building had faded to a few strobing torchlights flickering on the other side.

Behind him, one of the other wardens called out, 'We're ready, Lance Corporal.'

Raymond wasn't certain he himself was ready, but it wouldn't do to show the men that. He might not have truly been their commander, but tonight he was all that they had.

He reached out, drew the other warden alongside him. 'What's your name, sir?'

'Lockhart, sir. Craig Lockhart.' He was a stout fellow, fifty years of age, jowly and round. He liked his ale, by the look of him. His piggy eyes blinked rapidly, already stinging from the smoke.

'Do you see the lights, Mr Lockhart?' Raymond directed him to the blinking torchlights that marked the factory entrance. 'You're to head there – hand in hand,' he ordered. 'Do you understand me?'

'But what about you, sir? What will you be doing?'

'Making sure no man gets left behind,' said Raymond. 'Now go, go, go!'

Raymond pressed himself flat against the stairwell, held himself there as the wardens and their chain of survivors strained up the staircase, then disappeared into the murk above. Up there, the fire was still raging. Timbers creaked and moaned. Before the last survivor had slipped by, Raymond heard the crash of some rubble falling in a fiery landslide to the factory floor. Another, smaller explosion wracked the rubble.

But it was nearly done.

One last job awaited him. Gulping for air, he returned to the shelter below. At least, here, the air was cleaner. He filled his lungs, regaining some of his composure, as he flickered his torch into every corner, making sure no survivor remained. Only when he was certain that he was the last among them did he return to the staircase.

The smoke was impenetrable.

He was walking through interminable night, every breath filling his lungs with poison, every step disorienting. There was no torchlight to follow any longer, for the smoke was too thick. The only light at all came from the coruscating flames.

He wanted to cry out, but there was no breath in his lungs. He wanted to turn back – but, when he did, the smoke had closed its fist around him and he couldn't even see the place from which he'd come.

He was about to give up when he heard his name. 'Raymond!' it came, cutting through fire and smoke.

He thought, at first, that it was Nancy. Here, at the end of all things, it was Nancy calling his name, leading him back to the light.

But no – Nancy was far away, right where he'd left her, mere moments after she'd told him he was going to be a father. What a fool he'd been. And now he'd never get the chance to tell her.

'Raymond!'

Not Nancy, he thought. That voice belonged to Cathy. Nancy was far away, but Cathy was near.

He picked himself up, threw himself forward, and followed the voice.

With eyes screwed shut against the bitter sting of the smoke, he crashed forward. Twice he collided with some fallen debris and pitched to his knees; twice he picked himself up, listened out for the voice again and – seeking to reorient himself in the smoke – allowed it to draw him on. He opened his mouth to cry for her, found his chest wracked with pain where he breathed in the churning smoke, then dropped to his knees again. *Crawl.* He would have to crawl. So that was what he did, heaving himself onward like the child he would one day have – until, at the very last moment, when he felt certain Cathy's voice was almost upon him, the pressure in his breast was too much to bear. What little air was left inside him exploded outwards; when he tried to take a fresh breath, none was there.

'Raymond?' the voice came. 'Raymond, I'm here ...'

His eyes opened. By some strange mercy, the smoke had fleetingly parted, revealing a sliver of light in the noxious warehouse air. In grey silhouette, the air around its edges rippling with the heat that consumed him, was Cathy Everly: jet-black hair and crimson lips, her elegant hand outstretched as if it might take his own.

'Take my hand,' she spluttered.

He could hardly hear the words. No sight, no sound, no breath to take: not for the first time, Raymond de Guise hovered on the very edge of his life.

Take my hand.

Take my hand.

Take my hand.

He reached up to grasp her, but this was the arm he had fractured; the pain was just too much – so instead it was Cathy who, crouching down and stretching beyond herself, grappled with his good forearm and started to pull.

It shouldn't have been possible. He was bigger than her. He was a dead weight.

He'd be dead soon. He was certain of it.

'I've got you,' she told him. And perhaps it was only the smoke on the warehouse floor, but Raymond thought he saw some angelic look flitter across Cathy's face – as if, in this moment, she was fulfilling her purpose on earth; as if this moment had long ago been foretold, and now she was reaching it – the very reason for her existence. 'I'm here, my darling,' she told him. 'Your Cathy. I've got you now. I'll get you back home.'

Darling? he wondered. *Your Cathy? Get you back home?* He had certainly misheard her – because, in those otherworldly moments, her words didn't make sense; they were off-key, or off-centre, like an actor whose memory has failed him and he starts paraphrasing his lines.

But she was right in one thing. She *did* have him. Who knew that Cathy was that strong? She was hauling him upwards, heaving him on until he started lumbering forward once again, bound for some place he could not see nor feel: Cathy his guide, away from the edgelands of death.

'I have him!' Cathy screamed. 'Somebody, quick!'

Two dark, begrimed figures had pitched out of the gap in the factory wall, no longer able to stand. For a second, they simply hovered there, apparitions made out of fire and smoke. Then, Cathy – unable to keep Raymond aloft any longer – lowered him to the ground at her side. There she hung over him, wiping the dirt and soot from his face, pressing her fingers to his lips, entreating him to stay with her, to keep breathing, to *come back home*.

It wasn't long before the other wardens appeared. Moments after that, Lance Corporal Raymond de Guise was on a stretcher, soaring up the street to where the ambulances waited. There, among the milling survivors, the wardens set him down. Cathy – who had hurried in their wake – knelt again at his side, grasping his hand, urging him to wake. 'Raymond,' she whispered. 'Raymond, please. I'm here. Come back – come back to me now... Raymond!'

She'd shrieked the last word, convincing herself his hand had tightened on hers. Now his eyes were opening. She felt certain he could sense her, if not see her, from whichever faraway place he was stranded in.

'Oh, Raymond,' she said, 'you bloody fool...'

Suddenly, there was another figure crouching at the stretcher. At first, Cathy took it for one of the Red Cross nurses, for there were plenty of those working among the WVS; only belatedly did she realise it was the auburn-haired American who ran the Daughters of Salvation. Her face was a rictus of horror. 'What's he doing here?' she gasped.

'He went into the building. He knew the property. Said he could get the survivors out of the shelter. And that's what he did,' Cathy trembled. 'He got them all out, every last one. And now…'

The American woman sank down, taking Raymond's other hand.

Cathy bent down, pressed her lips to his ear. 'Please,' she whispered. 'Come back. It's your Cathy. Your Cathy. I'm here…'

The American woman stuttered before she said, 'Who *are* you?'

'My name's Cathy,' Cathy said, not looking up, her eyes fixed on Raymond alone.

'My name's Vivienne,' the American said. 'Vivienne Cohen.'

If the name meant anything to Cathy, she did not betray it. Or perhaps she was so lost in Raymond that she didn't hear anything at all.

'I think you should step away from him now,' said Vivienne, sternly. 'He needs space. He needs air.'

'No!' Cathy snapped, and for the first time she darted a look up, her glittering eyes taking in Vivienne's own. Her jaw was set, her stare piercing. She looked, thought Vivienne, as frazzled as if it was she herself who'd just been thrown out of the carnage. 'I won't leave him. I'm the one who led him out of there. I'm the one who saved him. He needs me.'

'Needs you?' mouthed Vivienne. 'He needs a doctor, a nurse…'

Vivienne was about to call for one when Cathy said, 'You don't know what he needs. *I* do. We've been through it all, me and him – side by side, ever since this began.' She snorted; the sound was half a laugh, and half a rebuke. 'Every night we've been out here. Death all around us. Death and destruction, everywhere

267

we turn. But…' She stroked the hair from his brow. 'There's light too, Raymond. There's love.' She looked back at Vivienne. 'Sometimes it takes the darkest night to see it, doesn't it? I didn't think I'd find a love like it. I don't think I really knew a future was possible – not until now, not until Raymond. He's the only reason I can stand nights like this. He's the only reason I know there's hope. That, no matter what they throw at us, we'll find a way through. *That's* why I'm not leaving his side, Mrs Cohen. Because we're in love.'

Vivienne loosened her grip on Raymond's hand. 'You must be mistaken. Madam, I'm not sure you know—'

Cathy lifted her left hand and presented it to Vivienne. There was no mistaking this, for its surfaces caught the light of the fires and dazzled along their every edge. On her ring finger was a simple silver band, and at its heart three diamonds in a row. 'We're to be married,' Cathy declared, and smiled madly, for all the torture of the night. 'He asked and I wasn't sure, but I said yes. I say *yes*, Raymond.'

She turned back to him and started brushing the hair from his eyes again. Slowly, by increments, they started to open.

'Cathy?' Raymond croaked, his voice a broken whisper.

Finally, Vivienne let go of Raymond's hand. None of it made sense. It was like she'd slipped into some second, shadowy world – a world of illusions and mirrors, showing only cracked reflections of what was real.

But one thing she could not mistake: on Raymond's own ring finger, where once his wedding ring had lived, there was nothing at all.

'You're here,' Cathy said to him, 'it's me. Your Cathy. You're going to be OK.'

But she was wrong, thought Vivienne – because, if what she was seeing was true, nothing was going to be OK ever again.

Chapter Eighteen

The damage was more striking, the further she travelled north. In the heartland of London, the ruins made of the city were quickly corralled and tidied away – but here, in the north, the buildings were left to gape open, too many roads closed where craters had been carved by falling bombs.

Mathilde had left the Buckingham Hotel directly after the afternoon demonstration dances and, having travelled by Underground, now stood just off the Regents Park Road in Finchley, following a devastated terrace out towards the Dollis Brook. The last time she'd been here, the world had been different. Back then, of course, the Underground hadn't stretched this far – but, looking at the craters that pockmarked the streets like a plague, that was only the tiniest of the changes that had been wreaked since she'd been away. Had it really been four years? These were the streets where she'd been brought up. Those were the school gates where she'd last seen her father: on a winter's day in 1924, he'd been standing underneath that ash tree, watching for her as she left. By then two years had passed since he walked out on her mother – just another drunk, her mother's family used to say, hardly ever acknowledging the reasons he drank, the constant wheezing from the gas attacks, the fitful dreams he'd been keeping at bay ever since the Third Battle of

Ypres – and she'd seen him on only a smattering of occasions since. This was the corner where her grandmother once lived. This, the park where she'd played. Memories could be nasty, vicious things – they showed you all that had been good in life, only to remind you that it hadn't stayed that way forever.

The corner shop where she used to stop for pear drops had gone; now it looked like one of the old ruins, from the first days of the bombardment. That age could be counted in weeks but it felt as if years had passed. She stood there for a moment, looking at the boards and debris, and tried to picture how it had been – but the memory wouldn't materialise. She wondered if that was to do with the bombs or to do with the thing she'd come here to do.

To meet her mother.

Sometimes, the mind just blotted out the past.

Camille Bourchier did not, of course, know that Mathilde was coming. In the four years since their last encounter, Camille had written letters – and in particular a flurry of them when she discovered Mathilde had been signed up by the Buckingham Hotel – but Mathilde had studiously ignored every one. Now, as she turned onto the street where she'd grown up, she wondered if that had been wise.

It was the strangest thing: she remembered the cracks in the pavement, the ones she'd skipped over and avoided on her way to school. Then, at last, she was standing in front of the old front door.

It was a statuesque, Victorian property, the place where Mathilde's family had lived since the middle of the last century. The gleaming black door had been repainted since she'd slammed it behind her on that fateful day. It all came back to her now.

Her mother had been standing at the foot of the stairs,

bawling at her that she should come back this instant, unpack her bags, that they had an appointment to keep. 'This man could make you, Mathilde! He's asked for you *personally!*'

She'd announced it the previous night, like a general declaring victory in a battle. 'Gregory Marner wants you for his son, Mathilde. We'll meet him tomorrow.' And it had been the last straw, the thing that broke her, the thing that made her snap. It wasn't that there was anything wrong with Peter Marner; he was a perfectly talented dancer, who'd already won plaudits in the competitions that summer. No – it was the way they behaved, Mathilde's mother and Peter's father, like they were the 'powers behind the throne', the clever courtiers, the kingmakers. 'Mother!' she'd screamed. 'It's like you're arranging a marriage!'

'No,' Camille Bourchier had grinned, 'this is much more important than a marriage. Where does a marriage lead you? Debts – debts and divorce.' The last word was unutterable; of course, Camille had never divorced Mathilde's father – because such a thing was unthinkable; no, it was far more acceptable to be *abandoned* than it was to be *divorced*. 'This is a union that can prosper, Mathilde. One where triumphs can be achieved. You and Peter can be stars. All you need is a little guidance.'

It was the last word that made Mathilde erupt in fury when it was repeated the following morning. Camille had been delicately applying rouge and kohl to Mathilde's face when she'd started rhapsodising again about the things this new partnership could achieve.

'I'm not a bloody sheep, Mother! And you're not a sheepdog!'

Such a preposterous image for such a charged moment. With her face half-painted, Mathilde was up and on her feet, packing bags, declaring her fledgling dancing career finished. 'You don't want it for me, Mother. You want it for yourself – all because you *couldn't!*'

It wasn't the first time Camille had slapped Mathilde – but it was the first time Mathilde, anticipating the blow, caught her mother by the wrist, forced her backwards, and threw her onto the bed. Then she was taking flight down the stairs, suitcase in hand – and leaving home, at seventeen years old, declaring she would never return.

And here she was.

She knocked on the door.

After some time, when there was no reply, Mathilde knocked again. Perhaps it was a sign, she told herself. Perhaps some God above was telling her to forget this scheme, to forget about her mother, to return to the Grand Ballroom and get on with the business of preparing for One Grand Night. Everything else, she told herself, was just a distraction.

But still she knocked. She'd come this far; there was no point in backing down now.

This time, though there was no movement behind her mother's front door, one of the neighbours' doors opened – and out waddled the elderly Mrs Law, who'd often looked after Mathilde when she was small. It took a moment for the old woman, with her snow-white hair and spectacles like milk-bottle tops, to recognise the woman standing on the step. Then she started windmilling her arms in surprise, like somebody losing balance and scrabbling for something onto which they might hold. 'Little Tilda!' she exclaimed. 'Tilly, my girl! You came home!'

Mathilde blushed. She remembered Mrs Law with fondness, because Mrs Law would bake cakes for her, or take her blackberry picking – or sit with her, on the carpet in her sitting room, and make pictures and solve puzzles. She'd loved it back then; a day with her mother meant a day of tuition, focus, concentration – but a day with Mrs Law meant cakes and tea parties and picnicking by the brook.

'Mrs Law,' she said, summoning all that old affection, 'it's been a long time.'

'Oh, too long, Tilly,' she said, 'please, come on in, I've got some rock cakes in a tin. I've heard so much about how you've been getting on, of course. The Buckingham Hotel! I always knew you'd make it, dear. Come on, come on – I've just put a pot of tea on.'

The pull of that old house was strong in Mathilde, but she feared that, if she stepped through those doors, the determination that had driven her to this street would simply evaporate away. 'Mrs Law, I was looking for my mother.'

Mrs Law's face blanched. There was no doubt she'd heard the fight that last morning; no doubt she'd been watching from behind the edge of a curtain as the seventeen-year-old Mathilde marched away.

'Well, she's at her studio, love. I should think so, anyway. She's there almost every day.'

Mathilde faltered before saying, 'Her ... studio?'

'It's down by the crematorium, love. The old church hall.' Mrs Law wracked her brain. 'She used to take you dancing there.'

'It wasn't *hers*, the last time I was here.'

'Aye, well, your mum's got lodgers in and out. She's earned a bit in the last few years. I reckon, after you left, she needed someone else to tutor or train. Camille never was one for taking it easy.'

No, thought Mathilde. She was one for cracking the whip. One for driving you past the point of exhaustion. One for making sure nothing else mattered but that you might, one day, take the place in the ballroom world that should have been hers.

'I'll come soon, Mrs Law,' Mathilde promised – and reached across the garden fence to touch her hand. 'I'd love to have one of those rock cakes.'

'And tell me all you've been up to,' Mrs Law said, grasping her hand in return.

'I promise,' said Mathilde.

It was a promise she intended to keep. It was a boon to remember that there really were good things about having lived here.

Now, however, she had to face the bad.

The crematorium was only a short walk away. At least the streets didn't show signs of devastation out here, where London's outermost fringes gave way to small wooded areas, green fields and, in one or two places, open pastures. The hall sitting leeward of the crematorium had once belonged to a church, where it was used for various fetes and fayres, but it had also been leased out to parties celebrating wedding receptions, commiserating with each other at wakes, or otherwise just gathering for a special occasion. There'd been a time when Camille Bourchier hired this place every Saturday morning from dawn until noon, as well as three evenings during the week, for the sole purpose of tutoring Mathilde and whichever partner she could rope into the 'ballroom' that week. Mathilde had rather expected Camille to have relinquished this habit the day she stormed away; it was only now, approaching it along the autumnal thoroughfare, that she realised she'd gone the other way – embraced it, somehow turned the hall into her own, and found other dancers to train.

She could hear the music as she approached. There was little to see through the thick, velvety curtains that had been hung in the windows, but she could hear a record playing. It was Tommy Dorsey – she was sure about that. How many times had she danced to that particular refrain?

Here it was – the last opportunity to turn tail and flee. The idea was tempting, because standing outside this hall was more nerve-wracking than standing backstage at the Grand had ever been.

This time, she decided not to knock. She simply opened the door and walked through.

The hall was not quite the same as she remembered it. Velvet curtains hung in every window, and across the little stage at the front, giving the hall the appearance of a minor ballroom in miniature. That was all it was: a small room, cocooned in rich burgundy. But across its floorboards two couples waltzed. A young man, perhaps no more than sixteen, had taken a slender blonde girl in hold; they had some rudimentary talent, Mathilde observed. A much bigger young man – perhaps seventeen, and dressed in an evening jacket not quite big enough – had a flame-haired young beauty in his arms. By their looks, Mathilde took them immediately for brother and sister. Partnerships like that could often flourish.

But it was not to them that her eyes were drawn – because there, standing between the dancing couples, barking out instructions in that shrill, harpy's voice that had haunted her for years, was her mother.

Mathilde had to focus to stop trembling. Her last chance to turn away was rapidly disappearing.

Then her mother saw her and it was gone.

Suddenly, that miniature ballroom seemed as vast as an ocean. Two petite women stood on each shore, staring at each other across the expanse.

Then Camille, who was trembling herself, turned away, marched to the edge of the room and silenced the gramophone. 'We'll take a break there, ladies and gents,' she said to the dancing couples – who, with puzzled expressions, stepped out of each other's arms. 'I said that's enough. Get out there, get some air. We'll reconvene in ...' Her words failed her. 'Let's leave it for today. Gerald, you've work to do on your pivots. Charlotte, your side-step's much improved. I'll see you on Saturday. Well, come on – chop, chop! Fleet of foot and fiery of heart! In your own time, please!'

By now, the young dancers had seen Mathilde standing in the doorway. If any of them understood who she was, or the significance of her sudden appearance, they tried not to betray it. Mathilde stepped aside as, stumbling out of their dancing slippers and into their regular walking shoes, they bustled past.

Then there was only one set of footsteps sounding in the room.

Her mother Camille was tentatively approaching.

'Hello, Mother.'

Camille had opened her mouth twice to say something, then stalled on each approach, when Mathilde blurted out, 'I know you're not expecting me. I know I'm the last person you thought would come through those doors.' She paused. 'I didn't know you were training again. It wasn't in any of your letters.'

Camille was taller than Mathilde, but had the same dark colouring: olive complexion and black hair, cut short. Mathilde's green eyes had come from her father – Camille's own were almost as dark as her hair – but, in all other ways, Camille was an aged reflection of her daughter. Mathilde had sometimes wondered if that was what turned her mother into such a demanding, driven teacher: in Mathilde she saw not her daughter, but herself restored to youth, vitality and promise.

'You read my letters, then. I'd always assumed they went directly into the fire.'

'Mother, I didn't come here to argue...'

There was a moment in which Mathilde thought her mother might have mellowed – as if she might, right now, melt into Mathilde's arms, all the years of separation and enmity simply vanishing into the air. But then her face hardened, she crossed her slender arms across her breast, and stiffly said, 'Then why did you come, Mathilde? If you don't mind me asking, why – after ignoring the mother who gave you everything, for four long years, after denying you wanted to be a dancer at all, then suddenly showing up for a star turn at the Buckingham Hotel – why, after benefiting from the fruits of my labour, then casting me to the wind, are you standing on my doorstep, right now, when I'm trying to train stars for the future?'

Mathilde took a deep breath. It was going to take everything she had to say these next words. Part of her felt as if she was debasing herself – as if she'd made the right decision years ago, and didn't need to revisit it now. But the other part of her – the part, she supposed, that she'd got from her mother, the determined part, the ruthless part, the part that wanted success and stardom at almost any cost – was the part that won out.

'I'm here, Mother, because I need your help.'

They were the only words Mathilde could possibly have said that would make Camille unfold her arms, lock the hall door, and lead her daughter back to the old house. Soon – with Mrs Law watching from behind a twitching curtain – they were slipping inside, and for the first time in four years, Mathilde was standing in the home where she'd grown up.

Her junior trophies were still on the mantelpiece in the sitting room, pride of place among the cups and plaques Camille had won across her own dancing life. Even the smell of the house was the same: of perfume and candle smoke, a faint hint of peppermint and lemon. There were few signs of the lodgers Mrs Law had said her mother took in – just an errant pair of boots by the back door, and a bottle of whisky she was quite certain her mother didn't drink, in the cabinet in the alcove. In the window, the old gramophone player sat on an oak table, and beneath it her mother's records were arranged in a varnished crate. There were some of the all-time great recordings here – everything from Fats Waller to Cole Porter and Irving Berlin, and all the way to the smaller, half-forgotten British artists, the phenomenal Richard Allgood, the smooth pianist Samuel Salt. Mathilde had learned to love the jazz and swing standards that had filled this house – she spied Benny Goodman and Artie Shaw in pride of place – but there'd been a time when the first notes of so many of these records sent a shiver of dread down her spine. She'd heard them so many times, danced to each bar until she was sick of the sounds of them.

Mathilde was alone in the sitting room when she heard a crash from the kitchen, where her mother was making tea. Hurrying through, she found her mother nursing a bloody hand beneath the cold water tap, then wrapping it in a tea towel. In the sink basin there sat two shattered cups.

Her mother was holding herself rigidly. She turned, waspish, and glared at Mathilde. She'd been trying to keep it in, speaking of nothings all the way back to the house, but all of the bad feeling was etched on her face. The blood streaming out of the cut in her palm just made her spit it out. 'Why don't you just tell me what you're doing here, Mathilde? I'll assume it isn't just to play happy families, not after all this time. Not to tender an apology either, by the look on your face. Good God, Tilly, you walked out of here like I was the worst mother on earth – and all for wanting the best for my only daughter. All that hard work, all that effort, all that determination – you had it all, and you just threw it back in my face.' She tied a fierce knot in the tea towel. 'You can make the tea, Mathilde. I've had just about enough.'

This felt familiar too. Mathilde had always made the tea. A piece of her wanted to walk out of there now, but instead she fell back into old habits – and, having first rinsed out the sink, set about making a fresh pot. *Threw it back in my face*, she thought. Only a contorted mind could think like that. Mathilde had marched out of here because it had been *just too much*. There hadn't been a strand of hair on her head that was truly hers; everything she did, everything she was, had just been a creation of her mother's.

Mathilde set the tea down.

'You said that you needed my help. Well, out with it, Mathilde. I have to assume it's not dance tuition you're looking for? The last time I tried to tutor you, you wouldn't be tutored. Took yourself off to be a governess, as I recall.'

'Governess' was too grand. Four years ago, marching out on her mother had meant marching out on dance itself. For six months, Mathilde had lodged and worked as a nanny for one of the wealthier families she'd met on the ballroom circuit; secretly, she thought they held her mother in low regard and were only too pleased to help Mathilde escape from the family home. From that moment on, for Mathilde, dancing had become a thing of the past. A relic of her childhood, to be cast off as she ascended into the adult world. She wanted to carve it out for herself, just as she wanted to carve out her mother – to become her own woman, free of the constraints of all that had been. And yet, six months later, she'd set foot inside one of the dance halls of Soho. The Midnight Rooms, dark and cavernous, echoing with music, alive with the whirl of bodies consumed by song. There, on the edge of the dance floor, she admitted to herself that dancing was who she was; that it was a part of her, as inherent as the colour of her eyes, the timbre of her voice. Dancing was calling her back – but, this time, she'd find her own way into it; no longer the property and project of her mother, she would succeed alone.

'Marcus Arbuthnot,' she said.

The two words filled the room.

'What of him?'

'You'll have heard he became principal at the Grand. Don't pretend you haven't, mother. I see your copies of *Dancing Times* on the rack.' There they were, among all her copies of *Melody Maker*.

'A talented choice.'

Camille's eyes glowered at her, over the rim of her teacup, pregnant with expectation.

'And I suppose you know, already, that I didn't become principal in the Grand after Miss Marchmont left.'

Camille nodded, her face half-enveloped by steam. 'Tell me – why did they overlook you, my girl? Not your talent, one presumes. You always had the talent, Mathilde. Was it your … drive?'

The words were like daggers in Mathilde's heart. She'd heard the same thing so many times in her youth. 'You have the body, Tilly, but you don't have the mind. Where's your hunger? Where's your ambition? Dance, girl, dance!'

'I have an opportunity, Mother. I'm being courted by the Imperial Hotel to be principal in their refurbished ballroom. I'd be a star, just like you wanted.'

She said the last just to ingratiate herself with her mother, to give her what she wanted, but the words made her stomach turn. It was such a strange feeling, because Mathilde wanted this too; but it was also like admitting that she should always have stayed here, by her mother's side, taking her mother's direction, living the life that her mother ordained.

'The Imperial is a fine hotel. I've visited its ballroom. You would be proud to dance there, my girl.' She paused. 'Am I to understand a contract has yet to be signed?'

'They want something of me first.'

'Oh yes?'

By the way Camille's eyes considered her, it was almost as if she already knew. It couldn't possibly have been true – it was just her mother's way of taunting her – but, even so, it set Mathilde's teeth on edge. 'They want to ruin the Grand Ballroom. They want to discredit Mr Arbuthnot, and in doing so undermine the Buckingham Hotel. They seek to draw its guests to their own suites, and they want my help to do it.'

Camille had barely batted an eyelid. 'How?'

'Mr Arbuthnot vanished, in 1931. After the Exhibition Paris – his dancers were garlanded there, but then they fired him. Mr Arbuthnot wasn't seen, nor heard of, in two years.'

Camille was silent as she mused on the matter. Then, she said, 'I remember it being spoken of. They said he was sunning himself in the South of France, as a gentleman of his calibre often does.'

'The directors at the Imperial want to know the full story. They believe he hides a secret that could tarnish his reputation. I tried to prise him open, but I was too blunt – I startled him, I danced too close to it, and now I'll never gain his confidence.'

Camille whispered, 'So you came to me.'

'Archie Adams, the bandleader, had old photographs. And there you were – you and Marcus, in the same ballroom. So I thought you might have heard rumours. I thought there might be people you could ask.'

'Mathilde, Mathilde,' Camille smiled, 'my scheming little Mathilde. You're playing with fire, here – but you already know that.' She grinned. She was bewitchingly beautiful when she smiled – but Mathilde had long ago learned not to be put under her spell. 'You'd burn the Buckingham down, to get what you want? Are you sure, Mathilde?'

Mathilde snapped, 'You always wanted me to get to the top, Mother!'

'Come with me,' said Camille.

Together, they returned to the sitting room, and the archive of *Dancing Times*. At her mother's instruction, Mathilde sifted through the copies until the year 1931 was arrayed around them. There, in a summer edition, were the reports of the Exhibition Paris that year. In the centrefold, beaming for the cameras, were Victor Grace and Meghan Barr. In the corner, a smaller photograph depicted a young Marcus Arbuthnot standing between them, his arm draped lovingly over Meghan's shoulder.

'They were a handsome couple.'

'Oh, you'll find them all over these magazines,' crowed Camille, 'and then, just like Marcus, suddenly gone. Victor Grace and Meghan Barr should have conquered the world. Without Marcus Arbuthnot, they faded into obscurity.' Camille sifted through the next magazines. After a long, lingering silence, she set down an edition from the end of 1933 and said, 'Yes, there he is – the next mention of your dear Mr Arbuthnot, two years after Paris. Most curious, Mathilde.'

'It's the key to everything.'

'The key to your success.' Camille stopped. 'Do you really have the stomach for this, Mathilde? Do you want it enough?'

'You once told me that nobody gets to the top, not on talent alone.'

A look of satisfaction flickered across Camille's face. 'You always hated me for saying those things. But you see it now, don't you? The world is full of sycophants and con artists. To rise to the top in a world like this, sometimes a woman makes compromises.' A sudden fury descended on her. 'If you'd stayed with me, Mathilde, we'd both be on top by now. You'd be the Queen of the Ballroom; I'd be your faithful choreographer and courtier. But you spoiled it, girl. You ruined all the work we put in. And here I am, training *children* again, looking for my diamond in the dirt.'

Mathilde thought: I'm looking for my own kind of diamond. Then she looked back at the picture of Marcus in *Dancing Times*.

'I'm tired of playing second fiddle,' Mathilde whispered. 'Do you remember what you wrote to me, when you found out I'd been hired to the Grand? I was Hélène Marchmont's understudy, but you said …'

'You're no understudy. You're my daughter.'

Yes, thought Mathilde, I *am* your daughter – and I'm willing to do it, this time. I'm ready.

'I can't let the chance slip through my fingers, not again. It's this war, mother. It's the night after night, with the bombs falling down. It changes the way you think about things. We only get to live once, don't we? I could die tomorrow. Why shouldn't I take the chances in front of me? Why shouldn't I get the things I deserve? Why shouldn't I—'

'Stop at nothing to win what's yours by right?'

There was a pregnant pause. The truth was, Mathilde didn't need her mother to direct her in this one; she'd made her own decision many weeks ago.

'Will you help me, Mother? Will you speak to old friends, ask around, find me something – find me *anything* – I might use to unearth the truth of what happened to Marcus, in those missing years?'

She could almost see her mother's thoughts forming. She looked into her dark, sparkling eyes and could vividly picture what was happening on the other side: an image of Mathilde, stepping out as the star of the Imperial for the very first time – and there, in the crowd of admiring onlookers, Camille herself, back in the ballroom where she should have been a star.

'Come here, Mathilde,' said Camille.

Mathilde stepped into her arms. It was the first embrace they'd shared in much longer than the four years she'd been away – and she decided, as Camille closed her arms around her, that she would fall into it, that she would let herself be her mother's daughter for the first time since she'd been small.

'We'll do this together, Mathilde. You and I, like it always should have been. The Bourchiers of the ballroom. Well, it has a nice ring to it, doesn't it, my girl?'

Chapter Nineteen

It was now or never, Mrs Moffatt told herself. Then, reminding herself that she'd told herself the same thing half a dozen times, she toddled back from the dressing-room doors, turned to make haste to the safety of the Housekeeping Lounge – and walked directly into Archie Adams himself.

Archie was dressed, as he was always dressed, in his resplendent white dinner jacket. His hair, which was fading from the lustrous gold of old so that it almost equalled the white of Mrs Moffatt's own, glistened with the pomade he'd run through it earlier that evening. That made the forest green of his bow tie the only splash of colour in the whole of Archie Adams' outfit – that, and the blue of his eyes.

'Mr Adams,' she stuttered, 'Archie ... I've scuffed up your suit!'

She hadn't; Mrs Moffatt's fingers were scrubbed as clean as the bedsteads on her rounds. Even so, she started straightening out the barely perceptible crumples in his jacket.

'Emmeline, it's quite all right!'

He put a loving hand on her shoulder. Then there was a fraction of a second of silence, until he perceived that something was amiss. 'Emmeline, were you looking for me?'

Now or never, she told herself again. *It's now or never.* But how many 'now or nevers' could there be? There'd been at least four since she'd sat in the Housekeeping Lounge with Nancy. Everything seemed to make sense when you were saying it for the benefit of somebody else. Listening to your own advice was one of life's cruellest challenges. Every time she'd found the courage to come here, she'd faltered at this very moment. Poised to knock on the dressing-room door, her heart had skipped a beat, she'd toddled back to the Housekeeping Lounge and told herself 'never say never again'. It was the release she needed, the way she told herself 'you can always come back and try again'.

But Archie was here this time. It felt different. So, with a sinking feeling of finality – for certainly there was a chance she was ruining things forever – she reached into her apron pocket and produced a small ivory envelope, on which Archie's name was written in her delicate, cursive hand.

'Just a little note,' she said. Then, with a stutter, 'To wish you good luck tonight.'

Archie's perfect smile crumpled in puzzlement.

'Well, not luck,' Mrs Moffatt went on, increasingly flustered as – her task now complete – she toddled backwards. 'You've performed here a thousand times, of course ...'

'One thousand, seven hundred and forty-six, to be precise.'

'So you don't need luck,' Mrs Moffatt blathered. 'Just good wishes. Just – do your – best. Just ... you'll make the ballroom light up, Archie.' *You make me light up.* Those last words had almost stumbled from her tongue. She had to stop now, or else she'd tumble completely off the cliff-edge on which she was balanced. 'Have a good show. Have a ... jolly good show.'

By the time she got back to the Housekeeping Lounge, her embarrassment was complete. She dared not look in the mirror in the office, for fear of seeing her cheeks red and ruddy as a farm girl's. This time, not even a pot of tea was enough to steady the soul. Not even a handful of barley sugars. All that was left was to pace and fret, pace and fret – and wonder if words could ever be enough to change the course of a human heart.

The blackout began earlier and earlier as midwinter approached, but there had now been two straight nights without the sirens announcing the start of some fresh decimation – so, as Vivienne Cohen stepped off the Underground in the early evening dark, then picked her way across Regent Street and through the town-houses of Mayfair, she kept her fingers crossed that, tonight, she wouldn't be stranded away from home. She ought to have come sooner, but the day had been spent in trying to make some sense of the devastation at the Daughters of Salvation, in a conscience-stricken visit to Sir George Peel, the preparations for Warren's funeral – and, between it all, Stan squawking and squalling, as if he could sense in the atmosphere the fresh hell visited upon them. Thank goodness for Raymond and Artie's mother Alma, who was always there to take him in when Vivienne needed it the most. Between Alma and the refugee girl Leah, Vivienne felt as if she might *just* be able to tramp through the next year of her life.

But then had come the night the Daughters was destroyed. The night she had heard those enigmatic words from the WVS girl's lips. *We're in love. We're going to be married.* They'd been circling in her head, like carrion crows, ever since. So it was duty, now, that compelled her to walk across the open blackness of Berkeley Square. Duty, and friendship, which buoyed her along Michaelmas Mews and in through the tradesman's entrance to the hotel where, a time long ago, she had lived as a virtual prisoner to her step-father's hatred and conceit.

Vivienne never liked coming back here. She'd have preferred to visit Nancy at home – but that was where Raymond would be, for in the days since the fall of the Daughters, he'd been ordered to bed rest. A soldier, it seemed, always followed orders from above – even if he didn't acquiesce to the needs of his faithful, loving wife. Thank God, then, that tonight was the night when the Norwegian Fir tree was being delivered to the Buckingham Hotel. Tradition dictated that, once a year, as the 1st of December approached, the Buckingham Hotel sourced a grand Norwegian Fir from one of the plantations outside Trondheim; this year, things were to be a little different – the tree received, as a gift of the Norwegian King and harvested from a forest in the highlands of Scotland – but, in the hours before dawn tomorrow morning, the Housekeeping staff would gather to garland it with baubles and lights, to place the iconic cloth angel on its very top, and perhaps, once all that was done, there would be a moment in which they might forget that there was a war going on at all.

All of that, however, was immaterial to Vivienne. She'd already been facing up to her first Christmas without Artie, and the decimation of the old HJ Packer building had driven all thoughts of merriment and cheer out of her mind. There would be time for that next year, perhaps, when Stan was a little older and he might begin to revel in the majesty of the season – if, of course, there was still an England by then. Today all that mattered was that Nancy was sworn to spending the night in the hotel quarters, the better to be up with the lark and directing the girls in decorating the tree.

Vivienne looked for her first in the Housekeeping Lounge, finding only Mrs Moffatt in a flurry of time-sheets and rotas, and yet more application forms for seasonal posts at the hotel. Mrs Moffatt had always been kind to Vivienne – and soon she was directing Vivienne to the rickety quarters on the hotel's hidden seventh storey.

Vivienne had never ventured into the hidden, less well-polished corners of the hotel. She knew they had to exist, for no luxury hotel expends money unless it has a hope of reaping it in return, but as she stepped out of the service elevator, into a tumbledown hallway where the floorboards creaked underfoot and the rugs were threadbare, she got the feeling that she was in a different kind of establishment altogether.

At least she could see lights, and at least she could hear voices. The chambermaids' kitchenette was at the very end of the hall, past the rooms where the chambermaids all slept. Rosa's voice was the loudest of the lot (it always was), but it seemed like an early Christmas party was being hosted in the kitchenette. There was music and cheering, and Christmas lights seemed to be sparkling behind the blackout blinds.

Christmas was scarcely a month away. Vivienne had only spent one Yuletide as a married woman, before Artie shipped off to France and his undoing. As she approached the shindig, she felt like a ghost appearing at a feast.

Through the doorway, she could see Rosa and Frank, dancing where the coffee table – now propped in the alcove beneath the window – used to sit. The other chambermaids gossiped and cheered around the edges of the room. A red-haired girl with the definite look of a Brogan about her was jawing with Nancy, surrounded by cups and saucers, plates heaped with crumbs – and, Vivienne was surprised to see, at least one bottle of sherry, drained down to the bottom.

Across the crowded kitchenette, she caught Nancy's eye.

Almost immediately, Nancy was on her feet. 'Sorry, Annie, dear – I'll only be a moment.'

'Don't you hurry on my account, Nance – I mean, *Mrs de Guise*. I've a mind to show this lot how a Brogan dances. They won't quite believe their eyes.'

Almost certainly not, thought Vivienne, as the young Brogan girl launched herself into what could only be described as a highly cantankerous jive, equal parts youthful energy, jagged limbs and inability to see those around her. As Vivienne and Nancy retreated into the hall, even Frank was looking at her with a perturbed expression.

'Vivienne, what are you doing here?'

Nancy's voice was breathless with concern, for the sight of Vivienne in such unlikely surroundings had stirred some awful premonition in her.

'Mrs Moffatt sent me up. She said you were spending some time with the girls.'

Nancy nodded.

'How are you feeling, Nancy?'

Vivienne's eyes had taken in the contours of Nancy's belly, so of course Nancy understood. She lifted a finger to her lips. 'I haven't told the girls. I haven't even told Frank. I don't want it reaching hotel management, not until I have a plan. Oh, but Vivienne...' Nancy threw her arms around Vivienne and held her tight, '...the Daughters. I can't believe it. Is it really all gone?'

It wasn't what Vivienne had come here to talk about, but the thought of it now moved her to the edge of tears. She nodded, fiercely. 'Is there somewhere we can talk? Somewhere quiet?' Her eyes gravitated back to the dancing in the kitchenette. By the whoops and cheers and simultaneous commiserations, it seemed evident that Annie Brogan had just crashed down onto her behind.

'This way,' said Nancy, and took Vivienne by the hand.

As they walked, Vivienne was quite certain she could feel the cold metal of Nancy's wedding band still on her finger.

Nancy had been afforded one of the chambermaids' rooms, vacant since the last girl left London for less perilous climes, and they slipped inside it now. Nancy had once lived in a room just like this: cosy but functional, with a narrow bed, a dresser and a window from which she used to gaze out across their Mayfair surrounds. Now that she was here again, it seemed more poky than it used to do. She closed the door behind her, her nerves building at Vivienne's stricken face.

The first thing Vivienne said was, 'How's Raymond?'

And Nancy's mind cartwheeled back, to that night she'd told him she was pregnant and everything that had unfolded after she left . . .

She could hear the door, resounding as he closed it behind him. The back door echoed too, for she slammed it so fiercely as she went into the back garden that it scattered the birds from their roost in the fig tree outside the kitchen window. Moments later, wrapping her shawl around her, she was inside the tinny confines of the Anderson shelter, striking the storm lantern and watching its strange, spidery shadows cast against the half-moon walls. There was a new hardback here – *The Gallant Pimpernel*, she'd been reading it in the long nights – but she tossed it aside without even opening the covers. *Gallantry*. She'd heard quite enough about *gallantry*. Gallant Raymond de Guise, off into the night to do his duty – while here she sat, alone but for her child.

Most nights she sat here in fear for him. Most nights sleep wouldn't come, because whenever she closed her eyes, all she could see was him standing on some shattered street, the bombs falling down. Through all that fear, she'd had pride in him as well. Pride that he was doing the good thing. Honour that he was putting up a fight for all who were living, and those who had died along the way. But tonight those feelings would not come. Only moments ago, he'd held her and told her about the world they would have, the three of them together. Then he'd left.

What was 'duty', if not duty to the child you were creating? What was honour worth, if you chose sacrifice and risked death, rather than being there for your child?

Those feelings had dogged her through the night. They were dogging her still when she left the shelter, after the all-clear, and was settling into bed for a few scant hours sleep – and the knock came at the door.

She knew, straight away, that he was dead. That was why she hovered at the top of the stairs, not daring to go and answer the door. It was some time later, the knocking urgent and insistent, that she plucked up the courage to go out to the front step. The man who was standing there was named Mortimer Bond. He said he was Raymond's superior officer in the ARP. 'He's in St Thomas's,' the plump man said. 'You've a fine man at your side, Mrs de Guise. The finest of men. He saved more than sixty souls tonight – men, and women among them, who'd have perished if he hadn't been on site. Treasure that man, Mrs de Guise. And look after him – it's bed rest for Lance Corporal de Guise, and that's an order.'

Treasure him. The finest of men. All these plaudits rained around Raymond's shoulders, but Nancy didn't have faith in any one of them. Even as her heart skipped a beat with the knowledge he survived, a quiet fury rose that he'd been there in the first place.

More than sixty souls, Mortimer Bond had said. Well, for the rest of that day, Nancy ricocheted between fury he'd been there and relief that he had. The fact that it was the Daughters of Salvation that had been decimated made it all the worse; Nancy herself had given so much of her time and heart to the institution, before her promotion to floor mistress at the Buckingham Hotel. They said that Warren Peel was the only one to have died in the blast. A miracle, Mortimer Bond had said – but not for poor Warren. He'd had so much life left to live.

Of course, she went to Raymond, the moment that she could. She held his hand in the hospital bed, and walked with him, arm in arm, to the taxicab when the doctor permitted him to leave. She cooked for him, the Lancashire hotpot that meant so much to them both, and laid out clean clothes, stroked his hair as he slept. But, even two days later, the anger hadn't left her. He said all the right things, told her how it was the memory of her that had carried him through his darkest moment, how while he slept in the hospital bed he dreamt of her and their child – but so little of it touched Nancy. Sixty souls saved, they said. And perhaps it made her a shameful human being, but the thought that raged within her was: I'd have lost every one of them, just to make sure my child has a father.

It boiled out of her on the second evening. Mortimer Bond had paid a visit, told him it was good to see him back on his feet and that the whole team were eager to have his boots back on the ground. The way Raymond's demeanour changed made a devil grow inside Nancy – because she saw now that this was what he wanted; his boots on the ground, out on the streets where it *mattered*.

'You don't see it, Raymond,' she snapped, filling the silence of their kitchen with the smashing of crockery in the sink. 'We're having a *baby*. You've been hospitalised twice since September. We're having a *child*. And – and I want my child to have a father!'

The words had flurried out of her like a blizzard. Raymond, as he always did, rushed to take hold of her – but this time she didn't want his arms.

'You walked out of here, the night I told you. It's like you were … going over the top!'

'Nancy,' he said, in disbelief, 'they'd have all died. If I hadn't been there – all of them, dead.'

There was nothing she could say to refute this logic, nothing she could tell him that would change his mind. All that she had was the true feelings of her heart, no matter how destructive and disgraceful they might be. 'Then let them die, Raymond,' she screamed. 'Let them die so *you don't die.*'

Perhaps he understood, then. Something changed in his demeanour. He tried to take her in his arms once again, but Nancy brushed past, out into the hall.

She'd left so early the following morning that she'd scarcely seen him since.

'Might it be the baby,' Nancy ventured, sitting on the end of the bed in the chambermaids' quarters while Vivienne settled beside her. 'I've heard it said they can drive you crazy, even before they're born. Vivienne, it's like I'm feeling everything all at once. There isn't room enough inside me, so it just keeps spilling out.'

Vivienne took her hand. 'I was every bit as wild as you, Nancy, but I think you can be forgiven. What you said to Raymond – it was true. I said the same to Artie when he signed up. He kept trying to win me over with those wolfish smiles of his – but it didn't stop the rot I was feeling. The difference is, Artie *had* to go. He had to do his bit. Raymond's already doing his bit, and he'll *have* to go back to his division. But these nights, out on patrol…'

'Sometimes,' whispered Nancy, seemingly unable to confess this part of her heart, 'I don't know if I recognise Raymond any more. In my head, I know it's because of Dunkirk. I know it's because of Artie, just the same as it is for you. What he lost out there, what the war's already done to his body and his soul. But…' She was despairing, and heaved a great sigh, '…I don't want him to die a hero. He doesn't want to live life a coward.

But there has to be a middle way, doesn't there? That's just the compromise of life.'

Vivienne clung on to Nancy's hand, squeezing it tighter and tighter. For a time they sat together, in their respective silences. Then, finally, Vivienne seized the moment and said, 'Nancy, have you heard of a WVS girl named Cathy? Cathy Everly?'

Nancy said, 'Raymond knows her, from the patrols.' And the thought lanced across her, of Cathy at the end of her hall, Cathy wearing her nightdress, Cathy with the pin in her hair. Why did that image keep coming back? Somehow, it felt like the shadow she was casting.

'She was there, on the night the Daughters was hit.'

Nancy nodded, a cold creeping dread beginning to spread through her. There was something Vivienne wanted to say, something which she was struggling with in her heart. But now was not the time for fear to come between them. There was enough fear already in the world, too many relationships fraying and coming apart, so she looked her square in the face and said, 'Tell me, Vivienne. What's bothering you? What happened out there?'

So that was exactly what Vivienne did.

A story like this unfolded so strangely. All that Vivienne could think to do was to lay it out, exactly as she'd seen and heard. 'It was like Raymond was her light,' she ventured. 'Like Raymond was her moon and her stars. "I didn't think I'd find a love like it." Those were her exact words, Nancy. "I'm not leaving his side, Mrs Cohen. Because we're in love."'

Nancy absorbed it all in a rapt, contemplative silence. If Vivienne had expected her to break down, she had been mistaken; her eyes lowered, then lifted again, blinking only when Vivienne described the sparkling engagement ring on Cathy's finger and the lack of any wedding band on Raymond's own.

'He took it off,' Nancy whispered, thinking back, 'early in his patrols. For a few nights, he wore it around his neck. Then he left it at the bedside. They told him that, if anything were to happen to him, it was better it wasn't on his finger.'

'*Who* told him that, Nancy?'

Nancy shook her head. 'I just don't know.'

'She said he'd asked her to marry him. She said the danger had thrown them together, made them see what life was worth...'

Just the same as Mrs Moffatt, thought Nancy. *Wasn't she going to deliver her letter to Archie tonight?*

'Nancy.' Vivienne had grown more sombre still. 'The way Raymond's been. His distance. His coldness. Could it be—'

The mere hint of the question wrenched Nancy from the thoughts she'd been lost in. She let go of Vivienne's hand, snatched it away. 'No,' she said.

'He's been through so much. Couldn't it be he found comfort in—'

Nancy stood. 'NO,' she said, fierce in the denial. 'Vivienne, NO.'

Then the silence returned, stony as the earth.

Outside, the sirens had started singing. Nancy and Vivienne hung there, together, as they heard the chambermaids and Frank pour out of the kitchenette, off to do their duty escorting guests to the hotel shelters, then to head for the staff shelters themselves.

After the footsteps had clattered past, half taking to the stairs, half filling up the service elevator to reach the reception hall, Nancy said, 'I'm not angry with you, Vivienne.'

It was impossible to feel anger, because it was in this precise moment that she detected the movement of her baby for the very first time. It was the feeling of butterfly wings stroking the insides of her stomach, light and fleeting as the breeze. 'Vivienne,' she said, and reached for Vivienne's hand. 'Feel...'

There was nothing to feel any longer, but Vivienne's hand traced a line around the place where Nancy and Raymond's child lay.

'He wouldn't,' said Nancy. 'He's Raymond.'

For all of her doubts, Vivienne knew it too. 'Then something else has been happening, out there. She isn't who she says she is.'

'Perhaps,' said Nancy, 'she isn't who *she* thinks she is either.' A reverberation sounded, somewhere in the city. 'But I'm going to find out.'

'Ladies and gentlemen,' Archie Adams proclaimed, stepping away from his grand piano and standing, like a colossus, on the edge of the stage. 'Let us hope we can reconvene. In the meantime, it's my honour to invite you to the Buckingham Hotel's most elegant shelters.'

They were the same lines he said every night that the sirens started wailing, dispelling the magic and majesty of the Grand – but, tonight, he did not feel like the stately hero he often did when standing up here, directing the guests. As the dancers gathered them together – Marcus Arbuthnot leading two refined ladies through the ballroom archway and out towards reception – he hurried backstage, opened the drawer in his dresser and took out the letter Mrs Moffatt had given him moments before the evening's entertainment began. He'd barely had a chance to read it before he strode out onto stage, but its words had lived in him throughout.

Beads of sweat were trickling down his brow. He dabbed them away with the corner of a silk handkerchief. Why did words like these make him flush? It was the feeling of being a young man again – and Archie Adams wasn't sure that he liked it. There was a dependability, a reliability, a *certainty*, that came with the middle years of a life. It was a comfort, like a pair of old slippers. You didn't expect to receive letters like this at this time of life.

Dearest Archie

You will think me a silly old girl for writing to you in this way, but please know that I have tried to say these same things to your face, and every time they get lodged in my throat. I am moved to write to you because the war has changed me – as I believe it has changed us all. It has made me think about life in a way I have not thought about life in so long. And this has been frightening and enlivening in equal measure.

Archie, dear Archie, please forgive me for being so plain – but I believe I have never met a man who makes me feel the way you do when you come for tea in my little Housekeeping Office. I have cherished you as a friend these last years, and I have slowly come to the realisation that I cherish you more each day.

Please don't think unkindly of me for writing these words. Your company means the world to me. Your smile, your voice, your laugh. Reading these lines back, I know that I must sound like a lovesick girl – but, Archie, there is no sickness in it. It is just love. Whether you feel this for me in return, I do not know, but I am glad to have said it when I have been buttoning my lip so long.

Now give me the courage to deliver you this letter! If all else fails, I shall pass the job to Billy Brogan – but this is, perhaps, the kind of letter one should deliver one's self.

Yours in lasting love
Emmeline x

'Archie,' came Marcus Arbuthnot's rich baritone, 'we mustn't dally a moment longer.'

Archie looked up. The dressing room was almost empty now, as the last of the musicians made haste for the shelters. 'Mr Arbuthnot,' Archie declared, folding the letter delicately into his breast pocket, 'I'm right behind you.'

People were still milling in the reception hall when Archie emerged. Tomorrow, the Norwegian Fir tree would stand, pride of place, right here in the centre of the hall. No doubt there were some who would consider it a hazard – for a clear reception area had been deemed vital to ferrying guests to and from the shelters – but there were few in the hotel who would protest at its magnificence once it was raised. All of a sudden, Archie felt an old wistfulness come over him: what it had been like to be a boy, with a family, at Christmas. Nowadays, his Christmases were spent here, in the hotel – the musicians his family, the ballroom his home.

Beads of sweat were breaking out on his brow again. He dabbed them away as he hurried towards the Queen Mary, and the wine cellar shelters underneath.

It was there, framed in the restaurant door, that he saw Mrs Moffatt.

'Archie,' she gasped, as he stumbled into sight.

'E – Emmeline,' he stuttered. His eyes darted left and right, quite unable to settle on anything at all – and least of all Mrs Moffatt's wide, expectant face.

'Archie, about my letter...'

He froze. It was like all the music in the world had stopped. Like his fingers were dancing up and down the ivories, reaching for melodies and chords, but finding no sound at all. 'Your – your letter,' he said.

Mrs Moffatt nodded.

He should have said something, then. He should have said anything at all. But it felt like worlds were exploding inside him. His throat was desert dry. And, instead of saying anything about the letter, he simply strode past Mrs Moffatt, onto the restaurant floor, and said, 'The shelter, Emmeline. I've got to get to the shelter.'

So did Mrs Moffatt, of course. But instead it felt as if the ground was opening underneath her. As she watched him go, Archie's silence hung around her, like a shroud – so smothering that, for a time, and until Nancy appeared behind her, Vivienne in tow, she hardly heard the sounds of the sirens, or, indeed, anything else in the world at all.

December 1940

Chapter Twenty

Christmas at the Buckingham Hotel: that most feted and magical of seasons. In the reception hall, the Norwegian Fir might not have stood quite as tall as in years past – but what it lacked in height, it more than made up for in splendour. Baubles glittered, candles burned, while sprigs of holly ripe with red berries garlanded the branches in a specific, swirling design. Billy was bowled over by the beauty of it. Last Christmas, he'd sat in his billets in France, breaking bread with the boys and singing the old songs. They'd roasted chickens from the local farms, told stories and opened the packages that had made it over the Channel from home – but it hadn't been the same. He hadn't even had Raymond and Artie to jaw about the Buckingham with back then.

Seeing it now reminded him what Christmas could feel like. He allowed himself to linger over it for a moment, breathing in the perfect pine needle scent, before he marched on with his duties: the usual letters, bills, and demands to the audit office; the letters of enquiry from esteemed parties directly to Walter Knave, who would write personally – extending the hand of welcome where possible, politely demurring where not – to each one; until, finally, there were only what he called the 'love letters' left. These were not always missives of undying affection (though he was quite certain he'd delivered a few of those), but often letters of gratitude, thanks, congratulations – and not one or two personal entreaties – directed to the dancers and musicians of the Grand. Sometimes, a guest would feel so incredible, having waltzed with Marcus, that they would invite him to their country house; when Miss Marchmont had danced here, she had had so many admirers that the old director, Maynard Charles, had employed a typist to respond on her behalf. Half the letters in Billy's hands would be from old guests grateful for the escape to a different *feeling* the Grand had brought them on their last visits here. He slipped along the back passage towards the dressing rooms and passed through the door.

Inside, Mathilde and Frank were rolling through the various waltzes and quicksteps that were to pepper One Grand Night. These were the showpieces to be performed between each round of the auction, designed by Marcus to enliven proceedings and to get the wealthiest of guests delving into their pockets for future bids. As Billy watched, Mathilde and Frank turned sharply, turned sharply again, and described a wild spiral around the room.

'B – Billy!' Frank stuttered, on seeing him appear. 'I didn't realise we had an audience.'

Billy grinned. 'It's looking so polished, Frank. You too, Mathilde.'

Mathilde, who looked suddenly like a rabbit caught in some motorcar's headlights, nodded and gave a wan smile, as if masking some discomfort. Then, if only to break the awkward silence that followed, Billy said, 'I'm sure there are some letters here for you, Mathilde.'

In fact, there was only one. She took it and, upon seeing the slanting hand on the front of the envelope, her startled eyes widened further.

'Nothing for you, I'm afraid, Frank,' grinned Billy. 'Hey, you ought to get Rosa to start writing a few admiring letters and sending them through. We wouldn't want you missing out now, would we?'

Then, before Frank could jocularly admonish him in return, Billy took off, through the back door, across the empty dressing rooms and into the Grand Ballroom...

...where the first full rehearsals for One Grand Night were in full flow.

The music hit him like a wave. It was strange, bursting into the Grand through the backstage doors and suddenly finding himself on the dance floor itself. Suddenly, it was Billy Brogan who was frozen in a motorcar's headlights. There were no guests in the ballroom, but the dance troupe were arrayed around the balustrade, watching two dancers in full flow. At first, Billy thought it was Marcus and Karina – but, no, his eyes were deceiving him, because this was an image of yesteryear, of a simpler, golden time in the Grand: Raymond de Guise, resplendent in his midnight blue, dancing with none other than Hélène Marchmont.

It was almost enough to start Billy shaking. He'd never been much of a dancer – in fact, he'd made a fool of himself too many times, having gone with Frank and the rest to the clubs in Soho – but the very idea of Raymond and Hélène, together again, threw him back in time. Three years ago, when Raymond and Hélène last danced together, there'd been no war. Three years ago, Artie was alive. Three years ago, his brothers and sisters were scrabbling around back home, instead of flung out to Suffolk for safekeeping. Three years: how much had changed...

Three years ago, he wasn't indentured to some filthy profiteer, compelled to betray the very hotel that had looked after him half of his life.

He limped off the dance floor, then joined the others at

the balustrade. Around the edges of the ballroom, joiners and carpenters were all busily engaged. Ladders had been erected to string up the decorations for One Grand Night. The chandeliers had been brought down for polishing and refitting. These were the machinations behind the magic, thought Billy.

And there were the chambermaids, with their polishes of vinegar and beeswax, down on their knees around the fallen chandeliers as they restored them to glorious life. As Billy limped towards the archway that led back to reception, Mary-Louise looked up from her work and caught his eye. Separated by the ballroom's breadth, all that Billy could do was stare at her until, too overcome by a strange mixture of yearning and shame, he tore himself away and vanished from the Grand.

Down in the post room, there were yet more packages to bundle up for Uncle Ken.

With every one that he dispatched, he sent another little piece of his soul.

Perhaps it was only his enforced absence from the ballroom, but Raymond de Guise wondered if he had ever felt the same thrill of anticipation that came with the approach of One Grand Night.

He'd last danced in the Grand almost a year ago, returning from his basic training and stepping out onto the dance floor for one last hurrah, before the war came to take him away. The place had changed so much in that short time, but the moment he'd entered through the archway – to find the resplendent Hélène Marchmont already waiting here, a vision of old-world elegance with her striking gold hair and winter-blue eyes – he'd started *feeling* it again.

'Lance Corporal,' Hélène had said, with a gentle incline of the head that spoke of love, respect, and the deep bonds that once tied them together. To Raymond, she looked a little older, perhaps a little paler, but apart from that, so little had changed. Even as he took her in hold for the first time, it seemed as if they had never been apart. He knew every contour of Hélène's body; there had never been an inkling of romantic feeling between them, and this had only made them stronger as dancers. Her body fit with his; with her back in his arms, the months melted away. He felt as if he could fly.

Billy Brogan had not long departed the ballroom when Raymond and Hélène's dance came to its conclusion. As the trumpets died away, and Archie Adams struck the final chord on his grand piano – Raymond was not certain why, but he did not seem his usual self somehow, as if, even while he played, his heart and mind were many leagues away – Marcus Arbuthnot led the troupe in wild applause, sweeping onto the dance floor to take both Raymond and Hélène's hands. 'And that, ladies and gentlemen, is *elegance*. That is the old-world poise our guests will die for. Raymond, Hélène – would that you were permanent members of the troupe. We would close all the other ballrooms in London, for none could compare!'

Some of the joiners on the edges of the room looked quizzically upwards, seemingly unable to believe Marcus's grandiose flourishes – but Marcus saw nothing of them. He led Raymond and Hélène back to the edge of the balustrade, and declared, 'Now, Karina, perhaps you and I ought to show everyone our tango for the King! Archie, if you will…'

This time, Raymond and Hélène stood together at the balustrade while, waiting only for the enigmatic tinkling of Archie Adams' piano, Marcus and Karina began.

The tango was a passionate dance, thought Raymond as he watched. There was no doubting Marcus's passion for the dance itself, but he wondered if something else was missing: passion, perhaps, for Karina herself. Not real passion, of course – dancing was, first and foremost, an act – but the dramatic passion of the stage. If Raymond were still leading this troupe, perhaps he might have dropped an observation like this in at the end of the dance. As it was, he whispered it only to Hélène, who gently demurred. 'Any more passion from Mr Arbuthnot, and I think every soul in this ballroom will faint clean away.'

Raymond smiled.

Then, with her eyes still fixed on the dance, Hélène said, 'How are you bearing with it all, Raymond?'

Raymond and Hélène hadn't often spoken since the day she left the ballroom. In the summer before war was declared, he and Nancy had taken the trip down to Rye where she now lived – with her mother and daughter, in the old house by the sea, her daughter Sybil's other grandparents occupying the old coach house in the manor grounds – and Hélène had brought Sybil to the new house in Maida Vale once. But old friendships can endure even the longest of separations, and in that moment it seemed like she had never been away. With that simple question, she seemed to be reading Raymond's innermost thoughts.

'It's been a strange year, Hélène – strange for us all.'

'But perhaps you more than many.'

In Raymond's heart it was growing stranger still. It had now been seven nights since the devastation at the Daughters of Salvation, and only this evening was he due to return to his patrol. Seven nights, but it seemed incalculably more. If anyone could understand this moment in his life, perhaps it was Hélène. Once upon a time, she'd carried her own secrets: the child she'd borne in secret, and kept in secret until the day came when she was compelled to leave the ballroom forever. Hélène knew more than a little about the vagaries of chance and fate. He hadn't told anybody yet, for he still prickled with shame about that night he'd left Nancy alone, but he turned to Hélène now and said, 'Nancy's carrying a child. I'm going to be a father.'

The ballroom was alive with music. On the dance floor, Marcus and Karina led the tango to its dramatic, impulsive conclusion. Frank and Mathilde had appeared at the dance floor doors following their backstage rehearsal. As Raymond understood it, they were next to take to the floor – but Mathilde looked sickly somehow, as pale as Archie Adams, and Raymond began to wonder, then, if there were fresh secrets in this ballroom, if the veil of magic was just that – a simple veneer, as easily shattered as the pretence of peace had been last summer.

'But Raymond,' Hélène said, and clung to his arm, 'that's the most incredible news.'

It was. It really was. And yet too many other things were pulsing in Raymond, 'Nancy's been fuming. Hélène, I did a stupid thing. On the night she told me, I was due to go on patrol. She'd been begging me not to, though I was too blind to see why. It's what happened to my brother, how it left Vivienne alone with their child. That same fear's been building in Nancy, and I knew it – there's no denying that I knew – and yet *still* I went out there.'

'Oh, Raymond...'

She was not admonishing him; that was not in Hélène's nature. Her fingertips caressed his arm in a loving, sisterly way. She was, he realised, sympathising – and this moved him more than anything else.

'I should feel ashamed. Sometimes I do. But that night, Hélène, I saved more than sixty souls, stranded in a factory basement out east. Destitute souls, who'd found shelter – then got trapped inside. Nancy was afraid that I'd put myself in harm's way, leave her alone and our child without a father – I promised her I wouldn't, and then I did it anyway. I just walked into the storm with hardly a second thought.' He stopped. 'I don't believe she's forgiven me. I don't believe she can.'

'Have you told her how sorry you are?'

Raymond shook his head. 'We've just been existing. Sliding around each other, trying hard not to speak of it. It's like dancing through a veil. Like you and I are out on the dance floor, with a velvet curtain between us – we're there, with each other, but there's this thing between us.' He paused. 'I haven't told her I'm sorry – because I don't think I am. She said she'd rather sixty souls died than our child not have a father. But sixty people are alive in London tonight because of what I did. How could I ever take that back?'

The dance came to its end. Marcus released Karina from his hold, then started presenting himself in ostentatious bows to the troupe.

'Having a baby is a miraculous thing,' said Hélène. 'You'll never know what it feels like, to nurture your child with your own body and blood. It can make you fierce. I think, even, it can make you a little wild. There's not a thing you wouldn't do to protect that child. Perhaps it's impossible for fathers to feel it. Certainly it must be, before a child is born. But I believe, Raymond – knowing you as I do – that, the moment you hold your baby for the very first time, you'll understand why Nancy said the things she did. You'll understand what she meant. But until that moment – you mustn't lose her, Raymond. You mustn't keep dancing through a veil.'

Down on the dance floor, Frank had taken Mathilde in hold. The next dance was about to begin.

It was late afternoon, the sky heavy with cloud above the old heart of London. Heavy clouds, at least, would keep the bombers at bay – there was this to say for winter. It had not snowed yet, but as Nancy and Vivienne walked along the edge of Hyde Park, then disappeared along one of the broad thoroughfares leading north, the whisper of it was in the air. A winter city in siege – what a thing that might be to live through.

'Is this the place?' asked Vivienne, drawing her woollen coat around her, scarfs piled up high around her neck.

According to the scrap of paper Nancy held in her hands, this was exactly the place: just another of the old townhouses a stone's throw from Lancaster Gate. The blackouts were fixed in the window, so there was no way of knowing if the building was empty or a hive of activity within. In the end, all that either of them could think of to do was knock – so that was exactly what they did.

'Mr Bond?' Nancy began, when a portly, round, bewhiskered face came to the door.

He looked much less harassed than the night he had come to Blomfield Road, bringing with him the news of Raymond's brush with death. His face was not begrimed and his whiskers were not dripping in soot – but he still looked as if he'd been too busy to stand in front of his shaving mirror for several days. His shirt – worn without a tie – was crumpled and he had the hangdog expression of somebody who had woken up on the wrong side of the bed. Indeed, by the sleep in his eyes, he looked as if he'd only just arisen.

'It's *Captain* Bond,' he began. 'And, by the looks of you, you have the wrong address. Ladies, please, how can I help? The WVS area office is down the road.'

The man yawned so widely that Nancy saw the very back of his throat.

'Captain Bond, it's Nancy – Nancy de Guise. You visited my home, last week, when my husband was hospitalised.'

Mortimer looked her up and down. 'By God, it *is* you. You'll have to forgive me. The nights have rather scrambled my mind. Get in here, Mrs de Guise – the man's a hero. A bally hero! Come in, come in – you'll have to excuse the clutter, of course. We had a fresh hell on our hands last night, and without your good husband on patrol, we took a battering. I've six men out of tonight's rotation.' He stopped. 'Of course, the good lance corporal's back on the street tonight, so things are bound to look up.'

He was turning to lead them inside when Nancy, disgruntled already at the eagerness they had to put Raymond back on the streets, said, 'I'm afraid we can't stop. It's only that we're looking for somebody – a WVS girl Raymond knows from the patrols. He said she's done work for you, when it's been needed. She's the one who went into the Daughters of Salvation after him, after the explosion.'

Mortimer Bond said, 'You mean our Miss Everly!' with a broader grin than Nancy had thought imaginable under those improbable whiskers. 'A fine member of the service – I'm pleased to have had her spotting fires, instead of making casseroles in the canteens. As invaluable a service as that is, of course. There's many a cold night been saved by a warm broth.'

On the edge of being exasperated, Nancy said, 'We wanted to thank her, personally, for what she did for my Raymond. Raymond's to dance at the Buckingham Hotel this Christmas. We wanted to extend her an invitation.'

Mortimer Bond said, 'You know, *I* have dancing feet too,' and performed an ungainly prance – more like a crippled foal than a ballroom impresario – in the open door.

'The thing is,' Vivienne intervened, 'we know that poor Miss Everly was bombed out of her lodgings. We wondered if you knew where she might be staying? So we can pay a visit, you understand.'

Mortimer Bond's puffed his cheeks out, as if in deep thought. 'Bombed out, you say?'

'Yes, sir.'

He exhaled, long and loud. 'I can't say I know a thing about it – but if you wait here, for a moment, I'm sure I can rustle up an address for you. She's on my Christmas card list, don't you know? Oh yes, Miss Everly's quite the shining star around here – it isn't just your husband who's in her debt. The world would be a poorer place without Miss Everly marching through it.'

The address was in Holland Park, scarcely a mile from where Mortimer Bond stood, his top lip wobbling as he bid them farewell – but the time was not yet right to venture there; the day was still too young, with only the first hints of darkness drawing in, and there was every chance Miss Everly would be at the property, resting in anticipation of the evening to come. Nancy, who was already exhausted by the day's endeavour, found a tea shop on the Bayswater Road – and there they waited, drinking tea and eating scones, until dusk was heavy and the blackout began. Then, with night-time hardening – and the first fragments of the season's snow beginning to tumble down – they took off through the bracing December air.

The streets, here, did not look bombed out. To Vivienne's eyes, these stretches of London were an idyll, compared to the ruin being made of East London. Perhaps this was what came of being so far from the docklands. Along the Bayswater Road, the only signs of a city at war were the ARP wardens emerging on their nocturnal patrols. Nancy supposed Raymond was soon to join them. He'd spent all day in the ballroom, preparing for One Grand Night – but, if the promise of a child would not dissuade him from stepping out beneath the searchlights, then surely the ballroom would not. No, she thought, he'd be back out there tonight, up and down, spotting for fires and betrayals of the blackout – waiting, eagerly waiting, for the sirens to come.

Cathy Everly would be out there as well, of course. Nancy and Vivienne were banking upon it.

The address Mortimer Bond had given them was a townhouse much the same as the one in which his offices had been located, the middle house of a leafy street quite untouched by the bombs. By the time Nancy and Vivienne approached its gate, the first rags of snow had fattened into ripe, plump flakes, and the black railing surrounding the house was rimed in white. Nancy looked up. She counted four storeys, and a window in the attic above. A lodging house, she realised, and knocked at the door.

'She told Raymond it was bombed out,' Nancy began, shivering as they waited. 'He took her back to our house.'

Vivienne was cautious as she said, 'Are you sure that's what *she* told him? What chance it was just a lie that he told you, Nancy?'

Nancy remained defiant. She shook her head. 'Forget, for a moment, what's in his heart – unthinking and reckless as he's being. Raymond isn't foolish enough to bring a mistress back to his own house, not when he had every reason to think I'd be there. No,' she said, wearily now, 'it was a lie she told him. I just need to know *why*.'

It took some time before they heard the sound of a latch being drawn, and the door opened up. The lights inside had been snuffed out, the better to maintain the blackout, so at first they could not make out the face of the old lady who tottered to the doorstep, slender and bird-like, with thin grey hair instantly whipped up by the wind. In the gloom, the woman considered them closely, then said, 'May I help you girls?' in a voice rich with welcome, a warm tone quite at odds with her frail scarecrow's appearance.

'Mrs Yorke?' Nancy ventured. It was the name Mortimer Bond had given.

'Yes, dear?'

There was an inquisitiveness in Mrs Yorke's voice. She craned her head forward, and Nancy saw her lined, bunched features for the first time, lit up in the reflected light of the snow.

'Mrs Yorke, I'm so sorry to disturb you – and after blackout as well! We're friends of Miss Everly. Cathy?'

'Oh, but she's not in, dear. It's her night with the volunteers. Matter of fact, almost every night's her night with the volunteers – it's been that way since summer. I'm afraid you'll have to call another time. I've a pencil here, if you'd like to leave a message.'

It was Vivienne who spoke next. She took a tiny step closer to Mrs Yorke, the better to be heard. 'That won't be necessary, Mrs Yorke,' she began, hewing close to the script Nancy and she had decided on the way here. 'We were rather hoping we could leave a little something here for her. It's something of a surprise.'

They had expected old Mrs Yorke to look suspicious – but instead the old woman's eyes dazzled as she smiled, 'Well, go on then, dear! I'll make sure she gets it. A girl like Cathy needs a nice surprise, here and there. Something to pick up those spirits. Something to remind her life's worth living. Let's see it, girls. What is it?'

Nancy steeled herself as she produced the envelope from her shoulder bag. There was, of course, nothing in it – just a scrap of card she'd taken from the drawer in the Housekeeping Office – but on the front, Cathy's name had been inscribed in elaborate script. It didn't matter; it was only a prop, something to get her through the front door, something to win the old landlady's trust. 'It's a ticket,' she explained, 'for a ball at the Buckingham Hotel.'

'The Buckingham Hotel?' Mrs Yorke reeled back, with

disbelief. 'Well, I suppose Miss Everly comes from the blue bloods, after all. Hand it over, girls. I'll see it gets to the right spot.'

Mrs Yorke was reaching out with her papery hand, but Nancy – feeling a frisson of discomfort at deceiving the old dear – pulled the envelope back.

'Don't trust me, do you, girls? Well, I'll have you know – I'm the most reputable landlady this side of Shepherd's Bush. This was my father's lodgings. He ran it like a palace, and I'm the same. The utmost discretion. I'll see to it, girls – you've got a widow's word, and there's no stronger promise than that.'

'It isn't that we don't trust you, Mrs Yorke – far from it! It's only … Well, we rather hoped we might leave it in Cathy's rooms ourselves – arrange the place a little, so that she comes back to the nicest surprise. She'll have been out all night – I'll warrant she could do with a little cheer, after that.'

This time, old Mrs Yorke really did eye them suspiciously. 'Enter one of my lodgings, girls? What do you take me for?' She looked left and right, along the snowy street. 'If you didn't look as sweet, I might think you were looters. The night's alive with them these days. People out for what they can get, while there are others giving their lives up above.' She crossed her chest, and whispered the name of the Lord.

'Mrs Yorke, you're right. The night really is alive with people out for themselves – but I promise you, we're not those people. In fact …' Nancy set down her shoulder bag and opened it up. From inside, she produced a jar of glistening Royal Gardens Honey, a wax paper parcel of bacon rashers, a wedge of ripe Lancashire cheese, and a small cloth bag of oranges, figs and a single lemon. The bounty of the Buckingham Hotel. It had almost felt dirty, pulling these things together – until she remembered she was taking them from those who ate better every single night. 'A gift, Mrs Yorke. Well, you don't mind helping us a little, do you?'

Mrs Yorke's smile was so broad it revealed three missing molars. 'Oh girls,' she said, 'you do know the way to a poor woman's heart. Come on in – but you'll have to have me as a chaperone, I'm afraid. Those are the rules, you understand – it's like I said, I'm the best landlady this side of Acton Green.'

Nancy's heart was beating like a baby bird's as they followed Mrs Yorke into the lodging house, along the darkened hallway and up the first flight of creaking stairs. In the dark, she reached out and squeezed Vivienne's hand.

'Oh yes,' said Mrs Yorke, pausing for breath on the first landing, 'Cathy's been lodging here for more than a year. It helps, of course, that she draws an allowance – so she's never short on rent.' Mrs Yorke set off again. 'If you ignore the occasional blasts of music coming from that room, you might consider her the perfect lodger.'

Nancy caught Vivienne's eye. 'A whole year,' she whispered – and Vivienne knew instinctively what Nancy was thinking. The last chance that Cathy had been telling the truth – that she'd been bombed out of her original accommodation and found herself compelled to take temporary lodgings here – had just evaporated. The lie held true.

'Of course, a woman like Cathy's been through so, so much. It's hard to believe how much a life can change in such a short time.' They'd passed the second landing, and at last they came to the third. 'Well, here we are, girls. Let me find my key.'

The door to the apartment opened up, revealing a long, dark bedsitting room with a kitchenette in the window and two doors, one leading to a larder and the other to a washroom. Mrs Yorke was the first through, and fumbling to illuminate the lamp on its stand by the door. Moments later, the lamplight flared – and

Nancy stepped into a cluttered room, where the bed lay unmade, the bedside dresser was piled with unwashed crockery, and the washing basket was overflowing with laundry left untouched.

'Oh dear,' said Mrs Yorke, with a grandmother's judgement, 'oh dear indeed. I'm sure darling Cathy wouldn't want a soul to see her quarters quite like this.' Mrs Yorke seemed almost embarrassed for her; she gave them a weak, half-smile, and shrugged her shoulders in apology. 'She's been run off her feet, quite run off her feet with all her WVS duties. It's been the most awful few months. Every night, I thank my lucky stars we're still here.' Then she paused, took stock, and said, 'Well, if it's a surprise you want to make, maybe we could do dear Cathy a service and get this place ship-shape? Then she can find your invitation up there on the mantel, in her sparkling clean room.'

Vivienne's eyes seemed to have been drawn to a pile of envelopes and letters left on the bedside dresser, but with Mrs Yorke's words, Nancy lifted her own gaze up to the mantelpiece.

It was then that her heart skipped a beat.

There were still embers glowing in the hearth, which meant Cathy had kindled a small fire during the cold December day. In the low orange light they cast, Nancy saw a silver photograph frame sitting on the mantel. At first she couldn't be sure whose face was peering out of that frame, so she stepped a little closer. 'Vivienne,' she said. 'Vivienne, look.'

Nancy lifted the frame. The picture behind the glass had a ragged edge, as if it had been torn out of some greater picture.

It was a picture of her husband.

A picture of Raymond de Guise.

Mrs Yorke had appeared at Nancy's side. 'Oh, he was a handsome man, and no mistakes,' she said, with such an air of sadness that it near filled the room. 'Did you know him?'

'Know him?' mouthed Nancy, unable to fit the pieces of this particular puzzle together.

By the bedside, Vivienne was grasping the envelopes in her hand. 'Nancy,' she said, 'you have to see these…' With the letters in hand, she too gravitated to the hearth and the silver frame Nancy was holding. Then her eyes took in the image. 'Nancy, but that's—'

'There's a lot of tragic stories being written in this war, girls – but, I have to say, this one touches me the most. I suppose you girls have only known Cathy since she came to London to fight this bloody war, have you?'

Mrs Yorke's words seemed dreamlike and faraway, for Nancy was still gazing, confused, at Raymond in the frame. She'd seen this picture before – she was quite certain of it. It was one of the iconic images from early in Raymond's career: the young prince of the ballroom, on the cusp of becoming king. Yes, she thought, and remembered unpacking boxes in their new home together in the days after they were married, finding the shoebox of Raymond's old keepsakes and going through it with him. His copies of *Dancing Times*, every issue where they'd chronicled his rise from minor championship to the palaces of Europe. Now that she thought about it, she could clearly see how this picture had been torn from a magazine just like that: its ragged, shredded edges were not quite concealed by the silver of the frame.

'She must have talked about him, though?' asked Mrs Yorke.

'Oh yes,' said Nancy, because it seemed like the right thing to say, the thing that might goad Mrs Yorke into revealing yet more, 'she talked about him often.'

'Second Lieutenant Michael Bonneville. It has the proudest, most debonair ring to it, doesn't it?'

Nancy fixed Mrs Yorke with a look. 'What did you say?'

'The gentleman in the picture, dear. Second Lieutenant

Bonneville, as was. But hasn't Cathy told you about him?' Mrs Yorke's face took on a look of grief. 'I've let the cat out of the bag, haven't I? It's something she wanted to keep private, isn't it? And why shouldn't she? Why not, after everything that happened?'

Suddenly, this didn't just feel like intruding into somebody's private property; it felt like intruding into somebody's private pain as well. Nancy forgot, for a second, that the face in the picture was not 'Michael Bonneville', overlooked the material truth that it was Raymond in the frame, and said, 'What did happen to him, Mrs Yorke? Cathy's been so private. She didn't breathe a word.'

Mrs Yorke was suddenly tongue-tied. 'Perhaps, if Cathy hasn't even told her friends, it's not my story to tell.'

'Mrs Yorke,' Vivienne intervened, 'we just want to help her.'

'They were betrothed,' Mrs Yorke said, her voice cracking as the sadness of the story she was about to spin took hold. 'Sweethearts, and due to be married. They'd even set a date. Twenty-first of December, 1939 – an autumnal wedding, because it was the season they'd first been introduced. And then...'

'This blasted war,' said Nancy, and felt it too: this *blasted* war, which had upended everything, transformed so many lives, stolen so many others.

Mrs Yorke nodded. 'Michael Bonneville went to the War Office on the day of the declaration. He said it was his duty. Well, he came from old army stock – good men, who'd served out in Africa – and he couldn't let them down. They took him as an officer, of course – the Bonnevilles had class – and that was that. Second Lieutenant Michael Bonneville was off to France with the British Expeditionary Force, to serve his King and Country.'

Vivienne whispered, 'And he never came home.'

'They wrote to each other all through the winter and spring. The wedding was postponed, but never cancelled. He'd made her a promise, bought her a ring …' Vivienne recalled the sparkling, diamond-encrusted band she'd been wearing outside the Daughters of Salvation, 'When France fell, he made it to the beaches at Dunkirk. His boys saw him there. They swear he was on the boats with them, heading out for one of the destroyers. But he never again set foot on English soil.'

Mrs Yorke hung her head, but it was Vivienne who started holding herself – for hadn't it been the same with Archie? Hadn't she been that woman, patiently waiting for a man who would never come home?

Nancy reached out and took her hand.

'Well, by then,' Mrs Yorke went on, 'Cathy had been in London for six months. The way she told it, she just couldn't sit around and do nothing while her sweetheart was risking his life. So she'd signed up with the WVS. I don't think she ever expected to be out on the streets, night after night, bombs falling down … but after Dunkirk, everything changed. I've begged her not to go out into it – but she's always been adamant. She's doing it for Michael. Doing it in his honour.'

Nancy recognised this kind of behaviour. How many times had she strained on Raymond's arm, telling him the same thing? How many times had she tried to make him see that nothing he did, now, would bring Artie back home, that he didn't have to throw himself into the fire every night, that what he'd already been shouldering was enough – more than enough – for any man.

But none of it explained why Raymond's picture was in the frame.

None of it explained why Cathy had lied about her lodgings being bombed out. Why she'd been standing there in Nancy's nightdress. Why, on the night the Daughters fell, she'd told Vivienne they were in love.

Or did it?

Mrs Yorke was wiping a tear from her eye. 'Well, let's sort this out, shall we, girls? Give our Cathy something to lift her heart. And a night of dancing at the Buckingham Hotel – that might be just the ticket to make her see there's still *life* to be lived.'

As Mrs Yorke set about collecting up the dirty crockery, Vivienne sidled even closer to Nancy and revealed the letters in her hand. Through the tumult of thoughts in her head, Nancy saw how each one was prefigured. 'Dear Raymond,' read the first. 'Dearest Cathy,' read the second – signed off at the bottom with Raymond's own name.

'They're full of love,' Vivienne whispered. 'Adulation. Promises to be married…' She turned to one and read a single sentence: '*I am so glad you made it home, my treasure, and after I thought, for so long, that you were lost…*'

Nancy felt a great, yawning chasm inside her. Grief, she thought, had changed Raymond; it had worked its dark magic on him, turned him to stone, made him reckless and foolish and single-minded, even to the detriment of the people he loved. What might it take to push somebody one step further, to find them on the cliff-edge of madness and, with a whisper, cast them tumbling over the edge?

'It's not Raymond's writing,' whispered Nancy, taking the letters. Yes, she was quite certain of it now. Raymond had written to her often enough – she would recognise the curls and flicks of his letters every time, his inkpen dancing across the page. 'It's just not his hand.'

'Then whose is it?' Vivienne whispered, in reply.

That chasm inside her was deep and vast as the world – and Nancy thought she understood, in that moment, everything that was going on. When a person lived on the edge between fear and safety, between grief and love, the mind played tricks. It manufactured ways to feel safe again. To feel love. *Madness,* thought Nancy – *madness running unchecked, because we're in a mad, mad world.*

She folded the letters, slipped them into her pocket, then replaced the picture of her husband on the mantel.

'Vivienne,' she said, 'we have to find Raymond – before he goes on patrol tonight.'

Chapter Twenty-One

In the same moment that dusk first touched Berkeley Square, the carpenters, joiners and chambermaids toiling in the Grand Ballroom began the task of tidying their work away. In one hour's time, the ballroom doors would open and – should the sirens allow – an evening of resplendent, carefree dancing would begin.

'Taxicab for Hélène Marchmont,' came a voice from the ballroom doors, one of the hotel pages zealously fulfilling his commission. On the dance floor, Raymond and Hélène stepped out of each other's arms and walked, together, to the doors. Behind the page, Walter Knave was waiting to thank them both for their appearance. 'Every dance will be worth it, Miss Marchmont,' he said. 'The Board are intent on having One Grand Night splashed across all the Society Pages. We've invited the director of *Harper's Bazaar*.'

It was the magazine that had once made Hélène famous. 'I rather suspect they'll find me more lined and less supple than they once did, Mr Knave.'

By now they had reached the reception hall and stood in the fragrant shadow of the Norwegian Fir, its kaleidoscope of lights shimmering above. Hélène gave Raymond one last look, grasped his hand and said, 'Congratulations, Raymond. Find your way through this next moment – and allow yourself to dream again. Having a baby, Lance Corporal – it will be the best thing you ever do.'

Hélène ought to know, thought Raymond as he watched her leave, into the snow settling on Berkeley Square, the waiting taxicab and the blacked-out city beyond.

Lance Corporal, she'd called him. He'd be a lance corporal again soon. Christmas was already here; some time in the New Year, if he kept his body unbroken, he'd be on a transport ship, off to join his division, or else on some new posting. All that he had between now and then was the treasure that would be One Grand Night, his return to the patrols – and Nancy.

He wished he could see her now, but she was not in the Housekeeping Lounge. He wished he could sit down with her and tell her what was in his heart, make her see that life had thrown him an impossible decision and he hadn't meant to hurt her – but it seemed she was nowhere in the hotel. He'd have to go straight from here to his patrol, he supposed, but there were still hours to kill. He wandered, instead, down to the hotel post room, where Billy Brogan was waiting.

'Billy?' he ventured, as he stepped through the doors.

And there was Billy, on his hands and knees, brown paper and string all around him, a wooden crate packed with bottles of wine and screwed-up newspapers to cushion them. Billy looked up, his face a twisted mask. 'Raymond,' he said – and Raymond could tell the battle going on inside him, for Billy's voice was fractured and low. 'He's asking for more. Every time I see him – more, more, more … It can't go on. *I* can't go on. I need a way out.'

At least here, doing 'good' was black and white, thought Raymond. At least, here, he might be able to see the answers.

The clock on the wall was ticking, but there was still time until he had to be on the streets.

'Pull up a chair, Billy. We're going to figure this out.'

The last of the chambermaids had left the Grand, the joiners were hoisting the chandelier back into place. Most of the dancers had scattered now, off to their rest and relaxation before their evening's work began – but there was Marcus Arbuthnot, just where Mathilde had known he would be, standing alone in the middle of the ballroom floor, breathing it in.

Mathilde watched from the edge of the balustrade, the letter straining in her hands. She could still walk away, she thought. She could tear up this letter, forget she'd ever read its contents, and dance with Frank at One Grand Night with all the passion and talent of her heart. She wondered if that was the right thing to do – but, every time she was on the verge of slipping out through the backstage doors, she remembered her mother's voice, the thought of dancing as principal for the first time at the Imperial Hotel prickled in her, and she found that she had not moved.

Once you boarded a train, she thought, you did not leave until you reached its destination. She'd already started this thing. And what did she owe him, anyway? He'd had his chances. He'd had his rich and storied career. People remembered the name Marcus Arbuthnot, while the name Mathilde Bourchier was scarcely a footnote, even in the history of the Grand.

'Mr Arbuthnot,' she said – and, down on the dance floor, Marcus opened his eyes.

'Ah, Miss Bourchier,' he exclaimed. They'd danced, of course, since the last time she probed him, right here in this ballroom, but they hadn't spoken – at least, not away from the prying eyes of the rest of the troupe. That knowledge seemed to flicker in

Marcus's eyes now, but he was professional enough to squirrel it away. 'You've been working hard, Miss Bourchier. I've sensed it in your balance. Dare I say it – there will come a time when you and our very own Mr Nettleton might make a formidable duo in the competitions.' He shook his head sadly. 'Should we ever see the competitions unfolding again, of course. Mathilde,' he declared, 'I'll make you a promise. When the world reopens – as we must pray it shall – I should like to instruct you and Mr Nettleton for a season. Let's see what we can get out of you. You know, of course, that I've won the World Championship before ...'

It was all misdirection, thought Mathilde. It was all stagecraft – wasn't it? Or had he really forgotten the discomfort he'd felt the last time they'd been alone together?

She had to admit that it was a tantalising prospect: Marcus the champion instructor, Mathilde and Frank on top of the world. She hadn't, until this moment, envisioned a lifetime dancing with Frank Nettleton – talented as he was, there must have been someone with more natural refinement better suited to her needs, somebody with the instinctive elegance of Raymond de Guise – but the prospect did have a certain romantic appeal.

If it wasn't for the contents of the letter in her hands, she might have abandoned the Imperial dream and rushed straight into it.

It didn't feel good as she wended her way to the dance floor – but, she supposed, the act of betrayal wasn't meant to feel good. It was what came after that mattered – and, in this, it was not so very unlike the war: to reach peace, first you had to fight. Well, she would do her fighting today. She would do it right now.

As she reached the dance floor, she said, 'It sounds perfect, Mr Arbuthnot – you'd really do that for me?'

Marcus said, 'Of course, Miss Bourchier. There is no finer

feeling in the world than to share in the success of a talented young artiste.'

'To take them to the very top?'

'Indeed, Miss Bourchier!' Marcus declared, his arms theatrically wide.

'By all means necessary?'

'By talent, and pluck – and the unstoppable force of the imagination.'

Now, she told herself, *now's the moment*.

So she brandished the letter Billy had delivered to her and said, 'Or by cheating, Mr Arbuthnot?'

The shame prickled at her almost immediately. It was an intense feeling, as if she'd stabbed not just Marcus in the back, but herself as well. That was the feeling she had to fight back, if she was going to be successful in this. One bad deed, in exchange for a lifetime's happiness and success; in exchange for the true vindication of her talent. That was a pact that Marcus Arbuthnot knew well.

'Mathilde,' he said, without a hint of his usual grandiosity now, 'what's the meaning of this?'

'I asked you once about the Exhibition Paris, Mr Arbuthnot. I asked you once about why you vanished from the ballroom for two long years. You shied away from me then, but now I know why.'

It was all in the letter. She'd been right all along – if anybody could dig out the sordid rumours of times gone by, it was her mother, Camille. Camille, with her encyclopaedic knowledge of the ballroom world; Camille, with her little book of addresses and telephone numbers; Camille, with her bitterness at those who had succeeded where she'd fallen away. All she'd had to do was ask a few little questions, make a few polite enquiries, remind a few people of the favours they owed her from the old times. In the envelope there was a page torn from a copy of *Dancing Times*, and another letter, still in its blue envelope and signed in the hand of 'Mr Victor Grace'.

'Mr Arbuthnot, I know why you left the ballroom. I have it here in black and white. We can talk about it properly – or … or …' At the last moment, her words were failing her. She'd been through this moment in her mind's eye so many times, but fighting imaginary foes was so much easier than ones of flesh and blood. Looking at him now, Marcus did not look like the sort of man who ought to be destroyed – but the revolver was already in her hand, bidding her to shoot. 'Or you can leave the Grand, leave it forever.'

'Leave the Grand? Miss Bourchier, what's the meaning of this? What's the—'

'Please don't insult me by pretending you don't know what I'm speaking of. I deserve better than that.'

You don't deserve a thing, a little voice inside her said, *not if this is the only way to get it.*

Then her mother's voice came in return:

Nobody gets to the top on talent alone. The world is full of sycophants and con artists. To rise to the top in a world like this, sometimes a woman makes compromises.

'Do you want me to lay it out for you, Marcus? How you tutored Victor Grace and Meghan Barr. How, for some reason, you picked them out of thousands – though they were thought so little of in the ballroom, hardly proficient enough a prospect for a man like you. Just part-timers, with little hope of reaching the top. It's all over the *Dancing Times*, Mr Arbuthnot. There's no secret in it. You steered them from nothing to crowning glory at the Exhibition Paris. Meghan Barr, a perfectly ordinary dancer – and suddenly they were speaking of her as if she was a prospect for the World Championships.'

'The right instructor can work wonders,' protested Marcus, though his eyes would not settle on hers. 'Meghan had a talent. She simply needed it unlocking.'

'Yes,' Mathilde declared, 'and you unlocked it with a bribe.'

The word fell like a bomb in the ballroom.

'A bribe, Mr Arbuthnot. Meghan Barr wasn't strong enough to win the Exhibition Paris. The whole dancing world knew it. And then – *voila!* The championship was hers. The world beckoned. *Dancing Times* sang your praises, as if you'd sprinkled magic dust across her. But it wasn't so, was it? Because the truth was, you paid your old friend on the judging panel. You took him for dinner and slipped him a bribe, and the next day they made sure Meghan Barr was garlanded beyond her wildest dreams – and beyond the merits of her talent. And how do I know it, Mr Arbuthnot?' She pulled the smaller envelope out of the first. 'Because Victor Grace himself told my mother.'

Marcus's face changed. In an instant, he looked older, more lined, as if every expression of pomp and glory he'd ever made was just an affectation – and this crestfallen man had been hidden within.

'Camille Bourchier,' he whispered. 'I knew I remembered the name.'

'It turns out that my mother was only a few steps removed from Victor Grace. It turns out that he was only too happy to spill your little secret. It was the secret that cost him glory – wasn't it, Mr Arbuthnot? Because he's the reason you left the ballroom. When he found out what you did, he couldn't bear it. He wouldn't cripple Meghan's career by exposing you – but nor could he stand by and allow you to remain. So he told you to leave, to leave their side – and to leave the very ballroom itself. For two years, you did as you were told. Then, with Victor and Meghan long gone from the ballroom scene, you re-emerged from the stone under which you'd been hiding, and picked up where you left off.' She stopped, surprised at the vindictiveness of her own tone. Well, she supposed, she really was her mother's daughter after all. 'Well, Mr Arbuthnot, do you deny it?'

Marcus breathed deeply, 'Why, Mathilde? Why are you doing this? Why now?'

It was the one thing she could not truly tell him. 'Because,' she exclaimed, 'I care about integrity. About honour. I care about truth!' And so swept up in her own brio was she that she barely even felt the hypocrisy of it; the anger was simply carrying her through.

'You don't understand, Mathilde. Victor wasn't Meghan's only partner. I—'

'You cheated and you lied, Mr Arbuthnot.' Mathilde sat back against the balustrade, affecting despair. Her mother would have been proud; she ought to have been strutting on the Palladium stage. 'What's going to happen, Mr Arbuthnot? What will become of us all when everyone finds out? They hired you to save this ballroom. They idolise you here. You're Hercules. You're the hero to see us through the war. Mr Knave has kings and princesses in his suites, and all because of the reputation of this ballroom. But it's all built on a lie.'

Marcus took a panicked stride towards her. 'Mathilde, you're young, you can't possibly understand. The stresses of that moment, the desperation, the yearning to win ... I made a foolish mis-step, but it was the only time I ever strayed from a true and righteous path. I've paid for that mistake.'

'It's the rest of us who'll pay, when people find out. It's the Grand which will suffer. The dancers, the musicians – but it won't stop there. If the hotel starts losing guests, what then? What if there's some other ballroom, where things aren't played dirtily, where the magic holds true? What happens when the kings and queens and crown princesses find some other playground, better to their liking?' She hung her head. 'It's impossible, Marcus – and it's all on you.'

There was a long, lasting silence.

'Mathilde,' he eventually dared to say, '*how* would they find out? This has been my secret for almost ten long years.'

Mathilde allowed the question to linger, just long enough for the doubt to creep into his mind, just long enough that he might start believing in the reality of which she was capable.

'Mr Arbuthnot, it's *reputation*. Your reputation, and this ballroom's reputation. How many times do they tell us? It's the only currency we have. And you could undo it, in one fell swoop.' She stopped. 'I was thinking – I'd have to tell Mr Knave. Mr Knave would know what to do with a scandal like this. He'd know if it could be tidied away ...'

'Mathilde, please.' By his tone, Marcus Arbuthnot was already on his knees. 'There's no need to be so rash.'

'I just can't see another way,' she told him. 'Not unless—'

'Unless what?'

She drew herself up. 'Unless, perhaps, you were to leave the ballroom again? The Grand would suffer, I know, but it would recover so much more quickly than if a scandal like this were ever to erupt.' She stopped. By the look on his face, he still needed another gesture. She hated him for that; hated him, in that moment, for making her stoop so low. *Just one more time,* she told herself, *one more moment of ill in exchange for a lifetime's joy.* 'I think you need to leave, Mr Arbuthnot. I think you need to leave right now.'

Marcus filled his breast, kept his head held high, tried to convince himself – by poise and posture, as every good dancer does – that he was still in control of the dance.

But the dance was no longer his. He was being led, led by a partner who wanted only his destruction.

He did not start sobbing until he was out of the ballroom.

The last anyone saw of Marcus Arbuthnot was him streaking out through the hotel's revolving brass doors, then vanishing into the snowy darkness of Berkeley Square.

'One last delivery,' said Billy Brogan, down in the hotel post room. 'A delivery big enough and prized enough that he'd just let me go. What about that?'

'It wouldn't work,' said Raymond, his jaw set in determination. 'A man like Ken doesn't know kindnesses. It would take a kind man to say thank you and send you on your way – he'd have to empathise with your plight, and he's already shown himself unwilling to do that. If you tried to buy him off, Billy, it would only show him what you're capable of. Take him half the wine cellar, and it wouldn't be enough – he'd just tell you it proved you could get him the other half. No, there has to be some other way…'

Billy sank into his seat, all the various papers and manifests of his day's work ranged around him. He'd been forging a document moments before Raymond arrived, something to disguise the fact he was sending yet another delivery up to Camden Town. He hadn't even started the most important job of the day yet: tomorrow, the chambermaids would start packaging up all of the ball gowns from the dressing rooms behind the Grand for shipping off to the hotel laundries. The hotel laundry, once part of the hotel basements, had long ago been shut down – and now all of the hotel's relentless tide of bedsheets, towels and other linens were sent to an industrial laundry south of the river; it was one of the many cost-saving measures put in place by the former director Maynard Charles, back when the Great

Depression had threatened to end the Buckingham once and for all. Billy was supposed to have ordered the vans, instructed the driver, taken an inventory of everything that was being sent off to be laundered. It was, Mr Knave had told him, how Billy himself could contribute to One Grand Night, but he'd been so swept up in thinking about Ken that he was yet to begin.

'But Raymond,' he said, feeling his way with another errant thought, 'what if there was one big delivery… and he was caught in the act? If I packaged up racks of Champagne, and somehow he was caught receiving it?'

Raymond prowled the post room. 'Could it be traced back to you?'

'What if there was a way it wasn't?'

'Then what's to stop Ken throwing you to the wolves, Billy?'

Billy threw his head back, kneading at his brow.

'If he thought for a second it was you, Billy, he'd drag you into it. That's what men like this are like. You'd be in the dock alongside him. He'd do anything to try and save his own skin.'

'It's hopeless, isn't it, Raymond?'

It felt it, tonight. Billy's head crashed onto the table, his cheek smeared across the list of ball gowns due to be delivered to the laundries this week. Forty-six gowns of chiffon, silk and lace – what Ken wouldn't do for those, thought Billy. What a prize they would be. What a price they might fetch on this black market.

Somewhere, in the back of Billy Brogan's brain, a spark caught fire. Embers turned into flames. Flames turned into a raging inferno. Silk, chiffon, lace – the biggest prize at the Buckingham Hotel, bigger than anything he'd provided for Ken so far. And it was all leaving the Buckingham already. In a few days time, it would all be packaged up and in the back of a van – everything in one place, waiting to be found.

It was what Raymond had said that niggled at him, though. How to stop Ken knowing it was Billy who'd set him up? If the police swooped in and caught him red-handed, how to stop Ken howling Billy's name in vengeance and fury?

'Raymond, I think I have an idea...'

It was only half-formed, an idea full of holes and pitfalls and traps – but at least it was something. Billy was about to say more, when suddenly the door opened – and there, panting in its frame, stood Frank Nettleton, dressed in his charcoal grey dinner jacket and dancing shoes.

'Frank!' Billy exploded, leaping up to hide the packages he'd been wrapping. 'You know you ought to knock, I've got very sensitive information in here – not for prying eyes, certainly not for a dancer!'

In unison, Frank and Raymond shot Billy a puzzled look. Then, Frank turned his panicked eyes back on Raymond. 'Raymond, you're needed in the Grand.'

'The Grand?' Raymond baulked. 'Frank, the evening must be about to begin – there isn't any rehearsal time left. And, besides, Hélène's already...'

'It isn't rehearsals,' Frank implored. 'It's Mr Arbuthnot. Raymond, he's gone. Nobody's seen him since the rehearsals ended. They say he just marched out through the guest entrance. There's been hide nor hair of him since.'

Raymond's bewildered expression only invited more panic from Frank.

'Mr Knave's asked for you, Raymond. He's waiting backstage right now.'

Frank turned and hurried away from the post room, his dancing shoes making light percussion on the floorboards as he went.

'Billy,' said Raymond, 'don't give up, and don't lose heart.'

That was advice easier said than taken – but, as Billy watched him leave, his eyes fell back on the list of ball gowns due to be packaged up, and some deep, churning feeling at the bottom of his gut told him that the answer lay here, that in this simple piece of paper was the key that would release him from this mess, that – if only he could figure it out – his future was spelled out in front of him, in rows of chiffon, silk and lace.

The moment Raymond stepped into the dressing room behind the Grand, two dozen eyes turned to see him. Frank stood skittishly in front of a mirror, repeatedly failing to fix his bow tie. Karina Kainz was taking Archie Adams' counsel. Mathilde Bourchier stood, apart from all the other dancers, wearing an inscrutable expression. Alone among the musicians and dancers, she had a strange look that hovered somewhere between defiance and blind panic.

In the midst of them all, the diminutive figure of Walter Knave looked like a strange aberration – a man completely out of place and time. Dressed, as he always was, in a suit that seemed a size too big, with his gold watch as loose upon his wrist as a bangle, his owlish eyes glimmered behind their thick spectacles. 'Well, Mr de Guise,' he croaked, 'are you up to it? Those lungs of yours not too badly scarred by smoke, I hope? Your body not too battered?'

'Mr Knave,' Raymond said, 'when the ballroom calls, I'd ordinarily come running – but tonight I'm on patrol.' He looked around the room. 'Doesn't anyone know where he is?'

There were manifold murmured voices. Out of the unsettled chorus, Frank finally said, 'He might be at the Academy. He has friends there. He takes supper and drinks.'

The Academy des Artistes: the club on a cobbled Covent

Garden lane where Raymond had once spent many long evenings, alongside his mentor Georges de la Motte.

'There isn't time,' Walter Knave croaked. 'Mr de Guise, give us one hour – one hour of your waltzes. That's all I ask of you. After that, we'll take intermission – and, should we be fortunate enough not to be called off by the sirens, the whole ballroom will cheer you on your way. But I have guests expecting a debonair dancer tonight, somebody of Mr Arbuthnot's stature – and you're standing in front of me.'

Raymond wasn't sure if he could protest any longer. He looked at the clock on the dressing-room wall. It was mere moments before six o'clock, two hours before he was due out on the streets.

Walter Knave picked his way through the dancers, approached a wardrobe set into one of the alcoves in the wall and, opening it up, revealed a familiar suit of midnight blue. 'Somebody get some pomade,' he declared. 'That hair's been crushed under a warden's helmet for too long, Mr de Guise. Tonight, for one night only, you're back where you belong.' Walter Knave draped the suit over his child-like arm and presented it to Raymond. 'Time to get dressed, Raymond. The hour is nigh.'

Stepping through those doors, Karina Kainz on his arm, was like waltzing directly into the arms of the past. The short, sharp jabs of the trumpets – like buglers, announcing an arrival; the wild, untempered way Archie Adams' fingers danced up and down the piano, building the tension of the song until it was at an almost unbearable peak; the sound of the applause, starting in isolated pockets and growing together until it was a joyful, percussive storm. Here he was, no longer a lance corporal, nor even a warden of the ARP – just Raymond de Guise, King of the Ballroom, back home at last.

Raymond had danced with Karina only rarely before, back

when Karina had been part of a Viennese troupe visiting the hotel, but even with an unfamiliar partner in his arms, the sensation was unsurpassable. Dancing with Hélène this afternoon had reminded him of the way a body could move on the dance floor; it had reinvigorated some part of him sent to sleep while he served his King. But rehearsing could not compare to the feeling of being on the dance floor, cantering through the quicksteps, turning a waltz into a slow, meaningful thing of beauty while an esteemed audience watched on, ready to take your hand.

The sirens came before the intermission, while Raymond – nervous at first, in a way he hadn't been since his earliest days – danced with the wife of a French dignitary, staying at the hotel while her husband held talks with officials from the Free France movement. As Archie Adams took to the stage to announce an 'early intermission in tonight's entertainment', and to welcome the guests to the Buckingham's luxurious shelters, Raymond took his lady on his arm and, following the etiquette displayed by others in the troupe, led her up through the archway and into the reception hall.

At least the lights in the Norwegian Fir weren't blacked out. They glittered an array of enchanted colours as Raymond joined the flock of other guests and staff shepherding the hotel's residents to safety.

He was halfway across the reception hall when he saw Nancy and Vivienne, standing in the rainbow halo of the Norwegian Fir. They seemed out of place, somehow – as if they were standing in the eye of a storm, with all the guests and other staff milling frantically around them. Raymond could see, by the look on Nancy's face, that something was wrong; she had fixed him with a peculiar look, one that demanded his attention. At first he thought it was because he was in his midnight-blue evening wear, and he looked like a ghost from the past (even without the pomade in his hair). Then he sensed it was something more. 'Forgive me,' he said to the lady on his arm, then called for Frank, who was already scurrying back from the shelter, having delivered his first charge there. 'Frank will guide you. You couldn't be in safer hands.'

Through the hubbub, Raymond approached Nancy.

'I knew you wouldn't be at home,' she said. 'I only hoped I could catch you here, before the patrols.' She screwed up her eyes, taking in his midnight blue. 'I didn't think to find you dancing,' she added, with a smile.

'Marcus took off. Nobody knows where.' He paused. 'But Nancy – what's happened?'

There was a small stack of letters in Vivienne's hand. She peeled off the first one and handed it to Raymond.

'Dear Cathy,' it read, *'my Cathy.'* His eyes flickered over the rest. Phrases leapt out. *'The feeling of walking out with you under the stars... You saved my life... like I dreamt of you saving me from Dunkirk...'* But it wasn't until his eyes reached the very end of the letter, and the words, *'Your love forever and all time, Raymond'* that he felt the fists closing in around his heart.

The reception hall was still a hustle as guests and staff flocked towards the shelters. In the centre of it all, Raymond looked at Nancy with eyes disbelieving, panicked and wild. 'Nancy, what is this? Where did it...' He wasn't sure whether her eyes were accusing or just in despair. 'I didn't write this, Nancy. These aren't my words.'

There was a pause. Raymond fancied he could hear the sirens more keenly now – though perhaps that was just the sirens wailing inside him, the alarm call of some disaster he hadn't foreseen.

'I know, Raymond. I know it wasn't you.'

Just a few small words to dispel such a vast fear.

'I know what's in your heart, Raymond, and I know what's in your head. I can see it all now – I know what you've been going through.' Nancy took his hand – and it felt, to Raymond, as if some fresh understanding was being reached, as if some bridge was being rebuilt, as if the waters of the ocean that had been keeping them apart were separating, and they were walking through to meet each other in the middle. 'And I know what Cathy Everly's been going through too.'

The reception hall was emptying at last. Raymond watched as Billy Brogan limped forlornly through – his head evidently still wrapped up in thoughts about Ken and how to drag himself out of the mire into which he'd stumbled.

'Raymond, we went to Cathy's lodgings tonight,' Vivienne explained. 'She told you she'd been bombed out, didn't she?'

Raymond nodded.

'She wasn't bombed out, Raymond. She's been living in the same lodgings for a year, ever since the war started and she came to London. She lied to you,' Nancy said. 'She lied so that you'd invite her back to our house.'

Raymond stood, dumbfounded in the lights of the Christmas tree. 'But why?' he asked. 'Why would she do that?'

So Vivienne told him, all about that night at the Daughters of Salvation, about how Cathy had screamed out his name in horror at him being trapped inside the burning factory building, how she'd ministered to him on the stretcher, told Vivienne they were in love, that they were to be married. How her diamond-encrusted engagement ring had dazzled in the firelight of the White Horse Road.

'But I think we know, now, why she said what she did. I think we know that Cathy wasn't lying either.' Nancy saw Raymond's face paling and cut him off before he replied, 'Because she truly *believes* it, Raymond. Somewhere, in the storm in her head, she's started to believe you two are fated. That you're already betrothed.'

'It was her landlady who told us,' Vivienne interjected. 'Cathy Everly was due to be married, more than a year ago. But her sweetheart took himself off to France. They lost him at Dunkirk.'

Dunkirk, thought Raymond. Yes, Cathy always spoke about Dunkirk. And, now that his mind was cartwheeling backwards through the last days and weeks of his life, he suddenly remembered the words she'd said to him as she bore him out of the burning Daughters of Salvation: *I'm here, my darling. Your Cathy. I've got you now. I'll get you back home.*

'Raymond,' said Nancy, and there was both compassion and warning in her tone, 'she isn't who she says she is. I'm quite certain it's not her fault. I want to speak to Doctor Moore, to ask him about what grief can do to a mind. But ... don't go near her, darling. She has your picture, torn out of a magazine, and in a frame where her husband's used to be. She's concocted letters from you to her and back again. She talks about love and marriage as if it's here, here in the real world, and not plucked from the imagination.'

Outside the Buckingham Hotel, frighteningly close, some fresh explosion shook the city's foundations. Every eye still in the reception hall turned, as one, to the revolving brass doors. Raymond looked over his shoulder, his gaze gravitating back to Nancy only when he was certain the danger had passed.

'Raymond, please,' she said to him, 'not tonight.' Her hand moved to her belly. 'I need you tonight. *We* need you.'

There were men on the streets who needed him too. There was Mortimer Bond and all the rest, awaiting his return. There was no way of knowing what might happen tonight – what other desperate souls might suddenly be in need. He didn't want to let them down. He didn't want to let any of them down.

But there was Nancy, standing in front of him – his Nancy, reaching for his hand, even while the world crashed down around them.

He took it. 'To the staff shelters,' he said, 'we'll sit it out with our friends down there. And in the morning...'

In the morning, he thought, we'll work this all out – every last sordid detail of it, until the world's set back on its axis once again.

Chapter Twenty-Two

It was in the dead of night, lost in dreams of devils and delivery vans, that Billy Brogan knew how it had to happen.

The raids had been short and sudden that night, the all-clear coming some time before midnight – so that, together, Billy and Annie could pick their way, through the blackout, to No. 62 Lambeth Yard, leaving Frank behind to get some shut-eye in the chambermaids' kitchenette. By the time they crossed the river beneath the palaces at Westminster, the city was cloaked in white – yet, when they looked east, along the snaking Thames, they could see the orange glow of the fires, lighting up the dome of St Paul's Cathedral.

Annie had insisted that she wasn't tired at all – 'I could work a ten-hour shift, Billy, and don't you doubt it!' – but, by the time the key was through the door, Billy was exhausted beyond measure. It wasn't just the exhaustion of limping all the way from Berkeley Square, though his leg felt as if it had gone to sleep somewhere along the Horse Guards Parade. It was the exhaustion of living under a shadow, the exhaustion of a man in a cell. That exhaustion dragged him straight into sleep, the moment his head hit the pillow; but it dogged him through his dreams as well. In those dreams, Billy Brogan walked through a London of shadows and smoke – and, every corner he turned, there was Ken, watching, waiting, quietly saying, 'Just one more, Billy? You'd help me *once* more, wouldn't you, son?'

Silk.

Chiffon.

Lace.

Suddenly, he knew what he had to do.

He thought it was the revelation that had awoken him, and perhaps that was part of it, but when he opened his eyes – the clock on the wall not yet reaching 5 a.m. – he heard movement downstairs. His father wasn't due at Billingsgate this morning – thank God fish had not yet been rationed, for Billy didn't know how his father would bear it if his work was taken away – so it certainly wasn't him. Nor would it be Billy's mother, who rose every day alongside his father to get him ready for market. No, thought Billy – and heard, now, a gentle sobbing as well – it was neither of them.

It was Annie.

Wearily, with phantom images of ball gowns and delivery vans still swimming in the back of his head, he picked himself out of bed, levered his way down the crooked stairs, and stood in the sitting-room door. There was Annie, just the same as he'd found her that first morning after she returned – only, now, she wasn't ferreting through the sideboard, looking for a knife and fork; now, she was sitting, scrunched up in a ball with her arms wrapped around her knees, stifling the occasional sob and letting the tears roll, unchecked, down her face.

'Annie?'

She started at the sound of his voice, sprang up out of the armchair and immediately began dusting herself down. 'You're up early, Bill,' she said, completely ignoring the tears on her cheeks and the glistening rings around each of her nostrils. 'Up

344

and at them early, is it? I'm not on shift today. Matter of fact, they haven't given me a shift all week. I'm—'

'Annie,' Billy said, approaching her cautiously, 'you haven't been to bed.'

'Me?' said Annie, with a snort. 'I don't need a bed, Bill. I sleep where I drop. That's just how I am. I've never needed a bed. Give me a corner, and I'm out like a light. I swear, I fell asleep sweeping up the other day – it's a good job Mrs de Guise didn't catch me, or she'd have had my guts. No, I don't need anything, Bill, don't you worry about me, I'll be right as rain in a minute or two, I just need to get my...'

It was the words that had been keeping Annie's emotions at bay, but once they ran out, the tears returned with fresh urgency. There was no use hiding them any longer; she fell back into the armchair, wrapped herself up in her arms again, and quaked.

Billy hurried to her side. 'Annie Brogan, what's wrong?'

'It's nothing, Bill.'

Billy looked her up and down. 'It doesn't look like nothing.'

'Well, it is.'

'Well, maybe you ought to tell me about this nothing. Maybe we ought to talk about nothing.'

Annie snorted out a huge laugh. 'You talk about nothing all the time, Bill. It's all you ever jabber about. That big ol' nothing, bouncing about your head.'

There was room on the armchair for two. Billy pushed his way into it alongside her. This had been easier when they were younger, Billy reflected. Seven years separated Billy and Annie; there'd been a time when she fit snugly into the crook of his arm.

'You'd better tell me, Annie. If you don't tell me, I'm bound to be worrying about you all day long – and I got enough to worry about.'

It was the only way a brother could truly approach the

unbridled emotion of a sister – to make light of it, to pretend it was nothing, when really it was everything in the world.

'It's just – just … everything,' Annie sniffled. 'I've been doing my best, Bill. I've been doing everything I can. But it's never good enough, not for the Buckingham. There's always some spot I've missed. Some wrinkle I haven't smoothed out. There's always a hair left in the washtub – or that time I scrubbed that carpet clean, but just didn't realise I was tramping around in my own dirty boots, so that when Mrs Moffatt came, it looked like a dog had been running all over the suite.' Annie gave a loud, porcine snort. 'I think it's why they haven't got me on shift, Bill. They don't like me. They're not going to give me a proper job, even after how hard I've been working. I'm just not polished enough.'

Billy grinned. 'You sound like our Frank, mooning about getting his chance in the Grand on an evening, because he's just not elegant enough.' Then he put an arm around Annie. 'You silly girl, you never said. You've been bouldering around like you owned the place!'

'I just wanted to make a good impression.'

'You got to get to know the feeling of a place like the Buckingham. It's like its own world. You've got to get to know its rhythms. It's going to take time.'

'I haven't got time. They're going to throw me out. I can tell.'

'Who says?'

'I can just feel it. Mrs de Guise isn't being friendly like she was, and …'

'That might have something to do with you jabbering on about her being pregnant, Annie.'

'I only told you.'

Billy grinned. 'I seen the way you've been winking at her, when you think nobody's watching. You've just got to learn to keep your head down, Annie. Keep your head down and not get into trouble …' Billy's words petered into silence, because this was a lesson he himself seemed not to have learned, even after all these years working at the Buckingham.

'I miss the rest of them, Billy,' Annie finally whispered. 'Patrick and Roisin, Daniel and Gracie-May. Even Connor, little wild animal that he is. Maybe I shouldn't have come back. I'd be more use out in Suffolk. At least *they* couldn't throw me out. Brogans stick together.'

'They do,' whispered Billy, and thought suddenly of that insidious threat Ken had made. 'Annie, it's all going to work out fine.' He was saying it to himself as well, for even as he sat here, holding Annie tight, he was thinking about Ken – about a delivery van, about chiffon, silk and lace, and the words Raymond had said: *there's only one way out of this, Billy. Ken's enterprise has to be put to an end.*

'You'll see,' he said. 'By Christmas, it's all going to be splendid. I can feel it, Annie. You just got to hold on to that hope. Splendid – for you and me as well.'

'You're a good brother, Bill,' she said, in a rare moment of sincerity. She held him tighter. 'I'm sorry about you and Mary-Lou. I thought you'd found someone there. Thought there might be wedding bells.' She paused. 'She still likes you, you know. I heard her talking to the girls.'

'That's good,' said Billy, with a distant, faraway tone.

It really was. It was going to make what he had to do next just a little bit easier.

The snow was lying thick across Berkeley Square when Billy arrived the following morning. The smell of smoke, drifting in from the east, seemed to have been crystallised, somehow, by the snow; it seemed riper this morning, as if it might linger long into the day. That would be Christmas this year: not the bewitching smells of sage and cinnamon wafting up from the Queen Mary, but the smell of smoke rising up from the ruins.

Billy had just about slipped through the tradesman's entrance, then up along the hall that would take him to the post room, when Mary-Louise appeared at the bottom of the service stairs, dressed in her plain grey dress and white apron, ready for another day in and out of the suites. For a moment, they faced each other in silence – like two dogs, Billy thought, eyeing each other up before a fight. But there was the glimmer of something in her eyes, something that seemed like hopefulness, and the moment he saw that, Billy knew that Annie had been right. 'Mary-Lou,' he said, and nodded his head.

'Billy Brogan.'

Those were the only things either of them said, but the silence that returned was different somehow – less frozen, with the merest hint of thaw in the air.

Then, as each of them took off for their destinations – awkwardly dancing round each other in the hall – Billy dared to say, 'It's nice to see you, Mary-Louise,' and waited with bated breath for her to say it in return.

'It's nice to see you too, Bill.'

Billy's heart filled as he walked on. His stomach settled too. Indeed, the only thing that prickled at him at all as he wended his way to the hotel post room was his conscience – because, whether Mary-Louise had known what Ken was up to all along or not, she was the one who was going to help him out of this.

And she wouldn't know a thing about it.

In the hotel post room, he sifted through the papers on his desk until he found the list of ball gowns for delivery to the hotel post room. Quietly, he studied it. There was elegance in this idea that he'd had. There was simplicity in it too. He hadn't known, until the dead of night, that he could be as calculating as this.

Annie had told him it would start at midday.

For the moment, all he had to do was wait.

There were no demonstration dances in the Grand this afternoon; indeed, almost all of the usual early December dancing had been set aside in anticipation of One Grand Night. Consequently, at lunchtime, the backstage area was filled not with dancers and musicians, but with Nancy and a group of the other Housekeeping staff, emptying the wardrobes and laying out the crepe paper into which each ball gown would be folded, before being shipped off to the hotel laundries. Mrs Moffatt herself, who was overseeing events, seemed peculiarly distracted, as the girls said she had done of late – but there she stood, battling through her unease to rally the girls to the task. It was a shame Annie hadn't been included, thought Billy as he picked his way across the rehearsal studio and into the backstage throng. The girls here seemed to have quite forgotten the importance of the occasion and, before they tided each gown away, they were roaring with laughter, holding it up against themselves, gazing into the mirrors and declaring, 'I wear this better than Karina Kainz!' or 'Hélène Marchmont doesn't have a thing on me!'

'Here with your checklist, are you, Billy?' asked Mrs Moffatt, who upbraided the girls only when Rosa seemed on the verge of actually climbing inside a gown of ivory silk.

'It's right here, Mrs Moffatt.' Billy produced the list he'd been perusing, the list that had dominated his dreams. 'I just need them ticking off, to make sure they match yours. We'd both be for the chop if one of these gowns went missing, isn't that so?'

'Mr Brogan, I don't think we earn enough in our lifetimes to pay back the debt. Girls!' Mrs Moffatt declared. 'You're to get packing, now. Billy's got a van coming. We can't be late.'

The groans of displeasure were, at least, matched by an increased fervour. Across the dressing room, Billy caught Mary-Louise's eye. Smiling deliberately, he made sure his eyes sparkled at her. Then, sensing somehow that this was the perfect moment, he gripped his leg as if reacting to a sudden pain, staggered back and propped himself against the wall.

'Billy, are you OK?'

It was Nancy's voice, across the room.

'Just the ol' war wound, Mrs de Guise,' Billy said, giving a wince he was quite certain was completely over the top. Billy Brogan hadn't been to the theatre, but he thought suddenly of what a difficult time those actors had, falling about all over the stage. 'It's nothing.' And, with a theatrical wince again, he let his checklist of ball gowns fall to the floor.

The second wince brought the attention of the other girls. In a moment, Mary-Louise had dropped a silvery silk gown to the floor and hurried across the room. 'Bill, what happened?'

The genuine concern in her voice only prickled Billy's conscience more. He had to remind himself that she'd struck him across the face to build up the courage to see this next moment through. 'It's nothing, Mary-Louise,' he said, contorting his face into such a unique expression that it looked like a most unusual pain. 'I just need to sit for a bit. It's been nagging at me ever since this cold came on. It's just...' And he gave a howl.

'For goodness sake, Billy, you should get yourself sat down with a nice cup of tea,' said Mrs Moffatt.

'I need to tick these gowns off my list, Mrs Moffatt. Unless – maybe – no,' he said, shaking his head, 'it's asking too much. It's my duty. I've got to do it.'

And his eyes landed on Mary-Louise, who immediately said, 'I'll do it, Bill. You take yourself off. You can leave it with me.'

Billy said, 'Are you sure?'

'I'm quite sure,' she declared, and snatched up the checklist from where it had fallen on the floor.

'And maybe you can bring it down to me when you're finished?' Billy ventured, levering himself back upright. Then he lowered his voice, 'And maybe have a cup of tea?'

The whisper hadn't been low enough that the other girls didn't hear it. All of a sudden, they were tittering and whooping again – until Mrs Moffatt opened her arms, declared, 'We've a job to do, girls!' and rallied them to the cause.

'I'll help you back, Billy,' said Nancy. 'Come on, take my arm.'

As Billy left the dressing room, he looked once over his shoulder. Mary-Louise was looking at him too.

He hadn't expected it go so swimmingly. He even felt a little flicker of guilt.

It felt wrong to keep up the act all the way back to the hotel post room, but by the time Nancy had taken him there, it was almost second nature. Perhaps this acting lark wasn't so difficult after all. Idly, he wondered if there were ever any opportunities on the stage for half-lame Irish lads who'd never performed in front of a crowd. Perhaps he'd even make it to Hollywood: Billy Brogan, star of the silver screen.

Before Nancy left him in the post room, Billy said, 'Nancy, about my sister...'

Nancy had been expecting it. She cocked her head to one side, as if in sympathy. 'She's a great girl, Billy.'

'But...'

'But what?'

'When people use that tone, Nancy, there's ordinarily a *but*. "She's a great girl, Billy, but she's bloody useless." That sort of thing. Well, she's *not* useless, Nancy. She's trying too hard, that's all. She's a fast learner and she's dedicated and she wants, so badly, to make a name for herself here. I've told her to slow down, to just get good at the job first – no frills, no airs, no graces. But she's feeling down. She thinks you don't like her – that none of you like her.'

Nancy's face blanched. 'Oh, Billy! I can't think of a soul in the world who wouldn't like your sister. She's bright and she's eager – and that's all to the good. But, Billy, be honest with yourself – she's *not* a fast learner. We're tramping around after her, polishing the spots she's missed, sweeping up the bits she's left behind. A guest found a feather duster propped up by their bedside. There's love and patience for new girls in Housekeeping, but—'

'*You* tested Mrs Moffatt's patience, didn't you, Nancy?' Billy blurted out. He hadn't meant to be provocative, but by the look on Nancy's face, he supposed that was what he was being. 'It wasn't easy for you, starting out, was it?'

Nancy paled. 'I suppose it wasn't.'

'And you're going to need good girls in the department, aren't you? If you're going to be leaving?'

Nancy's eyes opened wide. 'Billy Brogan, if you're talking about what I think you're talking about…'

Billy smiled, tenderly and sincerely. 'Congratulations, Nancy. You're going to be the best mother. And that means something, coming from me – because, well, *I've* got one of the best too. But, listen, you're going to need good, loyal girls in the department. Give Annie one more try. I promise she won't let you down.'

Nancy thought about it for a long, lingering moment. 'I'm not going anywhere, Billy,' she said. 'I'm not sure how, and I haven't scratched the surface of speaking about it with the people who matter… but the Buckingham's my home. I'm not about to give up.' She stopped. 'And I'm not about to give up on Annie either. You can tell her to report in for the breakfast service tomorrow morning.' Nancy strode to the door. 'Oh, and if she could kindly refrain from adding sugar directly into the teapot, the girls would all hugely appreciate it.'

Then, with a smile, she left.

Billy was smiling too. At least that was one good deed for the day – one good deed in a day when he was about to do something that bordered on terrible.

He was still brooding on it, some time later, when there came a little knock at the door – and Mary-Louise appeared, with the checklist in her hand. 'Billy,' she said, slipping through the door and pushing it closed behind her, 'how are you feeling?'

Billy remembered his theatrical talents and, with a look of pained bravery on his features, said, 'It's getting there, Mary-Louise. I just didn't know winter would be so hard.'

Mary-Louise looked around the chill room. 'You need a little fire in here.'

'Oh, Mr Knave would never allow it. Just think of all those important letters, going up in smoke!'

Mary-Louise picked her way gingerly across the room. 'I sorted your checklist. The girls have got all the gowns wrapped now. I've marked off every one. Mrs Moffatt said the driver's to go straight to the dressing room?'

Billy nodded and, reaching out, took the checklist from her hands. The page was crumpled now, but she'd marked a tick against every last gown.

'Oh …' he ventured.

'Is something wrong, Billy?'

Billy looked up. 'It's stupid. It's nothing.'

'What is it?'

'It's only … Well, I might as well say it.' He hung his head in mock embarrassment. 'It's just, the way things have been, I thought – well, I thought you might have left me a little note. Something to say I've still got a chance with you. Something to say that, even after being such a fool, you might still...'

It was all the encouragement Mary-Louise needed. Seizing her chance, she snatched a pencil from Billy's desk, reclaimed the checklist and scribbled something across its bottom. If a girl could be described as writing something with passion, this was it.

Then she returned the page to Billy.

'To the man I love,' it read, 'Mary-Lou.'

Love. The word didn't just prickle at Billy's conscience; it near eviscerated it. He saw the way she was looking at him with those chocolatey eyes, the air heavy with expectation and promise, and all of a sudden it felt like that first moment she'd approached him, that first time she'd wanted to be in his company. And he knew, then, that she hadn't been lying. She really hadn't known about Ken. It had all been real.

It was just a shame the knowledge had come too late.

'Maybe we could start over, Bill. No trips up to Camden Town. Just you and me, and a walk along the river. Or, if that pains your leg too much, a café and a cup of tea.'

Billy said, 'I should like that, Mary-Lou.'

And she left him with a deep, warm smile.

After she was gone, Billy unfolded the paper. It took him a moment of courage before he picked up the same pencil Mary-Louise had been using. Then, trying to stop his fingers from trembling at the deceit of it all, he wrote his own sentence squeezed between Mary-Louise's own words, imitating her letters as best as he could.

When he was finished, he sat back and considered it. It didn't look bad at all. As well as acting, Billy Brogan had discovered yet another talent.

This is what it read:

'To the man I love,
Laundry South Lambeth Rd unguarded by night. Gowns being picked up in two-mornings' time: 6th December.'
  Mary-Lou'

He'd made the calculation in the dead of night. It had suddenly all seemed so clear. If Ken was caught stealing ball gowns at Billy's behest, there was every chance he'd drop Billy straight in it; if the information had come from somebody he treasured and loved, he'd keep his mouth shut.

Billy felt a strange, preternatural calmness descend over him. A rat in a trap – that's what he'd been. Well, he wouldn't be the rat any longer. *No*, he thought – and slipped the checklist into an envelope already marked with Uncle Ken's Camden Town address – *this time I'll be the trap.*

Chapter Twenty-Three

Raymond lay awake, Nancy nestled in the crook of his arm. It had felt good, these past nights, to keep the rhythms of the days with her again. To eat together in the evening, to sit together as the blackout came down, to hold her as the sirens began and hurry, arm in arm, into the shelter at the back of their house. Perhaps it wasn't dance that was the restorative after all. Perhaps it was only Nancy, sleeping soundly in his arms.

Tonight, though, Raymond couldn't sleep. The all-clear had come some hours before, but his mind was too active, the pictures in his mind too vivid for sleep to easily come. He hadn't been on patrol again; he'd delivered his excuses to Mortimer Bond, promised him he'd return as soon as he was able – but, if the feeling of having let his fellow wardens down still dogged him, it was at least leavened by the sense of peace he had, lying here with Nancy, and the peace he'd brought her too.

No, it wasn't the thought of the patrols that was keeping him awake. It was the thought of Cathy Everly, and what it all meant.

The letters that she'd written. His picture in a frame. Those words, as he'd helped her out of the Daughters of Salvation – and everything she'd said to Vivienne. In his dreams, he relived their nights on patrol, reading into every look that she gave him or word that she spoke some sinister, tormented objective. It had only been Nancy's innate kindness that had stopped him broiling with fury at the thought of it. To think of the jeopardy he'd been living through each night, the fires and the bombs – without ever truly knowing that the true jeopardy was the one into which his marriage had been thrown, and all at the hands of Cathy Everly.

At least it would all be over soon. Oh, the raids would go on – for, however steadfast the RAF remained, the Luftwaffe only seemed to match them in might – and the patrols would continue, from now until the war was either won or lost. But, by New Year, Raymond's part in the battle for London would be over.

The letter had arrived that morning, his summons back to the war lying on the doorstep when Nancy set out for the Buckingham Hotel. *'To: Lance Corporal Raymond de Guise. You are instructed to report to Bulford Camp, Salisbury, Wiltshire, on Monday 6th January 1941.'* The battle was calling him – but first there would be One Grand Night, the opportunity to dance with Hélène again, and Christmas, a chance to gather his family around him, fill them with love to bulwark them against the uncertainties to come.

There was just one thing he had to do before he gave himself to the festive season. A promise made to a friend who'd stood with you at the gates of death could never be betrayed – and Billy Brogan deserved all the help he could get.

Raymond stroked Nancy's sleeping face, kissed her on the brow, and made a silent promise that he would be hers, hers entirely, until the New Year sent him back to battle.

But first there was Billy's problem to sort out.

Raymond only hoped this plan of his stood a chance.

*

The snow fell wild the following evening. Raymond had spent the day ruminating on this scheme Billy had cooked up, and as darkness returned to London, he knew it was time to put his own part of it into motion. The rest was already unstoppable; with a half-forged note and a postage stamp, Billy had made certain of that.

He'd explained everything to Nancy, so when she returned from the Buckingham, only to kiss him goodbye, she understood. It wasn't as if he was stepping out on another patrol. In fact, though he took his ARP arm-band and tin helmet with him as he left the house that night, he was never going to wear them again.

He was going to hand them in.

'You'll stay safe, won't you, Raymond?'

He'd explained Billy's plan to Nancy, which meant divulging the sticky mess Billy had found himself drawn into. Nancy, as was her way, listened in silence, absorbed every word, and tried to understand. 'Poor Billy,' she finally said. 'But promise me – you won't put yourself in harm's way tonight. Whatever happens, you'll look after yourself.'

'I will,' Raymond said, and slipped out into the snowy night.

Great fat flakes were falling as he reached Mortimer Bond's office, the corners of the city somehow softened by the settling snow. The sirens had not started wailing yet, but he fancied he could still smell smoke in the air from the evening before. There was a part of him, he had to admit, that wanted to join the patrols tonight. It wasn't just the guilt at letting his fellow wardens down – or even the guilt at letting down London itself. There was, he'd decided in the last days, a strange pleasure in the exhaustion of it – of tramping home at the end of each patrol, spent and exhausted beyond measure, knowing that you'd put yourself on the line for something that mattered. He'd miss that, no matter how many nights he spent in Nancy's arms, or turning a quickstep in the Grand.

The rotund officer's face opened in a toothy, whiskery grin upon seeing Raymond march in, his helmet under his arm. 'Lance Corporal!' he declared. 'I'm glad to see you back on your feet. You're a sight for sore eyes, de Guise. We've missed you. Now, look here, we're down a man in Holborn – I've had a call in. How do you fancy a stroll through the old Inns of Court? The bastards have been peppering the east. We've an inkling they're throwing darts at St Paul's.'

Raymond didn't have the right words – but actions always spoke louder. He crossed the room in two military strides and, with great ceremony, laid his helmet and armband on Mortimer Bond's desk.

The cigar drooped in Mortimer's lips. His eyes flashed between the helmet and Raymond's helmet-less head. 'Say it isn't so, Lance Corporal!'

'I'm summoned back to Salisbury, sir. My time here's done.'

Mortimer hung his head – as theatrically, Raymond thought, as Marcus Arbuthnot. 'I knew this day would come.'

'My wife is having a child, sir. I shall be spending the Christmas season with her.'

Mortimer Bond shook his head, sadly. 'There isn't a soul can say you haven't played a part, Lance Corporal. A man might wish you'd been invalided out of the bally war altogether, so you could stick around on our streets.' The dumpy fellow got to his feet and, with a significant waddle, came round the desk to clasp Raymond's hand. 'I trust you'll name your son Mortimer? It's a good, solid name – falling out of fashion of late, or so I'm told. See that it doesn't die out, de Guise.'

Raymond wasn't certain if the older man was joking or not;

his expression was unchanging as he doffed Raymond on the shoulder. 'Godspeed, de Guise.'

Then Raymond returned to the snowy streets above Hyde Park.

She was there waiting for him, half-hidden behind the rippling veil of snow.

'Raymond?' came Cathy's voice.

He heard her before he saw her – but, in the parting snow, there she was, wrapped in grey lambswool and a scarf piled high, almost occluding her entire face. The moment she saw him, she hurried forwards – and, in her green eyes, Raymond thought he saw a kind of release; she was, he thought, like a girl who, having been told she will never see her father again, suddenly sees him waiting at the school gates. And wasn't that what it was like, in the tormented labyrinth of her head? Her betrothed's life snuffed out on the beaches at Dunkirk, and Raymond somehow stepping into that void in her heart?

But she was reaching out for Raymond now, kidskin gloves held in her other hand so that Raymond could see her engagement ring sparkling in the snowy light.

He recoiled.

'You're back on patrol, Raymond.' She looked at the skies. 'It's going to be a wild one.'

The chances were it would be deathly quiet tonight; with the sky banked in so much cloud, the ARP would be dealing with infractions to the blackout, passers-by lost in the dark, plunderers eyeing up the bombed-out shops – but all of this was preferable to the fire from above.

Raymond's breath plumed, mixing with Cathy's. He tried to hold on to what Nancy had said – 'Your heart goes out to a woman like that; she doesn't know her own mind' – but his wife had always been able to see the light in the dark; that was how she'd helped Vivienne over her addictions, in an age that felt so long ago. Raymond himself could only feel the fire. He had so little idea what to say.

'I've missed you, Raymond.'

He felt pinned in place. There was no sidestep, no sashay to weave away from Cathy right now.

'I'm not patrolling any more,' he blurted out. 'I've been recalled to my division.'

It was the only thing he could say that felt as if it might curtail the stilted conversation, but the moment he said it, he knew it was the wrong thing. The other WVS girls were rushing past in the snow, but Cathy stood stock still and said, 'No, Raymond. No, don't let them. You can't leave London, not again. You might never—'

'I have to,' said Raymond, and turned on his heel to march into the dark. 'There isn't a choice, not any more.'

She took off after him, up the road. 'But when? Where?'

'I'm to leave in the New Year. First to barracks. My division's in Africa. Chances are I'll board the first troop ship to join them.'

'Then we have Christmas. We have New Year. You'll still dance at your hotel. We have a whole month, Raymond.'

It was on the tip of his tongue to say, 'We don't have anything, Cathy,' but, when he risked a sideways glance at her, he saw the desperation in her eyes.

It was already getting too late; if he missed this chance, it wouldn't come again. Then Billy, having crossed a line he couldn't cross back, would be Ken's forever.

'Cathy, I'll see you soon. Just because I won't be on patrols, it doesn't mean—'

'Do you promise?'

Raymond tensed. Promises ought not to be broken. Trust

ought not to be squandered. But Cathy had done all of that in the months just past; taken his friendship, contorted it, lied and fantasised and tried to make that fantasy real. Nancy had counselled sympathy – but, standing here, Raymond felt a strange frisson of anger and fear. 'I promise,' he lied. 'But Cathy, I've got to go.'

She reached up, as if she might mean to kiss him goodbye – but, this time, Raymond's sashay was enough. He left her standing in the snowfall as he took off south.

Hyde Park was a crystalline pasture of white. He cut a trail across the virgin snow, hurrying past Buckingham Palace itself, where the armed guards were ever present and the barrage balloons loomed above, half-subsumed in the snow cloud. By the time he reached the river, his chest was burning from the cold. He was surprised, then, to hear the low call of the sirens beginning. He'd thought that London might be spared tonight, the English weather coming in to bat on behalf of the King – but, unless this was some accident, it was evidently not to be. He looked to the skies. The snowfall was slowing, gaps appearing in the cloud above. He could see a half-moon, beached in the sky beyond – and, in the east, the sweeping pattern of the searchlights.

But that only made it more likely that Ken would have fallen for Billy's bait. The cover of snowfall was perfect for Ken to follow the trail Billy had so calculatedly left for him, and to turn up at the laundries, seeking to liberate forty-six perfect Buckingham ball gowns – but the cover of the sirens was better yet. At least, then, the ARP wardens wouldn't be poking their noses in where they weren't wanted.

Raymond picked up his pace, crossing the river by the Vauxhall Bridge. It had been so long since he'd ventured into this part of the city – a lifetime since he'd danced at the club underneath the arches of the Vauxhall railway line – and the city looked more different still, under its cloak of December snow. He stopped at the foot of the bridge, reaching with frigid fingers for the map Billy had scrawled. In the failing light, he could just about recognise the conflux of streets. If he was right, the hotel laundry was less than a mile away now, occupying a corner plot on the South Lambeth Road.

'Raymond!'

He froze.

He hadn't been mistaken; that really was Cathy's voice, whirling at him out of the night. He dared to look over his shoulder – and there she was, appearing out of the ragged snow that whipped along the Vauxhall Bridge.

She looked almost ghostly as she tumbled from the bridge – while, up above, the parting snow cloud revealed yet more of the moon.

'I knew you weren't going home,' she gasped, out of breath as she approached. 'Raymond, you lied to me. Why did you lie?'

By her tone, it was an affront to the decency and trust between them. Nothing could have startled Raymond more. 'You followed me?'

'I had to. Raymond, you're hiding something. Tell me what it is.'

Raymond had been wrong; her voice wasn't laced with accusation – it was laced with concern. Somehow, this seemed worse. He looked again at the skies, as if in the movement of the moon and clouds he could discern how much time was passing. *Too much*, he thought. *Ken might be at the laundry by now.*

'Cathy, you shouldn't be here. You have duties of your own.'

Cathy opened her mouth, aghast. It was as if she'd heard a priest denounce God. 'Raymond, my love, my duty's to *you*.'

There was no time for this. He turned sharply, started marching along the street, floundering only when he sensed Cathy striding in his wake. 'Raymond!' she was calling. 'Raymond, darling, what are you doing down here? What's going on?'

She reached for his arm; he pushed it aside. She grappled for him again; this time, he pushed her aside too fiercely, and her feet – finding scant purchase in the snow – flew out from underneath her. Moments later, Cathy was lying spread-eagled in the snow, winded and bruised.

He should have walked on. Raymond knew he should have walked on. But the better part of him won out. Soon, he had taken her by the hand – he could feel the studded points of the engagement ring, even through her kidskin gloves – and was heaving her back upright.

The moment she was on her feet, she fell against his breast. This time, Raymond's impatience won out. He braced her by each shoulder, as if she might have some sense shaken into her, and held her fast. 'Listen to me, Cathy,' he said. 'You've no business following me down here. I'm running out of time.' There was nothing else for it; the words spilled out of him. 'There's going to be a looting tonight. A gang, robbing the laundry that serves the Buckingham Hotel. That's where I'm headed, Cathy – and you've nearly ruined it all.'

He released her, more suddenly than he'd meant, and had to reach out to stop her from falling again.

'Raymond,' she said, suddenly contrite, 'I'm sorry. I wasn't to know. But what am I supposed to think, when I haven't seen you? What am I supposed to *feel* when you nearly died in that building, then vanished for so long, without even a word? I've been out with the WVS every night since. Every night, just wondering where you are, how you are, *if* you are. Don't you know what that's done to me? And then you just appear tonight, and act as if nothing's ever happened?' She wrapped her arms around herself, started shaking. 'Don't you have any idea what's in a girl's head? What's in a girl's heart?'

Raymond could only stare at her, lost in that no-man's-land between horror and outright disbelief.

'No, Cathy,' he whispered. 'I don't think that I do.'

From somewhere along the monochrome streets of south London, there came the sound of an engine. Raymond was trying to turn away from Cathy when he saw the delivery van appearing out of the dark. Scything apart the waves of snow, it guttered past the place where he and Cathy were standing, then vanished somewhere ahead.

A terrible premonition hit Raymond. He was already too late.

'Cathy, go back to your patrol!'

'No, Raymond. No I won't! Not until we talk about this properly. Not until we—'

'Then you're going to have to come! Come, but keep quiet and out of sight – and don't breathe a word unless I say so. Do you hear me?'

'Raymond, you can't—'

'DO YOU HEAR?'

Cathy reeled back. She nodded.

Then Raymond started to run.

The streets were a labyrinth in this part of Lambeth. The craters and closed roads left by the bombings only made it worse. By the time Raymond and Cathy reached the South Lambeth road, the delivery van was already parked up on the kerb alongside the laundry building. A single torchlight flickered, somewhere in the grounds. The fools might as well have been shouting their presence from the rooftops. But that was what the blitz was doing; making the criminals among them as brazen as bombers.

Raymond had been right. It was the very van that had guttered past them as he and Cathy stood rowing on the edge of the road. He pressed himself to the edge of the road, instructing Cathy to do the same, and hurried forward, ducking down in the shelter of the low brick wall that ran around the laundry yard.

'They're already inside,' said Raymond, barely concealing his fury at how Cathy's appearance had slowed him down. 'There isn't time.' He clenched his fists. 'Never enough time.' And his mind flashed back, once more, to those nights he'd spent cradling Artie, trying to get him back to the beaches, trying to keep him alive just one more day, just until he could find a way across the Channel and home.

He shook himself, told himself those thoughts weren't right, that now was not the moment to get lost in dreams of the past. 'Cathy,' he said, with force, 'you're here now, and I need your help.'

By the look on her face, it seemed like she'd received some benediction from above. 'Anything, Raymond.'

'You need to go now – go and find wardens. Go and find police constables. Bring them here, and do it now.'

She was about to do his bidding when some thought entered her head and she faltered. 'Raymond, what are you going to do?'

He took a deep breath, trying to remain calm. 'I'm going to slow them down.'

She grabbed his hand. 'You'll stay safe, won't you, Raymond? Promise me – you won't put yourself in harm's way tonight.'

The echo of those words – the exact same things Nancy had said, mere hours ago, before he set out. He wanted to scream it at her: *you've no right to say those things*. But instead he made her the same promise he'd made his wife. 'Now go!'

At least, this time, she did as he asked. He watched her vanish, back the way they had come, and then turned his attention to the laundry.

The doors were opening up. Out of the blackness within, two figures emerged.

'She was right, wasn't she, Ken?' one of them crowed. 'That niece of yours came good. Look at this lot – you won't find finer outside Buckingham Palace...'

'Just load them up, boys,' came a deeper, older voice, as a third figure appeared from the laundry behind them. 'And do it quick. There's no use dallying. Time means money, boys.'

Raymond dared to lift his head above the brick wall and watched the three silhouettes as they crossed the laundry grounds, opened the back of the van, and started piling the ball gowns they'd found inside. Forty-six of them, Billy had said. At least that gave him a little time. They'd need to ferry that number out of the laundry in several trips. The seconds were flowing freely through his fingers, but at least they weren't gone yet.

As soon as the figures returned to the laundry, Raymond knew what he had to do. Counting the seconds until they reappeared, he threw himself away from the cover of the wall, bent low and hurtled across the open ground until he reached the delivery van. Then, throwing himself down into its own cover, he reached for the pen knife he'd been keeping with him ever since those earliest patrols. Blunted now, the blade precious little use for anything except jimmying open a tin can, he pressed its tip against the front tyre, leaned all his weight into it, and listened for the tell-tale tear of a puncture being made. Then, with the knife embedded in the rubber, he began working it back and forth. There didn't need to be elegance in this, at least. A jagged scar would do. He wrenched it free, the hiss of air behind it, and was working on the second, rear tyre, when he heard the voices again.

'Hurry up, boys, hurry up!'

It was the man he now knew was Ken, barracking the younger men in his employ. Raymond stopped what he was doing, took a deep breath – and then, leaving the knife embedded in the tyre rather than risk the disruption of drawing it out, he gently lowered himself to the ground and slipped underneath the chassis of the delivery van itself.

Thank goodness for the snow, for it masked his every sound as he slipped into the narrow space. From here, he could see the shadows of the men's boots as they tramped around the van, opened it up and deposited the ball gowns inside.

'How many's that?' Ken asked.

'Sixteen, I reckon.'

'Keep loading, boys. I'll stick with the van now. See we don't have no trouble.'

Underneath the van, Raymond stifled a groan. Moments later, he heard the front door unlocking and the van quaked as Ken clambered inside. Moments after that, the engine choked into life.

Exhaust fumes billowed around him. Smoke and thick grease. He'd breathed in enough rot this winter, but there was at least a pocket of clean air he could inhale by craning his face to the right. This close to the edge of the van, he could see the full face of the laundry – and was only too aware when Ken's cronies appeared again, ferrying another two armfuls of gowns. He waited for them to pass; then, if only for the extra ounce of courage it might give him, he reached out with one arm, fumbled blindly for the penknife still embedded in the rear tyre, and wrenched it free.

Raymond didn't intend to use a knife tonight, but nor did he intend to let them find it sticking out of the rear tyre while he was still hiding here.

The question was: how long would he have to hide?

With the oil of the exhaust beginning to coat his skin, he tried to count the ball gowns as they came out of the laundry. Each trip by Ken's cronies seemed to account for six or seven gowns. At a rough calculation, that meant it would take only four or five trips to complete the load, after the sixteen they'd already acquired by the time Raymond arrived. In his time hiding here, they'd been in and out twice. At his best guess, that left him with fifteen minutes before the game was up.

The minutes cascaded past. He thought of making a break for it, rolling out of the van's undercarriage and – taking the chance that Ken didn't see – scrambling for the safety of the low brick wall. Yet, every time he readied himself, Ken barked out, the boys appeared from the laundry, and he pressed himself back against the ground. Sandwiched between the heat of the chassis and the cold of the icy ground, he wanted to scream.

One minute.

Two minutes.

Three minutes.

Four…

An hour ago, he would have done anything to get rid of Cathy; now, all he wanted was for her to reappear, a flotilla of ARP wardens in tow.

A reverberation shook the ground, the echo of an incendiary landing somewhere along the river. The Luftwaffe hadn't demolished one of the Thames bridges yet, but surely it was only a matter of time. Raymond tensed, then tensed further as Ken's stalwarts appeared from the laundry once again, barking out, 'One last load, Ken. Then we can get out of here.'

'Hurry up, boys! I'm freezing my delicates off out here!'

With a laugh like that, Raymond had no idea how Billy had found the man charming enough to be hoodwinked into his schemes. But people showed different faces to different folks.

People wore masks. And no sooner was he thinking this, than he was thinking again of Cathy – of the mask she'd been wearing all year, and all the calamity hidden inside…

'Got 'em!' came a voice from the laundry, and Raymond's heart sank. He turned, to see the boys reappearing with the last of the gowns. Moments later, the back doors of the van were opening up again, the gowns were being thrown inside – and then, making the van shudder beneath their weight, the boys were climbing aboard too.

The engine roared.

Raymond shut his eyes.

He couldn't wait here a second longer. The van might slew on its punctured tyres. Muttering a prayer, and holding an image of Nancy vivid in his mind, he rolled sideways, scrambling between the tyres, and sprang to his feet.

The van took off – but with two flat tyres, it banked sharply, and Ken slammed his foot on the brakes. He'd know, soon enough, what had happened. It wouldn't be enough to stop him climbing back in the van and taking to the roads. Perhaps it might slow him down, perhaps it might make him easier to catch – but all it had really done was give Raymond a few more moments to think.

The van stopped dead. Ken's face craned out of the driver's window, to look back along the side of the van. 'What in hell?' he cursed. He seemed to know, already, what had happened. 'Boys, we've been foiled. These tyres are—' He'd been stepping out of the cab, but now he froze – for his eyes had lit upon Lance Corporal Raymond de Guise, battered and bruised, holding himself aloft in the laundry yard with a blunt penknife in his hands.

'Who in hell are you?'

The words felt futile, even as he spoke them – but they were all that he had. 'I'm here to put you under arrest – for profiteering, for plundering, for acting against the best interests of King and Country.'

Ken was silent. He hammered his fist on the side of the van, and soon the back doors opened, disgorging his two cronies again. 'Did you hear that, boys? We've got a do-gooder here. Somebody popping up to spoil the party. What do you think we ought to do about that?'

For the first time, Raymond got a good look at the two young men. They were burly sorts, of an age where they really ought to have been wearing a uniform, off with the rest in North Africa and the Middle East, and everywhere else the British army survived. Either that, or up in the skies, battling the enemy – instead of down here, becoming the enemy themselves.

'Go on then, lads. That's what you're here for. To solve problems. And here's one, standing right in front of you. Have a go. It's been a while.'

The knife was knocked out of Raymond's hand with the very first blow. Probably that was for the best; Raymond had no intention of killing a man tonight. The blow sent him reeling, but somehow he kept his balance. It was the second blow, blindsiding him from behind, that toppled him. Then he was down on the ground, and the boots were in his sides, his back, his ribs. The pain rushed over him, but so did the sense of where he was and what he must do. He reached out, took hold of one of the boys as they kicked him – and, by heaving on his boot, brought him crashing to the ground alongside him.

Fighting one was much easier than fighting two. This time, he could dodge the blows as they came – and, by scrabbling backwards, somehow he scrambled to his feet. It occurred to Raymond, then, that he'd been injured so much more seriously – and so many more times – here on the streets of London than he had in France. This was where his war was. He was fighting it now.

He threw a punch, but missed. Threw another, and it glanced off the man's jaw. He was just readying to throw a third when the boy he'd felled before lifted himself from the ground and wrapped his arms around Raymond's leg. It took too long to shake him off; the other man recovered his wits, and set about Raymond with punches of his own. Raymond wore each one well, but each one knocked a little more strength out of him. He could hear Ken bawling – 'Just finish it, boys, we need to get going!' – and the thought struck him that, every moment he clung on was another moment he was giving to Cathy. Another moment for the wardens she had surely found.

So he did not tumble. He did not fall. He caught the punches and ducked the punches – and, where he could, threw them back in return. Every second a victory. Every moment a prize.

'You've had your fun, boys,' snarled Ken. 'Give him here.'

Through blurred vision, Raymond saw Ken barrelling over the laundry yard. For a second, he vanished from view; then he reappeared again. Too late, Raymond realised that all he'd really done was bend down – and that now he was brandishing the pen knife in his hand. He felt his legs get swept out from underneath him; then he was lying on the stone and ice once again – only, this time, Ken was lowering himself over him, the knife outstretched.

'Arrest me?' he scoffed. 'Arrest *me?* Who do you think you are, to come here and tell me what I can and can't do? This is war, son. There'll be winners and there'll be losers.' He grinned. 'We've all got to pick a side. I reckon you just picked yours.'

'No!' cried Raymond, through bloodied lips. 'Here! I'm ... here!'

'I know where you are, son. It's right where you're going to stay...'

But it wasn't Ken Raymond was speaking to. It was the silhouetted figures now appearing on the edge of the yard. The wardens in their tin helmets who, blasting shrill whistles and hollering orders, leapt over the low brick wall, raced past the stalled delivery van, and ripped Ken off Raymond's prostrate form. They seemed, to Raymond in his haze, to be coming from every direction. Two wrestled Ken to the ground; others flocked to Ken's cronies and, stopping them from fleeing, yanked their arms behind their backs.

Raymond picked himself up. The world was spinning, but his feet were on solid ground.

Cathy appeared out of the wardens, rushed to him and threw her arms around his shoulders. 'I'm here, my love,' she told him, tenderly. 'I did it again, didn't I, Raymond? I got here in the nick of time. Didn't I tell you? I always will.'

Raymond stiffened. His body, which wore so many bruises, felt broken again – but at least he had the strength to disentangle himself from Cathy's arms. 'I need to go home, Cathy. I'll give my statement to the wardens and go. Perhaps – perhaps there's a car...'

'Home, Raymond?' She seemed to take stock of the phrase, then nodded sharply. 'I'll take you there. I'll make sure you're safe on the way. Wait here, Raymond. Wait right here.'

'NO!' he yelled.

Cathy stepped back. Her face creased, deep lines spreading on her brow and around her eyes. 'Raymond?'

'I'm going home, Cathy. I'm going home to Nancy. Do you understand?'

'Raymond, you're not well. You need help. I'm here for you, my dear.'

'I'm not your *dear*,' Raymond said, spitting blood onto the snow. 'Please, Cathy, don't you see? This is madness, Cathy. *Madness*. I can't be a part of it. Not now, not tonight – not ever, actually. I'm grateful for what you've done, but I need Nancy. I want to be with her now.'

Raymond barely saw the crestfallen look on Cathy's face as, feeling heavier than he had in days, he tramped past her, past the place where the wardens were shackling Ken and his cronies, past the place where the first police car had arrived, and the van where the stolen gowns were still waiting.

Nancy, he thought. Nancy and their baby, for now and ever more.

In the end, one of the constables took Raymond home. He watched the snowy city flicker past, wearing all its craters and scars, and wondered what it might look like when he next came back to it, after who knew how long away. Time was advancing more rapidly than ever. Artie was fading into history, while new life hoved into view on the horizon.

When he got home, Nancy was waiting. It was all that he needed. He didn't know how he'd ever thought otherwise.

Chapter Twenty-Four

You are Cordially Invited to:

ONE GRAND NIGHT

A celebration of dance and song in aid of
The Buckingham Hotel War Relief Fund

Saturday 14th December 1940

The Grand Ballroom
Buckingham Hotel
Berkeley Square

Featuring…

Raymond de Guise
Hélène Marchmont
Karina Kainz

And King of the Grand, Marcus Arbuthnot

With music by the Archie Adams Orchestra

'Let's Dance…!'

~

Mathilde held the simple, ivory invitation in her hand as the taxicab arced round Marble Arch, then ground through the traffic blocking Park Lane. There was bomb damage here, but the hold-up was primarily because of the guards stationed along the edge of the park: the war, on the very doorstep of Buckingham Palace itself. The traffic seemed to be infuriating Camille – who was dressed up to the nines and sitting alongside her daughter, tapping her long fingernails on the glass – but Mathilde found that she was almost grateful for the delay. The feeling had been curdling in her stomach ever since that moment with Marcus, as sour as turned milk. This journey, to the gilded environs of Knightsbridge and the Imperial Hotel, was the final furlong in the race she'd been running. Victory was tantalisingly within her grasp. But why, then, did she feel as knotted and nervous as a girl about to go to her first ball?

'It's the last time you'll pay for your own taxicab,' said Camille as they reached the corner of Knightsbridge and Lowndes Square, and the imposing turrets of the Imperial Hotel hanging above. 'Well, smile, my girl. Here you stand, at the gates of Heaven, and you have a face as miserable as sin.'

The barb stung, because it wasn't the first time Camille had used this particular image to denigrate Mathilde. 'Your face, girl! You look as if you've been slapped!' She'd said things of this ilk, and worse, at the end of so many of Mathilde's junior competitions that she'd lost count. But the truth was – these sorts of comments were the very reason Mathilde had brought her mother with her today. It was the reason she'd gone to her childhood home in Finchley last night, allowed her mother to raise a glass in her honour at suppertime, and even worn the clothes her mother had lain out. If she was going to complete this journey, she *needed* her mother breathing down her neck. The haunted look on Marcus's face as he fled the Grand had been dogging her ever since. The only way to battle through the guilt of it – to reach the joy on the other side – was Camille.

It was a talent to be able to stab someone in the back and not feel disheartened with yourself – and Camille had been practising it all of her life.

'It's single-mindedness you've always lacked,' Camille had once told her – when, having expected Mathilde to rehearse all weekend, she had instead discovered her lounging on the banks of the brook with friends from school. 'Nobody reaches the top without determination, Mathilde. Footwork's fine, but character is *everything*.'

'Well,' said Camille, some time after the taxicab had come to a halt, 'aren't you going to step out?'

Mathilde was still staring at the invitation. Trying to ignore the feeling of regret that had started to flower inside her, she took her mother's hand. 'Yes,' she said, trying to be certain. 'Yes, I am.'

For the first time, there was something approximating tenderness in Camille's eyes. 'You *deserve* a chance like this, Mathilde. It's never easy. Show me a world where we all get what we want without a hint of horror along the way, and I'll show you a fairy tale. But look at you, my girl. You're ready to bloom. Go through those doors and tell them. Take your rightful place.' She lifted her hand and stroked Mathilde's hair. 'I'm proud of you, Tilly. I never thought I'd be as happy as this.'

Tears were pricking Mathilde's eyes. How long had she waited to hear those words? *I'm proud of you*. She felt foolish – because here she was, a grown woman, and still overcome with emotion at the kind words of a mother, a mother who had used and belittled her all her life. She didn't have any words in return – all she could do was squeeze her mother's hand back; then she stepped out, into the frigid December cold, and walked up the granite steps into the Imperial Hotel.

A concierge showed her into the ballroom, with its scent of beeswax and pine needles heavy in the air. The ballroom had been garlanded with wreathes of holly, mistletoe, and branches of fir. A new chandelier had been hoisted since Mathilde last set foot here. It hung directly above the dance floor, silver and studded like a crown.

It was Mr Cockfosters who appeared first. If anything, he was a little rounder than the last time he and Mathilde had met – evidently the restaurants at the Imperial Hotel had no problems sourcing rich, extravagant ingredients for their guests – and he approached her across the ballroom with his pudgy hands folded together in expectation. 'Miss Bourchier, am I to assume you've come to visit your new home?'

Mathilde stood in the centre of the dance floor. Some day soon, she'd be standing here with a king on her arm. They'd call her the Queen of the Ballroom. Her mother would be up there, at the balustrade, watching the spectacle and knowing, deep in her heart, that every step they'd taken along the way had been worthwhile. Mathilde felt as if she could feel her mother's eyes on her, even now. They were eyes full of adulation, but they were eyes full of goading as well – goading Mathilde to finish her part in this, to reap her just rewards.

Before Mathilde could reply, the Hotel Director Mr Gove appeared in the ballroom doors. Mr Gove's whiskers had been tailored, presumably in anticipation of the Christmas season and all the festivities the Imperial was to host. He stroked his moustaches as he wended his way to join them.

'We've been waiting on you, Miss Bourchier,' he declared as he approached. 'It would, perhaps, amuse you to know that my good friend Cockfosters and I have indulged in a little wager over whether you might keep up your end of our bargain or not. I see, by your appearance here, that I am suddenly out of pocket to the princely sum of ten English pounds.'

Perhaps that was the reason for Mr Cockfosters' glee; or perhaps it was just professional pride that the scheme he had put into motion was finally paying off.

'I must admit, however – after a few weeks, we thought you'd quite forgotten about us. By the end of November, we were quite sure. But tell me, Miss Bourchier, did you get to the bottom of Mr Arbuthnot's little secret?'

She nodded. 'It's all done. Marcus Arbuthnot won't be dancing in the Grand again.'

Cockfosters and Gove turned to appraise each other. For a moment, they looked like a comical vaudeville act, each of their intrigued expressions mirroring the other.

'He's finished, gentlemen,' Mathilde said, surprised to find the lump in her throat. 'He walked out of the ballroom, and won't return.' She handed them the ivory invitation in her hands. 'One Grand Night is a little more than twenty-four hours away. See here – in all the invitations, they're calling Marcus the King of the Grand. But Mr Arbuthnot won't be dancing on One Grand Night. The fact of the matter is, he won't be dancing ever again. When he doesn't appear, questions will start to be asked. Rumours will begin. One Grand Night won't be the triumph they're heralding.'

There was a silence. Mathilde watched their faces for some sign of things to come.

Then, with a furrowed expression, Mr Cockfosters said, 'Tell me, Mathilde, what exactly did you do to drive Mr Arbuthnot from the Grand?'

Mathilde felt their prying eyes on her. 'I did as you asked me. I confronted him with the truth about his missing years.

379

I told him that, if he didn't leave, I'd reveal it to the world.' She stopped. There was something wrong with the way they were looking at her, some hint of bewilderment, some hint of disappointment. 'Well? Isn't it what you wanted?'

Mr Cockfosters lifted his folded hands to his lips, like a man preparing to break bad news. 'It *is*, Mathilde. That *is* what we wanted. But, you see ...'

'What my ineffectual colleague is trying to say,' interjected Mr Gove, with exasperation, 'is that this news falls some distance short of the effect we had been anticipating. Yes, it is all to the good – and beneficial for our own project – that Mr Arbuthnot has exiled himself from the Grand. But, Miss Bourchier, where's the spectacle? Where's the scandal? That, my dear, is what you were commissioned to create.'

Mathilde flashed looks from one man to the other. 'I don't understand. I did what you asked – I carved Mr Arbuthnot out of the Grand...'

'You seem, Miss Bourchier, to have accomplished it with barely a ruffled feather. Yes, people will be let down. Yes, this One Grand Night the Society Pages are – in my view, quite unwarrantedly – trumpeting about will be undermined. But, tell me, where's the lasting damage? Where's the fallout to drive dukes and other dignitaries from the Buckingham suites?'

'We don't want a little hiccup for the Grand,' Mr Cockfosters added, having dusted himself off from his director's insinuations. 'We wanted disaster.'

'So tell us, Miss Bourchier, what *did* you dig up about Mr Arbuthnot and his missing years? What secret is he carrying that's dreadful enough for him to flee the ballroom?'

'And how,' Mr Cockfosters added, 'might we make use of it?'

Mathilde stuttered, 'I – I ...'

Mr Gove heaved a great sigh. 'Second thoughts is it, Miss Bourchier? That would seem, to me, to be a terrible shame.'

'The man is gone. Isn't that enough?'

'Look at where you're standing. All of this could be yours. You have the knowledge in your possession. You have the treasure within your grasp. Why not just say it? Or are you simply not *hungry* enough?'

Hungry ...

The word cast her back in time. 'You're not hungry enough!' Camille would shriek, when Mathilde failed to be honoured in some junior championship. 'You lack the passion! You lack the drive! Tilly, we've been working for this all of your life. What's holding you back? What's stopping you now? Hunger, Tilly! Only hunger!'

Mathilde shook her head.

'I don't want it,' she whispered. 'Not like this.'

'What?' Mr Cockfosters whispered.

'You're like *she* is,' she gasped, and thought of her mother sitting in the taxicab outside. Already dressed up as if she was about to attend the ballroom herself. Already celebrating her daughter's rise to the top. 'I can't believe I went to her. I can't believe she had me convinced.' What was it she'd said? *To rise to the top in a world like this, sometimes a woman makes compromises.* But no, she thought – not like this. There were good compromises and there were bad. There were compromises you made for yourself, and compromises you made for others.

'All of my life,' she said, 'I'm dancing to other people's tunes. Dancing for my mother. Dancing for you. But all I want – all I ever really wanted – is to dance for myself. Whether I'm good or bad, queen or not, just to ...' The shame of it was palpable. The realisation, short and brutal. She thought of Marcus Arbuthnot, labouring under his secret, and she thought: I don't want some secret of my own. Labouring under the realities of life is struggle enough. But to labour under a secret? 'I'm sorry, gentlemen. You had me wrong. *I* had me wrong, and I've only just seen it. I shouldn't be standing here. I shouldn't be with you at all.'

She'd crossed half of the dance floor, making for the exit, when Mr Gove called out, 'Let's not be hasty, Miss Bourchier. Miss Bourchier, please. The calls of our conscience are many, but all is fair in a time of war. If Mr Arbuthnot committed some foul deed, it's right that he pays for it. That you might prosper from such a situation isn't a question of character. This is the ballroom, madam. Think of what you could have.'

Mathilde turned at the doors. 'I *am* thinking of what I could have. It's the first time I've seen it clearly. A lifetime of suspicion. Beholden to a secret. A lifetime knowing that I didn't really *earn* it, that I was here because I cheated.' She did not say what was truly on her mind, for to do so would have been to give the truth of Marcus's missing years away: Marcus had, once upon a time, cheated his way to a championship; how could she expose it and, in doing so, prosper from a cheat of her own? What kind of life awaited after that? 'I'm sorry, gentlemen. The Grand is the greatest ballroom in the greatest hotel in London. I'd be a fool to forsake it. Better to be an honest workhorse there, than a deceitful queen here.'

Her heart was beating, wild and unordered, as she hurried back through the Imperial doors, down the granite steps, and onto the snowiness of Knightsbridge. Her mind was a whirl. It was still a whirl as she took off down the street, sliding in the snow – so much of a whirl that she glided straight past the place where the taxicab was waiting, her mother standing anxiously beside it, cigarette smoke trailing from her hand.

'Tilly!'

Mathilde turned round, catching a lamp post to keep herself from falling.

'It's done, Mother. It's over!'

Camille smiled. Snuffing out her cigarette, she approached Mathilde, took her by the arm – and was about to lead her back to the taxicab when Mathilde suddenly broke free and said, 'You don't understand. I told them no. I told them I couldn't do it.'

Camille's eyes narrowed. 'Couldn't do what? Mathilde, it's already done.'

'They want scandal. They want sleaze. They want it all over the Society Pages. It isn't enough, for them, that Marcus should leave the Grand. They want it being gossiped about in every corner. They want it in the pages of *Dancing Times*. "Buckingham Hotel Stakes Its Reputation on Liar and Thief." They expected me to go back to the Buckingham now, and blow the whole thing open.' She shook. 'The way you're looking at me, Mother – you're about to tell me to do it, I know you are! Well, listen to me – I'm not a cheat. I'm *not*. I won't be.'

'Tilly, you silly girl, this isn't about—'

'*Tilly*,' Mathilde snapped. '*Silly girl*. The way you speak to me, Mother – I'm a grown woman.'

Camille snarled, 'You're a foolish child, with her head still in the clouds. Mathilde Bourchier, if you'd applied yourself like I instructed – if you'd worked as hard as *I* worked – you wouldn't need to be standing here, dealing in other people's secrets at all. But you didn't, and here we are.' Camille reached for her arm again, but Mathilde retreated. 'My God, you're still the same useless, ungrateful girl you always were! I've spent my life trying to get you to where we are today, and I've had to battle you every step of the way. Don't forget, Mathilde – you're the one who came to me. *You're* the one who wanted my help. And yet, here we stand, with you throwing it back in my face once again…'

'I was wrong,' Mathilde declared. All of a sudden, she remembered standing in the Grand, the moment before she destroyed Marcus Arbuthnot's life. His offer to her had been so tempting and real: *I should like to instruct you and Mr Nettleton for a season. Let's see what we can get out of you.* That was the chance she'd been looking for all her life, *that* was the opportunity presented to her; all of the rest of it, what she was doing now, was a fraud. 'I remember, now, why I had to run away. In your world, mother, winning's the only thing that matters. Getting to the top. But that was never me. There's a reason I didn't train like you wanted me to train. There's a reason I used to sneak off to the brook for picnics with friends.'

'Because you weren't hungry enough…'

This time, Mathilde nodded, and snorted up her tears. 'Yes, Mother. Who could ever be as hungry as you? Who could ever want it like you wanted it? But you wanted it for yourself – not for me. By God, maybe I was right the first time – maybe I don't want to dance at all! Better a governess than this.'

It was like she'd struck her mother across the face. 'Do I have to do *everything* for you?' she snarled. 'I will if I have to. By God, Mathilde, I'm your *mother*.'

She turned on her heel. The Imperial Hotel still hung, stark against the winter city skyline above. All it would take was for her to march in there and reveal what she knew. The world of the Buckingham could still explode. The Grand could still be a laughing-stock.

'There's no point, Mother,' Mathilde called after her. All the passion and emotion was gone from her voice, leaving behind only reason and regret. 'I won't dance in the Imperial, even if you blow the Grand apart.'

'You'd be Queen!'

Mathilde drew a breath and dried her eyes. 'That's your dream, Mother, not mine.'

The taxicab was still waiting, the driver sitting there with a stony face, flickering and flinching with every bitter word he'd heard. When Mathilde slid into the back, he hardly batted an eyelid, just muttered, with a dour tone, 'Where to?'

'The Academy des Artistes,' Mathilde declared. 'Covent Garden.'

The last thing she saw was her mother in the rear-view mirror, a harridan in her evening wear standing alone in the snow, as dusk threw its cloak over old London town.

Chapter Twenty-Five

The sirens hadn't wailed last night – and, if ever there was an omen to prefigure the success of One Grand Night, this was it: Raymond de Guise had had his first good night's sleep in what felt like an age.

Even so, he was awake with the dawn. As he watched Nancy ready herself for her morning duties, he said, 'Do you remember the first moment we met?'

Nancy said, 'I could hardly forget it.'

It had been right there in the Grand Ballroom: Nancy, not long at the Buckingham Hotel, had taken it upon herself to enter the Grand one evening. There, swept up in the magic and grandeur of the occasion, she had watched the debonair Raymond de Guise dancing with Grusinskaya, an aged Russian ballerina who had lived half her life in exile. Little had she known that, four years later, she would be standing in front of her bedroom mirror, admiring the tightness in her belly that heralded their firstborn child.

'I'll have to tell them soon. I'm starting to show.'

Raymond nodded. 'We'll visit Mr Knave – together.'

Nancy looked at him tenderly, then crossed the room to take his hand and coax him out of bed. 'Darling, I have to do this for myself. Mrs Moffatt's going to arrange a meeting. She thinks there'll be a way. Well, it's war, isn't it? War changes everything.'

War and love, thought Raymond as he too got dressed. Then, side by side, husband and wife left their home at No. 18 Blomfield Road, making twin tracks through the snow as they made their way to the frozen omnibus that would take them towards Berkeley Square.

So wrapped up in each other were they that neither one of them saw the figure who was waiting, in her grey lambswool coat and scarf, at the bottom of the road. So rapt in each other's company were they that neither one saw her as she approached their house, stood at the garden gate, and looked up at its face.

And because they were so lost in their own dreams neither one of them saw the woman as, pushing through the garden gate, she took a single silver key from her pocket, slipped it into the lock and stepped into the home where the air was still heavy with the scent of the tea they'd brewed, and the toast they'd burnt.

By the time they were boarding the bus to take them to the Buckingham Hotel, the woman was already walking up the stairs.

By the time the bus was gliding off along the icy road, she was at their bedroom door.

Opening it.

Slipping inside ...

'Still no sign of him?' asked Raymond, stepping into the studio behind the Grand – where the rest of the troupe were already gathered. He'd taken breakfast with Nancy and Mrs Moffatt in the Housekeeping Office, then visited Billy Brogan down in the hotel post room. There'd been no word from Ken in the intervening days, and that could only mean he was still enjoying a cell courtesy of the Metropolitan Police. Now, with the breakfast service still going on in the Queen Mary, the dance troupe gathered. The clock on the wall was counting down the minutes: ten hours until the first guests arrived and One Grand Night began.

'Not a peep,' said Frank, hanging his head in the corner of the room. 'But not a peep of Mathilde either. She's supposed to be here already.'

'Has anyone checked her quarters?'

'If she slept there last night, she didn't get back until after midnight – and now she's gone again.' Frank threw his head back and groaned. 'It's hopeless.'

Raymond turned at the sound of the door, and watched as Hélène Marchmont appeared in its frame, a ball gown of rose pink satin over her arm. Taking in the startled faces, she looked at Raymond and asked, 'Has something happened?'

'We still have the day,' came a voice from behind Hélène. Walter Knave appeared at her shoulder, and Hélène stepped aside to allow the shrew-like man through. 'Mr Arbuthnot hasn't let the Grand down yet. He was hired for this very purpose – to steer us through our choppiest moments. The ballroom's in his blood, ladies and gentlemen. I have every faith that the man will appear.'

Hélène's face was etched in the same bewilderment the rest of the troupe had been feeling for days. 'But where did he go?'

'Does anyone think… might Mathilde be with him?' Frank ventured.

Silence fell over the dressing room.

'We still have a troupe,' Raymond suddenly declared. He turned on his heel, taking in his comrades – and the rush he felt then, on being back here, back among them, with the anticipation of a show in the air was almost overwhelming. 'Look at us!

Aren't we still the finest troupe in London? Isn't the Grand still the envy of the ballroom world? Can we not put on a spectacular tonight that lasts long in the memory, whether Marcus arrives or not?'

Frank Nettleton lifted himself up. His eyes sparkled with some renewed delight.

'It's not as straightforward as that, Mr de Guise – as laudable as your intentions might be,' clucked Walter Knave, taking off his glasses and polishing them on his long sleeve in anxious worry. 'I have early bids placed on quicksteps with Marcus and Mathilde. Guests we wouldn't want to let down have been most generous in their contributions, in exchange for waltzes and tangos with our dancers. I scarcely know how to tidy this away, if we let them down. One Grand Night is our spectacular of the season – what cost if our guests go away underwhelmed?'

Raymond took his hand, startling Mr Knave so fiercely he almost dropped his glasses. 'We can but try, Mr Knave.' He opened his arms to the rest of the troupe. 'We have until the first guests arrive. Enough time, perhaps, to concoct new dances to open tonight's show. Enough time, perhaps, to *create.*'

Raymond was getting quite carried away with himself; Frank Nettleton wondered if Marcus's theatricality was somehow contagious.

He seized Hélène's hand, led her to the dance floor doors. When they opened up, the look on his face was almost as if the crowd was already there; as if kings and crown princes, ministers and lords crowded at the balustrade, hands outstretched.

'Let's dance!' declared Raymond – and the rest of the troupe, lifted suddenly from their despondency, followed him through the doors.

*

She'd waited until midnight last night, when the floor waiter came to her table and said, 'Mademoiselle, you must forgive us, but we have already been closed for some time.' Now, as lunchtime approached, she was here again, occupying the same corner table in the Academy des Artistes, nursing the pot of tea she'd been provided with – and debating just how long she'd dare stay, before hurtling back to the Buckingham Hotel. Mathilde had already let the Grand down once by betraying Marcus Arbuthnot, but she didn't intend to let it down again; she'd be there before the opening of One Grand Night, to step into Frank's arms and show the guests exactly what they should be bidding on, no matter what happened next.

'Is Mademoiselle waiting for someone?'

She'd been asked half a dozen times, and every time she said the same thing, 'He doesn't know I'm waiting. I was merely hoping he might be here. Mr Arbuthnot? Marcus Arbuthnot? Have you seen him?'

'Oh, of course, Mademoiselle, many times.'

The waiters at the Academy seemed to be chosen on account of their obtuseness. Mathilde said, 'And recently?'

'Perhaps.'

Then he drifted on.

At first sight, the Academy des Artistes was a small club, with a bar in the corner and innumerable little holes where men could entertain privately. The air was filled with a permanent reef of cigar smoke, but there was also the unmistakable tang of *Chanel* in the air – for the Academy, unlike so many other clubs of its ilk, had always welcomed its female patrons. But, while the Academy appeared tiny at first, this was only to the uninitiated, who knew nothing of the private chambers off the back staircase, nor the exclusive restaurant at the very bottom. The Academy's manageress, Almira – who certainly belonged in sunnier climes than London in the grip of winter, with her black hair and complexion that spoke of her ancestors in Persia – was as proud of their menu as any fine restaurateur in London. The rabbit cassoulet they served was said to be second to none.

The Academy had a long and noble history of hosting artists from the furthest corners of the world. The fact that it was quiet, of late, had done little to diminish that reputation, though certainly it had dented the Academy's coffers. Mathilde had waited hours already, and still not lost interest in the portraits that lined the walls – of the prima ballerina Anna Pavlova, who made the Academy her home in the years before the Great War; of Enrico Cecchetti, the Italian star who had, somehow, disguised the fact that he could only turn in one direction for his entire career; of Eduardo Corrochio, the world's first ever Tap Dancing Champion. All of these stars and talents had sat here, in the same place where she was sitting. Not for the first time, she felt a fraud. There would never be a portrait of Mathilde Bourchier gazing down from the Academy wall, but she could at least bask in their company; for now – perhaps forever – that would be enough.

She was still gazing at the portrait of Joe Frisco – the American vaudeville artist who had taken Broadway by storm with his tempestuous Jewish Charleston – when the door opened, and in staggered Marcus Arbuthnot.

It took Mathilde a moment to recognise him, because this was not the same groomed, gallant figure she knew from the Grand. Marcus looked part ballroom dancer, part vagabond as he lurched into the Academy, his russet-gold hair a tangled mess, his shoulders hunched like a man much older. He was still, quite absurdly, wearing his evening wear – and, though it could not possibly have been true, Mathilde wondered if he'd even changed out of it in the days since she'd seen him last. His eyes, famous for being such a clear, piercing blue, even seemed darker in the Academy light – though, perhaps, it was also the fault of the great bags of exhaustion hanging underneath.

Mathilde watched as he tramped to the bar, with all the elegance of a scarecrow. And that, she realised now, was exactly what he looked like: a scarecrow, dressed in a dead man's dinner jacket, jagged and broken.

'A bottle of Moët,' Marcus announced, as soon he reached the bar.

'As the gentleman requests,' replied the waiter, and soon a Champagne cork was popping and a single flute being filled.

'To elegance!' Marcus Arbuthnot drawled. 'To poise! To … honour!'

On the last word, he wheeled round, as if making a grand toast to a rapt reception.

It was then that he saw Mathilde, sitting in the corner of the half-empty Academy.

The horror caused his hand to tremble so violently that, soon, Champagne was sloshing all over his sleeve. The only thing that seemed to steady him was when he put the flute to his lips, threw back his head and swallowed the lot.

'Mr Arbuthnot,' Mathilde began, sensing he was about to flee and rising to her feet. 'Can I talk to you? Please? I've been waiting such a long time. I should be there now, at the Grand, but …' She'd said the wrong thing; the mere mention of the Grand had started Marcus shaking again. He reached for the Champagne bottle to refill his glass, but the waiter had already stepped into the breach.

'Might you want to take a seat with the young lady?' the waiter asked.

Marcus froze, giving Mathilde the chance to say, 'Yes please!' – and the waiter, like the very best of servants, leapt to attention, collecting both magnum and Champagne flute and transferring them to Mathilde's table.

Whether it was the draw of the Champagne or Mathilde herself, Marcus tottered across the room and crashed into the chair opposite. Mathilde tried to still her racing heart as she took her seat again too. The waiter had cleared her teapot aside, depositing a second Champagne flute – but, if Mathilde had any intention of drinking, the chance was quickly taken away. Marcus filled the second flute and kept it, churlishly, to himself.

'Mr Arbuthnot, I haven't breathed a word.'

Now that she saw them up close, she realised how bloodshot were his eyes. They were not glowering at her; they radiated the look of a scolded child.

'Come back,' she said. 'One Grand Night begins in scarcely seven hours. Eat, sleep, fortify yourself – and be there. I'm begging you, Mr Arbuthnot. I shouldn't have said what I said. I shouldn't have done the thing that I did. But I'm here now and I'm taking it back. I'll keep your secret for you, Mr Arbuthnot. I'll carry it to my grave. But the Grand needs you. Frank and Karina and all of the rest. The Buckingham Hotel. The War Relief Fund … Everyone's expecting you to be there, Marcus. Please don't let them down.'

Marcus drained another glass of Moët. 'You're the one who made me see the truth, my dear. My very presence has been letting them down all year. The way they look at me, Mathilde – they believe me their hero. But the truth is, I'm their fraud. No, my dear, you were right the first time – I don't deserve the ballroom. I haven't since the Exhibition Paris. The thing is, Mathilde, I did try and live life another way. For the better part of two years, I ran a cocktail lounge in Nice. The sea and the sun, Mathilde – the sea and the sun! I was good at it. It could have been a life. But, alas, temptation drew me back …'

'It's a horrible thing to be tempted by glory, isn't it?' Mathilde whispered, thinking of Messrs Cockfosters and Gove, and the devil's pact she had made.

'The strange thing is, my dear, that it wasn't for glory's sake that I connived for Victor and Meghan to win that competition. No, it's a much more ordinary story than this.'

'Then what was it?' Mathilde asked.

'It was for the sake of love,' he admitted – and this time, when he raised the Champagne flute it barely touched his lips. 'Meghan Barr is, perhaps, the only woman I have ever truly loved. Oh, it was a love that wasn't shared – I knew that, but it didn't matter to me, not one bit. I had come to believe, by then, that the purest love we can possibly hold is the love we have for someone who does not reciprocate those feelings. A love like that is unadulterated by the constant little complexities of life. It can soar and flourish – and yes, fade away – without ever being tarnished by the reality of a marriage, or even just by life. I held Meghan in such regard, but she did not have the talent to travel further in the competition. I wanted to give her that light, but for bestowing it upon her, I paid the ultimate price.'

'Two years, Mr Arbuthnot—'

'I don't speak of two years, Mathilde. I speak of the price I paid to the devil – the slow and gradual erosion of my soul. I always knew the day would come when somebody unearthed my secret.' He smiled, wanly. 'But I must congratulate you, my dear, because I never thought it would be you.'

Mathilde reached out across the table, but Marcus withdrew his hand.

'The directors of the Imperial Hotel approached me. They told me I could be their principal. Queen of the Ballroom. All I had to do was destroy the Grand…'

Marcus was silent, until at last he said, 'Oh, Mathilde.'

'I thought it's what I wanted. To sit on top of the ballroom world. And I was standing with them, ready to give them it all, when I realised: it isn't who I am. All of my life, I've talked about reaching the top. But those were my mother's words, not mine. God help me, but I turned to her for help. I suppose I should thank her, because it was this that made me see – what would be the point of reaching those heights, if I'd trampled on good people to make it happen? You made a mistake, Mr Arbuthnot, but it was born out of longing and love. My mistake was born out of malice and selfishness.' She paused. 'I was there with them, at the Imperial Hotel, and I realised – I just don't want it, not like this. I believe there *is* a love for dance inside me, Mr Arbuthnot, but the need to win? The need to be the best? That's something pressed into me by my mother.' She breathed out. It was the first time she had said it, but it felt so true. 'I don't mind not being the greatest, Mr Arbuthnot. I didn't realise it until the very last moment, but I don't need to be at the pinnacle of the ballroom world. If I'd told them your secret, they'd have put me there. But what would it be worth, if I cheated?'

Marcus exhaled. 'What indeed?'

For a time, they remained silent as both of them reflected on the mistakes of the past.

'I'm grateful that you didn't expose me, Mathilde. But I *feel* exposed. I feel exposed to myself. I've been running from that secret since 1931. Perhaps it's right and just that it should be the undoing of me, in the end.'

Mathilde shook her head, with a righteous conviction. 'I realised something else, as I walked out of the Imperial Hotel. My mother was waiting for me, shrieking that I'd let her down once again. And I realised: I'm not like her. She wanted me to be Camille reincarnated, but doing one bad thing does not make us bad people, Mr Arbuthnot. I'm going to cling on to that – I have to, or else, what's the point? I'm sorry I connived. I'm sorry I confronted and threatened you, and drove you to all *this*.' She took the magnum of Champagne, heaving it across the table and away from his grasp. 'But I'm a good person. I am. And you're a good person too. When we wrong-foot ourselves in the ballroom, we set ourselves straight again. Maybe it can be that way in life as well.'

'The rules of the ballroom are so very different from the rules of life, my dear.'

Mathilde shook her head. 'I don't think so. I *won't* think so. I want you to come back to the Grand with me, Mr Arbuthnot. I want you to dance tonight, and be where you belong. And I should like it, very much, if you would take me back there with you, right now, so that we can show them all what we're worth.'

By mid-afternoon, and the first inkling of the early December dusk, the first guests were arriving at the Buckingham Hotel. Though the ballroom itself would not open until 6 p.m., the Queen Mary restaurant and Candlelight Club were open for light meals and aperitifs, and as Walter Knave flitted from one to the other, he was filled with anticipation at the evening to come. His first Christmas in his second tenure as Director at the Buckingham Hotel – he felt a fluttering of quite unstatesmanlike nerves. Within the hour, the Hotel Board – led by the ballroom enthusiast John Hastings – would arrive for their private tour of the Grand. If all of the past year, all of the sirens and shelters and shrieks from above, had been building to this, then it should at least be spectacular.

Even from the hotel post room, Billy Brogan was aware of the change in atmosphere in the Grand. Christmas, it seemed, had come early. Wending his way along the Housekeeping hall, then around the edges of the reception area – where guests were bedecked in their fineries, already anticipating One Grand Night – he dared to venture into the studio behind the Grand. Here, the dancers were gathered, Archie Adams hunkered over the practise baby grand, while Raymond and Hélène danced their waltz. There was still, Billy saw, no sign of Marcus Arbuthnot; his absence seemed smaller in the studio, but it would be a gaping hole out in the Grand. Karina Kainz, who stood by the piano watching Raymond and Hélène, seemed to be wearing his absence more heavily than most.

But it was Frank whom Billy had come to see. 'Nettleton,' he whispered, and Frank turned round, 'I'm heading home. I just wanted to say – break a leg tonight, Frank.' Then he lifted his own lame leg and grinned.

Frank shook his head and groaned silently. 'You definitely belong on the stage, Billy,' he said.

'The post room's fine for me, Frank. Well, good luck anyway! With any luck, you'll be dancing with a duchess before midnight…'

The post room really *was* fine, thought Billy. It was more than fine. In the post room, you couldn't go astray. In the post room, you could keep out of trouble. And that was exactly what Billy intended to do now: keep his head down, attract no attention, limp on through this war doing the best he could – and never drawing the eye of a man like Ken ever again.

He hadn't made it to the tradesman's entrance before he heard Mary-Louise calling his name.

The cold December snow was flurrying in from Michaelmas Mews when Billy turned round to see her approaching. 'I was just heading home,' Billy began. 'Don't suppose you fancy a stroll? It's wild out there, but it'll be beautiful if we walk through St James's.'

That was when she struck him across the face.

It was the second time Mary-Louise had slapped Billy. This one stung more than the first. At least, back then, he'd known she was angry. This time, he reeled backwards, bringing his own hand to his stinging cheek.

'I know it was you,' she spat.

'Mary-Louise, what are you talking about?'

Here were those acting talents again – because, of course, Billy already knew. In the days that had passed he'd allowed it to filter out of his mind – but there had never been any escaping it.

'My Aunt Marge finally got to see him. Half an hour, in a cell in Pentonville Prison. All a big misunderstanding, we thought. My Uncle Ken's a good man. And, when he's not good, he's … clever. But then he told her, told her everything, Billy. How he got a tip-off about the ball gowns at the laundry on the South Lambeth Road. How somebody he loved and cared about told him where they'd be, and he decided the risk was worth it. And do you know who he thinks told him about those dresses, Billy? Do you know who he blames?'

Billy was silent as the grave.

'You set him up,' Mary-Louise snapped. 'And you used me to do it.'

Billy's silence continued. There were, he supposed, two ways this conversation might go: he might grovel and apologise, tell her he hadn't meant it, tell her it was all a big misunderstanding. Or he might tell her the truth.

'There wasn't any other way.'

'My Uncle Ken was good to you, Billy!'

'Good to me?' Of all the things she might have said, this was the thing that caught Billy off-guard. 'No, Mary-Louise, he wasn't *good* to me. He used me. He threatened me. He threatened my sister. And he wouldn't stop – so I had to stop him.' He shook his head, despairingly. 'If the tip-off came from me, he'd have come for me, Mary-Louise. But it didn't. The tip-off came from you. It was the only way he wouldn't know. He wouldn't think, for a second, that you set him up. So now it's straight: he won't be telling tales to the police and getting you in trouble, and he's where he belongs. I'm free of him. I'm out of his schemes.'

'Five years, Billy. They're saying he'll be inside for five whole years. He has children! He has a wife!'

Billy shrugged. It was strange, because Billy was ordinarily the kind of man to have sympathy with the spiders he accidentally trod on, but in this moment he hardly felt anything at all.

'He shouldn't have threatened me. I wasn't his puppet.'

Billy turned to venture out onto Michaelmas Mews, but Mary-Louise reached out and grabbed him by the wrist.

'How could you?'

'You were never in any danger, Mary-Louise. I wouldn't have done it if you'd been in danger, Ken would never land you in trouble. He loves you too much. As far as he knows, it was just an honest mistake.'

'I didn't mean for *me*,' she spat. 'I meant how could you do it to *them*? All the old folks my uncle helps. All the shopkeepers and families he's helping through this. He's been putting food on their plates. What's to happen to them now?'

'Food on their plates?' Billy balked. 'Ball gowns and Champagne, to put food on their plates? Mary-Louise, you're not a stupid girl. A few rashers of bacon, a bit of butter – that was just Ken making the tiniest gesture. He's been feathering his own nest from the beginning. Those bets he let us have at the dog track? Think, Mary-Louise! It was all for him, and he has more than enough…'

Mary-Louise said, 'What's in your bag, Billy?'

The satchel hanging over Billy's shoulder was bulging. He held it close.

'It's bread and butter, isn't it? Pastries and cakes. Bits you've picked up from the kitchen and room service trolleys. Well, isn't it? Open it up, Billy. Let's have a look.'

This time, Billy remained unmoving as Mary-Louise's hand shot out and pulled at his satchel clasp.

Inside was a heel of French bread; a wax paper holding some cuts of stewing steak; a pot of blackberry preserve, and three fat sardines.

Mary-Louise staggered back. 'You sent him to prison for the very same thing, and you used me to do it.' She folded her arms across her breast. 'Goodbye, Billy Brogan.'

The goodbye stung so much more than the slap had done. It was stinging him still as he wended his way through the December dusk, until he reached the bus stops on Regent Street. It was stinging him all the way south, across the river, and into the Lambeth dark.

The table was already set at No. 62 Albert Yard. Annie and his mother had spent the afternoon baking, and when Billy opened up his satchel on the table, their eyes lit up. 'Your father's due home any minute,' Billy's mother began. 'Let's make it a feast tonight. Our very own One Grand Night.'

As Mrs Brogan ferried the wares into the kitchen, Annie plucked an orange from the bowl on the table – it was old and past its best, pilfered by Billy two days before – and started unpeeling it. 'Stewing steak, eh, Bill?' she grinned. 'I could get used to this!'

Billy watched as she pushed the first orange segment into her lips.

He'd always been proud to provide for his family. Seeing the odds and ends he brought home peppering the Brogan table, bickered over by his rabble of brothers and sisters, had always made him feel like he was worth a damn.

Why, then, did it suddenly seem so ugly?

*

Backstage at the Grand Ballroom, the doors opened up – and Archie Adams appeared.

The ballroom was filling up. The guest doors had been open for almost an hour already – when Raymond last chanced a look out into the reception hall, he saw it milling with new guests, each of them bedecked in pristine dinner jackets and lavish gowns of rayon and silk – and, through the dance floor doors, they could hear the hubbub of anticipation that always came before a Buckingham ball. Frank Nettleton kept pushing the doors open the tiniest of cracks, just to catch a glimpse of the crowd that awaited him, only to be gently admonished by Karina Kainz. 'You know better than that, Frankie. Where's the magic? Where's the illusion, if they catch a glimpse of you before it begins?' The truth, though, was that peeking into the ballroom helped stop Frank thinking about Mathilde's strange absence. Without her, he would be taking Karina into hold the moment the music began. He'd danced with her for the very first time that afternoon, under Raymond's instruction – but a few scant hours was scarcely enough preparation for a moment like this. Karina was taller than Mathilde – taller than Frank as well – and something in it felt almost ungainly and odd. His first winter ball at the Buckingham was about to become a disaster.

'Still no sign of them?' Archie Adams asked, picking his way through the busy backstage area – where dancers were preening in front of mirrors, and the musicians polishing their instruments – to reach Raymond, who was tidying away a few stray strands of black hair with a liberal application of pomade.

'Not a word – but, Archie, we'll stay with the script. Everything, exactly as you'd planned it. We're capable enough. We'll march through the numbers before I take to the stage for the auction to begin.' Raymond caught Archie's blanched face in the mirror into which he was gazing and said, 'There's something wrong. Archie, what is it? You've led the orchestra through worse before.'

The corners of Archie's lips tweaked in the merest hint of a smile. 'Oh, it's hardly war, Raymond.' He shook his head. 'I've been distracted of late,' he admitted. 'I need to feel the music tonight.'

Raymond turned from the mirror, so that this time he was really looking into Archie's eyes. 'Archie, what happened?'

'Affairs of the heart, old boy,' said Archie enigmatically, and left Raymond's side to join his Orchestra.

Moments later, Walter Knave reappeared in the dressing room. 'Well, ladies and gentlemen, it appears my faith has been misplaced. One can only assume some terrible fate has befallen Mr Arbuthnot.' He looked owlishly around the room. 'And that same fate has somehow drawn in Miss Bourchier.' Whispering followed, in the corners of the room – but whether there was a real insinuation here, none could say. 'Are we prepared, gentlemen?'

Raymond nodded and, with his final hair put delicately into place, drew himself to his full height. His body had worn many scars this year – tossed about by the bombs, clawed at by fire, ravaged by smoke and the boots of a filthy profiteer – but it would serve him well tonight. 'Shall we?' he said.

It was the sign Archie Adams had been waiting for. At once, he rallied his Orchestra – the trumpeters and saxophonist, the percussionist and drummer – and turned them, like a regimented phalanx, to the dance floor doors. Frank, who was in danger of being trampled underfoot by sixteen defiant musicians, found himself hauled out of the way by Karina Kainz, and consequently he barely caught a glimpse of the Orchestra being met by the raptures of the ballroom, because he was too busy fixing his collar and tie in one of the floor-to-ceiling mirrors.

The Orchestra settled. The ballroom fell silent. The first trumpets blasted and Archie Adams' fingers charged up and down his grand piano in a succession of wild, unexpected chords.

Somewhere along the way, Walter Knave had slipped out of the dressing room. No doubt, now, he was somewhere out front, fraternising, like the Hotel Board, with kings and queens.

The music was building, building, building in intensity.

Raymond heard the saxophone glide in.

One bar…

Two bars…

Three bars…

This was his cue.

'Ladies and gentlemen,' he began, turning from the dance floor doors to the troupe gathered behind him. 'One more time, for the Gr—'

At the back of the dressing room, the studio doors burst open.

Mathilde Bourchier barrelled through.

The whole troupe turned to face her. She was dressed in her day clothes, with the most panicked of expressions on her face. Her cheeks were red and ruddy, her brow beaded with sweat, in spite of the December cold. Salt rimed the hem of her dress where she'd been tramping through the snow out on Berkeley Square.

'I'm sorry,' she panted, 'I've been trying all day – but I'm here, I'm here, I can still go on…'

Raymond's eyes were agog. Their moment was already here.

'Mathilde, quickly!' Frank yelled – and, tumbling across the room, threw open one of the closets where the freshly laundered ball gowns all hung. 'We can do it, can't we?' he said, turning frantically to Raymond. 'If Mathilde and I dance last?'

'Then who am I to dance with?' asked Karina.

A rich baritone came from the studio doors, which were still falling shut. 'You'll dance with me, my dear,' said Marcus Arbuthnot, stepping into the dressing room with a hand running through his glistening hair. 'I'm sorry to cut this so fine, my treasures. I'm afraid it's been a peculiar day in the heart of Mr Marcus Arbuthnot. But I'm here now – if you'll have me.'

Not a word was spoken in the dressing room.

'Then that's settled,' Marcus pronounced. 'Frank, please – my dancing shoes.'

Frank leapt for a dresser, rifled through it, and produced two shining black shoes.

'Well, what are we waiting for?' called Marcus, catching the shoes as they whirled to him through the air. 'There's a spectacle to be made out there. There's magic to be conjured. Lead on, Mr de Guise, lead on! I'm right behind you!' He paused – Frank was surely not mistaken when he saw him flicker a special, meaningful look at Mathilde – and added, 'I'm right behind you all.'

Chapter Twenty-Six

Stand with the crowd, now, in the heart of the Buckingham Ballroom...

The doors open. The dancers appear. In perfectly matched partnerships they spin onto the floor. Raymond de Guise and Hélène Marchmont, darlings of the Grand from an age now slipping into memory. Frank Nettleton and Mathilde Bourchier, the young hopefuls on whose shoulders the future of this majestic establishment surely rests. Marcus Arbuthnot and Karina Kainz, bastions of the ballroom from different ages and different lands, coming together in front of your eyes. Among and between them come the other dancers of the Buckingham troupe, eye-catching and dazzling, every last one.

But which one takes your fancy tonight?

In whose arms do you want to tango, to quickstep, to foxtrot and waltz?

Watch them carefully, my dears, for your time will soon be here...

In the very same moment that Raymond and Hélène appeared through the dance floor doors, Nancy poured the tea in the Housekeeping Office, arranged Mrs Moffatt's shortbread on a plate, and took it to the table where she sat. The armchairs

ANTON DU BEKE

seemed so inviting tonight, more comfortable and comforting than ever, and the shortbread couldn't have been welcomed more. In the past two days, the morning sickness she'd been feeling had turned into hunger – all-consuming, ravening hunger.

As Nancy sat down, she heard the roar of applause.

This far from the ballroom, the applause was muted – but it must have been filling the Grand Ballroom like a cavalcade of thunder, like an incendiary going off out on Berkeley Square. She shared a look with Mrs Moffatt. Smiles crept onto both women's faces: Nancy for Raymond, back where he belonged, and Mrs Moffatt for Archie.

It was Archie to whom conversation quickly turned.

'I was a fool to think he'd feel the same,' Mrs Moffatt began, 'but perhaps it doesn't mean I was a fool to write the letter. I've done a lot of thinking on this, Nancy – too much, you might say! – and it seems to me that the heart yearns for what it yearns. What I'm trying to say is that I *had* to write that letter. I couldn't find the courage to sit him down here, like you're sitting now, and let my heart out of its box. But I couldn't stop my heart from chattering away either. It would have been chattering at me forever, if I hadn't written to him. At least, now, I know.'

Nancy sipped at her tea. The initial applause had died away now, but every now and again she could hear some echo of a smaller celebration echoing around the hotel. 'And he didn't breathe a word at all?'

Mrs Moffatt shook her head, trying to hide her sadness.

'I don't believe it, Emmeline.'

Mrs Moffatt's eyes glimmered. 'You don't … believe?'

'There's another story here. There has to be. Archie Adams, esteemed gentleman of the Grand – just ignoring an expression of love? They say he replies to his Orchestra's admirers personally. I know, for a fact, how highly his band members regard him. He's like a father to each. A man like that doesn't just ignore a letter, Emmeline – no matter how unwelcome he finds its sentiments.'

Mrs Moffatt evidently wanted to speak no further of it. 'Well, Nancy, I feel better for trying. It's settled me, I suppose. I know what I need to do next.'

'Next, Mrs Moffatt?'

'Well, I should think that's a question that's been plaguing you as well, hasn't it?'

The time had come. Nancy had known that it must – and there seemed something in the air tonight, something wistful perhaps, that spoke of thoughts for the future and decisions that needed to be made. Perhaps it was the Christmas decorations that now garlanded the Housekeeping Lounge, in anticipation of the staff shindig to come; or perhaps it was the smattering of applause that periodically swept over them, all the way from the Grand.

Or perhaps it was the letter that had landed, summoning Raymond back to the war.

Whichever it was, the future was already here. She could put it off no longer; she needed to make it happen.

'Doctor Moore says I'll give birth by the start of May. I can already feel it changing me, Emmeline. I'm getting tired. I didn't use to get tired! I shan't be able to work by the last months of it, shall I? Pushing a trolley and changing beds, sweeping the floors and, down on my hands and knees, scrubbing the bathroom tiles. I can sense it coming. I'll go on as long as I can, but it's going to be beyond me.' She stopped. 'What happens next, Emmeline?'

Mrs Moffatt finished the shortbread she was chewing and softly said, 'What do you want?'

'Raymond leaves for his division soon after the New Year. Who knows when he'll return?' There was no need to articulate the things both women knew well, so Nancy did not say *if he'll return*. Mrs Moffatt had lived with the same fears, and found them fulfilled, during the Great War. 'I struggle to picture how life will look and feel. I'll have Raymond's army wage, of course, but … what would happen, if I didn't?'

'And if you *could* work, if there was a way, would you want to?'

'I don't see the Buckingham slipping from my life, Emmeline. I can't. I'm going to speak with Vivienne. I had a dream, a silly dream I know, that there might be a way she and I could help each other. Well, we are sisters by law, after all. Is it so foolish to think there might be a life where she returns to rebuild the Daughters of Salvation, and I remain here at the Buckingham, and our children play together? Where we both get to live our lives in the way we choose?' She was getting carried away with herself. She batted the idea away, like a fly. 'Will Mr Knave even want me, Emmeline, after he finds out? We'll have to tell him soon. The girls will start to see. It's a wonder Annie Brogan hasn't already told.'

'Annie Brogan, now *there's* a special girl.'

Both women paused and sipped their tea, with a warm, wry smile.

'Mr Knave's going to see the full picture, Nancy. He's going to know how valuable you are to this department, because I'm going to tell him. The Buckingham needs you now, more than it's ever needed you before.' Mrs Moffatt trembled before she said the next words, fortifying herself with what was left of her tea, and the delicious biscuitty sludge at the bottom of the cup. 'It's going to need you after I'm gone.'

The tea spilled over the rim of Nancy's cup. 'Gone? Gone, Emmeline?'

Mrs Moffatt smiled. 'Don't look so shocked, Nancy.'

'Shocked? I'll say I'm shocked! Emmeline, you're not – you're surely not leaving? But where to? Why? When?' The questions merged into one another as they sputtered out of Nancy's lips. 'Emmeline?'

'It's been preying on me, Nancy, ever since September. Ever since the bombs started falling, and Malcolm started flying up there, fighting the good fight. It's what Malcolm said when he came to London that day. It's the same thing that got me writing to Archie. How many Sundays do I have left on Earth? How many Wednesday afternoons? It's time I lived, Nancy. And if it isn't going to be with Archie, well, I could do a lot worse than living for my beautiful son, and my soon-to-be daughter-in-law, and ... and maybe I'll have grandchildren too. Wouldn't that be a twist in the tale? Emmeline Moffatt, who didn't get to raise her child, a doting grandmother, in some country parish, far away from London, far away from the bombs, far away from the whole bloody war.' She stopped. 'I want to know I'll come through it in one piece, Nancy, so that there's life still to be seized. Do you see?'

Nancy did. She said, 'And your mind's made up?'

'I think so,' said Mrs Moffatt – and, reaching into her desk drawer, pulled out the last two barley sugars in her supply. 'It's like I said before: sometimes the heart just knows; sometimes the heart just yearns for what it yearns.'

And, as if in answer to Mrs Moffatt's words, a fresh wave of applause roared out of the Grand.

Raymond de Guise took his leave of Hélène Marchmont, bowed graciously to her as he stepped aside, and, with his head held high, strode to the front of the stage.

Behind him, the Archie Adams Orchestra played a fanfare fit for a king. On the dance floor, in the precisely synchronised order that they'd rehearsed, the dancers knelt. Raymond himself looked out on a sea of faces. There were guests here who had been stalwarts of the Buckingham since the first days of the Grand – but tonight, more than any other night, he saw new faces. Not just the Buckingham's new, most valued guests – for there was King Zog and his entourage, and here the key ministers serving King Haakon of Norway and his government in exile – but others, too, who had been drawn in from London's other luxury hotels, hoping to catch a glimpse of what the Grand had to offer. Queen Wilhelmina of Holland was surrounded by her ladies-in-waiting, a sea of black in the ballroom's oceans of colour.

'Friends, allies, countrymen from home and abroad – I need bid you no welcome to the Buckingham Hotel, for we are proud that you can call this your home away from home. My name, as many of you know, is Raymond de Guise. This ballroom has long been my castle, and I am delighted beyond measure to have returned to it tonight – no, to have returned to it for this *One Grand Night!*'

The dancers and musicians had been instructed to cultivate the applause at this point, but they had no need, for the applause erupted spontaneously around the room. His eyes alighted momentarily on the members of the Hotel Board, surrounded by a coterie of Free France ministers, and among their number an elderly lady dressed head to toe in black, so that she looked like a shadow come to life in the heart of the ballroom. John Hastings, the American industrialist whose tenure on the Buckingham Board had been prompted by none other than Raymond himself, lifted his eyebrows in silent acknowledgement, his pride at what they were about to accomplish emanating across the room.

'One Grand Night,' Raymond began, calling to mind the speech Marcus Arbuthnot had written for him – and hearing the echo of Marcus's grandiose intonations in every word, 'is our way of pronouncing that, though we remain in the eye of the worst storm these good British Isles have ever encountered, we do not cower. We do not relent in our courage. We have not forgotten the difference between right and wrong, between the goodness in the hearts of men and the wickedness of which they are capable. We have brought you here tonight to celebrate the fortitude of London, the bravery of our boys in the skies, the common decency of every soul in this city. To do what we can, from this palace of dance, to honour those who have fallen – and give succour to those who, though they survive, have seen hardships that no good Londoner should have to suffer. It is, therefore, the honour of my lifetime to begin proceedings by opening this auction for the hand of my own partner in dance, the former – and forever! – Queen of the Grand Ballroom, Hélène Marchmont. Our first dance this evening will be a waltz, to the strains of Mr Archie Adams' very own 'Wings And Prayers.' I have in my hand three sealed bids from benefactors eager to take Hélène in their arms on this hallowed evening – but who else will join the fray?'

It began.

Because this was the Grand Ballroom, and not some common auction house, the auction was to be conducted in a stately, regal manner. Each guest had been given a stack of trimmed ivory cards, and onto these they inscribed their bids for the waltz. Soon, one of the concierges – decked out for the evening in a dinner jacket that made him feel as if he truly belonged in the Grand – was passing between the hallowed guests, collecting their cards in a jet-black top hat. This he delivered to the corner of the stage, where John Hastings of the Hotel Board had positioned himself. It was Hastings' responsibility to sift through the bids, his eyes goggling in pleasure upon seeing some of the more extravagant offerings. Then, with the winning card in his hand, he made a show of presenting it to the ballroom's true king. Raymond held it aloft.

'Ladies and Gentlemen, the honour of the first waltz of the night, in the esteemed company of my own Miss Hélène Marchmont, goes to Lord Rathcaven. Lord Rathcaven, you may step to the floor!'

A man of some considerable size, and even more considerable jowls, descended from the crowd to the hoots and applause of his fellows, wobbled down the steps at the balustrade and took Hélène's hand. At his side, Hélène looked more nymph-like than ever. Inwardly, Raymond smiled; the talent of a great dancer was in bringing the best out of those least capable on the dance floor – and Hélène had a veritable mountain to climb for her first dance back in the Grand.

'Let us begin the bids for the hand of Mr Marcus Arbuthnot, who has led the Grand so steadfastly in my absence!'

On the dance floor, the dancers turned as one to Marcus and began applauding. Soon, the applause was ricocheting around the rest of the ballroom too. Raymond saw Marcus and Mathilde sharing another meaningful look; then Mathilde began to cheer. Soon, that cheer was being echoed by others in the room. 'Hear, hear!' the collected lords and baronets exclaimed. 'Hear, hear!'

Marcus's hand went to the daughter of a French baronet; Mathilde herself, into the arms of a Norwegian minister – who, in contrast to Hélène's match, seemed light on his feet, a regular attendee at the Grand. Soon, Frank had been paired with a regal elderly lady in a gown of charcoal grey and jewellery as ostentatious as the chandeliers above; Raymond was pleased to see him standing as proudly at the old dowager's side as if his hand had been won by a beautiful crown princess.

The dance floor was almost full. All of the matches made, save for Raymond himself.

'Ladies and gentlemen, it now falls to me to auction my own hand for tonight's first waltz. Well, as they say,' and his eyes twinkled knowingly at the sea of faces, 'they save the best for last.' The cheers filled the Grand. 'Let us begin, friends – and quick sharp about it, for I can sense the Orchestra already growing restless. The Grand is meant for music. Ladies and gentlemen, your bids!'

There was a thrill that came with being back in the Grand. Raymond had danced on its inaugural night, featured in its Yule and Summer Balls; it was here, in this very room, that he had met Nancy, here that their wedding reception had been hosted; here, that he had returned to her, having been left for dead in France. Memories swirled about him. He was about to make one more.

With the ivory auction cards having been collected, John Hastings proceeded to sort through the bids – until, at last (and helped along by a crescendo of piano and drums from the Orchestra), he presented Raymond with the winning card.

'Tonight,' Raymond declared, and looked at the card, 'I shall dance the waltz with …'

He stalled.

The words on the card stifled him.

He looked up, with startled eyes, at the faces all anticipating the words he said next.

She had to be here somewhere, but he just couldn't see her. She was lost, between lords and ladies, between magistrates and ministers of the Crown, between dukes and dignitaries from all of Europe's fallen lands.

The anticipatory crescendo from the Orchestra died away. Now, there was only silence in the ballroom.

Hundreds of eyes fixed on Raymond. He heard John Hastings whisper, 'Raymond, they're waiting.'

'Cathy Everly,' Raymond announced.

Out of the crowd, she stepped onto the dance floor.

He hadn't recognised her, because he'd never seen her like this. Her jet-black hair was falling down around her shoulders; the kohl around her eyes made them seem more bewitching and green than ever. Without her grey lambswool coat, there was no doubt she was beautiful. And the gown she was wearing fitted her like a second skin; sky-blue chiffon, embroidered lace, simple and elegant and striking as the summer sun.

He'd seen that gown before.

In fact, he'd danced with it in his arms, right here in the Grand.

Suddenly, she was standing below him. The unstoppable forces of the ballroom were summoning Raymond to the dance floor, to take her hand. He thought of Nancy, gone to the Housekeeping Lounge to speak about her future – *their* future – with Mrs Moffatt. And it was then that he was certain: Cathy was wearing the very same gown that Nancy had worn at their wedding reception.

How it had happened, he did not know. But here it was – and, as Raymond was compelled to join Cathy on the dance floor, he felt it against for him for the first time in the two years since their first dance as a married couple. He was quite certain he could smell Nancy's simple, floral scent as well.

She nestled into him, but before he could breathe a word, the band struck up.

All across the dance floor, the men took their partners into hold. Seconds later, the dancing began. Frank sashayed past, with the elderly dowager in his arms. Hélène and her portly lord kept stately and elegant balance in the centre of the room.

But Raymond was frozen, his feet rooted to the spot.

'Hold me,' Cathy said, without a hint of awkwardness. 'Raymond, the music...'

She insinuated her way into his arms.

This was how it had to be. Raymond stiffened, welcomed her into hold, and began. He'd done the same on countless nights. Well, hadn't he? That was the lot of the hotel dancer – to take guests in your arms, to leave the outside world at the ballroom doors, to dance with them whether they were good or bad, highborn or low. He'd danced with those who'd sympathised and made allies with the very people he was going to war with; the very people who had killed his brother. He'd danced with fascists and fools. Professional pride would see him through.

'Raymond, my dear, won't you look at me while we dance?'

'This is the ballroom, Cathy. This is how we dance.' Raymond gazed over her head, turning her round. 'Cathy, what's going on? Why are you here?'

'Why, to dance with you, my love. Well, I *was* invited, after all. It was the strangest thing – my landlady swears blind that two friends came to my lodgings and left me a ticket for One Grand Night. A gesture, I think, of their affection for me. I couldn't find it anywhere, of course, but it seemed to go unnoticed as I arrived tonight. I've often thought, Raymond, that, if a woman comports herself correctly, she can go almost anywhere...'

The sky-blue chiffon slipped between Raymond's fingers. 'Even into another man's house,' he realised.

'I wanted to look my best tonight, Raymond. Do you like it?'

Somehow, she seemed oblivious to the madness of it. She stepped closer to his body; Raymond stepped back, his feet instinctively adjusting the dance as, in the corner of his eye, Mathilde and her minister wheeled by.

She must have taken a key, Raymond thought. She'd had it all this time. What a fool he'd been to ever invite her in...

'Cathy,' he whispered, 'this isn't right.'

'You're mine tonight, fair and square,' Cathy smiled. 'I've missed you, Raymond. I don't think you know how it feels. I've walked the patrols and manned the canteens. I've spotted the fires this week, and all without you by my side. It isn't the same on the streets, not without you. It's empty. It's hollow. I haven't been safe ...' The emotion was building in her; Raymond felt her tighten her hold on him. 'You promised we had a month, until the war took you back, but I've not seen hide nor hair of you. Raymond, my darling, I'm coming apart.'

Raymond stepped back. His instincts as a dancer – to keep on waltzing, no matter what – were fighting with his instincts as a husband, his instincts as a man. In the end, the only thing that stopped him from wrenching himself free were the other dancers, the complicated criss-crossing patterns of the other partnerships as they spiralled in and out of each other across the ballroom floor. Comportment counted in the ballroom. Elegance could be shattered by a single wrong move.

But he thought of her, walking through his bedroom door; he thought of her, rifling through Nancy's wardrobe to locate her wedding-night gown. If there wasn't malice in this, there was still danger. He could feel it in the way her fingernails prickled in his arms; the way she held on, cat-like, as he tried to pull away.

If he couldn't separate them with his body, he would have to do it with his words.

'Cathy, you're not in your right mind. Cathy, I know about Michael.'

She looked at him inscrutably, but still she danced on.

'No words, my darling. Just show me how you dance. It's been so long since we—'

'We've never danced before,' Raymond snapped, his whisper

severe and straight into her ear. 'Cathy, I can't pretend to know what happened to you. I don't pretend to understand – but these things you think just aren't true, not a word of then. The engagement ring on your finger is the one Michael Bonneville presented to you on the day that he proposed. I didn't give it to you, Cathy. We're not to be married. I'm married to the woman I love. Good God, Cathy, she's having our child!'

She'd danced on, oblivious to his words, until his final outburst. Now, Raymond sensed Cathy slacken in his arms. He felt her disentangle from his hold.

The waltz was coming to its conclusion, the Orchestra leading the song to its very peak, but Cathy and Raymond had already stopped dancing. The ballroom turned around them – but there they were, an island in the tempestuous sea.

'Don't you see, Cathy? I'm not *him*. He died at Dunkirk. This is all – it's all just a fantasy. It's just a delusion. He isn't coming back. Nobody can take his place.'

'Why are you saying this?' She wrapped her arms around herself, as if warding off the cold. 'Raymond, we're in—'

'We're not in love, Cathy. There is no love.'

But, by the way her eyes took him in, he knew that he was wrong; however fantastical and fraudulent its foundations, the love she held for him was vivid and real.

'I love Nancy, Cathy. This has to stop.'

As if on cue, the music came to an end.

Applause had filled the ballroom, so Raymond hardly heard it as Cathy opened her mouth and, through fits of tears, began screaming at him. He caught only snatches of it as the cheering ebbed and flowed. 'I saved you!' she seemed to be screaming. 'I brought you back!' He backed away from her, and she followed. 'You didn't die. You didn't. You didn't...'

She was drawing attention now. Hélène looked over, from

the other side of the dance floor, her eyes imploring Raymond to tell her if something was wrong. Frank, too, seemed to catch snatches of what Cathy was saying. As the applause faded, more and more people began looking their way.

Raymond took a panicked stride closer to her. He made to take her hand. 'Cathy, let's get you out of here. The ballroom's no place to—'

She ripped her hand from his. 'Don't touch me!' she told him, as ferocious as a wounded dog. 'You're a liar,' she howled. 'Every word you've ever said to me, it's been a filthy, rotten lie. You're having a child with *her?* This is my life, Raymond. You're trampling on my *life.*'

She slapped his hand away, turned on the spot and took off, clawing her way through the other dancers, scything through Hélène and her partner as she stumbled, arms and legs flailing wildly, to the balustrade.

She would have clawed through the guests crowding the cocktail tables if Nancy's sky-blue chiffon hadn't caught her around the ankles. Moments later, balance unchecked, she had crashed to the dance floor steps.

Raymond rushed to her, every eye in the ballroom tracking him as he ran.

Reaching out his hand, he said, 'Cathy, I can get you help.'

On the floor, she turned her face to take him in. 'I don't need your help,' she said, her voice broken and low. 'I need you.'

It was then, in the world outside, that the sirens started sounding.

Chapter Twenty-Seven

In the Housekeeping Office, Nancy heard the siren's call. Wearily, she rolled her eyes. 'One more night in the shelters,' she whispered. 'When will it end?' Then she was on her feet. 'Do you think they'll dance on, in the Grand?'

Mrs Moffatt shook her head. 'Let's hope it's short and far away tonight, Nancy. I'll catch you up. Hurry now, dear ...'

Nancy was loath to leave Mrs Moffatt, tidying away cups and saucers while the bombs came down, but even when you weren't on duty at the Buckingham Hotel, duty sometimes called. The moment she hurried out to the Housekeeping hall, she could already hear the hubbub in the hotel reception. Some of the girls were flocking down the service stairs, Mary-Louise and Rosa leading them, and soon they had fallen in line behind Nancy. 'You know the procedure, girls. Roll call in the staff shelters in fifteen minutes – chop, chop!'

In the reception hall, the concierges and pages had gathered. Nancy could hear the tumult in the Queen Mary restaurant as the guests were advised to leave their dining tables and progress to the shelters. Some of them, as was always the way, were putting up a protest. 'No meal of mine will be ruined by this damnable war!' one particularly porcine gentleman had declared.

ANTON DU BEKE

But minds were quickly changed when the first reverberation shook the hotel.

'That was close,' said Nancy to the girls, as they awaited the guests about to erupt from the Grand. She looked from Rosa to Mary-Louise, then back again. 'Stay sharp, girls. It isn't out east tonight.'

There were footsteps scrambling up from the Grand. The first guests were evidently running helter-skelter from the ballroom floor. Nancy stood fast, expecting to see Raymond, Archie or Hélène guiding the first guests onward. Then the figure appeared and Nancy stood, rooted to the spot in horror.

It was Cathy Everly. She was certain of it. Her hair was flowing freely, and she was wearing a sky-blue chiffon gown – a gown which made Nancy's heart leap, for it was so close in look and texture to the one she'd worn at her wedding reception. Her face was streaming with black where her tears had run through the kohl painted expertly around her eyes. There was no doubting it was her. She hung, for a second, in the archway that led down to the Grand, the glittering boughs of the Norwegian Fir spilling their enchanted light all over her. Her eyes darted one way, then the next, as if searching for a way out.

Then they landed on Nancy and everything seemed to slow down.

Other guests began bursting out of the Grand behind Cathy, buffeting her this way and that as they marched off to the shelters. Frank appeared, with a regal-looking lady on his arm, then Mathilde and – yes, Nancy was sure – Marcus Arbuthnot, each shepherding some highly valued guest. In the eddying chaos, Cathy stood shipwrecked. Then, wrenching her eyes away from Nancy, she clawed through the burgeoning crowd, through the hotel's famous bronze doors and out into the night.

Nancy shook herself out of her stupor. Whatever had happened tonight, she would find out soon enough. First, though, there were guests to ferry to safety.

Raymond appeared through the archway. 'Follow Frank!' he declared, directing three statesmanlike guests to Frank Nettleton, who was just disappearing behind the golden cage of the hotel elevators. 'Lead on!'

'Raymond,' Nancy exclaimed, weaving her way through the fanning crowd to reach him, 'I saw Cathy, Cathy heading out onto Berkeley Square.'

Raymond gripped her arm. 'I'll find you in the shelter. I'll explain everything.' Then he kissed her on the cheek and hurried on.

There came a crash, like thunder brought to earth somewhere in the south. Nancy, who by now had proudly introduced herself to two guests and was directing them onwards, fancied it was as close as Green Park, as near as Piccadilly. She turned over her shoulder. One of the doormen had appeared through the revolving doors, shaking his head stoically; by the scowl on his face, he was ready to roll up his sleeves and march into the fight.

After guiding her charges to the head of the basement stairs – where Walter Knave was standing, as he stood every night, to shake each guest's hand as they filed down into the dark – Nancy returned to the fray of the reception hall. There was still commotion in the Queen Mary, but the space around the Norwegian Fir was at least blessedly free. She picked her way through reception and under the archway into the Grand, where only a few stragglers remained. Among them stood John Hastings and the junior members of the Hotel Board. 'It feels like a nasty one, Mrs de Guise,' Hastings said. 'Let's pray it's over soon. One Grand Night can still go on – perhaps even better, without the sword hanging over us.'

'Have you seen Raymond, sir?'

'Doing his bit, I should think. You can't keep a good man down.'

She found him, at last, in the staff shelters beneath the Queen Mary restaurant. Here, having discharged their duties to the staff, the musicians and dancers were gathered together in one shadowy corner. The surroundings here were not nearly as opulent as the guest shelters – where the staff from the Candlelight Club were manning the subterranean cocktail bar, and the canapes provided by the Queen Mary were in the warming ovens, about to be served. Instead of velvety partitions, comfortable beds and the illusion of privacy, here the Buckingham staff crowded each other like rabbits in a hutch. Nancy appeared at their edges, squeezed Frank's hand – 'It was going so well, Nancy, better than you'd believe!' – and caught Raymond's eye. Soon, they were hunched together in an alcove where a wine rack used to stand. The black bricks above them were cobwebbed and dry; the smell of spilt Merlot still characterised the cellar air.

'She placed the winning bid,' Raymond began. 'Suddenly, there she was, in the middle of the Grand. Nancy, she's been in our house.'

As they were speaking, Archie Adams lifted himself from where he'd been holding court with the Orchestra and, mumbling apologies, brushed past. 'I'm sorry, Raymond, Mrs de Guise,' he breathed as he rushed to the cellar stairs. 'I'm sorry.'

Raymond and Nancy watched him go. Then Nancy, with a dawning realisation, turned to Raymond and said, 'It was my gown, wasn't it?'

Thunder, such as they had never heard, ripped through the Buckingham Hotel. The very earth seemed to shift underneath them.

All at once, the cellar shook. Brick dust showered down like rain. In the flickering underground light, faces turned to one another in consternation. 'It wasn't us, was it?' came Frank Nettleton's voice. 'Fear not, young Frank!' came the rich baritone belonging to Marcus Arbuthnot. 'The Buckingham Hotel is built of sterner stuff. A skeleton of the strongest steel. Sit tight, young man, and you'll be dancing within the hour.'

'And what dancing that will be,' Mathilde enthused. 'The all-clear come, the night all ours, the – the ballroom blitz!'

It was at that moment that the lights went out.

Archie Adams didn't knock before he burst through the doors of the Housekeeping Lounge. Nor did he knock when, having marched across the lounge, he appeared at Mrs Moffatt's office door. Inside, Mrs Emmeline Moffatt was nowhere to be seen. It was only when he stepped through and, calling her name, began to peer into its dark recesses, that he realised she was hunkered down, awkwardly filling the space beneath her desk. 'Archie?' she said, when she realised she was not alone. 'Archie, what are you doing here?'

It was more difficult to remove herself from the underbelly of the desk than it had been to slide inside – and this was not helped by her embarrassment at having to contort into such strange shapes in front of Archie Adams himself. Thankfully, Archie was a consummate gentleman and was only too happy to avert his eyes as Mrs Moffatt emerged. Only when he heard her say, 'Mr Adams, has something happened?', did he look back. Then, straightening his skewed bow tie, he said, 'I was going to ask you the same, Emmeline. I looked for you in the shelter, but you didn't come.'

She'd often found him in the shelter before. Sometimes, if he wasn't engaged in keeping the morale of his musicians up, he would sit with her and talk about the nothings of life. To Mrs Moffatt, Archie's life had been rich and storied; to Archie

Adams, Mrs Moffatt knew the meaning of home and the value of putting roots down in one place. Many a long night had been whiled away in conversation like that.

Until that letter, thought Mrs Moffatt ruefully as she said, 'I wanted to be alone tonight, that's all.'

'Alone, Emmeline? Alone, in the middle of the storm?'

Mrs Moffatt froze. Perhaps now was the moment she ought to say something. It would be that way in a book. But she'd said everything there was to say in that letter, and in return only silence had come. Archie Adams, who had built his world out of sound and noise and wonder, hadn't been able to dredge up a single word for her.

It was harder to think about it, now that he was here. In the days that had passed she'd been able to block out those thoughts, to scrub them away like a pesky stain, but seeing Archie face to face only brought the letter back to her mind. She'd written portions of it so many times that its words were near imprinted on her mind.

'Emmeline, talk to me. You've never not come to the shelter before.'

'Talk to you?' she gasped. She flushed red; it was not like her to speak out of turn, not like her to snap or chastise. She'd built her whole life around her talents for sitting down and talking problems through methodically and rationally with her girls. Everything solved by a simple cup of tea. But now she felt her skin prickling and her fingers start to twitch. 'Oh, Mr Adams,' she said, quite without meaning to, 'I did talk to you. I put everything in my heart onto a page and delivered it you by hand. It's you, Archie, who doesn't want to speak to me. No, don't say it! I've embarrassed you. I've embarrassed you and humiliated myself to boot. That was the risk I took, and I knew it all along. I'm no spring chicken, Archie – I've lived a life. So you mustn't come clucking around me now, just because I didn't fancy sitting down there in the dark with you. Sitting in silence, when we used to talk so freely. No, no, it wouldn't do. I'm quite content here, thank you very much – this desk's been in this office for sixty years. She's built of solid oak. She's as good a shelter as those Mr Knave ordered built under the hotel. I'm quite safe here, thank you very much.'

Mrs Moffatt gasped for air. She had, she realised, been speaking at length – and all without taking a single breath.

'If you'll excuse me, Mr Adams,' she said – and began folding herself, again, into the cavity under the desk.

She'd been cramped up in there for some time when she saw Archie Adams' legs, in their fine charcoal grey trousers, appear in her line of vision. 'Is there room for one more, Emmeline?'

Mrs Moffatt looked left. Mrs Moffatt looked right. On both sides, she was hemmed in by solid oak. 'Mr Adams, there's hardly a square inch!'

'Well then,' said Archie, and Mrs Moffatt saw him descend delicately into her desk chair, 'I'll simply have to say what I have to say from up here.'

Mrs Moffatt's heart skipped a beat. She'd heard of the term 'a captive audience' and now she understood what it meant.

It was at that moment that the lights went out.

She'd burst through the revolving bronze door, flailed wildly down the hotel's marble steps and through its grand white colonnade – and there, in the snowy heart of Berkeley Square, Cathy came to a stop. She'd meant to run further, of course. The searchlights were making a lattice of light in the London sky, and she'd meant to take flight underneath them, all the way west and to her lodgings in Holland Park. She'd tear his picture out of its frame. She'd shred the letters, burn the magazines, carve his name right out of her heart. But, by the time she reached the middle of the square, she stopped. Something deep inside Cathy told her that she had to stop and stand still. If she didn't, she would just float, float off, into the war-torn heavens.

The bomb landed.

Cathy knew nothing of it, for in the same second it happened, she was thrown from her feet, cast down into the snow. The noise had been deafening, but now there was silence.

The world came back to her, as if appearing out of a mist. The first sounds, of crashing and thunder, seemed so far away, ringing and echoing in her ears. She lifted her face from the snow, crawled forward, one hand patting every bit of her body as if to make sure it was still there.

The sounds were far away, but the smells billowed around her: dust and dirt and smoke, the smells she'd been confronted with for months.

She knew, then, what had happened. She flung herself around, still half spread-eagled in the snow – and with every beat of her heart, she knew that the Buckingham Hotel was gone.

But it wasn't. There it hung, a white fairytale castle, its copper crown so thick with frost it had nearly disappeared.

It wasn't the Buckingham that had been hit. It was the townhouse alongside it. The bomb had scythed straight through the roof, carving the building into two different wings. Fires lapped in the place where lives used to be lived. A great cauldron of dust and smoke roiled and twisted and spat out flame.

Sound rushed back into Cathy Everly's life. She heard somebody screaming. She heard the echo of some other bomb landing not far from where she stood. In the parting smoke, she thought she could see the townhouse's cellars open to the world; if a family had been sheltering down there, there was little hope they had survived.

She picked herself up. The snow had cushioned her fall, so that – even though she was still wearing nothing but a ball gown – she was not hurt. She could hardly even feel the cold.

She knew it was going to happen ten seconds before it did. The feeling of premonition came over her, as it sometimes does on the edge between waking and sleep, and she knew – in her gut, her heart, her head – that the wall of the townhouse still standing was teetering. Without the other walls, there was nothing to brace it in place; every rafter, every support strut was gone.

The wall plunged sideways, crashing over the top of Michaelmas Mews, piling straight into the walls of the Buckingham Hotel.

The side wall caved under the pressure. The sound of an avalanche reached Cathy's ears. Minutes ago, Berkeley Square had been a pristine pasture of white, an oasis in the ruin being made of London beyond. Now, the war was here, right in front of her – and the Buckingham Hotel, though still standing defiant, was open to the bitter cold of night.

Cathy started running, running back towards the hotel. Through the colonnade she came, hitching Nancy's ball gown around her; up the marble steps and towards the revolving doors. And she was not thinking of Raymond, now; it was not thoughts of Raymond that sent her clattering across the reception hall, under the boughs of the Norwegian Fir. It was the memory of who *she* was, and what she'd come to London to do. She wasn't a quiet little mouse, working in the WVS canteen. She was Cathy Everly, betrothed to the late, great Michael Bonneville; she was fighting this war, right here, on her very own front. If there was disaster in front of her, she wasn't going to turn away.

Just before Cathy had clattered back into the reception hall, the doorman standing sentry had rushed inside. 'Where is it?' she asked – though she already knew, for she was the one who'd seen it topple. She streaked past the reception desks, along one of the staff corridors and into the Buckingham's inner sanctums. It wasn't long before she could see the billowing dust. It wasn't long after that that she ran directly into the landslide of bricks and mortar where the walls had tumbled down.

The way ahead was blocked by ceilings caved in, banister rails blown apart, and the hotel's outer walls. She could feel the rush of wind and smoke from the burning townhouse next door.

'Hello?' she started crying. 'Is anybody in there!?'

In the guest shelter, Walter Knave's eyes darted upwards. 'Lights, gentlemen!' he called out, trying to keep the tremor out of his tone. 'Lanterns, please.'

Strobing torches illuminated the underground. Some moments later, pools of lantern light began to flare.

'Ladies, gentlemen,' Mr Knave said, as faces appeared from every partition to take him in, 'the Buckingham Hotel remains one of the strongest constructions in the whole of London. The steel structure around which our hotel is built is second to none. I assure you that you are safe here, even in the event that the Luftwaffe target us with precision. We are provisioned for a long night. We have food and we have the finest of wines. But we will not need it. One Grand Night will resume in no short order.' He could hear his own voice fading, just as his faith in his own words was frittered away. 'Let there be music,' he said – and one of the cocktail waiters quickly had the gramophones playing. 'Sirs, ladies, I shall return in but a few moments' time.'

Walter Knave had used up all his reserves of calmness and courage. Consequently, by the time he reached the shelter stairs, the tremors had taken hold of his body – and he had to cling to the banister rail to keep himself from keeling over. In faltering steps, he picked his way to the top of the stairs. At the top,

Victor Garlick, the night manager, ought to have been standing sentry – but his post was empty.

Walter stuttered forward. 'Hello?' he called out, struggling to summon more than a whisper. 'Hello?'

A doorway ahead of him burst open, and torches lanced him with their light.

'Mr Knave?' came a voice. 'Is that you?'

Walter cringed back from the light. 'Is that you, Victor?'

'Aye,' the voice returned. 'You need to get back in the shelter, Mr Knave. You need to keep them all down there and calm.'

'What is it?' Walter demanded. 'I'm the Hotel Director, sir. I should be where I'm needed.'

'Aye, and that's with the guests.' A second torch appeared behind the first, illuminating Mr Garlick's features as he said, 'Mr Knave, we've been hit.'

'Archie? Mr Adams? Mr Adams, are you there?'

A voice in the darkness – sometimes it's all a man needs to come out of unconsciousness. As soon as he heard Mrs Moffatt, Archie Adams stirred. His hand reached out blindly and, after three futile attempts, somehow connected with hers. Their fingers entwined, though neither one could see the other.

The darkness was impenetrable. The air thick with dust. Mrs Moffatt was spluttering, but Archie sensed that she was sitting upright. He picked himself up too.

'Are you hurt?' he asked. He thought he was facing her now, but he couldn't be sure.

Nor could she. She tried to take his other hand with her second, and in this way managed to orient herself. Was this what it was like to be blind? She could barely open her eyes for the dust – and, even when she managed to, there was only darkness, rich and deep as a starless sky.

'I don't think so,' she said, daring to let go of him for a second and touch her own body. 'I'm – I'm fine. But Archie – are you?'

He'd been thrown to the ground; this he already knew – but when he touched his body, his hands did not come away sticky with blood; he felt lost, disoriented, dizzy perhaps – but there was no discernible injury or wound. It was the thought of what must have happened that coursed through him now, the sudden knowledge that the Buckingham was hit; that he was sitting in some kind of mausoleum, some kind of tomb. By instinct, he turned round, trying to gauge how big the tomb was. He was a musician; he supposed he ought to be able to tell by the acoustics of their prison. But there was a ringing in his ears, everything felt dull and far away, and nothing made sense.

'Walk with me Archie,' Mrs Moffatt said.

'What?'

'We have to *know*,' she said. Something in her was stopping the shaking. The piece of her that always leapt into action for one of her girls had come alive at last. 'There might be a way out.'

Hand in hand, they got to their feet.

'What do you think happened?' asked Archie. 'Do you think the rest of the hotel...'

He could hardly say another word.

'This hotel is a fortress,' she said, defiantly. 'If it's hit, they're safe in the shelters.'

Archie said, with a dawning realisation, 'They won't know where we are...'

They had started tiptoeing gently forward, each holding the other's hand while reaching out with the other, trying to discern what was there. Mrs Moffatt's table, at least, was intact; whatever had happened, she'd been shielded from the blow by the old sturdy oak. A little further away, the armchairs where she had so recently been sitting with Nancy were covered in grit and dust; teacups rattled as she and Archie shuffled by.

'It's here,' said Archie, when at last his shoe collided with some pile of rubble.

'Archie, I don't know where the door is.'

That was because, she soon realised, there was no door. Nor was there any wall. In the place where the door to the Housekeeping Lounge should have been, there was only rubble, brick, and plumes of choking dust.

'Is that smoke?' Mrs Moffatt spluttered. Archie felt her turning away.

He drew in a breath, and almost immediately started spluttering too. 'Not smoke,' he told her, though the fear was nascent inside him now. 'I can't see fire. Emmeline, I can't see anything.'

Then, as one, the enormity of what was happening piled into them. Archie felt Mrs Moffatt's hand tighten in his; Mrs Moffatt felt Archie's fingers strain against hers.

'Help!' they both started to scream. 'HELP!'

Somebody had produced battery-operated torches. Raymond found one pressed into his hands. 'No candles!' somebody was bellowing behind them. 'If the kitchens were hit, there might be gas!'

'I'm coming with you,' Nancy told him, taking his arm.

Raymond thought of the child curled up inside her, that little formless thing that would, in a matter of months, emerge as his daughter or son. He wanted to disentangle his arm, to tell her to stay here in the dark – but the moment he opened his lips, he fell silent. He'd left her in the dark of a shelter too many times already. 'Stay close to me,' he told her instead. 'We don't know what's up there.'

Up there was only darkness. The Queen Mary seemed

undamaged, but its floor was carpeted in shattered glass, and the December wind clawed through the ruptured blackout blinds, bringing with it the ice and snow that strafed across Berkeley Square. Whatever had happened had sent its shock waves through the building; as Raymond and Nancy picked their way through they noticed that even the glass in the restaurant doors was shattered.

In the reception hall, against all expectations, the coloured lights in the tree still flickered. The glass in the revolving bronze doors, the whole front of the hotel, had been shattered too – but, in the icy cold that came in from the square, the Norwegian Fir was lit in iridescent greens, blues, silver and gold.

Walter Knave and the night manager were standing in its ghostly light. They turned, suddenly, at the crunch of glass beneath Raymond's feet – just as the doorman reappeared from Berkeley Square.

'It's the townhouse, across the mews alley,' the doorman confirmed, breathless and bruised. 'The place is gone. It crashed down into Housekeeping.'

Nancy's face was lit in vermilion light. 'Mrs Moffatt,' she breathed.

'If she's down there,' the doorman gasped, 'she's not the only one. Mr Adams went that way too. Just came out of the Queen Mary and marched down the Housekeeping hall. I told him he ought to stay safe – I did tell him it was close tonight, but...' He stopped, took a breath, allowed his torch to roam across every figure gathered by the Christmas tree. 'There's a guest as well, Mr Knave.'

'A guest?' Walter Knave gasped. His principal duty was to the guests. In times of both peace and war, it was the only thing that mattered. The idea of one sheep who had strayed from the flock, one lamb who had wandered into the den of a wolf – it was almost too horrific to comprehend. 'A guest?' he repeated – not to seek confirmation, but only because the horror was too much.

'A lady, sir. I watched her leave the ballroom – she just came streaking out of it. Then the bomb hit. She was out on Berkeley Square by then, but she picked her gown up and came streaking back in. She charged straight to it, sir. Straight past the elevators. It was like she was … hunting the storm.'

As the doorman spoke, Raymond had started gazing into Nancy's eyes. Her shock mirrored his; the plunging of his heart mirrored hers.

Without tearing his gaze from Nancy, Raymond said, 'This lady – what colour gown was she wearing?'

'It was blue, Mr de Guise. I remember it, because it stood out against the snow. Sky-blue, like a summer's day.'

'Cathy,' he whispered.

But it was Nancy who moved. It was Nancy who strode purposefully past the Norwegian Fir, paused briefly at the elevator, and then marched on – into that portal of darkness where dust still churned, and the hotel she knew and loved was now no more than a ruin.

With the torch in his hand, Raymond charged after her. 'Nancy!' he cried out. 'Wait!'

But Nancy didn't mean to wait – not while Mrs Moffatt was somewhere down there, not while there was a chance she still lived.

And not while Cathy Everly, tormented and trapped in the prison of her own head, was somewhere down there, fighting it alone.

In the darkness of the Housekeeping Office, Mrs Moffatt cried out, 'I've got them. Archie, I've got them …'

She'd let go of him some moments before, to ferret in the

drawers of her desk. Without holding on to her, Archie felt suddenly distant and alone. The Housekeeping Office was small in the light; in the dark, it seemed preposterously large.

It was Mrs Moffatt's words that anchored him again. 'Emmeline, I'm just not sure. What if there's gas?'

'We have to be able to see, Archie. If we can't see, how are we ever going to get out of here?'

A match flared. A candle flame ignited. Two seconds later, Archie dared to take a breath.

The candle flame illuminated the ruin that had sealed them within. The wall between the office and the Housekeeping Lounge was intact only along one half of the office; the rest had been crushed by some landslide from above, obliterating the door. It was only by some strange mercy that the landslide had not crushed them altogether. When Mrs Moffatt lifted the candle, she could see gaps in the landslide, but they were too small for them to have any hope of picking their way through.

'I never thought of it as a tomb,' Mrs Moffatt said, shivering. 'My little windowless office – I always felt cosy in here. Oh, Archie…'

The flame was flickering, dancing wildly. Archie watched it, mesmerised. 'There's a breeze coming from somewhere,' he realised. 'There has to be a way through.'

Archie marched out of the halo of flickering light, approached the rubble and, having located one of the chinks, dared to lift one of the bricks.

Immediately, three others gave way, skittering to the ground to smash at his feet.

'Archie, don't! You'll bury us!'

She was right, of course. Emmeline Moffatt was always right.

'A cup of tea,' she kept saying. 'There's hot water. I can fix us a cup of tea.'

A cup of tea in a crisis. A cup of tea at the end of the world. Archie wasn't sure he could drink a drop, but it seemed to calm Mrs Moffatt to go through the motions of refilling the teapot and finding the tea leaves in their tin.

They sat together on the dust-encrusted armchairs, the tea freshly poured between them, holding hands across the candle flame. The tea was gritty, of course, and barely lukewarm, but there was something in the ritual that settled the nerves.

'Did you hear something?' Archie suddenly asked.

Their eyes darted. Something had moved in the rubble.

A rat skittered out of the detritus, then skittered back in again.

'I've been telling Mr Knave. They live in the walls. Now their world's been upturned too.' Mrs Moffatt shook her head, trying to shake out the panicked thoughts that kept returning. Then her eyes, opening suddenly wide, fixed again on Archie. 'I'm glad you came, Archie. If I'm going to die tonight, I'm glad you're here.' She'd said something wrong; the words sounded so different, coming out of her mouth. 'That is to say, it makes me feel stronger to be with you – not that I think you deserve to die down here with me … Oh Lord, Archie, it's coming out all wrong! It always does. I just don't have the words. That's why I wrote that letter.'

Archie gripped her more fiercely by the hand. 'I'm sorry,' he declared.

Mrs Moffatt looked drained, pallid white even in the candle-light. 'I'm the one who's sorry. I put you in the most awkward position. You're my friend and I should have known better.'

'No,' Archie said.

'No, Mr Adams?'

'No, you won't say sorry to me, Emmeline. I'm not sorry you wrote the letter. I'm sorry only for my silence – which was cruel and unusual, and quite against the spirit we've built between us these last few years. Emmeline, since there's no running away from this moment now, I want to say it loud and clear: your letter frightened me. I should have been perfectly content to carry on in companionable friendship with you, but not because my feelings towards you pale in comparison with yours to me. I should have been content to carry on as we were, because I am *frightened*, Emmeline. Yes, *frightened*. I haven't dared to love in half a lifetime – not until these last years, and pots of tea right here in this office with you. When you handed me that letter, it struck me suddenly that this wasn't something I could ignore any longer. And it chilled me to my core.'

'Chilled you?' Mrs Moffatt was taken aback. 'Archie, I don't understand.'

'No, and I don't believe I did either. That's why, when I saw you next and you wanted to speak about your letter, I couldn't find the words. Emmeline, everybody in this hotel would tell you that music is my first love, that I'm married to my Orchestra, that my musicians are my family. I've told you the same thing myself. So what I'm about to tell you is something I speak of so rarely that it is almost as if it never happened.' He paused. 'I was in love once, Emmeline. It's a familiar story. It's been told a hundred times. She was a nurse, and I was in the field hospital at Arras, the last time there was war. I was a young man, then, of course. The young do fall in love more easily than the old, don't you think? But that love didn't last. It ended, one night, in a moment so very like this one that I can feel the dread of it, even now. A shell hit the field hospital where I was recuperating. It spared my life, but in exchange it took hers. War,' he said, sadly. 'War changes everything. I went into that war a hopeless young romantic, but I came out of it jaded and old. You mustn't think me defeatist though, Emmeline. I did try and love again. Some time later, just before my Orchestra was enlisted to the Grand, I thought I felt it again. An old family friend and I crossed paths that year. A ballroom dancer herself. But it couldn't compare to what I'd known in Arras, and love – love is doomed when it lives in the shadow of what went before. So I came to understand, then, that love visits us but once in a lifetime, and after that it rides on to find its next victims. It didn't matter to me, not in the end. I had music in my life, by then. My Orchestra was taking flight. There is nothing to heal the scars of a heart like music.' He stopped. 'Then there was you.'

For a little while, there was silence in the office – just the creaking of pipes, the occasional sounds of disturbance in the landslide as some brick shifted or some tile shattered.

'So you see, when you wrote me that letter, and confirmed the feelings I'd been telling myself weren't there – suddenly I was a young fool again, young and scared. I'm a middle-aged man, Emmeline. Does it sound so foolish that I should be terrified of love?'

Mrs Moffatt tenderly said, 'I don't think it sounds foolish at all.'

'It feels *different* with you, Emmeline. And that's why, Emmeline, that I'm glad I'm here too. I should have come sooner. Perhaps, if I had, we wouldn't be in this mess.'

A silence again, warm and companionable for the first time in weeks. 'Let's not think like this, Archie. There are three candles in the drawer. There's water in the pot. Oat biscuits – though not many; I'm not provisioned for an Arctic exploration down here. But perhaps we have a little time. Just to sit together.' She dared to laugh. 'I'm afraid I gave Nancy the last of my barley sugars. She'll be the Head of Housekeeping, after I'm gone.'

'Emmeline!' Archie gasped. 'All of those consoling words for me, and gloom for yourself?'

'No, Archie, you misunderstand. I'm leaving the Buckingham. Although I suppose, now, that I may have left it too late anyway.' She seemed preternaturally calm, now; the contentedness had washed back over her, and she sank into the armchair. 'It's what my Malcolm said to me. How many Sundays do we have left, before we go? I have to make a change. I have to seize what's left of my life. For years, now, I've been pottering along, making myself busy, making sure my girls are happy here. But I can't potter any more. I have to live.' She snorted in disbelief. 'Well, it seems I've discovered a lust for life, the very moment it's being taken away! Do you know, I would very much like to write a note. Something they'll find with us, when they finally dig us out. Something for my Malcolm.' The contentedness had broken a little, now, and a single bittersweet tear rolled down her cheek. 'I do wish we'd had this conversation some months ago, Mr Adams. But ... Why is it so impossible, when you're over the hill and looking old age in the face, to think of new beginnings? When you're young, you can get up in the morning and just start running. But now ...'

Archie stroked the back of her hand. 'Now what?' he asked.

Raymond caught up with Nancy at the end of the Housekeeping hall.

They'd seen, smelt, breathed in the dust from the moment they turned past the golden elevators, and here was its source. The blow had sent ripples through the very framework of the building, so that the walls along the Housekeeping hall were riven by three great scars. Great layers of wallpaper, paint and plasterboard had peeled away, revealing the brickwork underneath. Glass lampshades had shattered, picture frames and other fittings were torn from the walls. Even the floorboards underneath the rug that ran the length of the hall had been forced upwards in jagged spikes. Hot water was pumping from some burst pipe underneath. Sparks fluttered and danced where some electrical fitting, ripped from the brick, still had life.

'Hold my hand,' said Raymond.

'Here,' said Nancy, 'I'll hold the torch.'

She was careful with it, illuminating each step that they took. The further along the hall they went, the more apparent the damage. Raymond stumbled, had to catch himself against the wall; Nancy braced herself against him, using the fallen pieces of brickwork as stepping stones across the ruptured floorboards and scalding water below. Ahead of them, the torch beam swept and roamed.

Then they reached the corner. Nancy had stood here so many times, waiting to go into the lounge for the breakfast service, for the new rotas, or just for an idle chat with Mrs Moffatt, something to give ballast to her days. But not like this. Where the door to the Housekeeping Lounge should have been, there was only devastated stone, mortar and brick. Electric cables ran through the ruin like vines through some ruined castle. The water pipe must have been severed near here, too, because the ground underneath was a mulch of brick dust, floorboard and hallway rug.

Standing at the face of the landslide, working alone in the dark, was a figure. Nancy's torch beam picked out the sky-blue ball gown she'd been wearing on her wedding night, a head of buoyant black hair now turned to grey and white by dust; flailing limbs, a bloodied cheek, a woman in a fever as she ripped stone after stone from the landslide.

'Cathy?' Raymond began.

She didn't turn. 'What do you want?' she snapped, heaving another chunk of the old lounge wall out of the way. 'What are you doing here? Oughtn't you to be in your shelter? You're not an ARP man tonight, Raymond. You're a ballroom dancer. So go on – go and dance! And leave the rest of us to pick up the pieces. Just like – just like ...'

Her words petered away, and Nancy wondered if some element of Cathy's fantasy was, in this very moment, crashing into the reality around them.

'I might be a ballroom dancer tonight,' said Raymond, 'but it's my hotel – and they're my people – and I'll damn well get my hands dirty, midnight-blue dinner jacket or not.'

In fact, he'd already ripped it off.

When he was nearly at the wall, Cathy screamed, 'Get away from me!' with the ferocity of a banshee. Then she turned her eyes on Nancy, their glittering green caught in the torch beam. 'Take him away. I've work to do.'

Raymond was ready to ignore her, his hands seizing some piece of timber trapped in the avalanche, when Nancy said, 'Raymond, please? Raymond, a moment?'

Raymond heaved the timber aside and, gasping, said, 'A moment? Nancy, they might be alive in there!'

'They *are* alive in there,' Cathy cried. 'Can't you hear them, Raymond?'

Other footsteps were approaching along the devastated hall now, the doorman and a host of others coming to their aid – but Nancy, Raymond and Cathy stood still, holding their breaths, searching for voices on the other side.

But there was only silence.

Nancy and Raymond shared a look, as if to say this was another one of Cathy's delusions. Then Raymond, sensing that this was something Nancy needed to do, turned to the others advancing down the hall and cried out, 'Hold there! Hold! We need barrows – shovels, spades, anything you can find! Quickly, man! Quickly!'

At the landslide, Nancy dared to approach Cathy's side.

How to say this? How could she possibly begin? Was it better, perhaps, to just keep working? Better to ignore the tragedy unfolding in Cathy's mind, and focus on the tragedy unfolding right here, in the physical world? In a few moments time, the others would return with shovels and barrows, picks and tin helmets – exactly the tools they needed to have any hope of finding a way through. Then, she supposed, the decision would be taken from her.

So perhaps it was right that she tried. Grief, Nancy knew, drove people to the most terrible things. And was there ever an age more riven with grief than this?

'Tell me about him,' Nancy dared to say. She did not look at Cathy, but kept her eyes trained on a piece of brick. 'Tell me about Second Lieutenant Michael Bonneville.'

There was a moment in which Nancy thought Cathy might lash out at her, drive her away with raking claws and bitter invective. But she only paused in her labour, took a breath, and returned to it again.

It was dark in the Housekeeping hall. Nancy had set the torch down, so that it illuminated the base of the landslide. Consequently, she did not see Cathy's face when she said, 'I do wish people would stop calling him *Second Lieutenant*. I didn't know him as a second lieutenant. I knew him as my "Bonnie", my Michael. He was a second lieutenant to those who took him to his slaughter. He wasn't a second lieutenant to me.'

Nancy heard footsteps behind her. She glanced round and saw Raymond returning in a pool of lantern light. The other hotel staff were hurrying behind. She felt certain she could see ARP wardens among them now: tin helmets and long overcoats, men drawn to the site of the disaster.

'You were to be married,' Nancy said, waving frantically for Raymond to slow the others down.

'But war changes everything,' Cathy whispered. 'That's what my father said. He told me it would. "Michael will go off to war one man and come home quite another." He said he'd seen it before. That I had to think carefully – think about what I wanted from my life. Well, I wanted Michael. And if he was going to go to war, then so was I ...'

'So you came to London, and took the lodgings in Holland Park, and signed up with the WVS.'

'At first it was just manning the canteens. I was too late to help in the evacuations, but there was plenty to do in London. But then ...'

'Dunkirk,' whispered Nancy.

Cathy jumped. A huge slab of the Housekeeping wall crashed down at her side, and she and Nancy staggered backwards.

'You'd think the war was won. Afterwards, with the boys back with their families and Mr Churchill up on his podium, acting like all that was wicked in the world was suddenly vanquished – well, nobody spared a thought for the ones who didn't come home, did they? Nobody stood an honour guard for the ones they lost along the way. Michael Bonneville, the best man who ever lived, just forgotten. Just a footnote! They'll write the history books one day. Will Michael's name ever feature? Just one more dead in France ...'

'Like my brother-in-law,' Nancy said. 'They got swept back onto the beaches. He never made it off again. Raymond buried him in France.'

'Michael never got buried. Just lost in the madness of it. Lost to the world. Lost in my ...'

She was going to say 'head', thought Nancy – or she was going to say 'heart'. But the word never came out, because the tears she'd been holding back for so long suddenly burst forth. Waves of them crashed out of her. Her body was wracked in spasms as she let them fly. And this was the guilt of it, thought Nancy. For months, now, she'd been filling the Michael Bonneville hole inside her with an idea of Raymond, a fantasy concocted from delusion and desperation. But tonight all of that was gone. In the ballroom tonight – and right here in this hall – she was staring into the hole, overcome with the shame of how she'd tried to fill it.

By blotting out his memory.

By supplanting him in her heart.

Nancy put her arms around Cathy, and this time Cathy didn't protest.

The tears ended just as suddenly as they came. Cathy perked up suddenly, her head cocked to one side.

'Did you hear that?' she gasped.

Nancy hadn't, because at that moment Raymond and the rest closed in, dragging a wheelbarrow down the devastated hall. The night manager was somewhere behind them, conducting a survey of the ceiling beams, trying to judge whether any of them were safe to be standing here at all.

'Quiet!' Nancy cried.

The torch beams in the hall all turned on Nancy and Cathy. There they stood, side by side in the pool of light.

'I hear it,' Nancy whispered. 'Listen, listen!'

Two dull, faraway voices were calling to them through stone and brick.

'Help! We're here! Help!'

'It's no use,' said Mrs Moffatt. 'It's no use.'

Archie had drawn his armchair alongside Mrs Moffatt's own. Taking off his dinner jacket, he draped it over the arm between them, as if that might make a single chair big enough for them both. Then he put his arm around her. His throat was parched, as much from the dust as the shouting, but there was still tea in the pot.

Tea in the pot, until the very end.

Companionable silence, he thought. He'd been a man of music all his life, but never had he enjoyed silence more than sitting here, in the company of the woman he loved.

Yes, he thought, *loved*...

'I've been a bloody fool, Emmeline,' he whispered. His eyes were closed, and across the backs of his eyelids he saw scenes from the last years of his life; the roar of applause in the Grand, the camaraderie and good feeling of being backstage, segueing swiftly into the nights alone, with only him and his records.

'I wouldn't say that, Archie,' said Mrs Moffatt. She too had closed her eyes and, by instinct, she allowed her head to fall on Archie's shoulder. 'It gets more difficult as you get older, don't you think? There isn't time in life to make the mistakes, so you daren't risk anything at all.'

They sat in silence for a little longer.

'Do you think we ought to shout again, Emmeline?'

'Oh, I should think not. I think I should like to keep my voice. I should like to use it at the very end. To tell you – to tell you...' Even now, it was so difficult to say it. 'To tell you that I love you, Archie.'

Archie felt a tear in his eye. He tried not to let it loose, for he was still so parched that it felt a crime to lose a single drop. But he choked as he said, 'I love you too, Emmeline.' Then, after another moment's silence, he said, 'I should like to have music, if we're to go to sleep here. If there's not a soul to dig us out, I should like to hear my Orchestra.'

Mrs Moffatt sprang up. 'Oh, but Archie, perhaps...'

By the guttering candlelight, she picked her way across the office. There, buried deep in one of the sideboards, she unearthed an old gramophone player. 'It only gets used once a year – for the Christmas party out there in the lounge. You haven't been to one of our parties, Archie, not in full swing. Oh, you're far too busy in the Grand! But I'll bet my girls give the guests a run for their money in sheer joy.'

Archie smiled sadly when he said, 'We've no power, Emmeline. How could we even play it?'

At this, Mrs Moffatt just smiled. 'Well, Mr Adams, I do hate to contradict – but I'm an old-fashioned girl, and this gramophone has been with me since the very beginning.' She found a record, one of Archie's very own, and placed it on the turntable. 'It's wind-up, Archie. So we will have music. And, since we'll have music, perhaps we should dance.'

Archie said, 'I'm no dancer. I've never had the need, not behind my piano.'

'Oh,' said Mrs Moffatt, 'but that's half the fun of it, I'd say. My girls aren't ballroom dancers either, but it doesn't stop them putting on a good show. Come here, Archie. Please?'

He kissed her before they danced.

Perhaps it wasn't the perfect moment, but it was all that they had.

They'd been digging with fervour, revealing the Housekeeping Lounge and picking a way through to the hard-packed rubble that had decimated the chamber, when they heard the blasts of trumpet, the roar of piano, the smooth, sailing sound of a saxophone that Raymond was quite certain had been played by Louis Kildare, the former saxophonist in the Archie Adams Orchestra.

Raymond, Nancy, Cathy and the rest all froze as one.

There was still so much detritus between here and the place from which the music was coming. Where the townhouse had collapsed into the Buckingham, the wind was roaring through, flames flickering on the other side – and, before they could cross the old Housekeeping Lounge, they would surely have to buttress the walls against any further collapse, to guard themselves as they fought further on.

But now there was music. It felt so distant, tinny and small, but to Raymond, Nancy and Cathy it was like a lantern being lit in the darkness. It was a hand beckoning them forward. It was the knowledge that Mrs Moffatt and Archie Adams survived, somewhere on the other side of this hell.

'They might be injured,' Cathy said. 'There should be an ambulance waiting.'

There would be, because even now they were sitting out on Berkeley Square, as yet more ARP wardens and firefighters battled back the blaze next door, searching for survivors.

It took them some hours to dig through the Housekeeping Lounge. Along the way, the music came and went, the same three records being played time and again, like a beacon being shone from the world's deepest chasm. By the time they reached the devastated office wall, and began the hard labour of clearing a path through that wouldn't threaten further instability, the chances of saving One Grand Night were gone. Midnight had come, the all-clear had sounded, and guests across the Buckingham Hotel were being guided back to their suites with assurances that the rest of the hotel was as strong as it had always been, and promises of lavish breakfasts and future soirées to make up for the disappointment of the night.

But that didn't matter, not to those begrimed in sweat, blood and dirt down in the Housekeeping Lounge – for some time in the small hours, while the rest of London slept, safe in the knowledge that they had scraped through another night, Raymond and Cathy worked together to lever a smashed door out of place – and there, in the candlelit room beyond, they found two old friends (and, though they didn't know this yet, two new lovers) swaying in time to the music they played.

Music that had kept them company on this, their longest night.

Music that had helped them escape the creaking walls of their prison.

Music that had brought them together, and would keep them together, for now and evermore.

Chapter Twenty-Eight

Three days later, Walter Knave felt as if he had finally got a grasp on the work that needed to be done to steady the Buckingham's ship. The wall on Michaelmas Mews would be shorn up by the week's end, with scaffolds raised and a permanent reconstruction undertaken as soon as the weather allowed; the Benefactors Study had been hastily repurposed to serve as a standby Housekeeping Lounge; and, right now, glassmakers and window-fitters were working their way through the hotel, attending to every cracked and shattered pane. The Queen Mary restaurant was already back up and running, in the midst of its second lunchtime service since the night of the disaster. Of this, Walter Knave was inordinately proud. And at least they would dance in the Grand tonight; in spite of the rubble and the ruin, there would still be song and dance by the time evening returned.

He was just about to go and take luncheon there himself when there came a knock at the door – and, upon croaking 'Enter!', he was met with the anxious features of Mrs Emmeline Moffatt.

She hadn't worked since the disaster in the Housekeeping Lounge; it was a matter of honour, to Walter Knave, that his staff should be treated as the hotel's prized assets. Besides, he'd known Emmeline Moffatt back when she was a fresh new chambermaid, and had always admired her accomplishments at the Buckingham. A woman of such steadfast devotion deserved a few days to recuperate after a brush with death.

He hoped, as well, that it might deter her from going through with the contents of the letter she'd given him two days before. Here it was now, sitting on the desk in front of him as he invited Mrs Moffatt through to take a seat.

'Emmeline,' he began, 'how are you feeling?'

Now, *there* was a question. Even if Mrs Moffatt had been able to decide how she felt in her own mind, there were certainly no words for it. Fortunate and bedevilled; elated and afraid; anxious and yet inalienably content. The only thing she was certain of was that, for a few days, she had felt the most intense feelings of belonging and warmth; her heart kept skipping a beat, in a way she was quite certain was nothing to do with her new fear of the dark, and everything to do with the memory of her first candlelit supper with Archie Adams.

'Mr Knave, we've come a long way with this hotel,' she smiled, 'but I believe you know how this feels. You retired from the Buckingham once before.'

Mr Knave nodded sagely. 'And was drawn back in, for the twilight of my years.' He shook his head, as if some part of him still rued the decision. 'But you remember the reason the Board asked for my return? The Buckingham needs people who know it well, Emmeline. We may not be perfect, we may not be returning kings – Lord knows, there must have been someone younger and fitter they might have hired – but, in times like these, the Buckingham needs its old friends around it. I was hoping that, in light of this, you might have reconsidered.' He picked up the letter and tapped it twice on the surface of his desk. 'You promised me two days of careful deliberation. What say you, Mrs Moffatt?'

'The Buckingham does need its friends around it, Mr Knave. It needs good people fighting for it, up and down its halls every day. After a disaster like One Grand Nigh—'

Mr Knave interjected, 'Barely a guest has strayed. To our guests' eternal credit, many have even placed fresh bids on waltzes and foxtrots they did not dance. One Grand Night will no doubt live again – but, for now, our reputation remains quite intact.' Not that the workhorses at the Savoy and the Imperial hadn't been making subtle approaches to the Buckingham's feted guests, of course; two men from the Imperial had been thrown out of the Candlelight Club only last night for inveigling their way into conversations with just that intent. One of them, Mr Cockfosters, had found himself quite scuffed up in the course of his removal.

'Mr Knave, the Buckingham needs its loyal allies, and I will be one for the rest of my life. But my time here is done. I have a different loyalty now.'

'To your son?'

Mrs Moffatt paused – because of course she would remain loyal to Malcolm for the rest of her days – before she said, 'No, Mr Knave, I mean my loyalty to myself. My loyalty to however many years I have left, and my duty to live them as I need to live them. Do you understand?'

Walter Knave heaved a sigh. 'I only wish it was different, Emmeline.'

'The Housekeeping department needn't break its stride, Mr Knave.' She took a deep breath. 'I need to speak to you about Nancy de Guise.'

'Ah yes,' said Walter, 'Mrs de Guise. Nancy is but young, of course, and has served this hotel for only a little more than four years. But she has your confidence, am I correct?'

'She does.'

'And the other floor mistresses, will they not be put out by her sudden elevation?'

Mrs Moffatt said, 'No more or less than they should be. Nancy has their respect. She'll make this work.' She hesitated, for here came the hardest part, the part in which she had to scythe through all convention, the part in which she had to make an aged man see that the world had to change. 'There may be one hurdle to jump first, Mr Knave. It may take a little imagination. It will certainly take a great dose of confidence and forthrightness.'

'Oh yes, Emmeline?'

'Nancy de Guise is having a baby.'

The silence rang on in the Hotel Director's office.

Then Walter Knave said, studiously, 'I see.'

'Do you remember what it was like during the Great War, Mr Knave? How we got through, here in this hotel, when so many of our menfolk were in Flanders and France, fighting for the nation? You could see it all over London. Daughters and wives, who once stayed at home and baked bread, were in the offices across the city. We were clerks and shopkeepers. We were telegraph workers and factory assistants. You see the same now, Mr Knave, if you look closely enough.'

'Indeed you do, and quite rightly so. But a working woman is quite different from a working mother.'

Mrs Moffatt took a deep breath. 'Is it, really?'

Walter Knave's eyes goggled, as if Mrs Moffatt was challenging the very fact that the sun rises in the east.

'Nancy is the only one we have on staff at the Buckingham who I would trust with the Housekeeping Department. She has the respect of the girls. She has the knowledge to do this job. And she has a work ethic comparable to nobody else who has ever breakfasted in my lounge. I've made it a habit, in my working life, of finding ways, Mr Knave. Every time a girl came to me with a problem, I'd sit her down and talk it through. You'd be surprised just how much can be accomplished with a little conversation – and a little imagination. You would let Nancy de Guise go at your peril, sir. The Housekeeping Department would take flight with her at its helm. She's earned it. She's more than capable.' Mrs Moffatt stood and waddled to the office door. 'I'll leave you to brood on it, Mr Knave. But take a parting tip from an old friend? *Imagination*, Mr Knave. It's the solution to everything.'

There was a moment of silence. Mrs Moffatt was already in the hall when Walter Knave called out, 'Won't you miss it, Emmeline? The Buckingham's been your home.'

Mrs Moffatt nodded. 'The seasons change,' she shrugged. 'But one day they stop turning, for each and every one of us. Mr Knave, I want a few more seasons in the sun.'

In the hotel post room, Billy Brogan was inundated with letters. Most of these were tenders made to take part in the reconstruction of the Housekeeping department at the Buckingham Hotel, but yet more were missives of support from the various members of the gentry who had relied on the hotel over the years, with offers of credit and donations to aid the restoration. These, Billy had been instructed to set aside; Walter Knave was to reply to each personally, thanking them but declining the donations – which, the Hotel Board had decreed, would be better directed to the relief fund whose coffers were supposed to have been filled by One Grand Night.

He was sorting the letters into sacks, preparing to do his circuit of the hotel, when the door opened, without even a knock, and Annie stumbled in.

'There, Bill!' she declared. 'I done it!'

Billy's instinct was to scrabble the papers he was sorting quickly out of sight; it took him a moment to remember that there were no more secrets left to keep. 'Don't you know how to knock, Annie Brogan?'

'Oh, Bill,' she cawed, 'we're family, ain't we?' Marching forward, she perched on the edge of his desk, nearly toppling it over. 'They've hired me, Bill. Four mornings a week, and Sundays – because, Lord knows, these nobs can't possibly wait until Monday to get clean sheets. Well, what do you think? Proud of me, are you? I bet you never thought I could do it – but here I am, Annie Brogan, officially of the Buckingham Hotel.'

Billy was quite certain that it was he who'd told her she *could* do it, and that it was Annie herself who'd been riven with doubts – but he decided not to breathe a word of it; the joy on Annie's face was quite inspiring to see.

'And, Bill, there's a few perks to this Buckingham lark, aren't there? Look!'

She had a cloth bag over her shoulder and now she let it pool open on the table. Inside it were the remnants of half a dozen room service trolleys. 'That's a perfectly good bit of smoked salmon – look, the silly bugger's hardly touched it. And here, Bill, these nobs have actual lemons cut up and dipped in their tea.'

Something was suddenly twisted and knotted inside Billy. 'It's Continental,' he whispered.

'Well, it must be Continental to leave aside a whole boiled egg as well, Bill – and these little jars of Royal Gardens honey, for putting on toast. These toffs don't know they're born! But it'll look fine on the Brogan table, won't it, Bill?'

Billy remained silent for too long. The knots that had formed so suddenly in his stomach just weren't untangling. It had been several days since Mary-Louise lacerated him with that comment, and it had been replaying in him ever since. The image of

Annie happily tucking into a Buckingham orange, while Billy had single-handedly cut off Ken's supply to all the shops and families who'd come to rely on him, was there every time he closed his eyes.

'Here, Billy, you want this?' Annie was holding up an untouched finger sandwich – country ham with thick grain mustard, by the smell of it.

Billy shook his head. The fact of the matter was, his stomach was rumbling, but the thought of eating it turned his stomach.

'I'll leave it here for you, Bill. I've got to get on. They've trusted me with the Victoria Suite.'

Billy was certain the Victoria Suite had been vacated, one of the few that had seen a guest suddenly depart after the debacle of One Grand Night – which meant there was plenty of time for Nancy and the rest to double-check Annie's work – but, again, he kept quiet as Annie bounced out of the room.

He wished her joy was infectious. He wished he could bounce around the Buckingham like that, full of promise and potential. He'd thought that, the moment he forced Ken out of his life, he could start enjoying life again. It was a shame Mary-Louise wanted nothing to do with him, because there was nothing Billy wanted more than a sweetheart with whom to spend his days, but he was certain it wasn't this that had been bogging him down. In fact, he *knew* it.

The sandwich on the table was staring at him. Staring, he thought, directly into his soul.

Was there ever a more absurd image to move a man? Billy tried to summon a smile at the ridiculousness of it, but the knots in his stomach had reached his heart.

What was that old story, about a hero faced with a knot so tangled it could never be unpicked? The soothsayers said that only the man ingenious enough to unpick the knot would become king. Thousands tried, thousands failed – until, at last, along came a man who simply unsheathed his sword and cut the knot in half.

That was what Billy needed to do. He needed to slice through the knot in his heart.

There was no untangling this one. Mary-Louise was right: Billy might have freed himself from Ken, but in the very same moment he'd emptied the shelves of those stores in Camden Town; in the very same moment, he'd taken food off the plates of that old couple Ken had delivered to on the day of the races, and probably countless others.

Where did responsibility begin and end?

He was still knotted when he let his head fall down upon the desk. He was still knotted as he prowled the edges of the post room. Still knotted as the clock ticked past 1 p.m., then 2 p.m. and three.

By 4 p.m., he still hadn't touched the sandwich. He supposed he ought to be thinking about leaving the hotel now. Annie would be waiting for him somewhere above – no doubt she'd have strayed out to gawk at the Christmas tree, and Billy would have to subtly drag her away and remind her she was supposed to be 'invisible' here at the hotel.

It would all have been all right if Ken had stayed 'invisible' too. But putting food on people's plates hadn't been enough for Ken. No, it had turned into Champagne and silks. And all that talk of 'greasing the wheels', what had it amounted to? A nice house for Ken. A fluttering of cash at the dogs. *Influence* over the people in his 'employ'. That, Billy decided, was at the heart of the knot weighing him down. What Mary-Louise had said was true; but so was what Billy had observed: the good that Ken did and the bad, they were the strands that were knotted together.

Billy started laughing.

It was only after a moment of unbridled laughter that he truly understood why.

He'd realised, all of a sudden, how he could scythe through the knot.

There was not a sword in Billy Brogan's hand; there was only a telephone receiver.

The directory was in his desk drawer. He heaved it onto the desk and started thumbing through its pages. He had to wrack his brain for the memory of any of the shops Ken provided, but at last he plucked one out of his recollections: Cochran & Sons, up on the Camden High Road. Moments later, his fingers trembling as he leafed through the pages, he had found the listing.

The telephone rang for some time before the shopkeeper picked up. 'Cochran & Sons,' the voice began, 'how can I help?'

Billy had rehearsed not a word, but he didn't need to – because the knot in his stomach had been sliced in two, and now there was conviction in its place.

'Mr Cochran,' he began, 'you don't know me, but I understand you might be running a little low on some essential bits and pieces. I understand, sir, that the gentleman who used to find those essentials for you has been otherwise engaged for a little while, and isn't likely to resurface for some time. So I was wondering...'

'Who are you?' came the voice, warier now, the hint of panic in its tone. 'Who am I speaking to?'

'I'd rather not give you my name,' said Billy, 'not yet.'

Three short breaths came down the line. Then, just when Billy was certain Mr Cochran was about to slam down the telephone, he said, 'And how can I help you, then?'

'Mr Cochran, I'm thinking it might be *me* who could help *you*.'

'Oh yes?'

Billy had to grip the hand that was holding the receiver with the other hand, because it was shaking so much.

'I could deliver you those essentials, sir.'

Mr Cochran seemed guarded still, as if Billy was laying down the edges of some trap into which he was about to stumble.

'Well, it's true that I have people asking, of course. But I had the most favourable relationship with our mutual friend. He was a good, decent man, undone by this war – as we are all at risk of becoming. I suppose you'll be asking for pennies in every pound, will you?'

'No,' said Billy, 'no, nothing like that.'

'What do you mean *no?*'

Billy floundered. All he wanted to do was help, and that was what he said. 'I can't let people go hungry, Mr Cochran. I won't do it, not while there's breath in my body. I didn't fight in France to come home and see old people famished in London town. But...' Nothing more, he told himself. He'd be steadfast on that. No Champagne. No silks. No luxury goods. There had to be a difference between Billy and Ken – otherwise, what was the point?

'You're taking on Ken's old routes then, are you?' Mr Cochran asked, this time bold as brass.

Not quite, thought Billy. Ken had others he connived to get goods out of. He struck deals with farmers and delivery men, wholesalers and those, like Billy's father, who worked in the markets. All Billy could do was what he'd been doing for years – lifting a few bits, here and there, from the Buckingham trolleys; sifting through the bits the rich threw away, so that it might, at least, benefit the poor. And, in that, was it really any different from One Grand Night and the relief fund the Buckingham had promised to create? What the wealthy had in surplus making its way, somehow, to those who had little?

He wouldn't get trapped in it, not this time. He wouldn't owe anyone. And, this time, there'd be a line he wouldn't cross. Not profiteering, he thought, just good, old-fashioned charity.

'I could meet you tonight, Mr Cochran.'

There was silence on the line. Then, finally, Mr Cochran said, 'You know where we are.'

The line went dead.

On the desk, the ham and mustard finger sandwich was still staring Billy in the eye.

But now, he didn't feel bad about eating it at all.

Doctor Evelyn Moore left Nancy's bedroom and crossed the landing to clean up in the bathroom. By the time he joined Raymond downstairs, the blackout curtains now drawn tight and a fresh log thrown on the fire, Nancy too had emerged.

'Well, Mr de Guise,' Doctor Moore began, 'I'm pleased to say that things are looking every bit as strong and healthy as they did the last time I visited your home. Nancy is approaching the mid-point of this pregnancy – and, as any good midwife will tell you, many of the dangers unborn children face have now passed. I'm leaving Nancy with the details of a midwife I can heartily recommend. You can be confident the care she'll receive in your absence will be second to none – but it's time I stepped aside, and left you in more practised hands.'

'Doctor Moore,' said Nancy, 'Raymond and I can't thank you enough.' She paused. 'And as for the matter of Cathy Everly?'

'Ah, yes,' said the good doctor, who had spied the small cakes beside the teapot and was deliberating which one to accept. 'Well, it seems that, between the two of you, you did the hard work of liberating Miss Everly from those beliefs in which she had become so miserably entrenched. She is returned to Yorkshire, and her family estate.'

'Will she come through it, doctor?' Raymond asked.

Doctor Moore had settled on a cake. He perched it on the side of the saucer Nancy had provided. 'I first learned my doctoring in the last war. There were countless men who came back from those fields, fit as a fiddle in body but addled of mind. They did not, perhaps, receive the kindest reception on their return to England. It was easier to call them cowards than it was to admit that war corrupted men's minds even more than it could their bodies. But there were those among us, even then, who saw the writing on the wall for that particular way of thinking. There were doctors who undertook to find ways to help those whose nightmares wouldn't stop, whose personalities had become aberrant – who, in short, had developed maladies of the mind. The "talking cure", some of us called it. The idea that something as simple as talking could help exorcise the demon within. As good Englishmen, we are taught to conquer our demons in private. But, for people like Cathy Everly, it might just be that confessional *is* the cure.' The doctor smiled sadly. 'Your fellow at the ARP, Mortimer, began his career as an army doctor too. He's arranging that Cathy visit a doctor who could help ground her again. For all her faults, she is, by many accounts, an extraordinary woman. It would be a tragedy to lose her to those demons, wouldn't you say?'

After Doctor Moore left, Raymond and Nancy stood together, admiring the tightness in her belly, dreaming of that day in spring when their child would arrive. 'I should like to be there,' said Raymond, 'at the birth of my first child – if only to pace up and down the hall, and boil a kettle, and wait anxiously for it to be done. And yet…'

Nancy took his hand and pressed it to the place where their baby lay. 'There's Christmas first. Christmas and New Year. Our last together, without our child.'

Raymond set aside the thought that came over him – that there was no knowing where he'd be next Christmas, no knowing when he might first get to meet their baby – and held her instead. 'Have you spoken with Vivienne?'

Nancy said, 'She'll come tomorrow. I'll make dinner. I'll show her the back room.'

It was to be hers, if that was what Vivienne wanted – hers for as long as this war lasted, with Stan in the new nursery, sharing it eventually with Nancy and Raymond's child. Such a simple, elegant solution, Raymond had thought – and if it broke with conventions, well, perhaps that was exactly as it should be.

He was about to tell Nancy how proud he was of her when the telephone started ringing in the hall. Leaving Nancy to put her feet up with her tea, Raymond marched out to answer it.

Moments later, he was back in the sitting room.

'It was Mrs Moffatt,' said Raymond. 'It's done.'

Nancy set her cup down. 'I wanted her to have second thoughts – but after One Grand Night, I felt certain nothing was going to change things.' She had known it was coming, but even so, the announcement of Mrs Moffatt's resignation made her feel curiously empty inside.

'She's to gather the girls in the morning,' Raymond told her, 'and tell them at breakfast. But Nancy, there's something else she wants to tell them too.'

Nancy stood up.

'It's Mr Knave,' Raymond announced. 'He should like to see you this evening. We're to get in a taxicab right now.'

Mrs Moffatt closed the door of the Benefactors Study behind her, pottered across the room – it made a strange new Housekeeping Lounge, but the girls had done their best to arrange it in precise imitation of the old – and sat in the armchair at the end. There would be no Housekeeping Office, at least not until the restoration work was complete – and, now that Mr Knave had accepted her resignation, she supposed she would never get to see it. New Year's Eve would be her very last day at the Buckingham; a new year, for a new beginning.

Until then, though, the old habits of Housekeeping lived on. The Christmas rota was directly in front of her. The addition of Annie Brogan to staff would allow at least one of the other girls to have Christmas Day off, and perhaps Christmas Eve too. The only question was how far one trusted Annie Brogan. Mrs Moffatt chewed the end of her pencil in deep rumination. Well, somebody would have to trust her soon. Sometimes, the most unexpected of girls could rise to the occasion. If you put your faith in them, more often than not it paid off. Just look at Nancy.

There came a knock at the door. Perhaps that was Nancy now. 'Come in,' Mrs Moffatt called out.

But it was not Nancy who came through the doors. It was Archie Adams.

She'd seen him every day since that night in the old Housekeeping Office. Without the Grand to attend to, Archie had repaired to his club during the days – but there he'd been every evening, to take tea with her right here, and luxuriate in companionable silence.

The one thing they had not spoken of, however, was the future. She'd revealed her intentions to him, down there in that candlelit ruin; she supposed he had heard, by now, that she'd confirmed every word with Mr Knave.

'Archie,' she said, 'sit down.'

He did, but there was something almost frantic about Archie today. He wasn't dressed in his dinner jacket, but a navy blue jumper like a sailor might wear, so perhaps it was this lack of formality that was putting him ill at ease. 'Are you well, Archie?'

she said, but he could not reply. His throat was dry, or his tongue felt cracked – or perhaps the words just would not come.

In the end, he reached into Mrs Moffatt's pile of papers, found an empty leaf and, seizing her pencil, began to write. Moments later, he had folded his letter up and pressed it into her hands.

She opened it up.

This is what it read:

Let Me Come With You

Mrs Moffatt blinked rapidly, her eyes dancing between Archie and the letter.

At last, Archie found his voice.

'You may ignore it if you wish. As you sow, so shall you reap, as the old saying goes.' He stopped, running a finger around the collar of his jumper. 'My goodness, even my letter can't say it properly. Emmeline, the hotel will be empty without you. *I'll* be empty, without you. What was it you said, down there in the dark? How many Sundays do we have left, before we go?'

Mrs Moffatt sat in stunned silence.

'That's the question, isn't it?' Archie went on. 'How do you want to spend the Sundays you have left? And I've been think-ing, ever since that night behind the ruined office walls. Do I want to spend my Sundays at rest, looking back on the music and dance of the night before? Or do I want to spend them with you, out there in the country, wherever you land?'

Mrs Moffatt still didn't know what to say. 'Oh, Archie ... but your Orchestra! Your music!'

'The Orchestra will fly without me. And I'll take my music wherever I go.'

She stared at the page again.

'If you can choose a new life and leave your girls to take flight without you, then maybe I can do the same.'

Mrs Moffatt took up the pencil. There just seemed something right about it now. On the page, she wrote a single word, then handed it back to Archie.

This is what it read:

Always

'The Buckingham's going to be a different place without us, Archie. But perhaps that's right too. It's what I just told Mr Knave: the seasons change.'

Archie took the seat beside her and poured the tea.

"The Seasons Change'. That sounds like it might be the title of my very last song.'

There was no longer any way in through the old tradesman's entrance at the Buckingham Hotel. This was one of the principal problems with which Walter Knave was faced, because it simply would not do for deliveries to be made through the revolving bronze doors at the front of the hotel. As an interim measure, all deliveries were being arranged for dawn, when the blackout was over and the fewest guests might see – but even this was a lack of decorum the hotel would not tolerate for long.

Raymond and Nancy were distinctly aware of this as they stepped out of the taxicab on Berkeley Square and, arms around each other to protect themselves from the cruel December cold, came through the white colonnade, up the marble steps and into the hotel reception.

The warmth hit them like a wave. The smells of baked apple and spice flurried out of the Queen Mary restaurant. There'd been no siren for two nights now – and, though no Londoner was foolish enough to believe that this meant the Luftwaffe was defeated, neither were they foolish enough not to enjoy the briefest flicker of security this gave. Consequently, the hotel reception was a hive of activity, every table in the Queen Mary was full – and preparations were already afoot for the dancing to resume in the Grand, where guests were already taking cocktails at the bar.

Mrs Moffatt and Archie Adams were standing in the heart of the reception hall, gazing up at the tree. It did not escape Nancy's notice, as she and Raymond wended their way across the hall to join them, that they were holding hands.

'We came as soon as we could,' said Nancy, joining them in the glittering light. 'Mrs Moffatt, I feel certain I already know the answer to this – but are you sure?'

Mrs Moffatt smiled. 'I've played my part in the Buckingham Hotel. The Buckingham's played its part in my life too. But my waltz has finished. It would scarcely be an exaggeration to say that I've been married to this place. But war changes everything, Nancy. I'm sure you'd agree with that, Raymond?'

Raymond thought of Artie. He thought of Billy Brogan. He thought of Second Lieutenant Michael Bonneville, and every soul he'd seen on the beaches at Dunkirk.

'I think, perhaps, it's life that changes everything,' he said. 'Or perhaps it's just that change *is* life. All we can do is let it take us where it will.'

'A fine sentiment for a song,' said Archie Adams.

'But listen, Nancy,' Mrs Moffatt went on, 'as my time ends, yours is just beginning. I can feel it in my bones. We'll tell the girls in the morning, and we'll do it together. But you don't need my blessing. They love you, they respect you – and they'll follow you to the end. I suspect Annie Brogan will be at your heels for years to come, whether you want her there or not.' Only now did she hesitate, allowing her eyes to flicker fleetingly at Nancy's stomach. 'There's just one more thing you'll need to do. One more conversation you'll need to have. I've prepared him for it. I think, once he's deliberated, and perhaps spoken to Mr Hastings and the rest of the Board, he'll see it makes sense. Conventions are one thing, Nancy, but they'll see, soon enough, that conventions change just like everything else.' Mrs Moffatt paused. Her eyes had lifted from Nancy and over her shoulder, where a diminutive, mole-like figure had appeared behind the check-in desks. 'Here he is, Nancy. You should go to him now.'

Nancy turned.

There was Walter Knave, standing hunched behind the desks, gesturing to her with his tiny hand peeping out of his over-large sleeve. Then, without waiting to see if he was being followed, he turned and shuffled off, down the hall in the direction of the Hotel Director's office.

'Well then,' said Nancy, 'we come to it, at last.'

'Be honest with him,' said Mrs Moffatt. 'In the end, all he'll need to be convinced of is your devotion to make it work – and, dear Nancy, you have never lacked for devotion.'

Nancy took a deep breath. She squeezed Raymond's hand for the last time.

Then she detached herself from the crowd, crossed the reception and disappeared behind the check-in desks.

At the end of the passage, she knocked on the door. 'Mr Knave?' she called out.

'Come in, Mrs de Guise,' replied Walter Knave.

So that was what Nancy did.

As one door opened, and another fell closed.

New beginnings, she thought as she stepped into the office. They were happening all the time.

Acknowledgements

Thank you as always to my wonderful wife, Hannah, and my children, George and Henrietta. You put up with the long days away on the road, the time in the studio, and the various moments when I go into 'book mode'. Thank you for your patience and understanding and for being my daily inspiration. I dedicate every word to you.

A huge thank you to my manager and friend, Melissa Chappell. Book five! Who would have thought it? Thank you for always listening to my ideas, for making them happen, and for humouring me when needed!

Thank you to Kerr MacRae, my literary agent, for always being there with a wise word and a guiding hand. You started us on this path and I'm so glad you are still onboard for the ride.

Many thanks also to my dedicated publishing team at Orion: to Sam Eades and Lucy Brem for their editorial work, to Lynsey Sutherland and Brittany Sankey for their marketing expertise, and to Francesca Pearce and Frankie Banks for coordinating a spectacular PR campaign. Thank you also to the Sales team, with a special shout out to Victoria Laws, and to Paul Stark and Jake Alderson for my stunning audiobook edition.

To Lou Plank and the team at Plank PR, thank you for your

endless hard work, organisation and advice. We make a fantastic team!

A big thank you to Hollie Pratt, the person who, on a daily basis, makes sure I know exactly what I am meant to be doing and where I am meant to be. Without you I would be lost – quite literally!

Thank you also to Scott and David at Bungalow Industries. Please know that your hard work, unwavering support and dedication to everything you do is completely invaluable, and you are an integral part of Team Anton.

And finally, a massive thank you to booksellers and readers everywhere, for buying, reading and championing my books at every turn. I am so grateful for all your support, and it makes all the hard work worthwhile!

Much love,
Anton